EX-Terminator

Life After Marriage

ALSO BY SUZETTA PERKINS

A Love So Deep

Behind the Veil

EX-Terminator

Life After Marriage

Suzetta Perkins

SBI

STREBOR BOOKS

NEW YORK LONDON TORONTO SYDNEY

Strebor Books
P.O. Box 6505
Largo, MD 20792
http://www.streborbooks.com

ISBN-13 978-1-59309-183-5
ISBN-10   1-59309-183-4
LCCN 2007943469

First Strebor Books trade paperback edition May 2008

Cover design: www.mariondesigns.com

10 9 8 7 6 5 4 3 2 1

Manufactured in the United States of America

For information regarding special discounts for bulk purchases, please contact Simon & Schuster Special Sales at 1-800-456-6798 or business@simonandschuster.com

*"When one door of happiness closes, another opens;
but often we look so long at the closed door that
we do not see the one which has been opened for us."*
—HELEN KELLER

*"Love is a feeling, marriage is a contract,
and relationships are work."*
—LORI GORDON,
American marriage therapist, family therapist,
relationship coach and entrepreneur founder of PAIRS

ACKNOWLEDGMENTS

I give honor to God from whom all my blessings flow. I am nothing without Him. I marvel at what a literary journey this has been. As a dreamer, this journey has taken me beyond my wildest imagination.

I'd like to thank my family, who has been so supportive of me, not only in my writing but in every aspect of my life. To my dad, Calvin G. Goward, Sr., your constant encouragement has made me what I am today, and it certainly boosts my ego when I call and you say that you're reading my novel over again. I love you.

To my daughter, Teliza, and son, JR, thank you for always being by my side and singing my praises. JR, you've been a constant companion while on the road, so much so that when I'm at a Strebor affair and you're not there, the authors ask about you.

To my son-in-law, Will, I'm praying for your safe return home from Iraq. In the meantime, there's nothing like a good book that has your mother-in-law's name on it to keep you going. I love you.

To my sisters, Jennifer and Gloria, and my brothers, Mark and Calvin, thanks for being part of my experience. Jennifer, thanks for making my book popular in the friendly skies of American Airlines. Your co-workers are the bomb—buying my book like it was cotton candy at the fair. Mark, tell my nephew, Ezekiel, that he can't write any more book reports about his auntie's novels that are not geared for nine-year-olds. He will write his own someday that are sure to become bestsellers.

To my cousin, Doris, thanks for the wonderful brunch you had for me in California to celebrate my work. To be in the company of family is a great feeling. Having my dad, Uncle James, Dorothy, Virginia, and Stacey to celebrate before going to Underground Books with the illustrious Mother Rose to share my literary work was priceless.

To my sisters-in-law, Celeste, Dolly, and Gwen, I thank you for being so supportive—Celeste for telling the world about me and making me proud when I saw you walk through the door of the Underground Book Store, and Gwen and Dolly for the wonderful dinner on the wharf and the opportunity to sign my book. That was a moment captured in time.

I'd like to especially thank Dr. Shirish Devasthali, who gave of his time to share with me the nature of breast cancer—its progression in stages and a patient's treatment/outcomes as part of my research for this book. A special thanks also goes to Dr. Ed Dickerson aka/Coconut Shrimp of Cape Fear Aesthetics Day Spa in Fayetteville, North Carolina, whose day spa provided the model for the one in this novel. And to Dr. Saundra Shorter, one of my biggest fans, I love you.

To my publisher, Strebor Books/Simon and Schuster, you are the reason I've been able to succeed on my journey. Zane, you're at the top of your game. Thank you for believing in me. Charmaine, you are the best of the best. You have meant so much to me, and I appreciate you being part of my journey. A special thank you goes to Keith of Marion Designs for my beautiful cover. You're the bomb.

To my agent, Maxine Thompson, you make me smile. You and I have grown together and without you my journey would not have taken flight. Thanks for your love, understanding and the opportunity to soar.

To my publicist Donna Hill of Donna Hill Promotions, thank you for helping to put me on the map.

A special thank you to all the book clubs: Sistahs Book Club, Mary Farmer and the Sister Circle Book Club, Deborah Burton and Turning Pages Book Club, Deisdy Paige and the ladies of Alpha Kappa Alpha and others for letting me share my novels with them. A special thanks to Angela Reid, president of Imani Book Club, for always being there.

Last but not least, I appreciate the bookstores, especially Denise Skeels at Waldenbooks in Fayetteville; Mother Rose at the Underground Books in Sacramento; Bernard Henderson at Alexander Book Co. in San Francisco and for the spot on TV's ACCESSF's *The Bernard and Winifred Show*; Jason Rosenberg, Donna Walton, and Trudy Holden of the Army and Air Force Exchange System (AAFES) at Fort Bragg, N.C., Ft. Jackson, S.C., and Ft. Gordon, GA for being so supportive; and Sheri Brooks, CEO of Dynasty Publications, for the opportunity to promote my book with Detroit's listening audience on your television show *Wordz in Motion*.

Day of Reckoning

The clock sat quiet on the nightstand, its green fluorescent numbers shouting out three a.m. Heavy breathing was muffled under the layers of bed linen draping the large mass that lay in the middle of the bed. Every now and then the large formation would shift and a new pattern would occur.

In an instant, the still formation erupted—the mass tossing and turning under the bedcovers that rustled as the silk fibers rubbed against each other.

"No, don't go, please don't go," a voice cried out in the darkness. Then quiet.

The dreams were coming again, and Sylvia St. James let them play in her subconscious.

"What did you say, Adonis? I know I didn't hear what I thought I heard."

"I want a divorce, Sylvia. I can't say it any plainer than that."

"But why, Adonis? When did you decide this? I didn't know that our marriage was in trouble."

"That's the problem with you. You're always too busy to notice what's going on right under your nose. Too busy trying to kiss the boss' behind. Too busy trying to be something you're not. Think you're better than everybody else, and—if you remember before we got married, I told you I didn't like fat women."

"I'll get on the treadmill tomorrow, I promise, but can we talk about this…try to work it out? We have invested so much of our lives into this marriage. Our daughter, what is she going to think?"

"Sylvia, I'm unhappy. I've been unhappy a long time, and now it's *my* time. I've got to go."

"But…but what about me?"

"What about you? Look, Sylvia, the love slipped out of our marriage a while ago. Of course, you were too busy to notice. I don't have a lot of time left on this earth, and I'd like to enjoy a little happiness before I go."

"Time left on earth?" Sylvia muttered. "What are you talking about? Where are you going? No one will ever love you like I do, Adonis."

"Sylvia, please don't sound so desperate. You'll do fine. You always do."

"Don't go, Adonis. Don't leave me like this. Noooooooooooooo!" Sylvia screamed.

The cream-colored silk comforter slid to the floor as Sylvia rolled from side to side, caught up in her dream-memory.

"Nooooooooooooo!" she screamed once more into the early morning. "No. No."

Pulling her hand from underneath her, Sylvia began to beat the pillow on which her head rested. She pounded the soft down until her arm tired. She peeled her eyes open then sat up slowly, sweat pouring from her brow. She scanned the dark room, her eyes out of focus. After a moment, she was able to make out the outline of the "T"-iron that Adonis had left behind: his winning golf club that he had nicknamed "Tiger."

Sylvia slowly brought her hands to her face to catch the stream of water that ran from her eyes and threatened to soak her nightgown. Her breathing was labored as her sobs, soft at first, became loud wails. She sobbed and sobbed, then grabbed her throat to keep from choking. She wrapped her arms around her chest and shook herself from side to side.

"Why, Adonis, why? Why did you leave me? I loved you with all my heart and soul. Why, why?"

Finally, there was quiet…an occasional sniff. Sylvia unfolded her arms, drew her knees up to her chest and wrapped her arms around her legs. She laid her head on the bend of her knees and began to rock back and forth, willing her dream to recede. She sniffed again.

Sylvia lifted her head and turned toward the nightstand that held the clock. It was three fifty-five a.m. She threw her legs over the side of the bed and stood up, almost slipping on the comforter that had fallen to the floor. She moved to the bathroom and relieved herself, washed her hands, then looked into the mirror.

Almond-shaped eyes, which were framed by high-arched brows, stared back at Sylvia. She circled her eyes with her fingers. Even in the dim light, her skin seemed blotchier than it'd been the day before. Her face was discolored something awful, and the older she got the more defined the blotches became.

Sylvia's reflection stared back at her, daring her to speak.

"You don't need him."

Sylvia put her hand to her mouth, not sure whether it was she or the reflection that had spoken.

"Yeah, I don't need him. Get ahold of yourself, girl, and grab the world by its axis. It's time to take my life back and leave this pity party at the doorstep."

Sylvia was sure this time that the reflection in the mirror wasn't talking, but the face that stared back meant serious business.

D-Day

"Where's my purse?" Sylvia shouted to no one, moving from room to room, looking in corners and closets, pulling on her too-short linen dress every two seconds. "I've got lots to do and I want everything perfect before the ladies come. Ouch, darn! Not my stockings. This is not the time to get a run. Now I've got to stop and change them.

"Here's my purse," Sylvia continued to ramble out loud, her nylon-clad legs making a swishing sound as they rubbed together when she trotted back to her room to put on new hose. "Hiding from me again. I don't have time for this. I've got to get to the beauty shop by ten and I still have to stop and get gas before I go."

Brrng...brrng.

"Damn! Whoever it is, I don't have time to talk." Sylvia let out a sigh when she saw the name on the caller ID.

"Hello, Mother. I'm in a hurry right now. Getting ready to go to the shrink."

"The shrink? I thought you were having a men-hating party today? And hello to you, too."

"I'm sorry. Just got a lot to do and I'm running behind time. Our first meeting is tonight, and I've got to look good for the occasion. Arial, my shrink, is going to give me a touch-up. And I can't wait to get to the shampoo bowl to partake in the divine five-minute head scrub that causes you to have the most wonderful multiple orgasms."

"Sylvia St. James! I know you didn't just say what I thought you said."

"Mom, I'm a forty-five-year-old, good-looking woman—although lately my attention-grabbing curves have become a series of bumps on a line, hidden under my extra layer of fat."

"Stop beating yourself up. You just need to lay off some of those carbs and get some exercise."

"You're right. And today is the first day of my real healing. I've got a reasonable portion of my health and strength and I know that there is a world of somebodies out there waiting on me."

"Be careful what you ask for."

"A baby and twenty years of my life, Ma, and he had to go and—"

"Let's not talk about it."

"That's the problem. I need to talk about it." Sylvia paused. "I had one of my dreams last night."

"I'm sorry, baby. I wish I could be there for you. He's messin' up your mind and he ain't even thinking about you," her mother said.

"Thanks for the support, Mom. That's why I'm having this meeting. Now, I've gotta go. Love you."

"Love you, too." And the line was dead.

Sylvia stood in the middle of the room with hands on her voluptuous hips—gold bangles dangling from one arm—and surveyed her surroundings. In one corner stood a wooden African fertility statue that looked as lonely as she did. Six months had passed since the judge declared that the marriage of Adonis and Sylvia St. James was dissolved, but today, Sylvia made her own declaration that she was ready to live again.

Sylvia looked down at her watch. It was almost ten o'clock on a beautiful summer day in June, and she had to get going. Her adrenaline was high, excited about the prospect of sitting with other women who were divorced and sharing ideas about how to move on. She grabbed her belongings and rushed out the door. As she yanked open the door of her silver BMW 530i sedan, her hand slipped. "Aw hell," she muttered, surveying her broken nail, trying to will away the pain. After a couple of seconds she put the key in the ignition and headed for the gas station two blocks down.

xxx

Five minutes away, Sylvia thought. She would still be on time. At the corner, she looked in her purse for her gas card, then remembered she had taken it out and put it on the nightstand. Sylvia shook her head in disbelief. Her road to healing had some major obstacles.

She rummaged through her wallet, which was crammed with receipts. Adonis was always telling her that her purse was going to get stolen one day, and the robber would know her life story. She sifted through the papers until her fingers pulled up a folded twenty-dollar bill. "Thank You, God. You're so good. And I promise to pay careful attention to what I'm doing from now on."

xxx

Arial's mouth was moving a mile a minute when Sylvia walked into the beauty shop. Her petite frame was dressed to the nines: starched white linen slacks and a white short-sleeved blouse with lacy scallops running around the collar; hair piled high into a ponytail revealing the two-carat diamond studs that dotted each earlobe; and her immaculately manicured feet were stuffed in a pair of Dr. Scholl's comfort sandals made for standing long hours— her strappy gold stilettos sitting off to the side. Although Arial was in her late forties, she could easily pass for thirty. But more than that, the girl could hook up some hair. Arial had the gift.

"Be with you in a minute, sweetie…kiss, kiss."

Sylvia blew a kiss back and picked up a hairstyle book to pass the time.

Mane Waves was Arial's baby. Clients would sometimes drive an hour or two for Arial's services. The decor befit the queens the ladies believed they were—plush gold carpeting ran the length of the shop and a bird of paradise and large rubber plants were everywhere, their presence demanding attention. A black lacquered chest of drawers stood next to a large palm tree just inside the main entrance, displaying samples of the facial and nail products Arial also sold. A six-inch curved bar that served as the guest registry stood to the right of the chest, handsomely decorated with porcelain knick-knacks and a black lacquered business-card holder.

"Sylvia." Sylvia jumped. "What have you been up to, girl?" Arial shouted through the noise of the blow-dryer as she put the finishing touches on Ms. Jenkins.

"Preparing for a coming-out party."

"A what?"

"I'll explain later."

Fifteen minutes later, Arial took the towel from around Ms. Jenkins' neck.

"Looking good, Ms. Jenkins," Sylvia said.

"Thank you, baby. I've got a darned good stylist."

Sylvia gently slid into the chair vacated by Ms. Jenkins.

"How have you been, sweetie? I know you've been through some rough times." Arial picked through Sylvia's hair. "And you know you needed a perm three weeks ago. Next time you come in we've got to put some color in your hair, too."

"You're right. But to answer your question, I'm fine, Arial. In fact, I feel better than I have in the last year. I'm meeting with some other women tonight, and we're going to talk about life after divorce."

"A support group."

"Yeah. I'm looking forward to it."

"Who's in the group? I don't know about sitting around talking with a bunch of women…having them all up in my business, especially sistahs. You sure about this?" Arial began gathering products as she spoke.

"It's going to be a good thing, Arial. Sometimes your friends get tired of hearing your troubles over and over again. Some days you're up but there are many down days. Being able to connect with women who share the same experience and who may need me as well is the answer to my prayer. God knows I need this. Rachel Washington is going to be there. You might want to stick your head in and join us."

"You didn't have to go there. Lawrence and I are prehistoric news. I've been single for darn near fifteen years. Don't need no counseling, and I sure don't need a support group. Back to Rachel. It was a damn shame how her husband messed all over her, but that woman don't know how to pick a man. Isn't this her third divorce?"

Sylvia turned around to look at Arial. "See, that's what I mean.

So what if it's her third? Rachel is a sweetheart and one of my best friends. It's not her fault that these men take her kindness for weakness."

"I know you better hold your head up while I put this perm in your hair."

"You better not burn me, either. I'll take this shop from you like I took the house from Adonis." They laughed.

"Girl, you know I'm always here for you. Have you heard from Adonis?"

"You mean since he went to live with his ex-wife?" Sylvia hesitated. "No, I haven't heard from him."

"You still love him, don't you?" Arial accused.

"I don't love him like I used to love him. We've got history. We were married for twenty freakin' years!"

"Shhh, don't get yourself so worked up, sweetie."

"I'm sorry. Lost my head for a second."

"My next customer won't be here for another thirty minutes. I figured you and I need some downtime."

"I gave that man a beautiful daughter and the best years of my life. I still can't believe he just got up and walked out on me like that—without a decent explanation. Do you know that the self-confident, independent woman I was has turned into a whining, bitter, angry…"

"It's okay, sweetie," Arial soothed.

"But, Arial, it hurts to love a man as much as I loved and adored Adonis. He stabbed me straight in the heart. Declared that he was no longer in love with me and marched straight into another woman's bed."

Tears began to fall, and Sylvia let her head drop.

"I think it's time for your shampoo." Arial took off her latex gloves and with both hands kneaded Sylvia's shoulders. "I'll make it extra special today. We'll make it a ten-minute massage."

"You always know how to make a girl feel good."

"I love you, Sylvia. And I don't want you to take my shop! If we wait another minute, your whole head might be on fire."

Laughter ripped through the shop.

"I think you're gonna be all right, sweetie. And the way you're wearing that dress, showing all the thighs you own—Adonis might have to come back and rescue you from all the players that will be buzzing around the honeybee."

"Stop. I threw this dress on real quick. Just wait until you finish my luscious, reddish-brown mane. I'll be swishing my head from side to side, moving my hair like it was a merry-go-round."

"Girl, you're crazy. Knock 'em dead even if it's just going to be a bunch of cackling women."

"I see it like this, Arial. If we are going to get our lives back, we have to act as if we want change so we can close our Ex-Files for good."

"I'm with you, sweetie."

Meeting in the Ladies Room

The scent of hickory-smoked barbecued ribs permeated the room. Sylvia was pleased. The food was ready, thanks to the folks at Smokey Bones restaurant. Her 180-pound, five-foot-seven frame looked simply gorgeous in her yellow, green, blue and white napkin blouse and her navy blue pants. She exhaled and went about checking and rechecking things to make sure all was in order.

Once again, Sylvia stood in the large family room, her favorite. It was full of the remnants of war—the war of the St. Jameses.

An array of African violets sat on the mantel of the double-sided marble fireplace, their velvet flowers shining like jewels against lush, green leaves. In the center of the room, in its own L-shaped cluster, sat a cognac-colored leather couch with well-padded arms, a high back and deep seats, and a matching armchair and ottoman. A diverse grouping of mirrors in several shapes and sizes hung to the left of an arched, floor-to-ceiling window, creating an eclectic wall of reflection, while the latest state-of-the-art plasma TV hung by itself above an elaborate entertainment system. Polished hardwood floors were covered by imported throw rugs made of Chinese silk in hues of brown sprinkled with flecks of white. Crown molding snaked along the perimeter of the room while a five-armed antique brass chandelier with square silk shades and dimmers formed an architectural chameleon from the ceiling where it hung, changing the room at whim. African-American art hung throughout, and small family pictures sat on wooden wall ledges; everything was illuminated by a string of gallery-perfect track lights.

Sylvia stopped in front of one of the mirrors and admired herself. "Not bad, girl. Not bad at all." Arial had taken the time to make up Sylvia's caramel-colored face. Her almond-shaped eyes, the color of wheat, were dusted with a mixture of brown, tan and white eye shadow, and a rich lipstick the color of dark apricots set off her smile. "Fabulous."

"It's your loss, Adonis!" Sylvia hollered to the rafters. "It's your loss, man. I'm taking my life back and I don't need you to do it. I DON'T NEED YOU! I'll be fine all by myself…well, it wouldn't hurt to find a tall, handsome man who'd love to snuggle up every once in awhile. Your loss, man, your loss."

But she wasn't sure she was ready to be with a man. Her heart had a lot of mending to do, and she had to find a way to be happy with herself before she could give to someone else.

Sylvia picked up the remote and turned on the stereo. Light jazz filtered throughout the room—Sylvia became lost in her thoughts of getting on with her life.

Ding, dong. Ding, dong. The sound of the door chimes made Sylvia take a deep breath and one last look at herself. Again, she was pleased. She moved forward ready to get the party started, and opened the door to a smiling Rachel.

✗✗✗

"Hey, girl. Glad you were able to come tonight," Sylvia said. "Come on in and make yourself comfortable."

"Smooches," Rachel said, exchanging air kisses with Sylvia. "Had to be here." They hugged.

Rachel was sassy and stunning in her red, backless Calvin Klein cocktail dress. Her smooth skin was chocolate with three table-spoons of milk. Full Nubian lips perfectly suited her small, oval face with her long-lashed deep brown eyes, under perfectly arched brows, expressed her anticipation for the party. Her thick, relaxed, shoulder-length hair with a slight curl to it bounced on her shoulders when she walked in.

There was a slight hint of jealousy in Sylvia's eyes as Rachel's petite and firm body moved farther into the room. Sylvia wished her waistline was as small. She could probably wrap her hand around Rachel's waist. It was hard watching calories and trying to control the number of carbs and fats she ate, but she was going to give it a try—although tonight, she was going to lick the sauce off a half slab of baby-back ribs.

"Girl, you have any Excedrin?"

Sylvia stopped at the entrance into the family room. "You've got one of your headaches, Rachel?"

"Yeah, every time the atmospheric pressure rises, it feels like my head is falling down. I usually have my headache pills with me." Rachel paused as she looked in the room. "Doesn't look as if Adonis is gone. It's almost as if I can feel his presence."

"He's gone. Believe me, he's gone. Thank God for Adonis' mar-riage to IBM, though. It has allowed me to continue to live in the lifestyle I've become accustomed to."

The bell rang again, and Sylvia turned and headed back toward the door. "Go ahead and look in the medicine cabinet while I get the door. I should have some Tylenol in there."

Sylvia opened the door to a stunning, well-toned diva dressed in a pair of beaded floral silk pants and a knitted rose-colored cardigan and shell. She was at least five feet nine inches tall, with a long, oval face, dark chiseled features and high cheekbones. Her smooth cocoa fudge skin was blemish-free, and she wore long ruddy-red dreads that were pulled off her face with a silk scarf. A much shorter, heavyset woman with bleached-blonde braids stood next to her.

"Hey, Mona. You look absolutely gorgeous. Come on in."

"I see the single life quite agrees with you, my dear."

"Let's not go there."

"I thought that this was what this meeting was all about. Anyway, Sylvia, I want you to meet my hairdresser, Claudette Beasley."

"Hey, sister," Claudette said to Sylvia, shaking her hand.

"Hey, yourself."

"I thought this would be good for Claudette. She's a single mother, got a nine-year-old son, Kwame, and a daughter named Reebe who's fifteen going on sixty. She's been smothering that boy so long, no man can get close to her."

"Okay, Mona," Claudette cut in. "It ain't even like that. You don't want me to get loud up in here. I can get a man anytime I want. See, I loves my baby, and I want the best for him. Gotta keep him out of the streets."

"You got to give him a little breathin' room."

"Whatever, Mona, but he's still my baby boy."

"Why don't we go into the family room," Sylvia interrupted, pointing the way. "My good friend Rachel is already here. Mona, you remember Rachel."

"Yeah, yeah, married that crazy nig—"

"Not here," Sylvia warned.

"Okay. She married that crazy guy named…"

"Reuben," Rachel offered. "How are you doing, Mona?"

"Just fine," Mona said, a tad bit of embarrassment in her voice. "And this is Claudette Beasley, my hairdresser."

Claudette and Rachel shook hands, and the group moved into the family room.

"I love this room," Mona said. "It's got a touch of you and of Adonis."

"I just told her the same thing," Rachel agreed.

"I'm glad you like the room, but Adonis don't live here anymore. Get my drift?" Sylvia said pointedly.

"I think our sister is ready to get this meeting started," Claudette put in.

Sylvia looked at Claudette with interest. She noticed a two-inch scar that ran across Claudette's forehead. And if that wasn't enough, she had the nerve to have a tattoo plastered on her flabby arm that read *No More Drama*. In Sylvia's estimation, she should have had one that read *Do Not Feed Me, I'm Way Overweight*. Then she thought, who was she to call the kettle black? If Mona liked her, that's all that mattered.

"We will start in a minute," Sylvia began. "I'm waiting for one more person. I'll get you something to drink while we're waiting."

"I'm going to step outside and take a smoke since I don't see any ashtrays in here," Claudette said, pulling a pack of Benson and Hedges from her purse.

"You can smoke out back," Sylvia said, leading the way. "Ain't gonna be no smoking up in here," she added under her breath.

Mona looked at her watch, then in the direction of the door and then glanced at her watch once more. When she looked up, Rachel turned her face away. Mona sat on one end of the leather couch and looked over at Rachel again, who had now become fascinated with the collection of mirrors on the wall.

"Sorry, Rachel. I didn't mean anything by what I said," Mona finally said.

"No problem," Rachel replied. "Right now, all I want to do is get rid of this awful headache."

"I have some natural herbs that might help you with that. I used to have headaches bad until I started taking these herbs."

"I have a prescribed medicine that I left at home. Anyway, I just took a Tylenol that Sylvia offered. It's just the weather. I'll be all right in a minute."

"Suit yourself."

Ding, dong. Ding, dong.

"I'll get it," Sylvia called from the kitchen. She rushed into the room and handed Rachel the tray of iced tea, then headed for the door.

"For you," Rachel said to Mona as she handed her a glass.

"Thanks, and again, I'm sorry."

"You're forgiven."

Mona's smile faded when Sylvia returned to the room.

"Everyone, this is Ashley Jordan-Lewis. She works with me and is a very dear friend."

xxx

Rachel and Mona smiled and nodded at the newcomer. Ashley stood the same height as Sylvia but was rail-thin—with the exception of her ample bosom. She seemed much younger than the rest. A sharp, pointed nose jutted from her oval face and round, deep blue eyes stared back at the ladies.

Ashley was dressed in a smart navy Ralph Lauren silk blazer and a pair of off-white silk pants accentuated with a pair of two-inch, T-strap, off-white pumps. The soft collar of her off-white blouse lay obediently against the lapels of the jacket. Stunning two-carat diamond studs glittered from Ashley's ears: her blonde hair was pulled back in a ponytail that fell mid-shoulder. Mona looked at her watch once more.

"Let's get started," Sylvia began. Claudette rushed into the room, out of breath, the evidence of her activity outside still lingering about her like a cloud.

Sylvia St. James

Sylvia stood in the middle of the room, her reflection cast on the hardwood floor. Her audience seemed captivated as if she was on display at the Louvre museum, although she had yet to utter a word. Their eerie silence left her speechless wishing the spotlight were somewhere else instead of on her. Most of the ladies were friends, but serving your soul on a platter for everyone to judge took more than a little bit of courage.

Clearing her throat, Sylvia looked into the eyes of the eager faces. "Hi, I'm Sylvia St. James, and I've been an *Ex* for seven months." *There, it was out*, Sylvia thought. All of a sudden she stepped into her role and felt her self-confidence return.

"I'll tell you, this has been a wild day. I was trying to get to the hairdresser so I could look fabulous for you ladies tonight, and before I got out of the house, I lost my keys and tore my stockings, and when I finally got in the car, I broke a nail. Everything that could go wrong went wrong this morning. And it wouldn't have been so wild if I had Adonis—my Ex—here to remind me every five seconds to check and make sure I had everything. I'm not used to thinking for myself. My Ex thought I was dumb and stupid, and I have more credentials than he does."

The ladies snickered.

"Go ahead and get a good laugh in," Sylvia continued. "I'm sure you're saying to yourselves, 'No wonder he left her.'"

More snickering.

"But it's okay. It is…really okay. I'm here, and I'm glad you all are here. We are going to become very good friends. We are going to be an alliance of sistahs coming back from the divorce courts with our steel-toed shoes on. Yes, we are straight-from-the-divorce-court sistahs looking for healing—emotional healing, sexual healing, some kind of healing."

"Yeah!" the ladies shouted in unison, raising their fists.

Her voice a tad bit softer, Sylvia continued. "We all have a common trait: we are Exes with an Ex-File. It's time to clean up our Ex-Files and close them forever."

"*Yeah!*" Rachel screamed.

Sylvia gazed out of the corner of her eye at Rachel. Rachel's nerve had been pricked. She was the loudest one in the room. Sylvia smiled.

"How are we going to purge our Ex-Files? We will purge our hearts and souls, our minds, our anger. We will come ready for an extreme makeover. In doing so, we'll have to ask ourselves some very uncomfortable questions…questions about our exes and ourselves. The only way to heal is to purge those old feelings and keep walking straight ahead—run if you have to—never looking back and risking falling back into the clutches of the Ex-demons that constantly tell you that you're no good, you're too fat, I don't love you no more, you can't live without me, nobody wants you."

Clap, clap, clap, clap, clap, clap, clap, clap, clap.

"Let's close the Ex-Files," Rachel sang out.

"Yeah, Ex him out!" Claudette screamed at the top of her lungs.

Sylvia looked around the room at the four women who were assembled there. Though they were from all walks of life, they all had something in common. They all had an *Ex*. If they could go back in time, they would probably tear their Ex's heart out and jump on it to assuage their grief.

Sylvia realized she needed these women, maybe more than they needed her. She needed to reach out to someone—a shoulder to lean on. If it was four sets of shoulders, all the better. She needed to expose her files. She needed to get rid of her anger. She needed help…a crutch, and this meeting was just the thing.

Just as the applause subsided, Sylvia began again.

"We all seem to have the same objective—liberation, freedom, freedom to move on, freedom from being bound by the drudgery of our divorces, freedom from our Exes. You've got to leave your burdens on the table before your shackles can be loosed. And this is our aim, our goal. Are you ready?"

The four women applauded again, and Sylvia joined them. Their claps intensified. They sounded like six thousand women at a T.D. Jakes "Thou Art Loosed" convention. Finally, they fell silent again.

"So what I want you to do tonight, if you feel comfortable, I want each one of you to tell us as much as you would like to share about how you got here. You have to shake it off; you have to release it in order to move on.

"You might say, what can a support group do for me? You know, I think about the blues. I think about B.B. King—my man done left me and gone. But I'm going to tell you all right now: I'm not going down like that. I don't need a man to survive, I've got myself."

"YES," the ladies said in unison.

"I ain't goin' down like that!" Claudette Beasley roared, her blonde braids swinging about her face.

"I don't know about y'all, but I need a man," Mona interjected. "I've got to have a place for my twins to cuddle up to at night." Mona held her breasts in both hands. "But that freedom you're talking about, Sylvia, I'm all for that."

"Hmmph, she'll smother the poor fellow with those silicon implants."

"I heard that, Claudette," Mona said as she touched the tip of Claudette's nose with her pointed finger. She removed her finger and caught one of Claudette's braids in her hand and looked at it a moment. "You think blondes have more fun? My twins have more than their share of fun."

Claudette rolled her eyes. Sylvia glared at both of them before continuing.

xxx

"I woke up that morning in a peaceful, tranquil mood. I remember the day so vividly; it was a couple of days before Valentine's Day. When I focused my eyes, I found him staring at me from the foot of the bed—like something was on his mind but he didn't have the heart or the balls to tell me. I watched him as he continued to stare, then dropped his head and grabbed his chin as if the matter was too complex for even him to comprehend.

"I sat up and asked, 'What is it, Adonis? Why are you staring at me like that?'

"'Just thinking.' The two lone words fell from his mouth as if someone had slapped him on the back and forced them out.

"I knew I was in trouble; I had seen the look before. But I, with all the education and the good sense God gave me to know right from wrong, good from evil, I had no earthly idea how much trouble I was really in. The kind of trouble that makes you go and grab a gun and kill someone because if it wasn't for them, you wouldn't be in any trouble. The kind of trouble that makes you curse out everybody and use words you've never uttered in your life—and in the morning you can't remember a thing and wonder why in the world no one can stand your ass.

"But Adonis didn't release his troubled mind that morning. He kept it bottled up and left my brain twisted in agony because I just wasn't getting the clues he laid out for me. I would have done better playing *Jeopardy*.

"You all asleep? It's so quiet in here."

"No," Mona said, shaking her head in a continuous motion.

She, Rachel, Claudette and Ashley sat glued to their seats. They had become transfixed, drawn into Sylvia's Lifetime movie that played from the pages of her broken heart. Mona's pumps lay on their sides and her bare toes kneaded the carpet, while the others laced their fingers together ready to brace at the moment of discovery.

"Continue," Rachel encouraged. "You might have to get me a blanket and a bowl of popcorn. I'm in the room with you, girl. I'm waiting for Adonis to drop the bomb on you. We're ready to dance on his ass because we know that the news is gonna be bad." The others nodded in agreement. "So what happened?"

"He said, 'I've got to go to work.' And he headed out the room without his usual kiss good-bye. I screamed, '*Adonis*, come back here. *Adonis*, come back here.' A few seconds later, his body framed the doorway. He had a severe frown on his face like he didn't want to be there. He said he was going to be late for work, but I told him he started this mess and he wasn't leaving without giving me a reasonable answer.

"Y'all, he looked at me as if I didn't belong there…like I was some kind of stranger that he didn't know how to tell to get out of his house. His nose was twisted up like I had some kind of stench.

"It was horrible the way he kept looking at me, and then all of a sudden, as if someone took the cork out of his mouth, he said, 'I want a divorce.' Then I heard myself pleading and begging while he told me that he didn't want me anymore…that I was too fat… that I was too stuck on myself…that I spent way too much money…that I this and I that. I wanted to slap that smug look off his face, but I kept begging and he walked out the door.

"But what I didn't know until later was that he left me for his sorry ex-wife, Veronica. They were married three years before I met Adonis, but they weren't even married a year before he found her in bed with someone else. I fell in love with him, and we got married two years later. And to think he went back to that stank ho after all these years."

Sylvia's hands flew to her face. Rachel went to her side as the tears began to flow. She waved her off, wiped her face and looked into the faces of the other ladies. Rachel sat back down. Sylvia sniffed.

"I'm going to be all right, now." Sylvia started waving her hand in the air. "I vow that I will never look back. From this day for-ward, I am moving straight ahead. I don't care if my *Ex* marched in here right now, declaring his love for me, and told me he wanted me back. I don't care if he was crawling on all fours, I will never go back. I have been hurt by love. I'm through. I'm closing this chapter of my life. I need you ladies to help me. I need you to be there for me because I want to make it.

"The pain is there, and it's okay to grieve. It's time to get it out of our systems. It's time to acknowledge where we are, then move on."

All was silent. Each person looked at the next and finally Rachel rose from her seat and embraced Sylvia. Rachel stood and faced the others while they looked back at her expectantly. She hoped that she didn't have anything on her teeth and that she didn't look as scared as she felt. The way they were looking at her, she wasn't sure.

She cleared her throat and closed her eyes, trying to control her nervousness. The moment of truth had arrived, and she was willing to tell her story to this now-intimate group of women because she was ready to get on with her life.

Ding, dong. For a moment, everyone's attention was diverted toward the hallway.

Rachel Washington

Rachel stood with her head bowed and waited for Sylvia to return. Mona and Claudette chatted with each other, while Ashley drummed her fingers on her glass. There was conversation in the hallway, then Sylvia's light laughter. Footsteps from more than one person approached the group, and there next to Sylvia stood a tall, handsome gentleman with a well-trimmed mustache.

Mona immediately jumped up from her seat before Sylvia could introduce him.

"Ladies, this is a friend of mine, Marvin Thomas. He is the CEO of Thomas Technology Solutions, TTS for short." Rachel thought she saw him blush. "He's recently divorced, so I invited him tonight…that's if you ladies don't have a problem with a man being in our midst."

"Noooooo," everyone said in unison barely listening to Mona but sizing up the new member of the group.

"Well, he's an Ex and has every right to be here," Mona said.

"Thank you, Mona," Sylvia said. She introduced each lady to Marvin and brought him up to speed.

Rachel's mind wasn't on what she would say or that she would be the center of attention in a few moments. Her eyes were fixed on the man in the Armani suit. His cocoa-brown skin was a chocoholic's downfall and his dreamy hazel bedroom eyes almost made Rachel lose her balance, but she noticed that he still wore his wedding ring.

When Rachel came up for air she realized that everyone was looking at her.

"Why are you all staring at me?"

"Why were you looking as if you were lost in space?" Sylvia asked.

Rachel was embarrassed and dared not look in Marvin's direction. She shook her head, cleared her throat again, and stood still in the middle of the room. She wasn't sure she could share her pain with the group now that Marvin had arrived. He made her off-balance. Why? She wasn't sure. Rachel's nervousness returned, but she needed to move on.

Rachel's hair swung as she surveyed the group. She avoided looking at Marvin but felt his eyes on her. Eyes remote, Rachel took in a deep breath, stroked her top teeth with her tongue and began.

"Hi, my name is Rachel Washington, and I've been an Ex for three months. In fact, I'm an *Ex* for the third time. I guess I can't keep a man."

Rachel heard grunts in the audience, but when she looked at Marvin, he was staring straight through her soul. She shifted back and forth and clasped her hands together in front of her. If she was going to get through this, she had better do it now. Every eye was on her—waiting for her tale of woe, her tale of deceit, abuse and finally eviction from a marriage that was doomed from the start.

"Reuben and I met on my birthday, Christmas Day, four years

ago at my second ex's girlfriend's house. I'm not going to even try and explain to you why I was there because it's not even important to this story. The main thing is that I met Reuben. He was very nice to me, and when he heard it was my birthday, he turned a Christmas Day celebration into my birthday celebration. Imagine me and Jesus celebrating together."

Rachel was silent for a moment, searching for words, lost in a former place and time.

"Reuben was so attentive and charming; he made my day so special." She held her head down, remembering.

"He asked to see me again, and I agreed right away. I thought what a wonderful birthday present. A new friend, possibly a new relationship, and who knows what else? It was the latter that I'll never forget.

"After four months of dating, Reuben asked me to marry him. I had reservations because I had recently been delivered from an abusive marriage and didn't think I was ready to carry my baggage to someone else's house. I enjoyed dating Reuben. We went to plays, dinner, movies, and football games—he was a serious Atlanta Falcons fan, at least he appeared to be—and he always brought me flowers. He introduced me to his mother, which only proved that I was a special friend, but I never figured him for marriage.

"We stole away to Vegas and became man and wife. We had four absolutely fabulous days there. What I didn't know was that when the honeymoon ended, which I thought could have lasted a lifetime, so did the marriage. I was so enamored with the idea that I had finally found my soul mate, my true love, that I never saw the signs that were there from the very beginning."

Rachel paused again, trying to build up confidence and the

will to continue her story. Marvin was no longer a concern, only the desire to purge the demon that made her a prisoner in her own body.

"I was so blind, a year passed before it became clear to me that the man I married was using me. I provided the roof over his head, the food he ate, the clothes on his back. I was his drug dealer, I was his whore. I gave him everything he asked for without ever questioning him with the where, what, when and especially the why. And when I didn't comply—" Rachel looked down at the floor, then looked up into each person's face in turn—"he beat the hell out of me. The sad thing is I allowed it to happen."

There was a gasp from the group—each person covering their mouth, except Marvin, with their hand.

Rachel coughed and scratched her head. "Do you mind if I sit down? I've got to get this out now that the iceberg has melted."

✗✗✗

Sylvia pulled up a chair, and Rachel fell into it. She crossed her legs and leaned to one side, caressing the arm of the chair.

"I didn't know Reuben at all. I should have known that birds of a feather flock together. Didn't I meet him in the company of my second ex, Charles? I only went to Christmas dinner because my girlfriend Sherry, Charles' new girlfriend, had begged me to come. Reuben and Charles probably belonged to the 'men who abuse women' society.

"When we got married, all the dinners, flowers and movies ceased to exist. I was so stupid and naïve that I wasn't aware that Reuben neither owned nor rented the place he was living in—he was house-sitting for a friend in the military who was stationed in Germany. I never even thought about it until the divorce, when he had to tell the truth about his assets—or lack thereof. It never occurred to me that when we married and Reuben moved into my house that I was supporting a freeloading, didn't-have-a-job junkie.

"I don't know where the courage to leave Reuben came from. Someone somewhere was praying for me. I never shared any of this with my parents because they were done with me. They said I was wasting my life on the first two husbands, and time proved them right. And now I know it was best that they didn't know about number three.

"It was a rainy day in September. I had a terrible cold and left work early so that I could go home and nurse myself back to health. I remember when I drove up in the driveway, there were a couple of strange cars parked in front of the house. I cursed because not only did I have a terrible cold, but a migraine was threatening, too. The last thing I wanted to deal with were Reuben's freeloading friends up in my house.

"Woooo," Rachel sighed. "The key was barely in the lock when the front door flew open. Some crazy lunatic rushed past me. I looked on in horror because in the middle of my living room floor on my expensive Chinese rug were these three women and three men bouncing around on each other like monkeys… "

"You mean they were having sex?" Ashley gasped.

"Yes, that's exactly what I mean," Rachel said, a little annoyed. "Only they were all twisted and tangled up…you know…an orgy."

"Eewwww," Ashley, Mona and Claudette chorused. Ashley crinkled up her nose in disgust. Marvin looked at Rachel longingly.

Rachel pointed her toes straight ahead. She dropped her elbows to her knees and rested her head in the palms of her hands.

"And Reuben, well, he was sitting in a corner with a high-as-a-kite eighteen-year-old freebasing like they were taking medicine for the cold that I had. I was so mad. I was freaking *mad*."

Rachel jumped out of the chair. Her hands flew left and right, then around in a circle to prove her point.

"I was sooooooooo mad that I started swinging. I hit Reuben upside his head, and the stupid girl he was with started to cry which made my head hurt worse. And when your head hurts, you've got to hurt somebody.

"Yeah, they thought I was crazy. I hauled off and hit a home run on that girl's head. 'That's Mary's baby,' somebody said, 'and I said I don't care whose baby it is.' She had to get up out of my house. In fact, all of y'all get up out of my house. I laid some cussing and swinging on those folks, and before I could count to ten nobody was left in the house but me and Reuben—he wasn't gonna be there for long.

"I snatched whatever I saw of Reuben's stuff, opened the door, and threw it to the wind. You know the nig…I mean the brother had the nerve to try and raise up on me, pointing his finger all up in my face and shouting obscenities at me in *my* house. But yours truly pushed his ass through that open door, closed it, and wiped my hands of him. I know some of you didn't think gullible little Rachel had it in her, but it took a whole lot of being used, being walked over, pretending that it wasn't so, pretending that our marriage was real and denying what everyone was trying to tell me…that the man I had married was a no-good drug addict and I was his meal ticket for all his vices before I sent him packing."

Rachel took a deep breath and put her hands on her hips. She was exhausted, emotionally spent. She took another deep breath and placed her hand across her chest.

"I tried," Rachel cried. "I tried to be a good wife. All I wanted was for someone to love me."

Sylvia was at her side as Rachel wept openly. Another group hug was in order—even Marvin joined in.

The room was silent. When Rachel's sobs subsided, Sylvia helped her back into the chair. Rachel looked up, her head moving from side to side. She took another deep breath and sniffed.

"I didn't tell anyone; I knew they'd find out soon enough. And the streets proved me right. I know that I've been called everything from crazy to stupid to don't have good sense, but that was the old Rachel. Today, I'm taking my life back. I'm going to close my Ex-Files for good."

"Good for you," the women shouted.

And then there was this handsome man sitting in front of her named Marvin who had come to join their group. Rachel wasn't sure what the look on his face meant, but she wasn't going to be sidetracked by a friendly smile, a seductive wink or even a well-maintained body. She wasn't going to put up with any more crap from any man. Sylvia's voice brought her out of her daze.

"It's time to take a break. Let's close the Files for a moment. We've got a long way before they will be completely clean. This is a start. Now let's eat up. I've got plenty in the kitchen."

"I'm starved," Claudette said, "and I need a cigarette."

"Me, too," Ashley chimed in, "but I can do without the smokes."

"I know something smells good," Mona said.

"You ready to eat, Rachel?" Sylvia asked. "It might be a little messy, but I've got ribs."

Rachel shook her head no. She closed her eyes for a second. When she looked up, Marvin was standing in front of her offering his hand.

"I think if you eat a little something, you might feel better," came his baritone voice.

Rachel's hand shook like a palm tree in a hurricane as she tried to take his outstretched one. She wiped her eyes with the back of her other hand and said, "Okay."

EX-cuses don't count

"Girl, these ribs are kicking," Claudette said, swinging a braid out of her face to keep it out of the sauce.

"She didn't cook them." Mona groaned. "The least you could have done was asked me to cater this event for you, Sylvia."

"Girl, eat your food," Sylvia said, licking the barbecue from her fingers. "You know I don't spend much time in the kitchen."

"Well, it tastes wonderful, Sylvia," Marvin said. "My compliments to the chef, whoever it may happen to be."

The ladies giggled.

"You have to admit, Marvin," Mona interjected, "this ain't nothing like Mona's Cuisine. I've catered how many functions for your company?"

"Hmmm, five maybe six… "

"Too many to count. But this will do."

"That's not nice, Mona," Claudette cut in between spoonfuls of baked beans.

"Ahh, Sylvia knows I'm messing with her. If I didn't enjoy cooking myself, I'd probably be eating out, too."

"Are you all right, Rachel?" Sylvia asked.

Rachel sat on the bar stool listening to the others' antics. She seemed withdrawn, but managed to put a weak smile on her face.

"Yeah, I'm fine. I have a slight headache, but I'll eat something in a minute."

"So Ashley, how long have you been an Ex?" Mona inquired.

Ashley looked at Mona thoughtfully, then put the meatless bone on her plate. "It was final two weeks ago."

"Oh," Mona said. "Still fresh."

"Yes, the look of those eyes of his that wanted to kill when the judge awarded me the house and half of everything we owned is still fresh in my mind."

"I'm sorry," Mona said. "Didn't mean to open up fresh wounds."

Ashley got up from her chair and left the room in a hurry, with Sylvia close on her heels.

"There you go, meddling again," Claudette said.

"How was I supposed to know that she had just left the divorce court?" Mona replied.

Claudette waved a hand at her in disapproval.

✗✗✗

Marvin got up from his seat and walked over to the pan of ribs. There was something about Rachel that tugged at his heartstrings. She seemed so fragile, yet feisty—easy to break but tough enough to fight back. He thought she was courageous to get up before the group and share her story with them. It took a lot of guts to reach way down in your soul.

"Would you like me to get you some ribs?" he asked her. "They're pretty good."

Rachel placed her hand on Marvin's arm. "No, not at the moment," she replied. Then, as if realizing for the first time that her hand was resting on Marvin's arm, she jerked away, but not before Marvin felt the flutter in his stomach.

"Now, that's a fine brother, Claudette," Mona whispered.

"So why aren't you with him?" Claudette shot back.

"He's not my type. I like those dark, baldheaded brothers with a little more thickness to them."

"You're a trip, Mona. If he asked to jump your bones right now, you'd be waiting on him to get his clothes off."

"Looks like he's got his eye on Ms. Rachel. She wouldn't know what to do with a good man if he fell into her lap."

"Well, right now," Claudette said, "a man is the furthest thing from her mind. And I don't blame her with all the heartache she's been through."

"Yeah, I admit it was tough listening to her story. Makes you wonder what goes on in a woman's head when they see a guy like Reuben and 'playa' is written all over his face."

"What's done is done," Claudette said. "Right now, I'm going to have a second helping of ribs."

"Eat up," Mona said. "Our new divorcee is returning, probably ready to spill her Ex-Files. I like that *Ex*-Files."

"Ten more minutes before we head back into the meeting room to finish up," Sylvia said as she and Ashley returned to the their seats. "Four more files to open."

Marvin sneaked a glance at Rachel, but she refused to look in his direction. He picked up his plate and tossed the remains of his meal in the trash. He moved toward the door of the kitchen, then doubled back and stood before Rachel. She had a smile on her face as she slowly looked up into his, and it warmed him from the inside out.

"What is it, Marvin?" Rachel asked, her hand to the side of her face.

"I really think you should eat something. It might do your headache some good."

"That session wore me out, and I could stand to forgo a meal or two."

Marvin looked at her petite frame and thought she could pass for a fashion model. She was a breath of fresh air.

"No excuses. In fact, you could stand to put on a pound or two."

Rachel gasped and held her stomach to keep from laughing. "Marvin, you are funny. You really are funny."

"Why don't I get you a small plate—just eat a little something. See, you haven't heard my story yet. I've got some crazy stuff in my files, too."

Rachel grinned. She liked this guy. "Would you mind getting me a Coke, too?"

Ashley Jordan-Lewis

A shley closed her eyes and exhaled. She opened them and looked at the group waiting for her to empty her files. Ashley wasn't sure that telling her business was what she really wanted to do, especially with this group of hungry piranhas sitting anxious for the kill. She wasn't sure what she'd expected when Sylvia invited her to become a part of this group, but here she was in the wilderness—all alone, it seemed—and she had to make the best of it.

"I truly loved William," she began. "We met while we were students at Georgetown. I was running for student government president, and he was the only person that hung on to my every word. After that, I would see him every morning when I jogged along the Washington Mall.

"I remember the first time he spoke to me. The cherry blossoms were in full bloom. My body was soaking wet after running for an hour, and William turned a corner and bumped into me.

"'Oops, I'm so sorry,' he said, placing his hand on my arm to steady me.

"'I'm all right, but if I didn't know better, I would have thought you staged that,' I replied.

"'No, I would have done better than that to get your attention.'

"I think you already had my attention."

"William's raised eyebrows and quizzical eyes met my gaze. 'I had your attention. Hmmmm.' He wrinkled his nose and searched deep within for the moment I seemed to suggest.

'I ran for student government president.' I stopped to see if he was paying attention. "My platform," I began again, "concerned equal representation for all students regardless of their color, ethnicity, religion, or… "

"Yeah, I remember you," he said.

"I remember hesitating and then asked him how he got into Georgetown. William's eyes turned cold; the smile was completely gone from his face.

"You mean like affirmative action?" he asked me.

"Like affirmative action," I replied.

"So, you're telling us," Claudette cut in, bringing everyone back to the present, "that William is black?"

"Yes, he is," Ashley said without hesitation.

Quick glances went around the room; Marvin stared straight ahead.

Ashley continued, "I remember the day vividly. My thought at the time was what do I really know about affirmative action."

A loud grunt came from someone in the group.

Ashley swallowed hard and was silent longer than she had planned. She was up in front of the group now and might as well purge the demons that stalked her inner sanctum day and night.

"I had a mind to let this tall, dark, and handsome man continue on his way"—another grunt from the group—"but my intuitive nature pushed me where I wasn't prepared to go. I asked William again if he was the result of affirmative action."

"Somebody's about to get slapped down," Claudette muttered.

Ashley pretended she didn't hear her. "William did not move.

I was sure he was breathing, but those eyes of his pierced my soul as if I had detonated the atomic bomb. He looked at me hard when he replied.

"He said, 'My name is William James Lewis. I have two hard-working parents who are educators, three sisters who are educators and a brother who's a captain in the U.S. Air Force. I graduated undergrad at Howard University, in the top ten of my class with a 3.99 GPA, and you dare ask me if I was the product of affirmative action?' He kicked at a rock nearby. Then he asked, 'Why is it that if your skin is brown, black or tan people always wonder how you made it into college? I made it on my own merit, damn it. Not every black face is poor. Not every black person needs a handout. Not every black face needs financial aid, but thank God it's there for those who need it. Give me a break.'

"William was so mad that tears began to well up in his eyes. Not knowing what else to do, I reached out and hugged him… I kissed him. And to my amazement, William kissed me back. We were happily married for fourteen years, and two weeks ago it was all over—no salvaging, no pleading, and no good-byes. Finished."

Ashley bowed her head and twitched her mouth. She looked out at the ladies and Marvin, this somewhat unfriendly group. She was the only white face in a group of black ones. So what? The same kinds of things that happened to white women happened to black women. This group sitting in front of her was just mad because she was married to the finest black man on the planet—well, they didn't know that yet, but she couldn't be held accountable because she and William fell in love with each other, and yeah…he was black.

Ashley sighed. "When I caught William with another white woman, he had the nerve to say it was affirmative action."

"Serves you right," Claudette said.

"Serves me right? It's okay for him to cheat on me?"

"I'll say it again: serves you right," Claudette said. "There ain't enough black men to go around as it is for all the single black sisters out there."

Sylvia jumped up from her seat and stood between Ashley and Claudette.

"That's enough, Claudette. We have to respect one another. Everyone in here is a victim. We share a common denominator. We are all Exes and we're tired of the self-serving, ain't-going-nowhere pity parties that makes us eat a two-pound bag of Oreos and a half-pint of Ben and Jerry's Chunky Monkey just at the thought of our broken lives. We are all hurting and looking for a way to get past the hurt and the pain, and that's universal and extends to no one race. Let's let Ashley tell her story without further interruption, please."

"Maybe this is not a good time," Ashley said, looking at Sylvia but not at Claudette. "This was a bad idea."

"Yeah, it was a bad idea."

"Enough, let Ashley get on with it," Mona said in a high-pitched voice, shoving her hand in the air.

Claudette rolled her eyes at Mona.

Ashley stood still for more than a minute. She squeezed her eyes shut, then exhaled.

"I was angry when I caught him…them in bed together. But all I could do was just stand there because I was in such a state of shock I couldn't even scream. They looked at me like *I* was a stranger in my own bedroom and had walked into the wrong house.

"I asked William how he could do this to me, but all he could do was stare at me, wide-eyed. And the little bitch was so scared, she cowered underneath my husband to shield herself from what she believed was coming next.

"I didn't even have the energy to fight. I was pathetic. I walked out of the room and my husband didn't even beg me to stay or say that he was sorry. I could hear them whispering, planning what they were going to do next. I walked out and went to my parents' house.

"I loved that man—a part of me always will. There were many days and nights of pleading and begging for him to end the affair. Yes, I went back home, but it only made the pain greater since he ignored me. When I could no longer take the mental abuse, I told him I was going to file for divorce. I thought this strategy would wake him up and he would realize that he'd be losing a good woman. No such luck. He looked at me and said, 'Fine. I'll move out tomorrow'—no good-byes or apologies.

"He would slip back home, wanting to have sex with me because he knew it was good, and he knew I would let him. Even a couple of months before the divorce was final he showed up at the door—must have had a fight with the new girlfriend—and I let him in.

"Sitting in the courthouse listening to the judge talk about our lives, our assets, why we no longer could be husband and wife, chilled me to the bone. I looked at William with that smug look on his face—I'm sure he was thinking freedom at last. But when the judge announced my settlement and then proclaimed that our marriage was dissolved, a smile formed on my face. I said to myself, it isn't over yet. You see, Mr. William James Lewis, I'm carrying your baby—the one thing you always wanted...a baby."

"Ooooohs" and "ahhhhhs" came from the group.

"Ohhhhhhhh my God, Ashley," Sylvia said. "Why didn't you

tell anyone? The court would've figured the baby into your divorce settlement."

"No need. When I get up enough nerve to tell William, he's going to wonder what it will take to win me back."

"You go, girl!" Mona exclaimed. "You are one tough sister. Had me fooled."

"May I have a drink?" Ashley asked. "I've got nothing else to share. And I'd like a group hug, too."

Everyone laughed and huddled around Ashley. Claudette even rubbed Ashley's nonexistent stomach.

"Make him beg," Claudette said. "Make him beg."

"Who said I was going to take him back? I never said I wanted him back; I said, he'll wonder what it will take to win me back. There will be no going back. No, no, no, no, no. When I was begging and pleading, he turned a deaf ear. When I bared my soul, he looked at me in disgust. Now I've got something he really wants, but I'll have the power to deny him. He'll have visitation rights and child support to pay. Oh yeah, I still love that man, but me and my little one, hmph, we have other plans and they don't include the baby's daddy. Now, may I have a drink?"

"No!" everyone shouted. "You're going to have a baby!"

Claudette Beasley

"Whew," Claudette said. "Everyone's files are so tedious, but mine…they aren't full at all.

"I met Tyrone about sixteen years ago at the NCO Club at Fort Stewart, Georgia. My girls and me loved to go to Fort Stewart and check them fine servicemen out. There ain't nothing like a brother in a uniform.

"I was shaking my groove thang for real when Mr. Tyrone C. Beasley walked over to me and said, Lawd have mercy. I was still switching my tail—I was a size ten back then—and ooohhh my, those brown eyes could melt a sister down. He asked if I wanted to dance, and I told him I was already dancing, couldn't he see. Yeah, I had a smart mouth back then, too. He looked at me and said what the hell. Next thing I knew, we had the floor to ourselves because that brother was getting downnnnnnnnnn."

Claudette's arm went up in the air and around…then down to the floor. The group giggled as she demonstrated her point.

"Me and T, as I called him, dated awhile, and after a couple years we decided to make it legal. We were doing everything else anyway. The paper just made us respectable. We got married in a little church just outside of Atlanta. Had ten bridesmaids and ten groomsmen in that church—most of them were family.

"As stories go, the familiar gets old after awhile. We tried to keep it fresh, but we fell into that real marriage thing—work on the job, work at home, eat, sleep and maybe time to hang out with your boys or your girls. And it didn't help when I decided to go to beauty school on top of my part-time job. See, I had plans for my future.

"I forgot to tell you that two months before we got married, me and Tyrone found out we were pregnant with Reebe. To make matters worse, Tyrone got rifted from the military—surplus. That didn't do well for his ego. I think it hardened him and he never forgave the Army for treating him the way they did, especially after he put his life on the line for them during Desert Storm. He was a communications man, and he was still able to get a respectable job working with the phone company laying wires.

"After we got married, we began to argue a lot. We argued about what time breakfast and dinner would be ready. We argued about how much it cost for Pampers and baby formula. We argued about my weight since I seemed to be gaining ten pounds every year. We argued about the unwholesome shows he said I watched on television. We argued about how much water to put in the sink when I washed dishes like I'd never washed a damn dish a day in my life. We argued about washing the floor with a mop or getting down on all fours and hitting it like my grandmammy did back when she was washing the massa's kitchen floors. Yes, and there were days when I cried out and sang that old Negro spiritual, 'My Lord Done Delivered Daniel.'

"Oh, the blessed day arrived seven years later when we had a beautiful baby boy. We named him Kwame after T's uncle he liked a lot. Reebe was T's angel, but Kwame was his heart. He doted on Kwame day and night—couldn't wait for him to grow up so they could play ball together. And me and Reebe—soul mates.

"Then me and T began to argue again. We argued about my weight. We argued about what Kwame should eat. As he grew, we argued about what he watched on TV. When he grew into a bigger baby (you know they never grow up), we argued about what friends he could see. We argued about the violence that was on the video game T's uncle Kwame gave little Kwame.

"We were arguing so bad that day, the video game came to life. I tried to throw a karate chop on Tyrone, but he pushed me hard and I fell and hit my head on our kitchen table. And that's how I got the scar on my forehead. Tyrone felt bad and tried to help me up but not before saying, 'If your ass wasn't so big you might of kept your balance.' And one day after picking my children up from school, I didn't return home.

"Oh, he was still arguing. I just had enough. He complained about everything and wasn't happy about nothing, but he didn't do anything to make it better.

"Before we were divorced, I did open my beauty shop. That was a great day. I believe Tyrone was a little jealous about that. I was independent, didn't need him if push came to shove. Believe me it came to that. It took awhile, but I was able to get a good clientele—that's how I met Ms. Jacqueline Monique Baptiste—and her head needed me."

Mona rolled her eyes. "Nobody asked you to divulge my personal information, sugar."

Claudette shooed Mona with her hand and continued her story while the others giggled.

"And who says a full-figured woman can't have herself a man?" Claudette's braids swung wildly about her face as she became even more animated. Her curved, sculptured nails looked like a set of knives dancing in the air.

"Not a day goes by that some good-looking man who's had the

pleasure of my hands massaging his head doesn't make me an offer for dinner and conversation."

Claudette didn't miss the looks that passed between Rachel and Sylvia.

"Oh yes, I take them up on their offer. Sorry, Mona, but your beautician don't tell all her business. I smother Kwame, but occasionally I get smothered, too.

"I call them my disposable men—one exposure at a time. Dinner and a movie, dancing and drinking, even small trips to Birmingham for a hot, romantic interlude—lip smacking, hands pawing all over me. And it be's so good that in the key of G, I sing 'do, re, me, fa, so, la, tee, doooooooooooooooooooooe.'"

Marvin let out a mouth full of air. Eyes rolled around the room until they had nowhere else to go except back to Claudette, who had not missed a beat.

"I'd like to add that when I get up the next morning, only one egg, two slices of toast and two pieces of bacon will be on my breakfast table for me along with cereal for the children. I use them and lose them—disposable. Just so you don't go and misinterpret anything, I didn't say I didn't like men, because I love me some man, but the only clothes I'll be washing and the only food I'll be cooking will be for me, Reebe, and Kwame.

"Maybe I'm in denial; I don't know. I just don't want no one telling me what to do, how to do it and when to do it. I can do it all by myself when I want to. I guess I can close my Ex-Files because I'm doing all right, all by myself."

Claudette took a bow and looked at each member of the group. "If you have questions, I'll be glad to answer them. If not, I'm finished."

No one said a word except for an occasional giggle that seeped through someone's lips. Then a lone voice spoke up.

"So, why are you here?" Marvin asked, his eyebrows contorted as if trying to understand her purpose.

"Same as you, I'm sure. There are days when it's hard coping with all your household stuff, the children, the finances, an irate client and so on. For me, I was used to sharing those things with my husband and I valued his opinion, in between the arguing that is. And when T and me were together, I was a one-man woman. Can't trust all those diseases out there; I hate the feel of condoms. I won't risk my life, though. I've got Reebe and Kwame to think about. I can bounce things off of you all, and while I may not have been the most pleasant person here tonight, and I've apologized to Ashley already, I do feel like family."

Everyone got up from their seat and gave Claudette a sister hug.

"I hope you've accepted me into the family," Ashley said to Claudette.

"Oh yeah, you my white-skinned pregnant sister. And I've got my eye on you and that baby. I'll even baby-sit on Mondays since the shop is closed on that day if you need me."

"I'm going to hold you to it." Ashley smiled.

"Look, I'm ready to expose my files," Mona said. "Get back in your seats because Mona Baptiste is ready!"

Jacqueline Monique Baptiste

"I've got my own successful catering business, I ride around in a bad Jag, and I have a forty-two-hundred-square-foot home overlooking a beautiful lake. Does it look like I need a man?"

"You go, girl," Claudette said, while Ashley and Rachel traded glances.

"So the question becomes, what am I doing here? The answer is simple. I am here to help you divas—and this one pitiful man—move on with your lives."

The group erupted in laughter.

"If you don't need a man," Sylvia interjected, "why is it that every time I look around, you've got one either strapped to your bosom or sniffing around you like bees to honey?"

"You answered the question, honey. It's the nectar, and you can interpret that any way you like."

"That's not a hard one to figure out," Claudette said.

"Don't hate, Claudette."

Mona paused, blinked her eyes and shifted her body several times. She began to rock back and forth on her heels, as if contemplating what was to come next.

"When I was with Timothy, we were so young. Well, I was nineteen and Timothy was twenty-three. Anyway, I grew up in a wealthy family, sheltered by two older brothers and two older sisters. They treated me like a porcelain doll—too fragile to be touched. I had to be protected from all the elements—and that included the boys who tried to date me. So when I met Timothy that first year in college, I fell hard because I had been forbidden all my life to experience what it was like to have real male friendship.

"Timothy was from Trinidad-Tobago. He was a little dark for my liking, but his speech was smooth as butter. I spent a lot of time watching those lips and listening to the tone of his voice without ever really paying attention to what he was saying. I'm sure I fell in love with his rich, sexy voice that played out in Dolby stereo with lots and lots of bass that pulsated through every vein in my body. Oh yeah, I had died and gone to Heaven because he was definitely the man of my dreams.

"I wanted to take Timothy home to meet my family, but being from an old Creole family, I knew they would have issues with his color and possibly his age. Plus, Papa wasn't about to let anybody into the family that didn't bring a fortune with them."

Mona lifted a handful of her dreads off her back and let them fall before continuing.

"My sisters and brothers all have lucrative careers and married money. That suited Mommy and Papa both. When I told them that I was interested in the culinary arts they frowned at me. Papa said he wasn't wasting any money on me going to school to learn how to cook. He told me to take a good look at my siblings and what their lives had become because they understood honor among family.

"I was not like them. Papa could never understand that. They didn't like Timothy either. Papa swore up and down that Timothy crossed the gulf in a banana boat, got a free ride to Xavier and preyed on rich girls so that he wouldn't have to go back to live in a thatched-roof mud hut. Papa never gave me the opportunity to tell him that Timothy came from class and had a good up-bringing; he judged the outward appearance. That's when I made up my mind that I was not going to be ruled by Jean Claude DePaul Baptiste's iron hand. After I received my business degree, Timothy and I eloped to the chagrin of my fine, upstanding family.

"Timothy and I left New Orleans for Atlanta. Atlanta was a thriving city for blacks when we came here in the late eighties. My husband was going to medical school to become a surgeon specializing in obstetrics and I was studying at the Le Cordon Bleu College of Culinary Arts. Visions of becoming a renowned chef pulsated through me. Life seemed new and fresh for both of us. I didn't need Papa's money. My man and I were going to make it on our own.

"I remember the day that turned out to be a turning point in our lives. I was still in culinary school, and I became very ill. At first I thought I might have inhaled too much of the five or ten spices that I was using to marinate a pork shoulder. It could have been the smell of the fresh meat. At any rate, it felt like someone was dancing on my stomach muscles, twisting them every which way until I was unable to contain the contents inside of me. I sought refuge and comfort at the porcelain bowl in a back rest-room used by all the students. A friend of mine named Suzette found me in a heap on the bathroom floor and tried to pull me out of the stall so I could get some air. Sweat poured down my face, and when I opened my eyes, Suzette was staring at me with a strange look on her face.

"'Mona, are you pregnant?'" she asked.

"I gasped. Children were the farthest thing from my mind at the time. I was in the middle of my first year in culinary school, and whether I spoke to my family or not, I wanted to show them that I would not be just some ordinary cook, holding down the eggs and bacon in a greasy spoon. No, I would be a chef in the most prestigious restaurant in Atlanta.

"A baby. What was I going to do with a baby? Timothy was not overjoyed but didn't quite dismiss the fact that a baby would be a part of our lives; after all, babies would soon be his world day in and day out. A baby would disrupt our time together, especially since we would be in very demanding professions once our careers began to take off. What little time we would have had for ourselves would now have to be shared three ways.

"I began to daydream about the growing embryo inside me. Somehow, the idea of bringing a new life into the world struck me as my greatest invention. It would be better than a crepe Suzette or chicken Florentine. This new formation, flesh of my flesh, would take on the likeness of Timothy and me.

"As the weeks went by, I would rub my tummy every hour on the hour, fantasizing how labor would be and what my baby would look like. Although there was no visible sign on the outside that a baby was growing inside of me, I knew. I could feel my breasts preparing for the glorious day. I would cup them and rub my nipples as I stared into the room that would soon be turned into a nursery."

Marvin fidgeted in his seat.

"After awhile, Timothy seemed to take to the idea, often replacing my hands with his as I rubbed my stomach. We would talk about who the baby would look like—him or me. Then Timothy began to distance himself. I knew that Atlanta hadn't grown on him in the way it seemed to embrace me, but I figured in time everything would be all right.

"Timothy spent more time away from home. We were still

newlyweds, and I hoped that we could spend as much quality time together as possible before the baby came. Morning sickness was almost nonexistent in my pregnancy except for the day I puked in the toilet and nearly fainted. I always felt like a million dollars.

"Culinary school was going well, but my marriage was another matter. Timothy stopped coming home, stating that he needed some quiet time to study. Our home was modest, but there was enough space that privacy was his for the asking.

"I was still in my first trimester, and one night—it was a Friday—I began to have some minor cramping. I needed my husband. I couldn't call my parents, since we were estranged. I called Timothy's cell phone and couldn't get him, so I called the school. They told me that he had gone to New Orleans—and I was supposed to be with him! I couldn't believe my ears. I dropped the phone and began to cry. Somehow what was supposed to be my little miracle also disappeared. I lost the baby. You may call me cold, but I stripped that life off, strutted my stuff and never looked back.

"No, I never looked for him or tried to call him until he received a piece of mail at the house from Immigration. I felt I had every right to know what was in the envelope. My eyes nearly fell out of their sockets. He had applied for a green card because of his marriage to me. Can you believe that?

"I was pissing mad and for the first time in a month I called my nonexistent husband on his cell. A woman answered the phone. She had a distinct Caribbean accent. It could have been his mother. My breathing stopped for only a second, and when I got up enough nerve, I spoke.

"'May I speak to Timothy?'

"'Who may I ask is calling?' the woman asked.

"'It's his wife,' I replied briskly.

"There was silence; then the voice, now shaky, spoke. 'I don't know who you are or what kind of trick you're trying to play. I'm his wife. Timothy and I have been married for ten years.'

"In my best Caribbean accent I told her, 'Tell Timothy that his other wife lost their baby and he has papers here from Immigration.'

"The woman hung up the phone. I didn't blame her…in fact I had no beef with her at all. Timothy did her a disservice, but he was my husband, too, and I was going to get to the bottom of this. I didn't turn my back on my mother and father's advice about marrying Timothy for it to come to this so soon after we were married.

"Oh, Timothy called, hot as molten lava from an active volcano. There was nothing that man could say to me. Not once did he say he was sorry. I turned him in to Immigration and if they deported his ass, I don't know because that life was over. I began to live life for me, Jacqueline Monique Baptiste. I loved Atlanta, and I made it home. Men have come and gone, but I'm happy with Mona just the way she is. I didn't spend time crying about spilled milk. I took a rag, wiped it up, threw it in the trash can and moved on to greener pastures. I haven't looked back since. And life has been good.

"So, sister Mona is here to help you get over the hurdles and pass on some survival skills. These little meetings are fine, but I say don't take no stuff and get whatever is coming to you. I'm finished and I don't need a group hug.

"Whew!" Mona sighed as she looked around at the group. "Glad I got that off my chest. Didn't intend to go there, but there's something about purging your soul…Ex-Files, if that's what you like to call it."

Marvin Thomas

Marvin looked around at the ladies. Everyone was still caught up in Mona's Academy Award-winning performance. Her little act didn't get past him. Deep inside that exterior was a woman who wanted to be loved and had something to give in return. Mona painted over her loneliness with coats of self-confidence and expensive things to show the world that she had arrived and couldn't be touched. Marvin remembered how she'd thrown herself at him at one of the events she'd catered for his company, even though she knew he was married. Mona was very attractive but not the kind of woman he wanted to spend the rest of his life with.

He coughed into his hands.

"It's time for our fine brother to share his files." Mona laughed.

Marvin felt like daggers were penetrating his whole body as the ladies stared back at him. It might have been easy for Mona to stand up there and rattle on about the demise of her marriage, but Marvin truly loved his wife.

"Ladies, this is more difficult than I imagined. I didn't know I would be put on the spot and have to divulge my pain."

"You don't have to," Sylvia cut in. "Share what you want us to know. You may only want to tell us why you chose to come here tonight."

"I appreciate that, Sylvia, but I think I want to share with some-one how I've been feeling these last few months. I know we men are supposed to be macho, but I'm a real man with real feelings, and I've been hurt badly."

Marvin looked out and latched onto Rachel's eyes. She looked away fast as if she had been caught spying into his soul and was afraid of the repercussion. Marvin panned among the other ladies, wrung his hands, and dropped his head slowly without uttering a word. He looked up again and saw as much pain on the ladies' faces as he felt in his heart.

"If you don't feel like saying anything…," Sylvia said.

"No, I do. It's just hard getting started."

"Just pick a place in your life that was good and start there," Sylvia suggested.

His lips and mustache moved, but nothing came forth. Marvin beat his hand with his fist and sighed.

"Maybe if I take my coat off I'll be able to breathe." Marvin laughed uneasily. He took off his jacket and rolled up his shirt-sleeves. His muscles appeared to bulge through the soft fibers of his blue shirt.

"Take it off, take it all off," Claudette screamed.

There were short bouts of laughter.

"I'm a simple brother. What you see is what you get."

"I like," Claudette hollered out. Rachel rolled her eyes at her.

"So uncouth," Mona said, shaking her head.

"I had a good upbringing—wonderful parents and three sisters who doted on their brother. My cousin, Harold, was my best friend and business partner," Marvin said.

"I had three aspirations in life. They were to go to college, own my own business, and find the one woman in the world that would love me as much as I loved her, who would share my dreams and visions for the future while I acknowledged hers, and have a family.

"After working for several software companies, I branched out and started my own: Thomas Technology Solutions. I have been very fortunate, and I don't apologize for saying I owe everything that I am and that I have to God."

"All right, now. That's what I'm talking about," Rachel said. "Me and my God."

Marvin studied Rachel for a moment before continuing with his story.

"I don't want you ladies to get any ideas or think I've got my nose up in the air. I suddenly feel like sharing how good God has been to me. Not only did He bless me with the opportunity to start my own firm, but within a two-year time frame, I was able to enjoy a healthy income of $500,000 a year and maintain a portfolio of stocks, bonds, and mutual funds."

"Every girl needs to know that her man has bank," Claudette interjected. "I ain't mad at ya. Wouldn't mind sharing it with you." She batted her eyes. "Sorry for the interruption."

Marvin smirked. He didn't like loud-talking women. Claudette was the kind that would have your business on the gossip net, telling every head she shampooed what her man had done for her. He shook her image from his mind.

"After my business took off and I was in the best financial position I had been in a long time," Marvin began, "I knew that my life was not complete. I was a hardworking Black man whose ultimate goal was to reach the pinnacle of his career but I needed that someone to share it with. I hadn't dated much and wasn't sure if my old lines were still twenty-first century."

Rachel smiled.

"I met my ex-wife, Denise, while on a speaking engagement in

New York. When I laid eyes on her, I immediately fell in love. I couldn't keep my eyes off of that girl. We corresponded for a month or two, but found that we couldn't be away from each other. After a six-month romance, I proposed.

"Denise is very attractive, sophisticated—and very high maintenance. She has her hair, nails and feet done every week. Even after I married her, I showered her with gifts from the best stores, wined and dined her at the most fabulous restaurants, bought her the most elegant home in the most upscale neighborhood. But what I really wanted was children, and every time I approached Denise about it, she kept putting me on hold...her career, her figure... "

"I understand that sister," Mona said, cutting in on Marvin's train of thought.

"It would have been all right, Mona, if my wife hadn't assured me before we got married that she wanted children as much as I did and that she would be more than happy to be our baby's mother. I'm not a nag, and I didn't want to start being one. I had given my heart and soul to this woman...not just to please her but because I wanted to give her the best of me.

"My sisters told me I was a fool to lavish her with everything she wanted and everything I wanted her to have. I'm sure Denise came to expect these things, but she was always so appreciative.

"She missed her friends in New York, though, and the fast-paced life she'd led. She would often fly home to see her family and friends, and while I didn't begrudge her that, I think I was a little jealous. A couple of times I went with her to New York, as I often made presentations there. Sometimes my business partner, my cousin Harold, would go and that way I had someone looking out for my best interests.

"Three years passed and no baby. Denise became involved with a lot of the high-society folks in Atlanta and became an event planner for a lot of big names—that's how I met Mona: She catered a big shindig I had a year-and-a-half ago when my company reached another milestone on our way to Fortune 500 status. Denise was the perfect wife in every way—except for not wanting to disfigure her body for the only gift I ever asked for.

"About three months after the party, Denise announced that she would be in and out of New York to plan this big celebration for her family reunion because her grandmother was going to be eighty years old. It was a bad time for me to go because I was in negotiations for two lucrative contracts with some major players. Plus, I also had a large contract pending with a major New York corporation about the time Denise was heading that way. I really wanted to be part of closing that deal, but I sent Harold instead since there was no possible way for me to be in two places at one time. Harold had negotiated many contracts for us, so I was very confident in his work.

"I received a call late on a Thursday afternoon to say that the deal was on but they needed my signature as well as Harold's and they wanted the ink to be dry by Friday. I had no other recourse than to catch a flight to New York.

"I flew in and signed the papers before ten a.m. I hadn't called Denise yet, but I was sure she was staying at our town house on Long Island. I rented a car and set off to find my wife.

"I arrived at the town house; the parking lot was deserted—it was almost the middle of the day, and I figured everyone was probably at work. I was sure Denise was catching her breath before all the festivities that were to take place that evening.

"The blinds were still drawn when I entered the town house, even though I thought Denise would be up by now. I dropped my suitcase and briefcase on the floor in the living room and proceeded up the stairs. I walked into the bedroom and could hear the shower running, and I licked my lips in anticipation of jumping in with Denise and kissing her all over. Just as I was about to put my hand on the knob, the door opened and out walked Harold naked as a jaybird, drying his head with a towel."

"No!" Mona shrieked. The others gasped.

"You should have seen the look on my former business partner's face. *Shock* wasn't the word. It was *scared to death*. His whole body turned blue-black from fear. It was disgusting to see him that way. I was so angry, if I had a knife I would have done a Lorena Bobbitt on him.

"But Harold wasn't the person I came to see. I marched into that bathroom as Denise came out calling Harold's name. I'm not a violent man—'God-fearing' is what my church members say about me. But that was the first time I had hate for Denise— pure, unadulterated hate. I asked her why. Why with Harold? I had given her the world. I never complained about a thing even though there were some things I should have stood my ground about. I loved this woman, and now she had desecrated our marriage, desecrated the vows we made before God and man. I felt as if I was in the Garden of Eden with Adam and Eve. I caught both of them in their nakedness. And she claimed she was planning a feast for her family. Yes, she was making a spread all right, but it was her…her…her legs that she was spreading."

Marvin's body began to convulse and he began to cry. "I loved my wife. I was willing to do anything for her. All I wanted was the perfect family," he wailed. His chest heaved in and out while he gasped for breath.

"Enough," Sylvia sighed. She went to Marvin and held him and began to cry, too. Soon there wasn't a dry eye in the place.

EX-hale

Marvin's testimony zapped all the strength that was left in everyone's body. Well, almost. Claudette had enough strength left to make it to the patio to light up a cigarette and get in a few puffs. Various conversations about the evening's events were taking place, but Marvin had put his coat back on and was ready to bid good night.

Someone tapped his shoulder and he turned around to look into Rachel's face.

"You're still in love with her, aren't you?" Rachel asked.

"Why do you ask?"

"I noticed you're still wearing your wedding ring."

"My heart says I do, but every time Harold's nude body flashes in front of me, I turn into a madman. It's hard, though, to just forget the good times we shared as husband and wife—even when infidelity's involved. I read my Bible daily, and I was willing to forgive her, Rachel, but Denise thought it would be better if we dissolved the marriage…she was pregnant with Harold's baby."

Rachel's face turned from calm to anguish. Her mouth gaped open, but no words came forth. Finally she was able to say, "So, are your wife and Harold together?"

"No, they aren't. I find little comfort in knowing that. Every now and then my sisters give me little tidbits they hear since I bought out Harold and fired him from the company. I have not heard anything about Denise or her baby. If I never see Harold again, I'll be fine."

✗✗✗

"I want to thank you all for coming tonight," Sylvia said. "I'm sure it wasn't quite what you expected, but it has done me so much good to talk. I hope you feel the same way. We need to meet once a month and chart our progress. If you want to get together in the meantime, I'm open."

"Let's have a 'ladies' day at the spa," Rachel cried out. She turned and looked at Marvin. "I didn't mean to leave you out; you can go along with us."

He chuckled.

"That sounds like a nice idea, but I'll pass on the spa. I do have a suggestion, though. Maybe we can do a ski trip this winter. We have five months to plan."

"I don't ski," Claudette said.

"I don't, either, but I'd like to try," Rachel said. A sly grin crossed her face.

"I love to ski," Ashley interjected. "I won't be able to do any skiing because of the baby, but I'm all for going."

"I think that's a great idea," Sylvia said. "What about you, Mona?"

"Whatever the crowd wants to do, I'm in."

"Marvin, if you check on the location, cost for transportation and hotel, I'll do the rest," Sylvia said. "Is everyone in?"

"Yes," everyone agreed.

"When are we doing the spa thing?" Ashley asked.

"How about two Fridays from now? We'll take off from our jobs and make it our day," Rachel said.

"I have a doctor's appointment that day," Ashley replied. "But I could still join you later in the afternoon."

"No," Sylvia said. "We can change it to another time."

"You go on and tell me how it is," Ashley pressed.

"I can't go, either," Claudette said. "Fridays and Saturdays are my busiest days at the shop."

"Okay, everybody. We have a ski trip and a spa day in the works. Now let's *exhale* and close the files for tonight," Sylvia said.

Everyone thanked her for a great evening. Under the commotion of good-byes, Marvin asked Rachel, "May I walk you to your car?"

Rachel grinned.

The Road to Recovery

A brilliant sun shone in the spring sky just as the weatherman proclaimed. Temperatures in the high eighties and low nineties were predicted for the week and air conditioners would be working overtime, although it wouldn't officially be summer for another two weeks.

Sylvia jumped up from the table with the last of her bagel still in her mouth and an empty coffee cup on the table. She stretched her arms upward to the left, then the right and brought them down slowly in front of her, exhaling as she did. She lifted her arms again and locked them together, twisting her torso from side to side. When she finished her stretches, she walked to the small TV that sat on the brown granite island that sat in the middle of her spacious kitchen.

The kitchen was a mauve color with black and granite marbleized tiles creating a border between the black electric appliances and the large oak cabinets that adorned the walls. The kitchen boasted a large pantry, large enough for four adults to fit inside.

Sylvia had enjoyed whipping up gourmet meals for her husband in this kitchen, but today was not about him. For the first time in a long time, Sylvia felt rejuvenated. Last night's meeting had been a success. It had made Sylvia rethink her present state of mind. Hate, anger and distrust now had been replaced with joy, jubilation and rebirth—blessings.

T. D. Jakes' voice came from the TV. She sat down and brought one foot onto the chair and hugged her knee as she listened. She found him captivating and hung on to his every word. He admonished husbands and wives to love each other as Christ loved the church. Love begets love, and when you reward each other you honor God. Sylvia looked away. Then T. D. Jakes' voice rose to a crescendo. "Women, men who have been betrayed, mistreated, let down, and kicked to the curb by love, get up now and raise your hands toward Heaven, for you have been loosed to love."

Sylvia jumped up from her seat and raised her hands. "I've been loosed to love," she repeated over and over. "I've been loosed to love." Again, she felt the high she had experienced the night before. No more pity parties for her. She had just been given the key to new life, new hope and possibly new love if she'd just believe.

"I've got to get up from here and go to church," she said with enthusiasm.

Turning off the television, she looked at the digital clock on the microwave. It was ten a.m. She had enough time to make it to Mt. Calvary. Sylvia ran through the shower and put on a loose-fitting, rose-colored, silk chemise and a matching long jacket. A pair of Joan and David rose-colored pumps completed the outfit. She swung her hair from side to side, pleased with Arial's work. Sylvia applied makeup, took one last look and started to get Adonis' approval out of habit. She threw her hand forward to dismiss that thought, and walked out of the door.

Her neighbor, John Hendricks, was mowing his lawn when she exited the house. He nodded in approval. Sylvia smiled back and climbed into her BMW, showing more thigh than she intended. Mr. Hendricks continued to smile until Mrs. Hendricks wandered into the yard with a pair of gardening shears, catching Mr. Hendricks' attention. Sylvia laughed to herself. Old Mr. Hendricks couldn't do anything for her even if he was younger and single.

xxx

Church was dismissed, and Sylvia was still in good spirits. The pastor's sermon, "Don't Let Satan Steal Your Joy!" was still on her mind. She got in her car, waved to a few acquaintances and drove away.

Now that she was on her natural high, she wondered what she would do with the rest of the day. Her daughter, Maya, was still playing newlywed with her husband, Carlos, so this was not the time to be around them. She could stop by her parents' house, but her mother would get on her nerves ten minutes after she arrived.

She continued to drive and as she saw the after-church crowd— families five to six deep—pile into restaurants for their lunch, loneliness began to tug at her heart. Just at that moment, the pastor's message flashed by on a marquee in her subconscious: "Don't Let Satan Steal Your Joy!"

"It is resolved," she said aloud. "I'm going to fix myself a great meal and enjoy my own company."

Sylvia crinkled her face. There was nothing in her refrigerator except for last night's leftovers, and she didn't want that. She saw a Food Lion and pulled in. There were others dressed in Sunday frocks migrating to the store for a last-minute item they had forgotten to get to complete Sunday dinner; Sylvia felt she was in good company.

Sylvia looked in the rearview mirror and applied a tad bit of lipstick. She always had to look her best. She slid her tongue across her teeth for extra measure and, finding that all was well, got out of the car and headed for the store.

Colorful vegetables drew Sylvia in. Ogling over them, she touched each one as if it were a cashmere sweater or a pair of Prada boots. Yellow and white onions; red potatoes, sweet potatoes, baking potatoes, white potatoes; romaine and iceberg lettuce—so many varieties to choose from. She had forgotten how many since she ceased shopping the day Adonis walked out of her life. She'd been relying on takeout. That was about to change because she deserved to treat herself to the best, whether she cooked or a handsome gentleman offered to take her to the restaurant of her choice. She picked up some fresh broccoli and put it in her cart.

Clickety-clack went the shopping cart as Sylvia glided through the store like she owned it. She rolled past the pork section, the poultry section and stopped in front of the beef section and picked up several porterhouse steaks and a filet mignon. She examined them, finally settling on the filet mignon.

She wheeled the cart forward, headed for the steak sauce. She moved down the aisle as if she were on a mission and nearly bumped into her pastor.

"My, Sister St. James, we're in a bit of a hurry," Pastor Orlando Goodwin said.

"I'm so sorry, Pastor. My mind was on what I needed at the moment so I could hurry up and get out of here. I really enjoyed the sermon this morning."

"Well, thank you, Sister. And how have you been doing? I haven't talked with you much, especially since your divorce."

"I've been doing pretty good. I have a support group that started, and I think it's going to be a great help to me as well as others."

"Umm, a support group for divorced women. I don't know if you've noticed, but quite a few of our young people are opting for divorce instead of trying to make a go of their marriage. It's so sad."

"I know. Marriage doesn't seem to have the same staying power it did in our parents' generation."

"You've got me to thinking. I'd like for you to stop by my office next week. Call my secretary, Louise, and make an appointment. I think you can be an asset to the young women in our church."

"Okay, Pastor. I'll do that. Have a good day, and give my regards to Sister Goodwin."

"I will."

Sylvia watched Pastor Goodwin until he wheeled his cart off the row. A smile illuminated her face as she stood in the middle of the aisle digesting his request. *He's going to ask me to start a support group at church*, she thought. She barely had her own life together, but if this was God's way to help her through her trials, she was going to let Him help. She felt good and wheeled her cart to the frozen food section.

"Dessert to top it off," she said aloud to no one.

Sylvia leaned over the refrigerated bin and pulled out a Turtle Pie—full of calories and chocolate.

"Dessert would be nice," came a familiar voice that made Sylvia nearly topple over into the bin.

Catching herself, Sylvia turned in the direction of the voice and saw the finest piece of hard chocolate candy standing in front of her. He wore a white Armani suit and a white fedora sat on his head. His eyes were hidden behind a pair of dark glasses, and his sexy smile was framed by a neatly trimmed mustache.

"Excuse me?" Sylvia asked in a much too sexy voice.

"I like dessert, Sylvia."

"No, it couldn't be."

"I'm surprised you don't recognize my voice. The familiar will always be the familiar."

"All right, enough of the psychology lesson, *Kenny*. I've got to finish my grocery shopping."

"How are you doing?"

"I'm doing okay."

"How's that husband of yours? What's his name?" Kenny snapped his fingers.

"Adonis," Sylvia snapped.

"Yeah, yeah…cat from up North. Adonis. Strange name for—"

"That's enough, Kenneth."

"Well, how are you and your old man doing?"

"We aren't." Kenny stood at attention. "We have been divorced for awhile."

Kenny ran his eyes over Sylvia's body once again. His staring made Sylvia a little uncomfortable.

"I was wondering why a man would have his beautiful wife out shopping for food on a day like today. If you were my woman, we'd be sitting in a nice restaurant sipping on our second glass of Chardonnay, waiting on our steaks."

Sylvia stood still with a smirk on her face and hand on her hip as she listened to Mr. Kenneth Richmond spout out what he would do and what she shouldn't being doing.

"And I guess you aren't with anybody since you just happen to be in the store, also, Mr. Richmond."

Kenny laughed. "Busted. You look well…uhhh, more than well."

Sylvia shifted and placed her hands on the handle of her cart.

"You in a hurry? It's been…what…twenty years since I've seen you?"

"Yes, I am in a hurry."

"To go where?"

"That's none of your business."

"Slow down, my love. Just excited about seeing you after all this time. I just returned to the city a little over a month ago. Ran into Rachel's ex, and he gave me the rundown. You sisters know how to run men out—of town."

"That's where you're wrong. I did everything I could to keep my man happy and at home, but he wanted to fly. There was nothing left to do but let him go."

"I'm really sorry to hear that, Sylvia. He doesn't realize the treasure he left behind…just like I did so many years ago."

"Let's not go there," she snapped.

"Look, since we are both by ourselves, why don't we do dinner?" Kenny suggested.

"I don't know. I don't think it would be a good idea."

"Aw, come on. What harm could come of two old friends sharing a meal? You and I were good once."

"No, we weren't, Kenny. You know we weren't good for each other."

"I do know that this is another place in time. A beautiful woman is standing in front of me—a woman I've adored and would like to get the opportunity to know again. I would love to take you for a nice seafood meal at Pappadeaux. If I remember correctly, you enjoy Cajun seafood," he said in a wheedling tone.

"Your memory serves you correctly."

"It's settled then. There's no need for you to spend money on a meal that you would have been eating alone."

"I don't know."

"What's to know? I'm single; you're single; we're both hungry.

That equates to two people having a good meal at a nice restaurant."

Sylvia hesitated, then sifted through the items in her basket. She lifted her head and her eyes met Kenny's head-on. Not that the offer of dinner wasn't tempting or those sumptuous eyes uninviting, but visions of the old Kenny loomed before her— the one who had broken her heart into a dozen pieces.

As if he knew what she was thinking, Kenny moved closer and lifted her chin with his hand. "I'm not the same person from twenty years ago. I've matured and learned how to treat a lady."

Sylvia smiled, still not wanting to let down her guard. She put the cheesecake back into the bin and turned to Kenny.

"I'll meet you at Pappadeaux in twenty-five minutes."

"Great, I can't wait. And Sylvia? You look good, girl."

Sylvia stared into Kenny's eyes. Her head was telling her that she should get her groceries and go home, but against her better judgment, her heart said Kenny was a better alternative to being by herself today.

"I just want you to know, Kenneth, that having dinner with you is just that—two old friends sharing a meal," she said firmly.

"That's fine with me, but it's my treat."

Releasing a small amount of air from her lips, Sylvia turned on her heels and headed out the store, but not before turning around to see her old lover admiring the view. Kenny was going to be the death of her yet—even after twenty years. She smiled and walked out of the store.

Glitches in the Road

The drive to Pappadeaux was full of anxiety. Sylvia didn't know what to make of seeing Kenny after all these years. He looked amazing, like hot fudge dripping over a large scoop of chocolate ice cream. Of course, he had aged, but so had she. Although he was covered in fine linen, Kenny still possessed a muscular body. The thought made Sylvia shiver.

Interstate 85 ran through the heart of Atlanta. Sylvia was smiling as she drove along, waving to folks she didn't know as they drove past, admiring the Atlanta skyline that made the Peach State the most talked-about place to live. She realized that her speedometer was on 80 and immediately reduced her speed to 65. Was this a sign? Was she moving too fast with Kenny? She was only going out to dinner with an old friend. She needed to get a grip. The man only asked her to dinner; he never uttered a word about sleeping together.

S-c-r-e-e-c-h! Sylvia hit the brakes to avoid hitting the car in front of her. Daydreaming about Kenny was going to get her killed. A sudden chill came over her as she moved toward the right lane as she passed the mile marker for Jimmy Carter Boulevard.

The night Kenny walked out on her played out in her mind. They had a heated argument about Kenny running around with other women while they were dating. He denied it, but Sylvia had proof. She had done her own detective work, taken her own pictures. Kenny told her that she didn't control him and he was going to do what he wanted to—and if she didn't like it, there was someone else to take her place. Sylvia tried to block the doorway to her apartment to keep him from leaving, but he pushed her aside and walked out the door. Sylvia had not seen him since, although he had called her once or twice. And now, here he was after twenty years and a broken marriage, talking about dinner and who knew what else.

She pulled into the parking lot at Pappadeaux and reassessed her reason for being there. "Dinner, that's all," Sylvia said out loud.

Even at three in the afternoon the restaurant was crowded. She looked around for Kenny, but he hadn't arrived yet. She moved toward the hostess and put her name on the list.

"St. James, two, nonsmoking."

"It'll be thirty minutes," the hostess replied.

Fifteen minutes passed with no sign of Kenny. Sylvia's heart skipped a beat and she immediately regretted accepting Kenny's dinner invitation. Another five minutes passed, and soon her name would be called, but instead of two there would be one.

Fuming, she got up to leave. Just as she passed through the double doors, she bumped into Kenny. He was carrying a dozen red roses in his arms.

"You leaving?" Kenny questioned, his eyebrows arched. "These are for you." He pushed the roses into her arms.

"No, I...I...I was going to the car to see if I left my cell there."

"Didn't think I was coming, so you were going to call me."

"I don't have your phone number, Kenny," she pointed out.

"St. James, party of two. St. James, party of two."

"They're calling us," Sylvia said, thankful for the reprieve. "Thank you for the roses. They're beautiful and smell good, too."

"For a special lady who is more beautiful than the roses she's carrying."

A broad smile rose on Sylvia's face. "Thank you."

"Follow me," the hostess said.

Sylvia and Kenny were seated and gave the waitress their drink order.

"I love this place," Kenny said.

Sylvia continued to smile. "I do, too."

"Brings back old memories—good memories. I guess you might say that this was our spot."

"Something like that." At Kenny's puzzled look, Sylvia added, "I'm sure you brought all your women here at one time or another."

"Now why do you want to spoil a perfect day?"

"Am I telling the truth?"

Kenny laid his hand over Sylvia's as she fingered the cloth napkin. "I've been a lot of places in my life and time, but for your information, this was *our* place. You were the only special person in my life, although I didn't act like it much of the time. To answer your question, I only took the special people in my life to Pappadeaux. It holds a lot of memories for me, Sylvia. That's why I suggested it today. And I have changed."

"What was my favorite dish?"

"Salmon. That wasn't even a test."

"And you liked the steak and shrimp plate, and the seafood gumbo."

"You remember!" Kenny exclaimed, pleased.

"Why didn't we work, Kenny? My whole life was you," Sylvia said.

"That might have been the problem, Sylvia. You were holding on too tight. We weren't married, but you had me in this stranglehold, and I was way too young to commit to anything that sounded like forever."

Kenny couldn't keep his eyes off of Sylvia. He didn't look up when the waitress brought his iced tea and asked for their dinner order. At his silence, Sylvia said to the waitress, "Give us a couple of minutes, please?" *Snap, snap* went Sylvia's fingers. "What's gotten into you? You've left me again."

A rush of air escaped Kenny's lips. "I'm sorry. I'm amazed that I'm sitting with you in our favorite restaurant. My mind had gone back some years. You are beautiful, Sylvia. Wouldn't it be something if we got back together again?"

"I wouldn't count on it." Kenny looked hurt. "My husband and I have only been divorced nine months, and it has been a hard adjustment for me. Twenty years of marriage, a daughter, and… I truly loved Adonis. I don't know if I would take him back this very moment if he came running in here and asked me, but the consideration is there," Sylvia said honestly.

"I see. Why don't we order since we know what we want?" Kenny motioned for the waitress.

"Very presumptuous of you. I might have a taste for something different tonight."

Kenny smiled. "Taste for something different?"

Sylvia blushed. "Now, Kenny, you are making this difficult."

"I only repeated what you said, but I like different. Will I be able to get your telephone number tonight?"

"Ask me at the end of dinner."

"I will. This feels so right, Sylvia."

Sylvia blushed, then cleared her throat to speak. "Well, what has Kenny Richmond been doing with his life?"

"I've started my own computer support business."

"You what? I mean, I knew you were smart…but a computer business? I would never have equated the two."

"I'm your poster child for the wayward child found on the Damascus Road. I was given another chance at life, and I made good of it. Now I provide computer support to the school system. My clientele has grown since I've added the school system to my list of clients. I started with a few businesses, but my reputation is gaining."

"That's wonderful, Kenny."

"What about you? What has Sylvia been doing besides playing house with a man that doesn't know your worth."

"Remember, even though a lot of time has passed, you were not the most caring mate."

"Ouch! You're right; how soon we forget. But I promise if you give me a chance, Sylvia St. James, I'll show you what I'm really made of."

"What's that?"

"You answer your question first."

"I'm an event planner for a large corporation. I schedule high-profile meetings for some very high-profile customers. My beautiful daughter, Maya, recently got married and I now have the house to myself."

"Sounds lonely."

"It isn't." Sylvia looked up into Kenny's searching eyes. "I lied. It's very lonely."

"It doesn't have to be."

"Our food is here," Sylvia said, glad for the interruption. "Say grace."

Kenny said grace, and they tabled their discussion for later. They ate in silence.

"Thank you for a wonderful meal and good company," Sylvia said, trying to avoid Kenny's eyes.

"The pleasure was all mine. I'd like to do it again."

"Let's take it a day at a time."

"Okay. I'll walk you to your car."

Sylvia felt her adrenaline flow as Kenny walked close to her. They were silent until she felt his arm go around her shoulder. She stiffened, drew her lips together and let out a small bit of air but did not remove Kenny's arm because it was definitely the end of the road.

"Your hair smells good."

Sylvia did not respond. Her car was in view, and in a moment she would be driving home alone, left to recount the events of the day and contemplate her method of recovery from *this* Ex-file.

"This you?" Kenny said, as Sylvia stopped behind her BMW.

"This is me, and again thank you for a lovely meal."

"Now will I be able to get your phone number?"

Sylvia had hoped she'd get away without having to give up the coveted numbers. "I guess so. You were a good boy."

"Hmmph." Kenny smirked. "I was on my best behavior. I'd like to see you again, Sylvia. You stoked the fires of my heart tonight."

"Kenny, I can't promise you anything, but it would be nice to hear from you *occasionally*."

"Whatever you say," Kenny said, not oblivious to the word *occasionally*.

Sylvia wrote her telephone number on the back of the church program. She was upset that she didn't have another piece of paper to write on, but her memories of Kenny didn't include him worshipping at any church service.

"I look forward to hearing from you." Sylvia tried to sound sincere.

"It won't be long. If I could have come home with you tonight, I would have been at your side."

"No, Kenny. Not now or ever."

"We'll see, my love. Drive safe and until I see you again."

"Good night." *I hope this isn't the devil that's come to steal my joy because he'll have a hard way to go,* Sylvia thought.

Kenny swiftly pulled Sylvia to him—their mouths inches from each other. Sylvia's breathing was labored, and Kenny's eyes were hypnotic. He moved closer, touching her closed lips with his own. Sylvia's eyes were frozen wide-open—two large, almond-shaped nuggets pasted on her face for eternity.

Kenny held Sylvia in a tight embrace, his lips still seeking refuge. He let his hands rove the small of her back, hoping to thaw the stiff woman he held. Kenny kissed her lips again. Then there was movement. She kissed him back—those same frozen eyes fixed on him.

Feast Your Eyes on This

Green bits of cilantro crowned the tops of the Creole-seasoned crawfish cakes that Mona arranged on the porcelain platter. She delicately draped slithers of grated carrots mixed with red onions and a hint of parsley around the border of the platter, yielding an eye-catching and mouthwatering dish. Large urns were filled with delectable seafood gumbo—its rich aroma wafted from the pot and the steam kissed Mona's nose as she lifted the top to make sure there was enough crab in the thick stew. Fruit from the sea hugged the seasoned rice they called jambalaya as if it had ownership; hot oil bubbled from the searing heat that licked the bottom of the pan-fried, petite redfish fillets as they cooked, then relaxed when Mona pulled them from the skillet. Saran-wrapped tomato and crab salads were kept refrigerated, to be pulled out just before the 100 guests were to arrive.

Entertaining was Mona's forte, and she had built quite a reputation in Atlanta for catering the most lavish parties. Dress it up or down, Mona gave the best anyone's budget could afford.

The evening's clients were Atlanta's favorite philanthropists and socialites, Kessler and Kohara Gordon. The Gordons owned the only black cable television station in Atlanta, SILK—Soul

Interest in Life's Kaleidoscope—and, like their television company, they were visionaries about to change the world.

Tonight's affair was a fund-raiser to raise awareness about breast cancer, a disease that had almost wiped out Kohara's female relatives. She was a five-year survivor and had ridden some tough waves, but there was nothing mysterious about the prayers Kohara's family sent up for her down in the bayou. And she and Kessler were living the life, and Mona envied them.

With hands on her hips, Mona sashayed the length of the room in an Izzy Camilleri nylon tube top accentuated by matching belted wide-leg pants. A silk scarf of the same fabric pulled back her braids and hung just below her buttocks. She wore four-inch gold leather peep-toe heels. She sucked her teeth and marveled at her own knack for being able to turn the mundane into something spectacular. Mona posted herself on a high, leather-backed bar stool, crossed her legs and waited for the hosts to arrive.

Laughter streamed into the room and mixed with the slow, sultry voice of India Arie. Kessler and Kohara sauntered through the double doors of the SILK Palace dressed in black—a tux for him and a long halter gown for her. Mona slid from her seat ready to usher the Gordons to the colorful buffet table for final inspection, although one wasn't needed.

Thirty minutes later, guests began to arrive—the up-and-coming as well as the most prominent people in Atlanta society. They milled about greeting acquaintances or introducing a spouse to a new business partner, all part of a ritual already performed at least a dozen times this year.

Mona moved casually through the crowd in hopes of sighting Sylvia, hoping that she would come after the Gordons had so graciously extended her an invitation at Mona's request. There was no sign of her yet, so Mona eased farther into the crowd, checking and rechecking to make sure appetizers were being provided by her able staff.

Exotic and glamorous evening gowns dusted the hardwood floor, moving as effortlessly as the women who were draped in them. It was awe-inspiring, Mona thought, to see so many of her own kind, her Black people, so distinguished and well-refined.

One day, Mona would be one of them. She was nearly there, but she needed the perfect mate to complement her. She brushed back a braid that had slipped over her shoulder and daintily lifted a champagne glass off the silver serving tray as it passed by, giving a sly wink to the waiter.

Eyes closed, Mona let the fruited passion tumble down her throat. She puckered her lips in satisfaction, and when she opened her eyes a dark, handsome, bald gentleman filled her vision.

For a moment, Mona felt uncomfortable as the man stood off to the side, eyes locked into position, and analyzing every one of Mona's emotions.

The gentleman moved from his resting place and moved toward Mona. He took her hand, lifted it to his lips and placed a subtle kiss on the slope of her fingers. "Didn't mean to startle you."

Mona's eyes were quizzical, dancing and darting at the same time. She withdrew her hand from the man's gentle embrace. "I'm sorry. You did startle me."

"You were enjoying your drink, and I guess you never noticed me standing in the corner."

Mona eased up and let out a little chuckle. "You were not there when I put the glass to my mouth."

"Oh, but I was. I wasn't sure you had winked at me or the waiter, but it didn't matter because I saw before me the most beautiful woman I've seen all night."

Mona batted her eyes and smiled. "Flattery will get…"

"Michael Broussard."

"Mona Baptiste," she said, shaking his massive hand. She looked at him again two minutes too long to make sure she wasn't dreaming. "I'm sorry for staring, but you remind me so much of someone I used to know."

"Well, I've never met you before, and I hope to cause a different reaction if you'd allow me a second chance. Hello, my name is Michael Broussard."

Mona smiled again. Her smile was long and broad.

"I'm Mona Baptiste."

"Are you here with anyone? It would be a shame if you were."

"I'm the—"

"Mona." The voice rang through the crowd followed by a few *clickety-clicks*. Sylvia's timing was impeccable, Mona thought, although she couldn't believe her eyes: Sylvia was stepping up in this party with the likes of Kenneth Richmond! "Hi, sweetie," Mona said as she extended her right cheek and placed an affectionate sister kiss on Sylvia's left cheek.

"You remember Kenny?"

"How could I forget him," Mona said sarcastically. She rolled her eyes to the top of her head, and then turned slightly—right into the charming face of her new acquaintance. "Oh, Sylvia, this is Michael Broussard. Michael, this is Sylvia St. James and Kenneth uhh"—she snapped her fingers a few times—"uhh—Kenneth Richmond." A nasty smile crossed her face. "My dear friend Sylvia is newly divorced."

Sylvia jerked her head in disbelief and gave Mona an *I know you didn't go there* look—not with Kenny standing at her side.

Michael shook the couple's hands. Mona saw the puzzled look on his face, but she didn't care. She was having a little fun at

Sylvia's expense, and the champagne she consumed a few minutes earlier only egged her on.

"It was nice meeting you, Mona," Michael said. "Maybe we can talk later."

"That would be nice," Mona whispered in a sexy voice. He blew her a kiss, and Mona watched him become enveloped in the crowd as he walked away.

"Who was that?" Sylvia begged. "He is so fine."

"Some guy I met only a few minutes before you walked up. And what are you doing with that gonna-break-your-heart jackass?" Mona replied.

"Mona, he's standing right here."

Mona rolled her eyes and squeezed her lips together.

"Excuse me, ladies. Would you like something to drink?" Kenny asked Sylvia.

"Yes, I would. Thank you, Kenny."

"I'll be right back. Sounds like the two of you got some catching up to do. And I love you, too, Mona." He winked at her and headed for the bar.

"Damn, Sylvia."

"It's nothing serious, Mona. Ran into him at the grocery store a couple of weeks ago. You know how they say don't go into a store when you're hungry? Well, even though I was in the store to pick up a few groceries, I was also in need of some TLC. There he was, and he was it because he was there," Sylvia said with a shrug.

"I hope you know what you're doing."

"It's just a date. When you asked me to come to this shindig, it felt good knowing that I had someone to accompany me, and I didn't have to sit all night and watch married men parade around with their wives while the wives take sideway glances at me. I'm not sleeping with him, Mona; I'm smarter than that."

"You seem a little desperate, and he looks as if he already hit the honey pot."

"Don't be so crude; it doesn't become you. Don't make me regret that I came to this party. I don't care who's giving it."

"Lighten up, my sister. Didn't mean to pounce on you. It's just that Kenny was the last person I expected to see you with."

"Well, get over it and let me enjoy this evening. Anyway, that handsome guy is still watching you. I say your hands might be full."

"He *is* good-looking. I don't know, Sylvia. I get the distinct feeling I've met him before, but yet I can't recall ever seeing him before."

"All your running around is catching up with you. And you have the nerve to talk about me."

"Watch it, girl. No, I'm sure I have not met Michael Broussard before. My spirit says otherwise. Well, here comes Kenny. Enjoy yourself, but not too much."

Sylvia winked.

EX-cept This

Caribbean music floated through the air. A calypso band flavored the room with saucy beats and rhythms that had partygoers unloosening bow ties and lifting dresses so they would not be stepped on as they danced the night away. The Gordons' fund-raiser was a huge success, raising more than two million dollars for breast cancer research. While the elite gave for the cause, it didn't hurt that next year's tax return would reflect their generosity, too.

The seafood gumbo and jambalaya had been replaced with fine wine, and Mona sipped along with everyone else. Shoulders moved from side to side; Mona's did as well. Sylvia and Kenny were lost in the crowd, and Mona smiled, happy that Sylvia was enjoying herself. She stopped for a moment to contemplate the likelihood of Sylvia and Kenny getting back together, but it was their business. After all, she wouldn't want Sylvia interfering in her affairs.

Mona made a last check to see if her workers had enough wine and all was in order, sashaying around the room, stopping at different points, until she was satisfied. Everyone was having a good time, and the music continued as if there was no end.

"Would you like to dance?" whispered a male voice from behind Mona.

His breath was warm on her neck, and she felt her body tingle. She turned around slowly, and Michael Broussard stood nose to nose with her.

"You seem to be enjoying the music; if we hurry, we can get a in a few twirls before the song ends."

Mona looked into his eyes, not wanting to move. "I'd like that, Mr. Broussard."

"Michael is fine."

Mona kept quiet and followed Michael onto the dance floor. His movements were fluid and quick, and he moved Mona around with the air of a professional. He was light on his feet, and the wine Mona consumed caused her to loosen up and follow his lead. He swung her back and held her, twirled her around and lifted her at the waist giving the illusion she was a star flitting across the sky. When the music stopped, Michael had to hold Mona up to keep her from spinning out of control and landing on her behind.

She put her hand up when Michael begged for more. Mona was intrigued and wondered if he moved like that in every thing he did. At the moment, she needed a time-out to assess what had just happened.

Michael sat next to Mona and clapped to the music, glancing occasionally in her direction. He smiled, getting his second wind.

"Can't keep up with me, heh? I had you pegged for someone who could stay on the dance floor all night long."

"I believe it's the wine. It won't let me back on the floor."

"Had a little too much to drink?"

"Something like that. You're very discerning, Mr. Broussard…I mean Michael."

"I like you, Mona. You have class and style, and I love the way you walk."

Mona blushed. "I don't know what to say."

"Say you will have breakfast with me."

"Well, I don't know. I don't usually go out with someone the moment I meet them."

"I'm not just 'someone,' Mona. I've known you my whole life."

"Excuse me?"

"I mean that we were destined to meet. I've waited my whole life to meet someone like you. Tonight, I saw a first-class businesswoman handle a classy affair with ease and grace. Your flair and elegance are beyond words, not to mention the wonderful food the host told me was your doing."

"Well, thank you for the compliment. I'm glad you enjoyed."

"And breakfast…"

"There you are, Dr. Broussard," Kohara Gordon called. "Kessler and I wondered where you were."

"Enjoying myself, Mrs. Gordon. This has been a wonderful evening."

Did she just say Dr. *Broussard? He never said he was a doctor*, Mona thought. No, he introduced himself as Mr. Michael Broussard. *Who was this man?*

✗✗✗

"Mona is being swept off her feet by the gentleman who was admiring her earlier," Sylvia commented to Kenny as they watched the couple dance by.

"Good for him. Mona is not one of my favorite persons."

"Kenny, you know how Mona is. She's very opinionated and doesn't hold anything back. I believe it comes from her being so sheltered while growing up and experiencing quite a few disappointments in her young life. Now she has to prove to the world that she's confident about who she is. No one can pierce her wall unless she allows them to."

"Well, good for Mona. I'm with her as long as her opinions don't interfere with me and you."

"What do you mean?" Sylvia asked.

"I'm not going to tell a lie, Sylvia. You feel so right to me."

"Not so fast, Kenny. I'm just getting used to going out on dates."

"I know but I'm going to say this anyway. You have rekindled something in me. The person you knew twenty years ago is no longer the person you see. I'll admit that I've done some things in my life that I'm not proud of, but I've changed. I'm a better man."

"That's good to hear."

"The Kenny you see is the real deal."

"I don't know what to say."

"You can say that you'll give me a chance."

"Well, we're out, aren't we?"

"I'm talking about more than tonight, Sylvia. Let me show you how a real man treats a woman."

"I don't think I'm ready…for anything else."

Kenny reached into his pocket. "Hold out your hand."

"For what?"

"Close your eyes and hold out your hand."

Sylvia closed her eyes. Kenny laid a key in the palm of her hand. Sylvia opened her eyes. "What is this for?"

"Room 628 at the Intercontinental down the street—right next to your favorite mall. You can come with me or I can drive you home and let you think about it. I have another key. What will it be?"

EX-citement

The air was brisk and stung Kenny's face as he cruised down Peachtree Road with the window down. Soft sounds from Will Downing, Jr. floated in the early dawn.

Kenny hummed along with the music, tapping his fingers on the steering wheel. *"Maybe we can just get away…maybe lay in bed for a day,"* Kenny sang along with Will Downing. He rocked his head slowly to the beat, enunciating every word as if his life depended upon it, stealing the song away from Will. His thoughts were on the lady he had asked to come to his room. The tapping continued until the hotel came into view. Preoccupied with his thoughts, Kenny jerked the car left into the parking lot, cutting off a 1966 Ford Mustang barreling down the street heading north.

"Whoa, that was close," Kenny said.

Kenny found a parking space in the parking garage close to the hotel entrance, parked and then sat a moment, wondering if Sylvia would take him up on his offer. They were not the young, inexperienced kids of twenty years ago when life was an experiment in the making. They were two grown adults. Kenny drew his lips together and let out a stream of air. It was time to find out what Sylvia was thinking.

Kenny moved around the car until he came to the passenger's side and opened the door. There sat Sylvia, still beautiful in her evening gown—her ample breasts bountifully displayed above the bodice of her dress—not moving or saying a word as Kenny extended a hand to her. She looked at it as if it were foreign, then turned her head and looked at her lap as if searching for something. Kenny stood at attention, in no obvious hurry.

Creases formed in Sylvia's face. Kenny would have rather seen her dimples, but he understood that this was a big decision for her. Sylvia swung her legs out of the car and reached for Kenny's hand to pull her up. She looked into his face and gave a faint smile without saying a word.

They rode the elevator to the lobby floor and exited in a hallway that led to the lobby. Sylvia's head turned. Kenny's head turned.

"That was Boris Kodjoe," Sylvia said. "My God, he's fine."

"Look over there. It's his wife Terri with their baby," Kenny said.

Then Tyler Perry walked past. Sylvia and Kenny were speechless and their mouths hung wide open.

The Intercontinental Hotel still reeked of its brand-new smell. The lobby of the hotel was grand. Kenny led the way to the elevators. Sylvia was still at his heels, although she hadn't uttered a word since the Kodjoe family sighting.

The pair rode the elevator to the sixth floor in silence.

Ding…ding.

Sylvia looked at Kenny, and he nodded. This was it. They walked the fifty feet to room 628.

"Do you still have the key?" Kenny asked.

"I thought you said you had an extra key."

"I do, but I was curious to know if you were still holding onto the one I gave you."

Sylvia didn't answer. She reached into her small bag, produced the key and handed it to Kenny without a word. Without looking at Sylvia, Kenny took the key and opened the door.

Kenny saw Sylvia's eyes dart around the room, little flashlights trying to discern what lay hidden in the dark. He rubbed her back and gently ushered her into the room. Two queen beds were draped with heavy off-white spreads, and the pillows were fluffed to perfection.

Sylvia glanced at a bed, but stood in the middle of the room. Kenny strode to the window to close the drapes, then returned to where Sylvia stood and faced her. He raised her chin with his fingers and gingerly kissed her lips.

"What's on your mind, baby?"

"I can't do this, Kenny. I don't know why I came here."

"Is it me?" Kenny arched his eyebrows.

"Don't try and play me, Kenny. I know what you're trying to do."

"Sylvia, I want to be with you. It's as simple as that. And not just for the night. I hope this will be the night of all nights...and days...the beginning of a new friendship."

"Then this is all wrong, Kenny. We should try and get to know each other first. That's the biggest reason people get a divorce. They fail to become friends, and as their relationship moves ahead, they try to fill in the stuff that should have been there in the beginning and set themselves up for failure."

"Now where did all of this come from?"

"I've been thinking. After twenty-something years of what I thought was a marriage that had 'happily ever after' written at the end...somewhere, something went wrong and I have no clue what it was. Adonis leaving tore me apart. I gave my marriage everything I had and then some, but it wasn't good enough. Kenny, I still love my husband in a crazy sort of way."

"Then why are you here?"

"Because I let you talk me into it?"

"Oh, don't blame it on me! Yes, I want to be with you, but I didn't put you in handcuffs and drag you here against your will. I'm only guilty of forcing you to make a choice. All you had to do was say yes or no. It wouldn't have been the first time that you told me no."

"It was the look on your face."

"I'm not desperate, Sylvia. I've just been blessed to find the woman who I should have been with in the first place had I known how to treat her right."

"Listen to you, Mr. Kenny Richmond."

"Yeah, listen to me, Ms. Sylvia St. James."

"You smell good…real good."

"And your lips are fab-u-lous."

Kenny put his arms around Sylvia and held her tight. Sylvia's arms now hung around Kenny's neck. Their lips met in a tender kiss. Heads cocked to the side, they held each other tight and continued to kiss and let their tongues roam in search of all there was to discover. Kenny was afraid to let go—afraid that Sylvia would use it as an excuse to stop what was the beginning of what he believed was a lifetime together.

They stopped kissing and Kenny said softly, "Let me turn on the radio to a nice jazz station. That will help lighten the mood that is quite right at the moment."

Sylvia gazed at him as he moved to the radio. Kenny wasn't sure what to feel, but he thought that any minute Sylvia would pounce on him and lick him to death. She had that crazy seductive look about her. It wouldn't have been a bad thing, but Sylvia stayed glued to the spot.

"Do you want to get comfortable?" Kenny asked.

"You mean take my clothes off?" Sylvia responded.

He laughed. "If that will make you feel more comfortable, then by all means."

"Kenny, I'm serious."

"Let's dance. This must be a Will Downing night. They're playing my jam."

Sylvia fell into Kenny's arms, and they slow danced, punctuating every word Will sang with their bodies. Sylvia laid her head on Kenny's shoulder, and he stroked it until Sylvia was cooing.

A fast number played and they broke out into a swing number, throwing themselves at each other, making erratic movements at each bend and turn—foreplay by another name. Kenny and Sylvia were so lost in the mood they created, no one noticed that the music had faded and the disc jockey had gone to commercial.

Kenny touched the base of her neck. His finger slowly pulled the zipper down. The zipper moved like a train moving along the tracks, splitting the track in two. The top of the gown fell into his hands, and he laid her on the bed.

Kenny placed kisses on her breasts. Sweet adoration purred from Sylvia's lips as Kenny continued to climb up and down the mountain ranges. His kisses were potent, and Sylvia surrendered easily.

As Sylvia's lips continued to enjoy Kenny's, a sudden vision of Adonis invaded her subconscious. Almost as if someone had dropped a bucket of ice on the twosome to douse out flames, Sylvia sat up.

"Please, Kenny, I can't go there with you."

"We were so far along the way, Sylvia. Trust me."

"I have to trust what my head is telling me. I can't have sex with you. If we are to have anything at all, you'll have to respect my wishes."

"Didn't you feel what I was feeling, Sylvia?"

"What were you feeling, Kenny? What was your head telling you? You must have missed the signals that said I'm vulnerable, fragile, not sure if this is what I want to do although I'm is in the room with you. It's your…your…thang that's ruling your heart. You don't care about me."

Kenny was afraid that he might lose her again. "That's not true. I was caught up in the moment, but I do care about you. We don't have to do anything, but I'd like it if you would lay with me tonight. No touching and no feeling."

Her smile warmed his heart.

"Okay," Sylvia said, almost in a whisper. "I'll stay as long as you behave even though I know I've put myself in this compromising position."

"I'll behave. I promise," he said.

Sylvia smiled and kissed Kenny full on the lips.

"Thank you for understanding, Kenny."

EX-ample?

Sylvia walked back and forth on her tiled patio with a large glass of Pepsi in her hand. She took a sip and let the cool liquid roll over her tongue. With the other hand, she caressed her throat as the liquid went down, bringing her fingertips across her lips to hide her smile. Thoughts of her evening with Kenny swirled in her head, and the giggle that flew through her fingers contained secrets she shared with God.

Why she couldn't delete Kenny from her mind left her puzzled. He was an unlikely candidate on her road to recovery. She had wasted enough of her life on the man who had been her everything. Now that she was single and free, the only thing that blew her way was yesterday's leftovers.

Sylvia picked up a bottle of nail polish and sat on the chaise lounge. *He said he had changed*, Sylvia thought. *And there is something different about him.*

"I love this dark bronze color," Sylvia said as she began to paint her toes. "I liked that tall, dark bronzy man who held me last night, too. Ohh, wow. God, why am I having these crazy thoughts about Kenny? I'm strong. I didn't have sex with him. Yes, I lay in bed with him, and maybe he saw my breasts, but I didn't let him touch the temple of my familiar and I never saw what he was packing. God, take these terrible thoughts from me. I promise I won't let Kenny get that close again.

"Am I talking too loud, Lord? I don't want the neighbors to hear, especially nosy Mr. Hendricks. I thought I saw him peeking into my bedroom the other night before I slammed the curtains shut on him. Forgive me, Father, for I have sinned. I want to do right. It's all Adonis' fault for leaving me stranded with my needs unmet. Sorry, Lord. I just have no one else to talk to."

Sylvia bowed her head in silent prayer. She jerked her head, remembering that she was supposed to call the pastor. She reached for her cell phone that sat on the patio table and dialed the church number. *This will take my mind off of Kenny.*

"Louise? This is Sylvia St. James."

"Oh, hi, Sylvia. Pastor told me to expect your call sometime this week."

"Pastor Goodwin asked me to make an appointment to come by and see him to discuss starting a support group for young divorcees."

"They need it. It's so sad and alarming how many of our young people marry for the wrong reason. They get married, have a baby and wind up in divorce court."

Sylvia wrinkled her nose. *Who was Louise to condemn anyone?* Sylvia had heard that Louise's marriage had been on the rocks for years and was not the paradise she claimed it to be. Louise's husband, Lonnie, was rumored to be cheating on her. Louise was a sweet woman, though, and Pastor Goodwin sang her praises.

"Well, parents have to take a vested interest in their sons and daughters and tell them what marriage is all about," Sylvia continued.

"A lot of hard work. And these poor children can't do it with the role models they have."

"There are a lot of good parents out there, Louise, and I'm

sure many of them have sat down with their kids and had a long chat about what it's going to take to live with, love and support a spouse in this day and age."

"Hmph. I say these children don't have any role models. You should see them on TV with nothing on and darn near having sex in those music videos."

"That's what I mean. There is so much out there, but you have to monitor what your children watch and…but I didn't call to get into a discussion about black morality."

"Someone needs to discuss it. They get together, think they're in love, get married, have a baby, find somebody else and leave. Unreal."

"What do you think about women who know their husbands are cheating and they ignore it?"

"The Bible wants us to stay with our husbands. You must not have read that scripture," Louise said in a frosty tone.

"God didn't say be a fool. Now, may I have an appointment to see Pastor Goodwin?"

"Are you sure he said he wanted you to…"

"Louise."

"Thursday at three p.m. Don't be late." *Click*.

xxx

Sylvia stretched out on the lounger on the patio, letting the sun dry her newly painted toenails. Was she the example young adults should emulate? It had been less than six hours since she left Kenny's side, although nothing happened between them. Just the feel of his arms around her was sex enough.

Brrng…brrng…brrng.

"Hello," said Sylvia.

"Rachel here. How's my sister Sylvia doing today?"

"Why are you so happy?"

"Who said I was happy?"

"It's dripping all over your voice. Who squeezed your Charmin?"

"Wouldn't *you* like to know," Rachel said through a giggle.

"Not really."

"Ummm. You're in a stank mood. I don't know if I want to share my good news with you."

"What's up?" Sylvia said.

"I knew you weren't going to let any juice get by you. Girl, Marvin and I are going out on a date this weekend."

"I thought Miss Rachel was avoiding new relationships. Sounds a little contradictory to your announcement at the group meeting," Sylvia reminded her.

"People can change their minds, you know," Rachel retorted.

"That's why folks call you weak-men-ded." They both giggled.

"Whatever, but Sylvia, Marvin is so sweet and kind."

"Here we go again."

"No, listen. Marvin is different than any man I've known. You saw him firsthand at the meeting. He was polite and attentive to me when I was sharing my Files."

"And what are you going to do when he goes back to his wife and leave you with another broken heart? His wedding ring was hugging his finger real tight."

"Ouch. You don't want to see a sister happy. Just because you make yourself miserable waiting for Adonis to come home and ask you to forgive him doesn't mean everyone else has to be miserable, too!"

"I'm not waiting for Adonis. And I'd never take him back."

"Yeah, right."

"So what do you want to tell me about Mr. Marvin? You're in love? He makes your heart beat fast? He makes…

"Sylvia, please. You're the first and only person I'm sharing this with. There was chemistry the night we met. Tell me you didn't notice. And it certainly helps that he's so good-looking."

"Shallow."

"Whatever. But Sylvia, I'm telling you because I'm feeling something I've never felt before. Have you ever watched butter melt on a stack of hot, hot pancakes? That's how I feel…like I'm absorbing him into my system. We've talked on the phone every night since the meeting."

"You counted the times?"

"He loved his wife very much. I wonder if he could ever love me like that?"

Buzz…buzz.

"Hold on a moment, Rachel. I've got another call coming in."

Click. "Hello."

"Hey, baby. Just checking on you."

"Hey, Kenny. It's nice to hear your voice."

"I enjoyed last evening and this morning. I've thought about nothing else."

"I…I…I did, too. Thank you for accompanying me to the fund-raiser."

"You're welcome, but I want to thank you for accompanying me to a place I have not been in a long time."

"What do you mean?"

"Sylvia, I was on cloud nine, but what I'd really like to say is that I shared a wonderful moment with a wonderful woman. I adore you, Sylvia. I'm not sure how else to say this, but I believe I'm falling in love with you."

"Kenny, be serious. It's only been two weeks since we first saw each other and twenty years before that."

"I know what my heart says. You're like butter that has melted on hot bread. You saturate my heart. I can't think of anything else."

"Ohhhh my God," Sylvia said before she could pull it back. "Kenny, let's talk later. I forgot I have Rachel holding on the line."

"I'll go, but we can't afford to let love get away this time. I love you."

Click.

"Rachel, sweetie, I'm sorry," Sylvia said erratically.

"Kept me holding for ten minutes, girl. Must have been talking to your man."

"What are you talking about?"

"Calm down, I'm just kidding."

"You better be. And I'm not waiting for Adonis."

"You are crazy, Sylvia."

"So you and Marvin are going out this weekend. I think that's marvelous. If you're happy, Rachel, I'm happy."

"What happened between you putting me on hold and now? You weren't talking like this before. Is everything all right? Who were you talking to?"

"It was just an old friend I haven't seen in a while." Sylvia grinned.

"Oh, catching up on my dime."

"Sorry about that, sweetie. Back to you and Marvin. I want you both to have a good time, and you better give me the 411 when it's all over."

"Girl, you know I will, but I'll see you before I go on my date. Did you forget? We're meeting at the spa on Saturday morning."

"That's right. Still, I'm happy for you, Rachel. Kisses, and I'll see you Saturday."

"Smooches."

Click.

Sylvia smiled. Rachel wasn't the only one whose pancakes were saturated with butter. Sylvia shifted the small pillow under her head, closed her eyes, and curled her toes. The nail polish was now sunbaked, and so were her thoughts that were only on her night with Kenny.

EX-cuse Me

Brrng, brrng, brrng.

"Hello."

"Claudette, is that you?"

"Depends on who's asking. Who is this?"

"Ashley, your white girlfriend from the group."

"Well, hell-o, Ashley. What a surprise. Didn't expect to hear your voice so soon. Sorry if I seemed a little preoccupied. *Desperate Housewives* is on, and I don't talk to nobody while my show is on."

"I can call back, but I won't be but a minute."

"What's up, girl, since you've already interrupted me? You're lucky it's a commercial break."

"Just wanted to know if you meant what you said about baby-sitting for me when the baby came."

"Sure, I meant it, Ashley. But your baby ain't here yet, and *Desperate Housewives* is getting ready to come back on. Whatever it is you want, you better make it quick."

"Okay. Will you go with me to my first appointment?" Ashley blurted out. "It's tomorrow morning at ten. I'm nervous about it. You know what it's like being a mother, and I would feel comfortable if you accompanied me. I know it's your day off."

"I said I would baby-sit the baby when it came, which doesn't include going to prenatal appointments with you. Didn't you say your appointment was on Friday? I'm sure you said Friday because that's the day the girls were supposed to be going to the spa. I think they're going on Saturday instead."

"In my excitement I got the days mixed up. Don't worry about it. I thought… "

"That's what you get for thinking. Isn't Sylvia your good friend? Have you asked her? Even though it's been twenty-something years since she's had a baby."

"Don't worry about it, Claudette. I'm sorry I bothered you. I just thought we were in this group to support one another, and for some crazy reason, I felt you were the person I was supposed to bond with."

"What time is your appointment?"

"Ten o'clock. You don't have to…"

"Pick me up at nine. Don't make me regret that I said I would baby-sit for you."

"Thanks, Claudette. You don't know what this mean to me."

"I'm sure I do. I've got to go."

xxx

"You're right on time. If you were a sistah, I'd still be waiting on the curb."

"Huh?" Ashley said.

"CP time," Claudette said taking another drag on her cigarette.

"I'm sorry, Claudette, but this is a no-smoking ride."

"Ride? What does a blonde-haired woman know about a ride?" Ashley rolled her eyes. "Cigarette out, now."

"You do want me to go to the clinic with you, correct?" Claudette asked.

Ashley rolled her eyes again.

"I'm putting it out. I wouldn't want to give the baby second-hand smoke."

"Thank you," Ashley replied, wondering if it was a good idea after all to have Claudette go with her.

"I like you, Ash. Everything's going to be all right. There is nothing like giving birth. I remember the day Reebe was born. What a miracle. It was hard to believe that I brought that beautiful baby into the world."

"I hope my experience will be much like yours. My only regret is that William and I won't bring our baby home together. My baby will not have a full-time father. My man won't be there to take up the slack when I need an extra hour of sleep. I'll miss the moment when the daddy gets to change the baby's diaper, make cooing sounds, and take a nap with his son or daughter. Those are the things we talked about, and now I'll have to experience them all alone. I can't wait until I get to wear maternity clothes, though."

"It will be three or four months before you start to show as thin as you are. But I want you to know that you will not be all alone. The baby will have aunties to love up on it, too."

"You know what I mean, Claudette. Your children had a father in the home."

"Yeah, when he wasn't arguing and making everyone miserable."

"I just want to be happy. I want my husband to come home; I don't care what that piece of paper says. We can get remarried. What do you want, Claudette?"

"Truth be told, I want to quit smoking and find a wonderful man to spend the rest of my life with. Easier said than done."

"It'll happen. Here's the clinic. Thanks for coming with me, Claudette. Me and my baby thank you."

"Let's go, girl, before you make me cry."

EX-amine This

S wollen bodies entered the clinic. Some walked briskly; others dragged their feet, still others moved at a turtle's pace, hoping the finish line was not far away. Ashley had never seen so many pregnant women in one place at the same time, and it almost made her want to turn and run out the way she had come in. It seemed that each round stomach was the result of some curse, and they were all placed in a room and given a sentence of death, no…life or whatever. Ashley turned to find Claudette right by her side. She rubbed her stomach and relaxed.

Claudette escorted Ashley to the patient window, where she was handed a clipboard and some papers to complete. She and Claudette sat down. Ashley looked around at the other women who occupied seats. They seemed unconcerned as they watched the baby-oriented programs on televisions mounted around the room or entertained younger children who had accompanied them to their appointment.

Ashley turned her completed paperwork in and sat next to Claudette in silence. Every now and then, a nurse came through the door and called out a name, and when she didn't hear hers, Ashley wiped her brow and stared at the other mothers-to-be, wondering what was going through their heads. When her name was called, she insisted that Claudette come with her. Claudette picked up a magazine from the table next to her and shooed Ashley on. She would be right there when Ashley returned.

A half-hour later, Ashley emerged from behind the double doors.

"Claudette, I'm going to have a baby."

"No kidding. And what did the doctor say?"

"He told me I was in my first trimester. He told me to take my vitamins and iron and continue my exercise regime, and I should be fine. It was simple…it was like going for your yearly checkup."

"What else did you think was going to happen?"

"I don't know, but I'm going to have a b-a-b-y. Lunch is on me. Let's celebrate."

"Sounds good to me. I'm hungry and I need a cigarette."

Ashley stood by as Claudette gathered her belongings, then moved toward the hallway on their way out of the clinic. Before they had gone two feet, Ashley stopped abruptly, Claudette stepping on her heels.

"What are you doing here, William?" Ashley asked. She grabbed her stomach.

"What?" Claudette asked.

"I'm not talking to you, Claudette. The gentleman standing in front of me is William, my ex-husband."

"Ohhhhhh," Claudette said out loud. *God, he's fine*, she thought.

Ashley's eyes were fixed on William and the honey-blonde woman with him. Her roots were showing; Claudette should give her her number, Ashley thought.

"Why are you and that—woman—here?" Ashley asked again.

"What are *you* doing here?" William countered.

"I asked first."

"I asked second."

Ashley headed for the door. William was right behind her with Claudette taking up the rear.

"Come back here, William," the girlfriend called.

Ignoring his girlfriend, William grabbed Ashley's arm and swung her around to face him. There was hatred in Ashley's eyes. Claudette stayed back a couple of feet ready to come to her friend's defense.

"Why are you here, William?" Ashley demanded.

William sighed. He grabbed both of Ashley's arms and looked straight into her eyes. "I hate to tell you this way, Ashley, but I'm having a baby."

"Make that two, you son-of-a-bitch."

"Yeah, make that two!" Claudette repeated loudly after giving William another once-over.

Ashley snatched her arm away and rushed out the door.

"You're having our baby?" William seemed dazed for a moment. Then he suddenly gave chase to his ex-wife.

Startled mothers-to-be covered their stomachs to protect their precious cargo as he passed by, Claudette hot on his heels. They didn't have far to go. Ashley sat slumped over on a bench just outside the clinic, holding her face as she sobbed. When she felt William's hands on her shoulders, she shrugged him off and jumped up from her seat.

"Go back to your pregnant girlfriend," Ashley shouted and pointed.

"Leave Ashley alone," Claudette added. "You didn't want her before. She doesn't need you now. She'll do fine without you."

"Claudette—," Ashley began.

"Oh, just let me have him, Ashley. He'll wish he'd never seen the day he cheated on you. I'm going to call the girls because we need to have an Ex-family meeting."

William stared at Claudette and spit on the ground. He turned to Ashley. "Our baby, Ashley."

"No. *My* baby."

William twisted his mouth and shook his head, giving Claudette the evil eye before softening his expression to look back at Ashley. Air escaped from Ashley's mouth as she gazed from William to Claudette. She turned to William one more time and said, "My baby, and don't you forget it." She turned and walked away.

Disbelief was written on William's face.

"It's her baby," Claudette repeated, waving her finger in William's face. She half-skipped to catch up with Ashley.

"That's what you think," William said to no one in particular.

EX-treme Makeover

Sylvia followed the attendant through a labyrinth of halls before finally entering her treatment room. She placed her jacket on a coat rack in a far corner and forced a lid on her nerves as she examined her surroundings. The sound of soft music met her ears, causing her insides to tingle.

The room was serene and dimly lit by mod lamps that adorned the walls. Palm trees and exotic plants were strategically placed throughout giving the room the feel of a tropical island. The mood was enhanced by the sound of the small fountain tucked amidst the foliage. Cotton robes hung outside a marble shower that was separated from the main room by a bamboo divider. A black leather table with steel legs stood alone in the middle of the room—the table where her naked body would lie while experienced hands manipulated her muscles into obedience.

The door opened, and a male dressed in a loose-fitting white cotton jacket and gray slacks entered the room. A girlish smile crossed Sylvia's face in anticipation of what lay ahead. The masseur draped a clean sheet over the table, instructing her to take off her clothes, lay facedown on the table and cover her body with another sheet she was given. For the first time, Sylvia was able to see the masseur's face. He was of Spanish descent, but more than that, he was the handsomest man Sylvia had ever seen. She blushed as the masseur turned to leave the room so she could get undressed.

"He's going to get a big tip if he knows how to work it," Sylvia said to herself.

"First time?" he asked, startling Sylvia as he turned to face her, catching the glow on her face.

Sylvia thought she was going to melt. His voice was deep and romantic. This was not the time to get cold feet. What if his voice hypnotized her and she fell into his clutches, where he would do what he liked to her body at will? She shuddered and drew the sheet close to her body, although she still had on all of her clothes.

"Uuhm, yes," Sylvia said, a little embarrassed.

"I'll be gentle. You have nothing to worry about. My name is Andreas." And he walked out the door.

Sylvia looked around the room afraid to speak. She squeezed the sheet tight, then released it. This was the kind of moment when she needed to consult her girls. She wondered how Rachel and Mona were doing with their facials.

"Okay, Sylvia," she said out loud to no one. "Let's do this. You were the one who wanted to play in the mud, wanted to feel a man's touch, wanted her body rubbed, wanted to moan and groan while every muscle in her body was kneaded and twisted. Oh yes, I'm going to do this. My name is Andreas," she mimicked the masseur, shaking her head as she did so.

Sylvia eased out of her clothes and placed them neatly on a chair nearby. She crossed the room and stood at the foot of the table, inspecting it for who knows what. Then that crazy smiled skipped across her face again, and she crawled onto the sheet-covered table, placing the other sheet over her body.

xxx

"Rachel Washington?"

"Yes, that's me."

"Follow me, please. My name is Anika, and I'll be giving you your facial today."

"Sounds great."

"Your skin looks beautiful. It appears that you're doing all the right things to keep your skin looking healthy."

"I do try to eat right. It's the men in my life that cause my body stress. That's why my girlfriends and I are here today—makeovers to revitalize our bodies so that we'll be fresh when we meet our new somebody."

Rachel and Anika laughed.

"I think it's a great idea that you and your girlfriends came together to support one another," Anika commented as she ushered Rachel into her treatment room.

"Truth is, my girlfriend, Sylvia, brought a few of us divorced women together, and we now have what you call a support group. Sylvia calls it the Ex-Files. Our ultimate goal is to move forward in our new life as an Ex and help each other overcome emotional suicide after a bad divorce. And when we have made it, we will have cleaned out our Ex-Files."

"Hmmm, that sounds wonderful." There was a long pause. "Look," Anika continued, her voice now a soft whisper, "do you have room for one more person?"

Rachel jerked her head so that she could see Anika's face.

"Sure. I'll talk with Sylvia. She's getting a full-body massage right now, but I'll see her when we all come together for lunch. I've been going on and on and had no idea…"

"It's okay. Today is my lucky day, I guess. Sometimes, it's all about timing. Now sit in this chair so I can do your facial. I don't want to cheat you on what you're supposed to have since I have another client in thirty minutes."

"I'm not going to let you cheat me," Rachel assured her. "How long...how long has it been since you were divorced?"

"A month. He said he really wasn't ready to be tied down. If only I had known that before my parents spent ten grand on the wedding of my dreams two years ago, I would be a much happier person today." Anika began examining Rachel's face, but that didn't stop the other woman from replying.

"Shut your mouth. I ought to be giving *you* a facial and a massage. You've been through a lot. Girl, I've been down the aisle three times and divorced just as many, so I'm kind of numb when it comes to divorce court. Our group was the one thing I needed to make me look at life differently, though. We've only had two meetings, but I feel rejuvenated already, and if there should be a number four in my life, oh well, I'll just have to wait and see. It's not because I need a man, mind you. I like having a special someone to go out to dinner or a play with every now and then. Bottom line is I'm feeling good about myself again—confident."

"Well, my new friend Rachel, I'm your first stop today at the station called confidence. And if you don't mind, I'm going to ride with you."

"Well, come aboard, Anika. There's an empty seat with your name on it."

XXX

Sleep was an easy option as Sylvia lay facedown on the table, waiting for Andreas to return. The steady trickle of water and the soothing music relaxed her so much that she forgot where she was. Then she heard the door open, gently, then close but without the sound of footsteps. Then he spoke—his voice so soft and sensual that it paralyzed Sylvia from the head down.

"Are you comfortable?" Andreas asked.

Was she comfortable? She was darn near scared out of her wits.

"Yes," came her feeble reply.

"All right, we'll get started. I need you to place your arms by your sides and relax."

How am I going to relax, Sylvia thought to herself, *with his handsome body swooning over me and whispering sweet nothings in my ear*. She placed her arms at her sides obediently. "I'm ready."

"First, I'll start with our Signature Mud Massage. It will be a little cool to the touch, but when I'm finished you will feel renewed."

Sylvia felt a slight chill as the sheet was lifted from her left hip and leg. Strong, sinewy hands glided over her buttock in a circular motion, massaging a light mud mask deep into the muscle. Then Andreas' hands moved down her leg, applying more mud over her calf down to the ankle.

"Ahhhhh," Sylvia sighed.

After Andreas finished the one side, he repeated his performance on the other. Then he drew the sheet down to work on Sylvia's back, finishing at the nape of her neck. Sylvia was so relaxed she couldn't move. There had to be healing in those hands.

Andreas let Sylvia lie a few minutes on her stomach.

"It's time to turn over," Andreas said softly not wanting to threaten the mood.

Sylvia wasn't sure how she was going to accomplish this without exposing her goodies, but Andreas left the room as if reading her mind while she exchanged one side of her body for the other. Andreas returned on cue and worked on her legs and her arms.

Sylvia felt rejuvenated. She closed her eyes, casting her inhibitions to the sky. The feel of Andreas' hands was much too much for her, but she was anticipating the moment when he would touch her breasts, which were past due for an examination by a handsome gentleman. She was ready and waiting.

Then Andreas said, "Relax for ten minutes, then take a shower. Everything you need is behind the partition. When you're finished, lie back on the table for a final rubdown. I'll be back in fifteen minutes."

Sylvia's eyes popped open and stared at the ceiling. She moved the sheet from her breasts and stared. He hadn't touched them— *no mud, no hands, no sensation. She had been robbed of the one thing she had really wanted after succumbing to this handsome man. She'd been cheated, cheated, cheated!*

Sylvia swung her legs over the table and slipped off, holding the sheet tight around her body. As the music continued to soothe her, she loosened the sheet and let it slide from her bosom, draping it loosely around her hips. She waltzed to the music as graceful as a swan, performing several pirouettes before gliding toward the bamboo room divider. And for her last act, she dropped the sheet and shook her groove thing while extending her arms to the sky. She smiled seductively, then disappeared behind the divider and into the shower.

EX-foliate

Sylvia, Rachel and Mona were assembled in a medium-size room that held a table, a refrigerator, a TV and built-in shelves full of spa literature. Large palms sat among African artifacts—masks, statues, ceremonial robes—from the Ashanti tribe. The room was painted a dark salmon color, adding to the mystique. The same lamps that Sylvia saw in the room where she received her massage hung on the wall here as well.

Lunch was served on salmon-colored mats. Sliced turkey sat between a sliced croissant. A bag of chips and a glass of raspberry tea completed lunch. The television was on, the volume turned low.

"How was your massage, Sylvia?" Rachel began, anxious to get the details.

"It was divine—better than sex."

"At $300 a pop," Mona chimed in, "it better be."

"Details, details," Rachel pushed.

"A man with wonderful hands just gave me the most wonderful massage I've ever had. He massaged every muscle on my body."

"Mmm-mmm," Rachel said. "Sylvia looks pretty satisfied. Don't you think, Mona?"

"Yeah, there is something different about her. I want to know if it was so good that it made you want to do things you couldn't tell your mama about."

Sylvia smiled. "Eat your lunch. In fact, I think we should be talking about how Ms. Rachel is going to feel after her date tonight."

"Date? With whom?" Mona asked. She threw her hands up in disbelief.

"The one and only Marvin Thomas—your Mr. CEO," Sylvia offered.

"Oh really? And just what did you have to do to get his attention? Bend over backward or feign a headache so he would come running?" Mona said nastily.

"Mona, you sound as if you want Marvin for yourself," Rachel retorted. "I don't owe you an explanation for anything. Just know this my friend, me and the CEO are having dinner tonight."

"Umph, you'll mess that up, too."

"Okay, ladies," Sylvia cut in. "We're here on a healing journey."

"Speaking of healing, Rachel, did Sylvia tell you that she's hanging out with Kenny again?"

"Kenny? Kenny who?" Rachel asked.

"Kenny Richmond," Mona replied. "Our girl took him to the Gordons' fund-raiser. Can you believe that?"

"Oh," was all Rachel could say as she looked at Sylvia with disappointment in her eyes.

"Thanks, Mona," Sylvia said with disgust. "This trying to get on with our lives is difficult with the two of you. I'm going to get my facial."

"Speaking of facials," Rachel began, "I was telling the young lady who does the facials why we came to the spa, and she asked if she could join our group. Poor thing was only married two years, and she's so young."

"Sounds like a shoo-in to me," Mona said. "This place gives great manicures and pedicures." She stuck out her hands to show off her nails. "But right now I'm hungry and if you don't mind, I'd rather eat than talk."

They laughed and then there was quiet.

"We may fuss and get on each other's nerves," Sylvia said, "but I'm glad we're here together. It helps the pain."

"Same here," Rachel said.

Mona picked up the remote and began surfing through the channels. "Look at that," Mona exclaimed, pointing toward the TV.

"What is it?" Rachel asked. "You're messing with my peace and tranquility."

"You weren't studying peace and tranquility a minute ago. Yak, yak, yak," Mona said.

"What is it?" Sylvia asked.

"Now that Tiger is cute." Mona grinned. "I like that red polo on my man. This must be a recap of what happened this past Sunday."

"I'm not talking about Tiger," Sylvia said, her voice raised. "My God, Adonis is in the stands with that prehistoric hoochie."

"Where?" Rachel snapped, eyes glued to the TV. "I think you're imagining things."

"That is Adonis." Mona pointed. "Sylvia, your man is sitting in the stands at the U.S. Open with another woman."

"I can't believe the camera keeps panning his unfaithful face. Look at them, sitting up there like they're the king and queen of Pinehurst, Pinewood, Pinecrest...whatever it's called," Sylvia stuttered.

"Don't hate," Mona said. "Anybody that would dig up the past like yesterday's trash..."

"He never took me to a golf tournament."

"Because you never wanted to go, Sylvia," Rachel pointed out.

"They've just panned past him *again*. I'm going to call the TV station…"

"And tell them what, you crazy girl?" Rachel asked.

"That they have violated FCC regulations. Showing those two ugly faces on national TV is worse than Janet Jackson showing her breast."

Rachel and Mona giggled.

"You are too funny, Sylvia," Rachel said.

"I think Adonis looks tired," Mona quipped. Rachel covered her mouth to keep from laughing out loud.

"Can you believe Adonis has the nerve to showboat that piece of trash out in public? That man has no shame." No one responded and Sylvia fingered her sandwich, pouting as she did so.

Mona and Rachel stared at Sylvia.

"Don't act like you don't understand my pain," Sylvia said, refusing to let go.

Mona cleared her throat. "You have Kenny," she whispered.

Rachel coughed and cleared her throat. She pursed her lips to keep from laughing. "I don't believe it," Rachel said at last. "Kenny the asshole Richmond."

"Forget you wenches. I'm through trying to explain to you two fools what it's like to be with the same man for twenty years and all of a sudden he experiences the male change of life while you're having your own private summer and neither of you can put two and two together. Then he decides one day that he's going to venture out because he doesn't know what in the hell he wants, like he's been walking in this great big circle, and ends up in the arms of this ancient nightmare."

"You are so dramatic, Sylvia," Rachel said, still holding in a day's worth of laughs.

"'Dramatic,' am I? Nooooooo, you don't understand because

you've never had a man"—snap snap went Sylvia's fingers—"this long."

"That was a low blow, Sylvia," Rachel said. "This isn't about me or Mona. You didn't have to go there."

"Yeah. It was your man on national TV," Mona quipped.

Sylvia could feel the tears well up, and the last thing she wanted to do was cry in front of Rachel and Mona.

"I've had enough. I'm going to get my facial, and I'm outta here."

"You can't leave without me," Rachel said calmly. "I'm sorry. Didn't mean to hurt your feelings."

"I'm sorry, too," Sylvia said.

"Enough of this apologizing. Let's finish up," Mona said. "I've got a date with my twins' daddy."

Sylvia and Rachel looked at her. "Those twins aren't real, Mona," Sylvia said.

"You need to exfoliate Adonis out of your brain, Sylvia, and leave me alone. Leave that man with his ancient ho and live your life."

Sylvia was silent. Thoughts of Kenny bounced around in her brain. She needed a fix, but wasn't that why she was at the spa?

✗✗✗

Mirrors don't lie, Rachel thought, as she tossed her bangs about her forehead, batted her eyes and swiped her fingers through her hair like she was a contestant for *America's Next Top Model*. In fact, she thought she was much better-looking than any of those girls, and though she was petite, she could work a runway from Milan to Tokyo. And her body felt wonderful after the massage she had today.

Tonight had very little to do with how well she walked a runway or posed for a camera. It had everything to do with capturing a man's heart—yes, a man's heart, although less than two weeks ago she'd vowed to herself that men would be banned from her life. Rachel hadn't counted on Marvin Thomas making a liar out of her.

Although Rachel experienced disappointments in life, mostly self-inflicted, she was proud of what she had been able to accomplish. She was a senior account executive at IBM which enabled her to afford the beautiful house she now owned in the suburbs.

A smile crossed her face as she looked at her surroundings. Warm colors adorned the walls throughout Rachel's house. After throwing Reuben out, Rachel wanted something more tranquil, something more inviting to her soul. The strength of the colors warmed her, cuddled her, made her feel safe—the one thing Reuben or the other exes could never do. Marvin was somehow different, but tonight was all about fun, fine wine and dining. Discovery would be later. But that was Rachel's problem. She never took the time to discover if she had picked a weed or a strong, thick vine.

Rachel looked at the clock, dabbed a little more lipstick on her lips and sprayed herself with perfume. She hoped Marvin would like her green-and-white polka-dot, Italian cotton summer dress with a green patent-leather belt running around her waist. She bought it especially for their first date. She also picked up a pair of strappy green stilettos as well. He would be hypnotized by her beauty and style. And she would have Marvin right where she wanted him.

Nerves replaced self-confidence as Rachel paced from room to room. She looked at her watch. Marvin was fifteen minutes late. All those good feelings were starting to fade when the doorbell rang.

She ran to the door on jet fuel and jerked it open before the doorbell could ring a second time. Rachel could not contain the smile that was upside down only moments earlier.

"Hel-lo, Mr. Thomas," she said.

"Marvin is fine." He smiled.

"Hello, Marvin."

"Aren't you beautiful." Marvin was unable to take his eyes away from Rachel. "Wow, you are absolutely gorgeous. That dress looks stunning on you."

"Well, thank you." Rachel blushed. "Do come in."

"Ummm, nice home. Warm, inviting. I like it."

"I'm glad you approve."

"Oh, I do. I don't understand why the others—the guys in your Ex-Files—didn't get it."

Rachel blushed again, although it did conjure up bad memories. "I say it's their loss."

"Certainly is," Marvin agreed. "Certainly is."

"Would you like something to drink before we go to dinner?"

"Yes, I would."

Rachel went to the wet bar and brought back two glasses of Chardonnay.

"So tell me about your wife."

Marvin took a sip of his drink. "What do you want to know?" Marvin said, somewhat dejected.

"I know it's a hard subject to talk about, but I'm curious to know why the woman in your Ex-Files was crazy enough to forfeit the best."

Rachel sat down and motioned for Marvin to join her on the couch. She was sorry, almost as soon as the first word left her mouth, that she had steered the conversation in this direction. She felt terrible.

Marvin sat next to Rachel, arms folded across his chest. His voice was soft as he spoke.

"You remind me of Denise."

Rachel shrank back, not sure what to think.

"I mean…you're both petite and beautiful. She was the woman of my dreams, and I had big plans for our future."

Rachel realized that she had made a second mistake in the ten minutes since Marvin had entered her house. It was obvious that Marvin still loved his wife—rather, his ex-wife. Rachel had turned the windup toy on, and now she couldn't get him to stop. She tuned out his soliloquy—his sad, tale of an unfaithful wife—one second into his story.

Marvin was very handsome. Rachel digitized him into her memory one pixel at a time. She didn't realize he had stopped talking until he touched her arm.

"Are you okay, Rachel?"

She jumped. "Me? Yeah, I'm fine. I must have been day-dreaming. Sorry."

"No need to be sorry. I'm sure I bored you talking about Denise. It was so devastating, Rachel. But why talk about Denise when the most beautiful woman I've seen in a long time is sitting on the couch next to me?"

Rachel's cheeks ballooned.

"You're blushing," Marvin said. "And what pretty dimples."

"Why do you still wear your wedding ring?" she blurted.

Marvin sighed. "Sometimes it's hard to let go. You try to hang on as long as you can until one day you wake up and realize time has passed you by. And it cost a fortune."

Rachel laughed and Marvin joined her.

"Why don't we go to dinner?" he asked. "I've made reservations at a quaint little spot I hope you'll like."

"Just so long as you're by my side, it doesn't even matter," Rachel replied.

Marvin looked at Rachel thoughtfully. Rachel smiled one great big smile.

"I love green ones," Marvin said at last.

"What are you talking about?" Rachel asked.

"M&M's. You remind me of a bag of green M&M's—my favorite."

"I'm not sure what I'm supposed to say or think, but I'll assume it's a compliment."

"You're beautiful, and I love that dress. Let's go eat."

"Okay."

Escargot

The skyline was a canvas of orange, red and purple. Just behind the outline of a dogwood tree, the sun dipped on its descent beyond the horizon. Streetlamps illuminated the city, while men and women stepped into their favorite restaurants for a bite to eat.

Light jazz rippled through the Cadillac Escalade as Marvin and Rachel zoomed into the heart of Atlanta. Marvin took occasional glances at Rachel, while also keeping his eye on the road. Marvin made a right turn onto a quiet street and found a place to park. A small French restaurant hugged the corner of the block.

"*Oui, oui, monsieur,*" Rachel said, taking a stab at her French lessons of twenty years ago.

"Oh, we *parlez-vous Francais,*" Marvin responded.

"I love the French language. It is so romantic."

Rachel and Marvin turned in each other's direction and quickly turned away to disguise what their eyes were saying.

"Rachel, sweetheart, stay put until I open your door."

"*Merci, monsieur.*"

xxx

French music met their ears the moment Marvin opened the door to the restaurant. Rustic, medieval trophies hung from the rafters and room-size lampposts were placed throughout, giving the room a feel of sitting in a sidewalk café. Conversations were muted, with the restaurant's guests lost in their own Parisian fantasy, sipping Merlot and tasting the delicate garlic-infused escargot.

A dainty waitress met the couple and showed them to their table. They ordered a bottle of Cabernet Sauvignon and sat a minute browsing through the menu.

"This is so cozy," Rachel said.

Marvin eyed Rachel. "It certainly is." He smiled.

Rachel placed her hands atop of Marvin's. "I didn't take you for French food."

"Why, do I look like the country boy that I am?"

Rachel smiled. "No...well, maybe a little. You are so full of surprises."

"I just know how to treat a woman. I grew up with a houseful of women—my mom and three sisters. My father was a hard-working black man who took his responsibility seriously. Oh sure, there were times when we had to go without, but we were a family, a wholesome family—something I hoped to have when I became a man and could afford to offer my wife the things she needed and wanted."

"Where have you been all of my life, Marvin? I prayed for a man like you, but I guess God doesn't hear a sinner's prayer."

"That's not true. God hears everyone. You just didn't give Him enough time to give you what you asked."

"Hmph, you're probably right. And so wise. Let's toast."

"To what?"

"To us...the beginning of a new day in our lives, the beginning of friendship and possibly love, and the beginning of the music that's playing throughout my body."

"You feel it, too?"

"A little flute, a little bass… "

"I feel a drum beating…ohhhhhhhh…it's touching my soul."

"I'm serious, Marvin."

"So am I, Rachel. So am I."

The waitress returned with the wine. As she poured, Marvin lightly tapped the edge of the table. Rachel closed her eyes and lifted her head toward the ceiling. She thanked God for this moment—the beautiful music, the universal language she defined as love that danced all around her. She dropped her face and opened her eyes to meet Marvin's warm hazel gaze.

"I'm glad you like the place," he said.

"It's heaven, and I hope the food is as good. We better look at our menus before the waitress comes back."

"I recommend—" Suddenly Marvin jerked his head to the right and back.

"Are you all right?" Rachel asked. "Something wrong?"

"No, no. I was about to say that the duck à l'orange is very tasty."

"Duck is pretty close to chicken. That's what I'll have." Rachel thought this first date was headed in the right direction, even though he seemed a bit distracted.

The waitress took their orders and Rachel poured herself another glass of Cabernet. She looked at Marvin, who had a puzzled expression on his face.

"Are you sure nothing is wrong?"

"I'm sure, Rachel."

"We were talking and having a good time."

"Yes, we were."

"Is there something you need to tell me?"

"No."

"It's going to take some time, Marvin. You're a good man and you deserve better. Ex-Files brought us together, and it's going to help us get through our situations."

"You're right, Rachel." Marvin picked up her hand and kissed her fingertips. "Did I tell you tonight that you're beautiful?"

"Wellllllll, you did, but, I could stand to hear it again."

They laughed, then Rachel excused herself to the ladies' room. "Don't start dinner without me."

xxx

Marvin watched as Rachel walked the length of the room and disappeared. He picked up his glass of wine and held it tight. His nervous gaze wandered around the room, grateful for the salad the waitress placed on the table.

"So, who is she?" the voice demanded as Marvin stabbed at his salad.

"I thought I saw you. What are you doing in Atlanta, Denise?"

"I've moved back. Tired of New York."

"Moved back? To Atlanta?"

"Yes, to the A-T-L. Me and Danica, although Danica will be spending a lot of time with Harold."

Flashbacks of Denise and Harold put salt on an old wound. For an instant, Marvin wondered if Danica looked like Denise or Harold. Danica might even favor him since he and Harold were first cousins. Marvin shook the thoughts from his mind, hoping he could make Denise disappear for good.

"So you're already passing the baby off."

"You don't know what you're talking about."

"I do know that you probably would have been an unfit mother for our child, if we had had one. I am blessed not to have crossed that river."

"Don't insult me, Marvin. It won't change a thing."

"You're right, so…"

"Look, I actually came to Atlanta to talk to you."

"Don't go there, Denise."

"Please. Let me finish before you pass judgment on me."

"All the pleas I made that fell on deaf ears—too late now."

"Because you've found someone else to carry your seed?"

"You are so tacky, Denise."

"Well, that's what you always wanted, wasn't it, Marvin? A baby? A nice little family?"

"I'm sorry that I didn't recognize from the beginning that you were not my soul mate."

"You couldn't resist me."

"I resist you now, and you better leave before Rachel comes back to the table."

"Rachel…is it? I wonder what Ms. Rachel would think of you if she knew that this was *our* favorite restaurant? Didn't have enough intelligence to find one of your own."

As Rachel approached the table, she watched as he spoke with a petite and beautiful woman who stood over him.

"Is this your ghost, Marvin?" Rachel asked. "She looks nothing like me."

"You're quite right," Denise exclaimed. "Know this, Rachel, the ghost wants her husband back."

Rachel huffed and looked Denise dead in her eyes. "You won't get him. Know *that*."

Denise stormed off with egg in her face. Marvin glanced at Rachel, whose music had faded. It was replaced with red-hot coals that exuded ninety-degree heat. They sat there and said nothing. Marvin twitched uncomfortably in his seat. The waitress brought their food.

"I'm not hungry," Rachel said.

EX-cedrin Headache 101

Sylvia pulled the covers over her head. Andreas was massaging the length of her body. Not a muscle in her body was left untouched. Sylvia lifted her arms to lasso his neck and bring him to her, but his image faded along with the good feeling that had overcome her.

The room was pitch-black, just the way Sylvia liked it. Darkness was her security blanket against the evils of the world. She had learned to live alone but every now and then a small sound—the wind blowing through the trees, a squirrel scampering over the roof of the house—got her on edge, especially in the absence of any protector.

The bedspread shifted left, then right before sliding to the floor.

"No, don't go, please don't go," Sylvia cried out. *"What did you say, Adonis? I know I didn't hear what I thought I heard."*

"I want a divorce, Sylvia. I can't say it any plainer than that."

"But why, Adonis? When did you decide this? I didn't know that our marriage was in trouble."

"That's the problem with you. You're always too busy to notice what's going on right under your nose. Too busy, too busy, too busy, too busy. Think you're better than everybody else; and—if you remember before we got married—I told you I didn't like fat women."

"*I'll get on the treadmill tomorrow, I promise, but can we talk about this…try to work it out? We have invested so much of our lives into this marriage. Our daughter, what is she going to think?*"

"*Sylvia, I'm unhappy. I've been unhappy a long time, and now it's my time. I've got to go.*"

"*But…but…but what about me?*"

"*What about you?*"

Sylvia sat up straight and wiped the sweat from her face, panting, trying to place the strange sound that had awakened her. "Damn, the phone. What time is it?"

She reached for the phone and looked at the clock. It was eleven-thirty p.m.

"Sylvia, I hope I didn't disturb you," Ashley said.

"No," Sylvia said as coherently as she could.

"William wants to come back home."

"Isn't that what you wanted?" Sylvia blinked furiously, trying to gather her wits.

"I thought I did. But things have changed. He now knows I'm pregnant."

"What? How?"

"Last week when Claudette and I went to my doctor's appointment, guess who we ran into?"

"I'll take a wild one—William."

"Correct. A crazy thing happened on the way to the doctor. William was there with his girlfriend."

"Please don't tell me she's pregnant with William's baby."

"Right again."

"Jesus! What an ugly mess. Why are you just now telling me about this?"

"I don't know. Claudette has been very supportive."

"So the two of you have bonded?"

"Yes, and she was going to kick William's ass when he said that he was having a baby with that wretched woman."

"Oh, girl. What are you going to do?"

"There's more. The girlfriend lost the baby this morning. Now he wants to come home. Can we have an emergency meeting of the group? I'm desperate. I need to talk this out."

Beep, beep.

"Hold on one minute, Ashley. Don't go anywhere." Sylvia clicked over to the new call. "Hello?"

"Sylvia, this is Rachel. I've got to talk to you now. Can I come over?"

"What's wrong, Rachel?"

"My date tonight…it went sour."

Like you and Ashley are the only ones with issues, Sylvia thought. "I'm so sorry, Rachel. I thought Marvin—"

"He's a good man, Sylvia, but…"

"Hold on a moment, Rachel. I have Ashley on hold; she's got problems, too."

"Is she all right? It's not the baby, is it?"

"That and a whole lot more."

"Look, talk to Ash. We need to have a meeting. We ran into Marvin's ex-wife at *their* restaurant."

"What do you mean 'their' restaurant?"

"You heard me. Think about it a moment. Arrange that meeting because I need to talk to somebody, preferably without Marvin being there."

"Okay. Ashley wants a meeting, too. How about tomorrow after church? About three o'clock?"

"That's fine. Everyone can come to my house. I'll call Mona."

"You sure?"

"Yes. No Marvin, though. Give Ashley my love."

"Okay, sweetheart. It's going to be all right, Rachel. I'll see you tomorrow."

Click.

Sylvia took a deep breath before switching back to Ashley.

"Sorry, Ashley, that was Rachel. It sounds as if everyone is overdue for a meeting. Can you come to Rachel's house tomorrow at three o'clock?"

"That's fine. I'll call Claudette. I'm sorry to have disturbed you."

"It's okay, Ashley. I was wide awake. Try and get some rest. We'll talk tomorrow."

"Thanks, Sylvia."

Sylvia sat in the middle of the bed with her knees pulled up to her chin. She needed to talk to someone as well, but she had to be there for Ashley and Rachel. Putting other folks' needs before her own seemed to be the story of her life. It might sound selfish, but wasn't that why she started the support group—to get help for *herself*?

Well, she still needed to talk to someone. She clicked the phone back on and dialed the numbers.

"Hello?"

"Kenny, it's Sylvia. Can you come over? I need you."

EX-tenuating Circumstances

For those anxious to get a good word under their belt to carry them through the week, today was Sunday. Sunday was the day people went to church to get the blessings God had set aside for them. Sunday was the day to get your praise on for all of His goodness and mercies that kept you from an early grave. This was the day that the Lord had made, rejoice and be glad.

xxx

Right here, right now, on this Sunday morning, Sylvia felt like shouting. She left Kenny in bed to get the sleep she'd deprived him of. A nice breakfast of eggs, bacon, grits and Belgian waffles would be a great reward for coming to her rescue. Something else nagged Sylvia. She was falling in love or maybe it was a figment of her imagination. She wasn't sure, but there was some kind of chemistry brewing.

Fresh coffee brewed in the pot brought Kenny to the kitchen. "Smells awfully good in here; I could definitely use a cup of coffee."

"One cup of coffee with cream and sugar coming right up."

"This feels so right, Sylvia."

Sylvia turned and faced Kenny. She smiled but didn't say anything. Sylvia flinched at the sight of him and looked away to
regain her composure.

"I'm willing to wait. Didn't I share your bed last night? And
nothing happened? I didn't even complain."

"You were here to listen…help me get through the night."

"And you did, baby. Now, how about that coffee? And what
else do you have in here?" Kenny asked as he stepped completely
into the room, his taut muscles rippling on his bare chest.

This man was fine, and whatever Kenny Richmond had done
in the past was now forgiven. She took the towel that was in her
hand and wiped her face. When she looked up again, Kenny had
on her black-and-white polka-dot robe. How he'd managed to
retrieve it from the bedroom that fast was a mystery.

"Sit down," Sylvia admonished, giggling. "You're going to have
a real breakfast."

"Oh, you're going to hook a brother up. I'm telling you, I
could get used to this real fast. That cat messed up—oops. Sorry,
Sylvia. Didn't mean to bring up your ex."

With hands on her hips, Sylvia walked to where Kenny was
standing. "It's okay. Adonis had it coming. Now hold me, Mr.
Richmond. Don't let go until it's time for me to get ready for
church."

"Church? You're going to church?"

"My flesh wants me to stay here, but the Lord is calling my
name."

"My flesh wants you to stay," Kenny murmured.

"You can go to church with me," Sylvia replied.

"Maybe another time. In the meantime, don't let the devil get
in the way."

Kenny drew her close to him and held her in a warm embrace. Their eyes met, then their lips, gingerly tasting each other. Their bodies touched and Sylvia could feel Kenny through her flimsy gown. She wasn't fooling God. He was a know-all, see-all God.

A flood rushed through her body, and she knew that she should move away. Kenny's hands roamed her body like he owned her, taking control of the buttons that tapped into her emotions. Sylvia tried to resist, but she was weak. She had to get to church. She couldn't miss this appointment with Pastor Goodwin after missing the one on Thursday.

Kenny pressed buttons and Sylvia responded. She held on as Kenny examined and explored, testing her endurance and raising the bar. Fingers tore at the sides of her panties, while her negligee lay on the tiled floor. Moans of pleasure escaped from Sylvia's mouth. Kenny smiled and opened his eyes.

"Oh, Sylvia. We're going to burn the house down!" Kenny ran to the stove to put out the fire under the pot of grits that had boiled over onto the stove.

"My God," Sylvia wailed. "What is wrong with me?"

"Too late to call on God. You should have been getting ready for church."

"Shut up, Kenny. It's all your fault."

"The kitchen didn't burn down, and you can still make it to church on time. I'll admit, Sylvia, I wanted you bad, but not at the expense of losing everything. Dinner later?"

"Much later. We're meeting over Rachel's house after church. Some of the sisters need to talk. Thanks for coming to my rescue."

"You're welcome. Now what were you wearing last night that made you smell so delicious?"

"You mean my Warm Spirit mango soufflé?"

"Whatever you call it. It messed a brother up. It was hard to concentrate on what you were saying and very hard to be that close to you without…well, you know what I'm trying to say. If you're trying to live right, don't invite a brother to come and talk to you in the middle of the night, in your bedroom, drenched in mango soufflé."

"So everything that I was saying to you last night or early this morning, whichever it was, fell on deaf ears."

"I'm a good listener."

"I bet you were." Sylvia grinned. "I do owe God an apology, though."

"For letting the devil use you to get me to come over?" Kenny kissed Sylvia.

"Kenny, I was having a terrible nightmare about Adonis, and I couldn't—"

"So why were you smelling sooooooo good?"

"Get out," Sylvia said jokingly. "Put some clothes on because you're going to church with me."

EX-planation, Please

People spilled out of the sanctuary in a hurry to get home or to their favorite restaurant. Everyone was talking about the wonderful message Pastor Goodwin preached today. The spirit was still with some of them as they continued to praise the Lord.

xxx

"Mother," said the voice behind Sylvia.

Sylvia stopped in her tracks and slowly turned around at the sound of the familiar voice. Oh, she looked so much like Adonis—from her button nose to her petite frame. Even the texture of her wavy hair screamed his name. There was no mistake that Maya was his child.

Looking at her daughter made Sylvia queasy and prompted her to question whether she had fought hard enough to save her marriage. If there was any consolation, Maya had Sylvia's smile and cute dimples.

"Maya, Carlos, you look wonderful. How are you two doing? Honeymoon over?"

Maya looked Kenny up and down, giving him the once-over.

"We're doing fine, Mother," Maya said. "And we will be on our honeymoon for a long time. The question is, how are you doing?

We saw you tiptoe in late. Bet you didn't hear a word Pastor preached today—finding a virtuous woman."

"Mind your manners, Maya. I'm still your mama, and you're not too big to put over my knee. Right, Carlos?"

"Whatever you say, Mrs. St. James." Carlos tried to stifle a laugh but could not hold it back.

"Don't laugh at her, Carlos."

"I'm Kenneth Richmond, an old high school friend of your mother's." Kenny offered his hand. Carlos took it; Maya looked on with a twisted smile on her face.

"Look, I have an appointment with Pastor Goodwin, and I'm going to be late," Sylvia said. "Would love to stay and chat."

"Appointment for what?" Maya asked, looking from her mother to Kenny.

"Not that it concerns you, but Pastor Goodwin wants me to head up a class for some of the young members who are on the verge of divorce or have recently gotten one."

"Why did he choose you?" Maya mocked.

"Because he found out that I had already started one."

"Oh, so I guess it helped you get over Daddy." Maya took another shot at Kenny with her eyes. "You are a recovered divorcee."

"Maya, I love you, too. Now I have to go before I hurt you."

"Mother, I…I…just want an explanation."

"For what? If you're talking about Mr. Richmond, he has every right to be at church as you, Carlos and me. In fact, I was telling him about the Lord and how he should give his life to Him. The Lord is happy, and you need to mind your own business."

"Sorry, Mr. Richmond." Maya offered Kenny her hand. "Mother has been pining over Daddy so long, I can't believe she knows what another man looks like."

Sylvia would not look at Kenny. If Maya only knew that Kenny had spent the night, albeit nothing happened, she would have gone ballistic—not that Maya had forgiven her daddy for running off with his ex-wife of twenty-five years ago. Sylvia smiled internally, thoughts of Kenny sifting through her head.

"Gotta go, babies. Give me a kiss. Don't be a stranger. Stop and see your mother sometime."

Both Maya and Carlos gave Sylvia a giant hug and swift kisses on either side of her face.

"Nice meeting you, man," Carlos said to Kenny.

"I apologize again," Maya said to Kenny. "The Lord loves you. Come back again."

"It was nice meeting you both," Kenny said, glad they were going in the opposite direction.

"Whew," said Sylvia and Kenny at the same time.

"If they only knew," Kenny said.

"Well, we won't entertain that in the house of the Lord," Sylvia said.

"Look, go to your meeting and I'll catch up with you later on."

"I don't think you should come over, but do give me a call."

"Mango soufflé?"

"No, Mr. Richmond. You better get your mind on the Lord."

"I only came to be close to you."

"Don't talk like that in the Lord's house. He might strike you dead."

"Sylvia, you drive me crazy. I'm out."

"'Bye, Kenny," Sylvia said softly and seductively. "Call me."

Sylvia watched Kenny until he exited the building. Her knees were trembling and butterflies teased her stomach. It didn't take a rocket scientist to tell Sylvia she was falling in love. She composed herself, took a deep breath and turned and walked in the direction of Pastor Goodwin's office.

She wasn't sure that she wanted to take on this task now. She wasn't sure that she could be objective considering her somewhat contradictory feelings about Adonis. And now Kenny had resurfaced in her life. There was no denying it: Sylvia was messed up.

Sylvia knocked on the door to Pastor Goodwin's office, and he asked her to come in.

"Sister St. James, it is so good to see you," Pastor Goodwin said as he stood and shook Sylvia's hand. "Have a seat."

"I enjoyed your sermon today, Pastor. I'm trying to live the walk and be that virtuous woman you were talking about."

"Are you sure you were here today? Don't tell me you went to sleep on my sermon."

Sylvia sat back, embarrassed at the obvious mistake she'd made. She was going to kill Maya! What did the pastor think of her now? Was she worthy to lead a group of young adults in the direction that was intended?

"Don't worry about it, Sister St. James. Sister Goodwin nodded through the last part. 'Faith in God' seemed so appropriate since we have so many young people who are just getting started and find themselves at a crossroad in life—slaves to debt, victims of spousal abuse, survivors of failed marriages, you name it.

"I don't know what the statistics are, but I look all around me, right here at the church, and see that the number of divorces and domestic problems are astronomical.

"We have to pray for the world, Sister St. James. I want to impress upon the young people that God is their refuge and help in their time of trouble—they need not feel alone. If they need to talk to someone, there is someone they can go to. While the scriptures do not advocate divorce, the Bible, in the book of Matthew, chapter five, verses 31-32 gives legal justification to do so in the case of adultery. And for those who may want to get married again, I want them to know that God will send them what they need if they ask."

Sylvia fidgeted in her seat. Pastor Goodwin was preaching straight to her. Forget the young adults; she hadn't gotten that part herself. Now she had to share what she wasn't practicing.

It was moments like this that Sylvia felt so unworthy. But how could she disappoint Pastor Goodwin, who seemed to have so much faith in her?

"Pastor, I have one question," she began.

Pastor Goodwin's thick eyebrows arched upward. "Yes, Sister St. James?"

"Pastor Goodwin…" Sylvia paused. "Pastor, am I weak because I struggle to loose myself from my ex-husband? I saw him on television yesterday; he was at the U.S. Open. He was with the woman who was his wife twenty-five years ago—a marriage that lasted less than a year."

"Oh, I didn't know… "

"It wasn't a big deal until now. I became so angry looking at him sitting with that woman. How dare he? Pastor, how could he just get up and leave me after all the years we spent together as husband and wife? I was a devoted wife and mother. I worked hard to ensure that my marriage would be forever—in fact, I worshipped the ground Adonis walked on. I don't know where I failed, but I didn't see any of this coming."

Sylvia stood up and began to pace. Her face and hands became more animated as she continued speaking.

"I loved my husband with all of my heart and soul, but I'm honestly trying to move on with my life. It seems when I make strides, something sets me off that causes me to take two giant steps backward."

"Sister," Pastor Goodwin cut in, "let me try and answer your first question. You're not weak; you had expectations that you and your husband would be man and wife forever. When those expectations weren't fulfilled, you did what most people do in this situation. You fought to save what was yours, and the more it became unattainable, the more determined you were to make it right.

"Divorce is like death. It has that air of finality, and it hurts like hell to lose someone you love. You've said a lot of things this afternoon, but you have to be willing to step back, step out of the familiar and see the whole picture.

"It appears that Brother St. James didn't invest as much into the emotional side of your marriage as you did. There had to be a thread, though, that kept you together for twenty years or more. He seemed to be a good Christian and a decent man to me, but we don't always no what goes on behind closed doors."

"But he walked out, Pastor," Sylvia cried. "Said the marriage was over a long time ago, that I was too fat, oh I can't remember what else. I'm so sorry. I didn't mean to go on like this." She collapsed back into her seat.

Pastor Goodwin went over to Sylvia and handed her a tissue, then sat in the vacant chair next to her. "Perhaps now is not the right time for you to head up the young people's support group. You seem to have a lot of sorting out of your own to do. I'll speak with Sister Witherspoon about taking over that ministry."

Relief washed over Sylvia. "Thank you, Pastor. That would probably be best."

"Is your support group offering what you need?"

"We've only had one meeting. In fact, as soon as I leave here, I'll be on my way to our next meeting."

"Know that if you need me, I'm here. I'm sure it's good to be surrounded by a group of women who have similar situations and by sharing you help each other. Just remember God is only a prayer away," Pastor Goodwin reassured her.

"I do want you to talk with someone who may be helpful to you. My sister, Margo Myles, will be coming to Atlanta next week, and she has a testimony. Her husband, Jefferson, is serving time in Raleigh, North Carolina, for embezzling lots of money to purchase weapons that he and others then sold to a rebel group in Honduras. And he had an affair with his married next-door neighbor. It nearly broke my sister's heart. My sister chose to stay with him in spite of all these things. Margo is a strong Christian woman. Many women would have let Jefferson rot in jail. My sister loves her husband, but most important, she forgave him."

"My goodness," was all Sylvia could say.

"Margo is fine. Her children have been her rock."

"I'd like to meet her."

"You may want to invite her to your support group. I'll set it up if you like," the pastor offered.

"That will be fine. Again, I apologize for my outburst, and I appreciate your understanding. I was having doubts about leading this group," Sylvia confessed.

"God always has a way of revealing what we need to know. That was the reason for this meeting, I guess—to show us you weren't ready for this task, especially since young lives would be affected. God bless you, Sister St. James. Please stop by from time to time to give me a progress report."

Sylvia stood and shook Pastor Goodwin's hand. "Thank you again, Pastor. I will keep you updated. Good afternoon."

"Good afternoon."

Escape

"Legs carry me up out of here."

Sylvia was nearly out of breath when she reached her car. She was glad to be away from the pastor's office. She hadn't anticipated that her meeting with him would be so nerve-wracking. Instead of talking about the young people she had obligated herself to help, it became an "all about me" occasion. She was so exhausted, exposing herself to Pastor Goodwin that way—sharing all her inner turmoil, the soap opera that her marriage had become.

"Two-thirty-three," Sylvia said, looking at the clock on the dash. She needed her support group as much as Rachel and Ashley did. She was glad that she had only twenty minutes before she would arrive at Rachel's house.

EX-posed

A chilled bottle of wine and a box of candy? Or was it a bouquet of flowers and box of candy that made women take notice? Whatever the combination, Marvin wanted it to be perfect. He had a lot of mending to do to get back into Rachel's good graces. What was he thinking, taking Rachel to his and Denise's favorite restaurant? He never expected to run into Denise, though. The last he heard, she was still in New York, hobnobbing with the rich and slightly famous. Marvin had to admit seeing Denise last night made him long for her, if only for a moment, because he knew the scorpion's bite was lethal.

"That will be twelve dollars and fifty-nine cents," the cashier said.

"Marvin," came a familiar voice. He looked up to see Mona walking toward him.

"Hello, Mona, what you cooking today?" Marvin asked.

Mona sized Marvin up, taking inventory of his groceries.

"I should ask what you're cooking with that bottle of wine and box of candy."

"If you must know, I'm on my way to see Rachel."

"Rachel? You might not want to go there today."

"So she's told you about our date last night."

"In a roundabout way. Just a little advance warning: She's called the ladies together to talk about your situation. And when a bunch of sisters get together and they're dissecting a man, you can rest assured you don't want to be anywhere near them because they're sure to draw blood."

"I can't believe that Rachel would put our business out there like that. What happened should be between Rachel and myself," Marvin said angrily.

"Your ex-wife, Marvin? Was she really at the same restaurant you took Rachel to for your very first date?"

Mona looked at Marvin as if he had lost her mind. "Let me say this, Marvin. They are probably wearing your name ouuuuuuut."

"I've got to go, Mona. See you later."

"All right, cowboy. Go on and make it up to your girl." Mona snickered.

"Why aren't *you* at the meeting?"

"A handsome gentleman is my excuse. I met him at a fund-raiser I catered for the Gordons. Called me up and asked if I would like to go out to dinner. So I'll get the scoop another time. I wish you all the best."

"Thanks a million, Mona."

Marvin dropped his head and walked the few feet to his car. He threw the candy and bottle of wine on the backseat of his Escalade. Drama seemed to follow him, and he didn't understand why. He was a good man with a good heart, and all he ever wanted was to find a good woman to share his life with, settle down and have a family.

Trying to move on with his life was hard, but participating in a group that would help him get over Denise had seemed the way to go. Who would have thought that while he was lamenting over an ex-wife who didn't want him that he'd run into a beautiful woman who had also been hurt by love?

Marvin started the ignition and pulled out of the parking lot. Mona was probably right. The women were probably tearing his good name to shreds. Just like females to grab you by the balls and make mincemeat out of you. It was a mistake taking Rachel out when Denise wasn't completely out of his system. Maybe he'd just go home and drink the bottle of wine by himself.

The EX-clusive at Three

"Hold up!" Sylvia shouted. "We all can't talk at the same time! I know everyone has issues, but let's be calm."

"You're right," Rachel said. "I guess I was being selfish."

"We understand," Ashley said. "What was Marvin thinking?"

"Or William," Claudette cut in. "The nerve of him to try and handle Ashley when his girlfriend was standing over there with a pound of baby in her stomach looking stupid."

"So," Rachel began, "you ran into William at the clinic and found out that he's having a baby?"

"How about that," Ashley said sarcastically. "And of course I had to let him know that I was having a baby, too."

"Ooooooh, he was some kind of mad," Claudette cut in.

"Claudette was going to beat him up if I hadn't stopped her," Ashley continued.

"Claudette…" Rachel shook her head.

"The man is still in one piece," Claudette assured everyone. "He's lucky that Ashley is nonviolent. This sister was getting ready to get it on."

"He wants to come back home," Ashley blurted out.

"What?" Claudette and Rachel said in unison.

"His girlfriend lost the baby so he had the nerve to run back home to try and ruin me and my unborn child's life. I feel bad for the girlfriend, but he made his choice. And guess what, he's still without a child."

"You go, Ash." Claudette laughed.

"What do you propose to do?" Sylvia asked.

"I don't know. The divorce has been final just over a month. Now that jackass wants to unravel all that he's done because 'his wife,' so he says, is bearing his child."

Sylvia rubbed Ashley's back as she curled up into a fetal position on the couch. There was a blank look on Ashley's face and she finally closed her eyes. A small stream of tears flowed gently down her face.

"Stay strong," Claudette said. "Don't let no man dictate to you. He made his bed; he's got to sleep in it."

"When I wanted him, he didn't want me. Now that I've got something he wants, he wants to run home to mama."

Ashley jumped up from the couch. She looked from one lady to the next and held out her finger as she moved it back and forth in a semicircle like she was taking a meter reading. "William had his chance. I know a child needs his father, but I'm going to raise my baby by myself. What kind of man leaves a woman for another woman, then turns around and leaves that woman, who was pregnant but lost the baby, for the pregnant woman he left in the first place, although he didn't know she was pregnant. Sounds complicated to me."

"You're right. It does sound complicated." Sylvia laughed.

"I need your support to get through this," Ashley said. "William is intent on being with this baby and me. The fact of the matter is that I'm afraid—afraid what he might do to me if I refuse to let him come back."

"You have our support, Ashley," Sylvia said.

"Mine, too," Claudette agreed in a firm voice.

"Mine, too," Rachel said softly.

"You really need to talk with someone, Ash," Sylvia said. "You need to talk to a professional. This sounds more serious than we may be able to handle. But we're here for you."

Ashley sat back down on the couch and crouched in a corner, guarding her stomach for dear life.

"Rachel, why don't you go ahead?" Sylvia said, sensing Rachel's mood.

"No, I feel selfish in light of what Ashley's going through."

"I think we have all been through a lot in the past few weeks," Sylvia began. "In fact, Rachel and Ashley may have saved me from emotional suicide last night. Your telephone calls interrupted my anguish, while I probably didn't do anything to help yours.

"I was having those damn dreams again, and I swear Adonis was right there in the room making me relive that scene over and over again—the moment he walked out on me, telling me that he didn't want a fat woman and blah, blah, blah, blah, blah. I can't take it anymore. I want peace. I don't want to be afraid to move on, to be alone, to enjoy someone else if they should come along."

"Uhmm-hmmm," Rachel sang. "Sylvia is seeing someone from her past on the sly. Just found out about it myself. Yesterday."

"Good for you," Ashley said.

"This was a no-good man," Rachel interjected.

"Hold it, Rachel. You don't know Kenny now and I don't appreciate you making remarks like that about him," Sylvia said.

"Ohh, so defensive. I'm sorry, sis. It's your life."

"And don't forget it—after all, you haven't always been the best judge of character."

"I guess I deserved that."

"Well, what happened to you, Rachel?" Claudette cut it.

"Yeah, what's your issue?" Sylvia asked, miffed. *Don't know what to do with a man*, she thought, but refrained from saying out loud.

Rachel flew into her story about how wonderful the evening started out, with Marvin taking her to the quaint French restaurant. "It was so romantic," Rachel cooed. "We spoke French to each other; about the only thing left was to French kiss. I was already dreaming about what I'd be dreaming that night when out of nowhere the ex-wife is standing over Marvin when I came from out of the bathroom."

"No!" everyone said in unison.

Ding-dong, ding-dong.

"I'll get that for you," Sylvia said. "This is juicy, and I don't want you to miss a beat."

When she opened the door, her face went blank and she glanced back quickly toward the group. "Marvin!" she announced so that everyone could hear.

"Are you all having a meeting…without me?" Marvin asked as he stepped inside.

Sylvia closed the door behind them. She pursed her lips and rolled her eyes at the predicament Rachel now found herself in.

"Uhh…well, we were just… "

"There's no need to lie, Rachel," Marvin said. "Let me guess… you were right in the middle of a private matter between you and me."

"Hold on, Marvin," Sylvia interjected. "This is what this group is about. We get together to support one another in an effort to move on past our hurt and pain."

"I thought I was a part of this group. It makes perfect sense to me that if Rachel's problem involves me and I'm a part of the group, I should be part of the solution. Maybe it's best that I resign," Marvin added. "I don't think I want to be part of a group of hypocrites anyway. I think I was better off before I met you all."

"Now hold it, Marvin," Rachel finally spoke up. "Don't take it out on the group. You're right. I should have been woman enough to discuss this with you first."

"Well, that's on you. I was prepared to say something else—to apologize—but right now I don't feel like it. Ladies, continue. I'm leaving."

Rachel wanted to run after Marvin. She wanted him and she wasn't about to let the best thing that had come into her life in a long time walk away from her. But Sylvia would say she was weak if she did. Who cares what Sylvia thought? It was her man. Rachel slumped to the couch, her mind in turmoil.

"Not running after your man, Rachel?" Sylvia inquired.

"Kill it, Sylvia. I should not have been talking about what happened at that restaurant. I don't believe Marvin expected to see Denise. He was as shocked as I was."

"So why aren't you going after him?" Claudette asked.

"Good ones are hard to find," Ashley chimed in.

"I don't want him to think I'm desperate," Rachel admitted.

"You are desperate. We're all desperate for one thing or another. Why are you sitting over there like you lost your best friend?" Sylvia shook her head at Rachel. "I would have been gone."

"Whatever."

I'm every woman…sang Claudette's cell phone. "Y'all like my ring? Hold on a moment. I don't recognize this number… What? What did you say?"

Claudette's eyes got round as saucers. She shook her head—

hard—her braids flying as she made a fist. Fresh tears fell from her eyes. "Jesus, Kwa-me! Hell, why did you…"

"What's wrong, Claudette?" Ashley asked.

Everyone gathered around Claudette. She slammed the phone shut. Her voice was subdued. "Gotta go. Kwame was picked up about an hour ago."

"What?" sang the chorus of three as they smacked their hands over their mouths.

"Yeah, they're holding my baby at the jail. I can't talk about it now."

"I'll go with you, Claudette," Ashley offered.

"No, Ash. I've got to do this by myself. I'll call T when I get in the car."

"Let us know what's going on," Sylvia said. They huddled together and hugged Claudette.

"He burned my shop down. My livelihood. My independence. My shelter from the rain. My shop, my shop, my shop!" Claudette wailed. "My damn shop!"

Blame it on the Rain

M arvin drove blindly through the streets of Atlanta. How could he have given his heart so easily only to have it broken so fast? He wished that Mona had never told him about the support group.

Raindrops began to fall on the windshield. He was driving much too fast, but he wanted to get home. The sound of a siren brought him back to his senses, and the fire engine that flew by made him grab the wheel and cherish life as he knew it.

Twenty minutes passed and Marvin was glad to be away from the hustle and bustle of the city. A couple of blocks more and he would arrive at his subdivision. He glanced through the rearview mirror at the bottle of wine that lay on the backseat along with the box of candy. It would be his meal for the evening because the lady didn't deserve it.

The bark of a neighbor's dog announced Marvin's arrival as he rolled up the driveway of his spacious house in an upscale neighborhood. He drove the Escalade into the four-car garage and turned off the ignition. Marvin got out and looked around, then reached back in for the wine and candy.

The two-level house sat at the edge of a man-made lake. Tall pine trees stood like tall wooden statues all around Marvin's estate. A tennis court sat on the property nearest the lake and a swimming pool with Jacuzzi occupied the other end.

Marvin entered the kitchen through a door off of the garage. Brown granite countertops flowed throughout, stained kitchen cabinets set the right tone for the room with its modern appliances completing the décor. Marvin got a wineglass and went into the entertainment room.

ESPN the magazine, *Sports Illustrated* and *Black Enterprise* littered the tabletop of the marble coffee table. Marvin slumped on the brown leather couch and set the wine, the glass and the box of candy on the table next to the magazines. He picked up the remote and flipped through the channels until he found a golf tournament. He was going to learn to play golf one of these days, he thought.

Marvin filled the wineglass until it almost overflowed. He sipped until the glass was empty, then poured some more. Wrappers littered the floor as Marvin devoured the candy piece by piece.

Ding-dong. Ding-dong.

Marvin looked at his watch. It was only six-thirty in the evening, but it felt like ten. A smile formed on his face. Rachel had found him and wanted to make amends. He straightened his shirt and quickly picked up the wine and candy and set them in the kitchen, tucked away out of sight. Marvin smoothed his mustache and went to the door.

Ding-dong. Ding-dong.

When he opened the door, his smile turned to a frown.

"What are you doing here?"

"Are you going to let me in?" Denise asked as she brushed past. She wore a gold-flecked burnt-orange silk chemise that molded to her body, matching her four-inch heels and clutch.

Denise scanned the room half-expecting to see someone else.

"Go home, Denise."

"The place looks the same as I left it," she said, tossing her bag on the couch.

"Don't flatter yourself. I've been busy or otherwise I would have made some changes."

"Don't pretend with me, Marvin. I know it's been hard without me."

"Turn around and go back to where you came from," Marvin snapped.

"Come on. Let's not act like a spoiled child. We were married once."

"Were. Remember that."

"You are so hostile, Marvin. It doesn't become you."

"A lot of things about me have changed, Denise, and you are the major cause of it."

"Ouch. So, where is your girlfriend?" Denise asked as she sauntered over to peer into the kitchen, oblivious to Marvin still standing guard at the front door.

"She's at a meeting."

"So…you're by yourself. Ummmm."

"Not for long."

"You're expecting her later? This might be fun," she said, smiling seductively as she came back toward him.

"Denise, I'm telling you only once. Go home."

Denise suddenly lunged at him, catching him unaware. Smothering his mouth with hers was the easy part. Holding on to Marvin proved to be a little more difficult.

"Don't fight me, Marvin," she whispered against his lips.

"No…uhhh…no, Denise. Stop. Please stop," Marvin muttered.

Fingerprints left evidence around Marvin's neck and on his arms like a kindergartener's artwork. Denise squeezed and kissed Marvin as if her life depended upon it. Marvin held up the wall like a sergeant at arms—defiant yet accommodating as Denise continued her assault on his lips and neck, holding tight. This was the kind of moment Marvin relished—complete spontaneity— and Denise's aggressiveness drove him mad with pleasure. She slipped out of the dress and stood before him in nothing but heels, push-up bra and thong.

Marvin suddenly relaxed and enjoyed Denise's playfulness and her deceitful attempt to try and arouse him. He thought about Rachel sharing their ugly moment at the restaurant with the group. She'd probably ridiculed him in front of the ladies, made him look like a common street thug with no class or style even though he'd brought her to one of the finest restaurants in town. He looked at Denise and kissed her passionately on the lips. He grabbed her buttocks with both hands and squeezed hard, pulling her close to him until she could feel what she thought she wanted.

"Whoa, baby," Denise said as she pushed away. "I've got all night. Let's take our time. I like this, Marvin."

Marvin looked at Denise with contempt. He would have been all right if she had kept her mouth closed. The wine had warmed him inside and Denise had warmed him outside, but now Rachel's image floated in front of him once more. There was no way he could give in to Denise's sexual badgering.

Denise blew Marvin a kiss, then licked the tip of her index finger with her tongue, beckoning him to come closer.

She was beautiful, but he didn't love her anymore, he realized. Marvin looked at his left hand and pulled his wedding ring off. He went to Denise and placed the ring in her hand.

"Put your clothes back on, Denise. I remember the woman I fell in love with...the woman who completed me...the woman who crept into all of my dreams...the woman I would have died for. I don't see her anymore. I see a woman who would use her body to get what she wants...how she wants it. I would be lying if I said you didn't look good to me, but the truth of the matter is you don't look good enough. I'm sorry."

Denise's eyes shot daggers at him, but her voice was calm. "I'll leave, but just know that the little tramp you were hanging out with yesterday ain't half the woman I am. Remember that." She put a little extra shimmy into putting her dress back on.

"Let me be the judge." But Marvin was speaking to a closed door.

Claudette Beasley

The champagne-colored Nissan Altima swerved in and out of traffic as Claudette headed toward the beauty shop. Rain fell in buckets and visibility was low, but she plowed on unconscious of the blaring horns that warned her not to cross the line again. Pink fingernails gripped the steering wheel with one hand and a lighted cigarette hung from the other. Bleach-blonde dreads moved each time Claudette shook her head at the thought of what she would find.

She continued to drive in silence, whimpering softly as she tried to remain calm. She was within blocks of her shop and now could see the fire engine as it sat quietly against a street full of colorful umbrellas, whose owners had come hell or high water to view what the rain had failed to put out.

A policeman blocked the road as Claudette neared and motioned for her to detour. She waved the policeman down, and he approached her car.

"Ma'am, you need to turn and go the other way. We've got us a mess here."

"Is it bad?" Claudette asked, fighting back the tears.

"It's a total. The owner is probably glad it burned down, sitting in this run-down neighborhood. Probably got no insurance, either.

Now ma'am, you need to move on. You're obstructing traffic. You need to move before I give you a ticket."

"I'm the owner of the building that just burned down in this raggedy neighborhood. I worked hard to build my business, and when I collect on my insurance, I'm going to rebuild in the very same spot. And your hair needs washing; smells like old grease. Now move away from my car."

The officer moved back and stared at Claudette as she prepared to drive away. "We'll need some information from you—if you *are* the owner," he said.

"When I get back. I've got to check on my son." Claudette looked in her rearview mirror as she sped away. "I'll be back sooner than you think."

xxx

Rachel had some regrets about baring her soul to the ladies about her night with Marvin. She couldn't take it back, but she felt she needed her sisters at the time. But it was no longer about her.

She picked up the phone and dialed Mona's number. Mona wouldn't forgive her or the group if they neglected to tell her about Claudette's shop catching on fire.

"Mona," Rachel said when she heard Mona's voice at the other end.

"Rachel, how was the meeting? Did you get the candy and wine Marvin brought you for your make-up session?"

"What are you talking about, Mona?"

"I ran into Marvin just before…oh, I think I've messed up. Can I call you back?"

"Not so fast."

"Look, Rachel. I'm out on a date. It's very rude of me to be talking on my cell phone when I have a handsome gentleman feeding me caviar."

"Yuck."

"Look, I saw Marvin when he was on his way to your house, and I tried to warn him about the meeting. I guess it didn't do any good."

"No, it didn't. You could have given *us* a call to warn *us* that Marvin was on his way. But, no, that was too much for you to do. Selfish you."

"Yes, selfish me. Now I've got to go. Why did you call in the first place?"

"It's Claudette."

"Claudette? What about Claudette?" Mona asked with sincerity.

"Her shop burned down."

"What?"

"Yes, and Kwame might have done it."

"Thanks, Rachel. I've got to get to Claudette."

"Okay, I thought you'd want to know."

✗✗✗

Her knees felt wobbly as Claudette proceeded to the information desk to inquire about Kwame. There was little activity aside from the occasional guard who walked by and flipped a "what's going on" sign to the sergeant behind the information desk. Before Claudette could ask about Kwame's whereabouts the outer door to the police station opened and in walked Tyrone, looking like the young serviceman she'd married so many years before.

Tyrone moved swiftly toward Claudette dressed in an olive

dress shirt, off-white slacks and blazer and a tie that tied it all together. A diamond earring sat in the lobe of his left ear, and his hair was trimmed close to his scalp. Kwame looked so much like his father, she thought.

Claudette stood in the middle of the room, not knowing what to say. Tyrone met her and wrapped his arms around her.

"Hey, girl. We'll get through this together," Tyrone said. "Let's go find our son."

"Thank you, T. I appreciate you coming down."

"Claudette, Kwame is my son, too. I would have been here even if you hadn't called."

One for the Road

"Michael, I really hate to leave."

"Then don't. I don't think I could stand to have you out of my sight for even a second."

"Flattery usually works but my friend Claudette needs me. Her beauty shop caught on fire, and I know she's at her wit's end."

Michael sat the glass of wine on the table. "If you must, I do understand. The night is young, and there's yet so much to enjoy."

Mona smiled. She liked Michael Broussard's style. He was smooth as silk and he wasted no time in telling her what he wanted.

"I want you, Mona. Ever since I laid eyes on you at the Gordons' party, it became my mission to pursue you for this moment. Timing, I say, and it has been well worth the wait. I don't want to sound selfish, but…no, you do what is best."

"What if I come back? I need to know that Claudette is okay."

"Why don't I drive you? You can leave your car at the restaurant and we'll pick it up later."

"Really? I don't want you to go out of your way. I've already spoiled our evening."

"Not a problem. We can check on your friend and continue where we left off once we know she's all right."

"I'd like that, Michael. I feel lucky to be in your company."

"Mona, it's just the beginning."

Mona gazed into Michael's eyes and wouldn't let go. This man could not be real. It had been a long time since someone who was worthy of the society page crossed the threshold into her life. She blinked.

"Let me get my umbrella. It's still raining outside."

✗✗✗

A scared Kwame sat in a room with two chairs and a table. Claudette and Tyrone rushed in when the officer gave them access.

"Baby," Claudette wailed, "tell Momma what happened!"

Kwame looked at Claudette, then Tyrone, and dropped his head.

"Kwame," Claudette pressed, "what happened? Where is your sister? Why were you at the shop?"

"Take it easy, Claudette. Can't you see that he's traumatized?" Tyrone said.

"I just want to understand what happened, Tyrone. Why did they pick you up, Kwame?"

"Because they panicked and left me at the shop, and I was the only one there when the fire truck got there."

"Who is 'they,' Kwame?"

"I…I don't know." He shrugged his shoulders. "Some guys and Reebe."

"Where is your sister?"

"She's with the guys."

Ohhhhhhhh, Claudette sighed out loud.

"Kwame," Tyrone began, "what happened today?"

"It was an accident, Daddy."

"What was an accident?"

"The fire."

"What happened?" Tyrone pushed.

"I lit a cigarette like I see Momma do. Reebe was kissing—I mean, talking to this guy, and when she smelled the smoke she screamed at me to put the cigarette out. I threw the cigarette in the trash can. Then it caught on fire."

Tyrone took charge. "Where was Reebe when the police picked you up?"

"I don't know. I didn't see her anywhere after I ran outside. I guess she was scared and ran away with that guy she was with."

Claudette popped her knuckles and got up from the chair. There was fire in her eyes, but she didn't say a word. There were so many "what ifs" to be answered. What if she had stayed home and not gone to the meeting? What if she had been more responsible…had not left the cigarettes lying around? What if she had paid more attention to the company her daughter was keeping instead of making sure her own needs were at the top of her priority list? What if?

"Sit down, Claudette. Don't go blaming yourself for what happened," Tyrone said. "Kwame didn't do it on purpose. We have to make sure the law understands that."

"Oh, it's not that. You get a second chance at life T, and things are going fine. There's never a thought that things could go wrong again…ruin your life."

"You can rebuild the shop, Claudette."

"I keep thinking about how hard I worked to get to where I am today. What am I going to do? No income means I won't be able to pay the mortgage, the car note, the light bill, the phone bill…"

"Enough. It's not all about you. We have Kwame to consider, also. We can rebuild the shop, and I'll help you until you get on your feet."

"No handouts. I can make it on my own," Claudette stated.

"Have it your way."

"Momma, Daddy, I can't take it. I didn't mean to burn the shop down." Kwame placed his head down on the table and cried.

"Son," Tyrone said, "we believe you. We're going to talk with the police and see what we can do."

"I'm scared," Kwame cried. "Daddy, I'm scared."

Claudette and Tyrone went to their son and hugged him. "We're going to get you out of here," they assured him.

"I'm grateful for the neighbor who saw the building on fire as she passed by. Kwame could have been killed. Thank God for cell phones."

The door to the interrogation room opened.

"Is everything all right in here?" the officer asked.

"Yes, sir," Tyrone said. "I need to talk to someone about my son. He told his mother and me that it was an accident, and we believe him."

A Friend in Need

Anderson Cooper concluded another interview on CNN. An ad for Allstate began to play on the screen.

Caaaaaaaaaaaaaaaaaaaaaaaaaaaww. Caaaaaaaaaaaawww. Caaaaaaaaa-wwww. Marvin jerked his head up, then down. *Caaaaaaaaaaawwww. Caaaaaaaaawwwww.* His eyes popped open at the sound of the phone ringing. Groggy, he sat staring into space as the phone continued to ring. In slow motion, Marvin reached for the mobile that sat on the table.

"Hello," he mumbled.

"Marvin?"

"Yes."

"This is Rachel. Is this a bad time?"

"Rachel. No…oh no, this is not a bad time. I'm sorry, I fell asleep on the couch—a deep sleep—and I'm still a little out of it."

Marvin was happy to hear Rachel's voice. The incident earlier was childish, and he was going to make it up to her. He understood how she must have felt seeing Denise at the restaurant hovering over him, and she did what most women do: confide in a friend.

"I want to apologize for this evening, Marvin."

"No need, Rachel. I'm the one who needs to apologize. I want you to know that I had no idea Denise was going to be at that restaurant. In fact, I didn't know she was in town. I do hope we can start over…get a fresh start, because I do enjoy your company."

"I'd like that very much."

"If you're not busy, maybe I can drop by. I know tomorrow is Monday, but I won't stay long."

"Why don't you pick me up? Claudette's shop burned down tonight," Rachel told him.

"Oh my God."

"She got the call while she was at the meeting. Maybe we can check on her—she was not doing well and I'm concerned about her state."

"I'm on my way, Rachel. We have to help Claudette. That's what the group is all about—supporting one another during a crisis."

"You're right. I'm lucky to have you, Mr. Thomas."

"I'm the lucky one. I'll be there in twenty minutes."

"I'll be waiting."

xxx

"Mr. and Mrs. Beasley?" the judge asked.

"Yes," both Claudette and Tyrone said.

"Do you have an attorney for Kwame?"

"No, sir," Tyrone replied. "Our son has said the fire was an accident and his mother and I would like to take him home given this information."

"Sir, your son is being charged with a serious crime. Arson is a felony, and he was found at the scene of the crime. I recommend that you obtain a lawyer. Bail is set at fifteen-thousand dollars."

"Jesus," Claudette spat out. "Fifteen-thousand dollars. My baby can't stay the night."

"Ma'am, you and your husband are going to be asked about your whereabouts while your son was at the shop."

"Don't say anything else, Claudette. Let's get an attorney."

"Jesus, Jesus, Jesus!" Claudette wailed. "I'm going to kill Reebe."

"You can't talk about killing anybody," Tyrone tried to whisper.

"I'm going to—"

"Excuse my wife…"

"*Ex*-wife," Claudette corrected.

"Ex-wife, sir. Excuse my ex-wife. She's a little distraught."

"I need a cigarette," Claudette said.

"Not now, Claudette. Have you forgotten that cigarettes are the root of this whole problem?"

"I need a cigarette and I need to see Kwame."

"Okay. Then I'm taking you home and I'll try to work the other out."

Claudette was unable to move. She shivered at the thought of Kwame being left alone at the juvenile detention center. How she wished she could control fate and erase the moment that now caused her so much pain and frustration. She was a tigress when it came to standing up to Ashley's ex, William. Now here she was at the detention center, unable to save her own son.

She let Tyrone lead her from the room.

XXX

"What a nasty night. I would hate to see you out here in all this mess. I'm glad you agreed to let me take you," Michael said.

"I'm glad, too. Hopefully, the rain will have stopped by the time I'm ready to go home," Mona replied.

"We can remedy that, too."

Mona smiled. She wasn't quite ready to expose herself to Mr.

Broussard just yet, but she'd keep the offer in the back of her mind.

"Where to?" Michael asked.

"The south end of Stone Mountain. Claudette should be home. I'll call her cell."

Michael stole glances at Mona as she chatted briefly with Claudette. He held the steering wheel with his left hand and allowed the other to gently graze Mona's other hand which hung over the console. Mona flinched, then turned in Michael's direction, finally ending her phone call with Claudette.

"Claudette is on her way home."

"Your hands are soft," he murmured.

"Why me, Mr. Broussard?"

"Why not you, Mona?"

"There were so many good-looking women at that party."

"Need I remind you, most of them came with a date."

"Everyone except us." They laughed.

"You intrigue me, Mona Baptiste."

"You have a faint accent—islander?"

"West Indies."

Mona sat back and her mind roamed to the day she met Timothy in college. It was the accent that caused her to take another look at the dark-skinned guy whose pearl-white teeth glistened like a lighthouse on a foggy day. She shook the memory from her mind.

"You all right?"

"Yeah. I was thinking of home. Haven't been there in awhile."

"Maybe you should go for a visit. It might do you some good."

"I will eventually." There was a short pause. "Make a left, then a right. Claudette lives four houses from the corner. I hope I find the right words to say."

"Just be her friend. And think about getting an airline ticket home."

Mona looked at Michael Broussard. He was a lucky find. Her Ex-Files had been emptied long ago. She had plenty of empty space to accommodate someone in her heart. And she was ready.

xxx

Darkness fell as Mona and Michael waited for Claudette to arrive home. The night was silent, save for the hissing sound of the tires of the few automobiles that passed through the rain-soaked street. Another set of headlights beamed in their direction but slowed as it approached the house. Mona didn't recognize the car that turned into the driveway but she did recognize the driver as he got out of the car. Claudette herself exited on the passenger's side.

"Hmmph, Claudette's ex," Mona said. "I wonder what happened to Claudette's car."

"He must have come to Claudette's aid when he got the news."

"Maybe."

Mona and Michael exited the car when another set of head-lights stopped right in front of them.

"Marvin and Rachel? I can't believe they made up so fast. Just a few hours ago, Rachel was sulking," Mona said in surprise.

"These your friends?" Michael asked.

"They are part of our support group for ex-wives, even though I'm not sure why I joined. I've been an ex for awhile, and I've gone on with my life."

"Hmmm," Michael said, perplexed. "So, your life is fulfilled and happy."

"Well, yes, but there's always room for new adventure."

"I see. You are a very complicated woman, Mona Baptiste, but don't worry, I love puzzles."

Mona looked at Michael and smiled. *I am* very *complicated, Dr. Michael Broussard, and it won't be that easy to navigate my waters*, she thought.

As everyone gathered in Claudette's driveway and gave her hugs, another set of headlights approached. Out hopped Sylvia and Ashley, outdone by the welcome party who beat them there.

"Let's go into the house, everybody," Claudette said, throwing the butt of her cigarette down on the carport floor and smashing it for good measure.

The group followed and sat on the sparse furniture without taking off coats or wraps. Claudette stood next to Tyrone; his arm was wrapped around her shoulders.

"I love you all," Claudette began. "It's late and most of you have to get up tomorrow and go to work, but you cared enough to see about a friend." A tear welled up in her eye. "Standing next to me is Tyrone, my ex-husband." Claudette looked at T and dropped her head.

"Hello, everyone," Tyrone began.

"My...my...my shop is gone," Claudette interrupted. Tyrone squeezed her tight. "I drove by there after I left Rachel's, and there's nothing left. Kwame is in the juvenile detention center because the police found him outside. My baby is in jail and will have to stay there until we can make bail—fifteen-thousand dollars. Can you believe that?"

The group stood up to offer their support. Claudette let the tears roll. There was no more shame.

"Sit down, Claudette," Tyrone prompted and led her to a chair.

"Did Kwame set the shop on fire?" Mona asked.

"Not on purpose. He was at the shop with his sister, for what reason I don't know. He picked up a pack of my cigarettes and lit one. Reebe shouted at him and he threw it in the trash can, and it caught on fire. Accident. He didn't mean to do it. I don't know what I'm going to do."

"You can use your house as a shop," Rachel put in.

"Yeah, that's a great idea," Mona chimed in. "Go back to the roots. You know that's how we did it before these fancy, schmancy salons came along."

"I agree," Sylvia said. "It's an excellent idea. We'll help you notify your customers."

"I'm so grateful to you all," Claudette said. "I don't know what I'd do without the Ex-Files." She laughed for the first time.

Marvin moved toward Claudette. "I'll donate the money for Kwame's bail and help you get whatever you need to get your shop set up."

Everyone stared in awe at the gorgeous and gracious gentleman who had withdrawn from the group only hours earlier.

"Oh, oh, I...I can't, Marvin. That is so generous, but I can't take anything from you."

"Please, accept my offer. If we hurry, we can bring Kwame home tonight."

"And I'll purchase the hair supplies you need," Ashley put her two cents in. "You were right there for me, Claudette, when I needed a friend."

Rachel could not stop staring at Marvin. She went to him and kissed his lips. Marvin searched her eyes, which were full of tears, and he kissed her back passionately in front of a room full of friends.

Sylvia turned away unable to keep the tears from streaming

down her face. She had not seen such a beautiful display of affection in a long time. It was obvious that Rachel and Marvin were soul mates, and Sylvia knew she could mark the day as a pivotal one in Rachel's life—her resurrection day.

"Thank you, Ashley," Claudette said, giving her a hug. "I appreciate it, girl. Whenever you need a babysitter, Auntie Claudette will be here for you."

"Thanks, man," Tyrone said, shaking Marvin's hand. "I appreciate what you're doing for Claudette—for us. Kwame's my son, too. I'll hit you back, man. I'm going to do all I can to help my family."

Claudette glanced at Tyrone. She had gotten used to being by herself—gotten used to her independence. This was not the time for Tyrone to try and waltz back into her life. Maybe God was trying to tell her something. She would not dwell on Tyrone at this moment; she wanted to bring her baby home, and she had to find the other one. Reebe was in trouble.

"Before we go," Marvin began, "another thought came to mind. We should have a fund-raiser this Saturday to help Claudette."

"You have to plan for that, baby," Rachel insisted.

"Not if we do it right. We'll have a barbecue. I'll get the meat and ladies, you can make the dishes that go with it. Everybody is tasked with calling their friends and co-workers. I don't care who they are as long as they buy a plate. It's for a worthy cause, and I expect everyone to work. We can have it in the parking lot of the beauty shop—I'll check to make sure we can have it there."

"Take charge, baby. Take charge!" Rachel shouted.

"What happened between three o'clock and now?" Sylvia asked Rachel with a nudge to her rib cage. "You were singing a different story earlier."

"Break up to make up. It's a beautiful thing. Don't hate, my sister."

"I don't, Rachel. I'm happy if things are working out for you and Marvin. Give that ex-wife, Denise, a run for her money."

Rachel threw Sylvia a sly glance. "I'm not worried about Ms. Denise. I've got something for her if she thinks she's gonna try and reclaim my man. Plus I've got backup. We really are a team."

"Don't expect me to fight like a street hood," Sylvia shot back. "If I'm in trouble, you better come running."

"I'm happy for you, Rachel. I really am, sis."

"Thanks, Sylvia. That means a lot."

xxx

Sylvia longed for Kenny, but she knew he could not be a fix every time she felt she was in trouble. No one would ever say she was a junkie, but she wanted him. She needed him like a crack addict needed his rock. Kenny had become her rock. Yes, she had become very dependent on him because he offered shelter from the rain, his words soothed when she sought calm and he had become the man she had looked for to complement her life. Sylvia walked to her car and waited for Ashley.

The Prodigal EX

Sylvia drove in silence as she sped toward Ashley's house. Ashley must have sensed Sylvia's need to recede into herself because she interrupted the silence only to tell Sylvia that she was about to pass the turn onto her street.

There was a chill in the night as the light from the moon cast a sinister glow on the wet, black asphalt. When they were about to pull up to the two-story, three-car garage brick house, Ashley drew back in her seat, paralyzed. It was then that Sylvia noticed the black BMW sitting triumphantly out front.

Nervousness was written all over Ashley's face. She did not move for several minutes. A car door opened, and a tall man stood beside the BMW. Sylvia could not make out his features in the dead of night, but she could tell that he was dark and possibly bald.

Ashley sighed.

"You all right, Ash? Is that your ex-husband?"

"Yes, it's William. I'll be okay."

"Sweetie, you can come home with me, if you like. I'm not liking the vibes you are sending me."

"Nothing to worry about, Sylvia. It's…it's just that I thought I wanted my husband back, but since seeing him at that clinic with that pregnant woman, I feel differently. And what kind of man leaves the woman he ran off with because she lost his baby to turn around and be with the one he said good-bye to in a court of law because he found out she's having his baby? I don't understand William's psychotic reasoning at all. If my heart was bulletproof, then it would be one thing, but this man poked holes in my soul and now his all-of-a-sudden repentant heart wants to undo the wrong. I'm going to clean out my Ex-Files and label it 'case closed.'"

"I wish it were that easy, Ashley. Now you have a tie that binds the two of you together, forever—the child growing in your womb."

"Some miracle."

They watched as William advanced toward Sylvia's car.

"Call me if you need me," Sylvia said before Ashley got out of the car. Sylvia sat and watched as Ashley walked toward her ex. The fear in Ashley's eyes did not escape Sylvia, and for the first time, she was afraid for Ashley.

Sylvia began to back out, then turned and noticed that Ashley and William were still standing in the driveway. Ashley's hands became animated as she tossed them in the air to demonstrate her point. William was up in Ashley's face, territorial in his stance with no thought of backing down. Sylvia thought she saw Ashley slap her hand toward her, telling her to go. Sylvia was afraid and decided to sit in the driveway until she was sure Ashley would be all right. She circled around a couple of times to be sure.

✗✗✗

Claudette, Tyrone, Rachel and Marvin headed for the juvenile detention center in hopes of being able to bring Kwame home. No one said much of anything. Claudette took brief glances at Tyrone, and Tyrone squeezed Claudette's hand every thirty seconds. Rachel and Marvin sat in the backseat huddled together as if their lives depended on it, smiling at each other like lovebirds.

"I want to thank you again, Marvin," Claudette began. "First for being a true friend and for doing the unimaginable. If I can pay you back, I will. I thank you from the bottom of my heart."

"We thank you," Tyrone said.

"You are more than welcome. It's not a loan; I want to do this. But I would like to ask something of you, Claudette."

Claudette finished dabbing at her eyes. "What is it, Marvin?"

"You said that Kwame picked up your cigarettes and lit one."

Claudette felt her stomach tightening. Only Tyrone had admonished her about her smoking, and she ignored him. Now the man with the generous gift was going to give her an ultimatum. She was sure of it. But there would be no words to dismiss him because he was going to rescue her baby from the pit of hell.

"Yes."

"Do you think Kwame was trying to get attention?"

"I don't think so," Claudette said calmly. "I know I work hard, but I'm there for my son. I help him with his homework and take him to his sport activities…"

"And he's learning bad habits," Tyrone interjected.

"T, Marvin was asking the question. If Kwame had a father around, maybe you'd be in a position to say something."

"Just remember, Claudette, it was you who left me and took our kids away from their father."

Tyrone rocked his neck back and forth to ease the tightness, and he sealed his lips.

"Look, guys, this is not the time to get upset," Marvin offered. "You've got to get it together for Kwame. I'm sorry that I said anything."

"Marvin, I know where you're coming from," Claudette countered. "I want to quit smoking…God knows I do. And I will…if you will help me."

"We're there for you," Rachel finally said. "All for one. We're going to see you through this ordeal and any other ordeal you might have."

"That's so sweet of you, Rachel. I know you didn't like me very much when we first met, but I must say God knew what he was doing when he had Sylvia to organize the Ex-Files."

"Ex-Files? What's that?" Tyrone inquired.

Everyone laughed.

"We're all exes, man," Marvin piped in.

"I'm an ex," Tyrone said.

"Yeah, but I was trying to find a way to move on without my ex," Claudette said.

Everyone laughed again.

"This isn't funny," Tyrone admonished.

"Lighten up, man," Marvin said, still laughing. "You want to join our group?"

Claudette's bunched-up face met Marvin's. She was a funny sight. Rachel began to laugh and so did Marvin.

"What's going on?" Tyrone asked.

"Drive the car," Claudette said through clenched teeth.

"Man, our next meeting of the Ex-Files will be at my house… I'll have to get back to you on the date. It is going to feel good with another man in the group."

They all broke out in laughter. Tyrone joined them since it was the only logical thing to do.

Anything for my Man

Mona peeped out of the window for the third time in ten minutes, hoping to see Michael drive up. The candles were lit, and the dining room table set for two. Sparkles bounced off the crystal in the chandelier that hung above the dining room table as the light from the candles gleamed on their teardrops.

China plates with stainless steel covers sat at either end of the table. Under the covers were plates of veal tenderloin that sat in a river of brown gravy dotted with scallions. Steamed asparagus draped with hollandaise sauce and rice pilaf completed the meal. A vintage red wine sat chilled in a bucket ready to be poured at the right moment.

Mona jumped at the sound of the telephone ringing. She grabbed her throat, hoping the voice at the other end would not disappoint her or make her regret all the time and effort she had gone through to make this evening perfect. She grabbed the phone on the third ring and sighed when she heard Sylvia's voice.

"Ohh, don't scare me like that."

"What are you talking about, Mona?"

"Girl, I thought you were Michael calling to say you couldn't make it. I've prepared this scrumptious meal for him…and I'm so nervous."

"Girl, please. Not Mona the man-handler."

"It's not funny, Sylvia. I...I think I'm falling in love with this man."

"What? Not you."

"You don't think I'm capable of love?"

"I know you can throw a mean meal, and if Mr. Broussard doesn't show up I will."

"He'll show up. Got my stomach all in knots. No man has ever done that to me before."

"No man?"

"Well, maybe my ex-husband did, once." For the second time in two days, a vision of Timothy tried to penetrate her thoughts. "Guess what?"

"Tell me so that you can put me out of my misery."

"Michael and I are going to New Orleans."

"What?"

"Sylvia, you know I haven't been home in... "

"A long time, my dear. You're overdue. But why go with Michael?"

"He has family there. If things aren't well with my family, I'll just stay with Michael's family."

"Wow. How long have you known him? Two weeks, a month?"

"Poor, poor Sylvia. Can't stand to see anybody happy. I heard what you said to Rachel tonight. If Kenny was half... "

"Now hold on a moment—"

"Hold on, Sylvia. I think I hear a car."

Mona rushed the two feet to the window and pulled back the drapes. Wishful thinking. "It wasn't him."

"You are sprung."

"Like I said, Sylvia, I'm falling in love with this man. We're going to purchase our tickets to New Orleans tonight."

"Whatever you do, you best be at the barbecue fund-raiser on

Saturday for Claudette. We should let you cook the side dishes since it's what you do."

"You heard Marvin. Everyone must participate."

"We will. Hold on, it's Ashley. I'll put us on three-way. William was waiting for her outside the house when I drove her home last night."

"What!"

"Ashley, I've got you and Mona on three-way."

"Hey, ladies."

"How are you doing?" bellowed Mona.

"Sylvia told you about last night, I see. The baby and I are fine."

"So what happened?" Sylvia asked. "I drove around the corner and came back a couple of times after you went inside."

"So you checked on me. Thanks, Sylvia. William said that he was going to be a father to this baby. Said he was coming home and the divorce decree was just a piece of paper—that he paid a lot of money for, mind you—and it couldn't dictate to grown folks. That's what we were arguing about because it was very clear to me sitting before that judge that he was happy to get that piece of paper. And since he got what he wanted there was no need for him to come home."

"I had you pegged wrong, Ashley," Mona said. "You're a tough white sister. Can hold your own. How about that, Sylvia? I hear another car, hold on."

"What's that all about?" Ashley inquired.

"She's got a dinner date tonight with her Caribbean king," Sylvia said.

"I'm back on the line, heifer. Sylvia's hating, Ashley, because she don't have a man and I do."

"I thought Kenny was back in your life?" Ashley asked.

"She's better off without him." Mona moaned.

"Forget you. What is this? Rachel's calling. Hey Rachel, you are on a conference call. Mona and Ashley are on."

"Ohh. We're having a meeting and you didn't tell me?" Rachel mimicked Marvin.

"Sounds like a re-run," Sylvia said. "But I'm glad that you and your man have worked it out."

"Guys, I'm in love."

"Ohhh, I'm happy for you, Rachel," Ashley crowed.

"Here we go again with this love thing." Sylvia sighed.

"Who else is in love?"

"I am, Rachel. I am falling in love with Michael."

"But Mona, didn't you just meet him?"

"That's what I was trying to tell her," Sylvia put in.

"Isn't this what Ex-Files was supposed to do, Sylvia? Help us to move past our hurt and pain? And if we find love in the meantime, I don't think that's a bad thing. What do you other ladies think?"

"I slept with William last night," Ashley confessed. "And…I let him come back home. It's just temporary—to see how things go."

"You did what, missy? After all the worrying I did over you. Couldn't sleep." Sylvia snorted in disgust.

"Well, I am carrying his child."

"Ashley got her some." Mona laughed. "You go, girl; I ain't mad at you 'cuz I'm going to try and get me some, too."

"I heard that…, " Rachel cooed softly.

"I don't believe it. Hold on, it's Claudette. Hey…Claudette. Everyone is on the line—Ashley, Mona, and Rachel."

"Having a meeting without me?" Claudette asked.

Everyone broke into laughter.

"Look, I just wanted to tell you all that Kwame is home thanks to Marvin. I don't know what to say but thank you all for being there for me…and T."

"Don't tell me you two are getting back together, too," Mona sang.

"And would that be a bad thing, Mona? We're concerned about our family. I've got issues with Reebe. I just want to kill her. If it wasn't for Tyrone, she would be dead.

"Had the nerve to come waltzing back home like nothing happened. Didn't even ask about Kwame. Oooooooh, I could barely look at her. She gave me one of her flippant looks when I asked her what happened yesterday, and then shrugged her shoulders at me and said, 'I don't know what you're talking about.' Made me so mad. I tried to jump her because she knew good and well what I was talking about. Tyrone was back in high school playing football because he tackled me before I let loose on that girl."

"Claudette, could you hurry up?" Mona whined. "Michael is pulling up in the driveway, but I want to hear the rest of this."

"Go tend to your man. I'm about finished."

Mona sucked her teeth.

"Go on, Claudette," Ashley prompted.

"Tyrone and I talked about it, and I'm going to take Reebe to a counselor. In fact, we all need to go to counseling. I'm going to have to depend on Tyrone for a minute until I get my business back on track. You know, it felt good having him worry about me and take matters into his hands."

"Ashley slept with William," Rachel said.

"What?" Claudette hollered.

"Claudette, he felt good next to me and our baby."

"Shut up," Claudette hollered again.

"Look, gotta go," Mona interrupted. "My man is ringing my bell. Talk to you heifers later. Ashley and Claudette, put a check mark up there for me, too. Bye."

EX-plain this to Me

"Sylvia, we need to talk."

"No hello? No how are you doing, Sylvia? It's been awhile, Sylvia? Arial, you disappoint me."

"Honey, we need to talk… "

"About my head. I know. I'm terribly overdue."

"Sylvia, are the rumors true? Are you and Kenny an item?"

Sylvia rolled her eyes. She came to relax and get her head massaged…not answer a battery of questions that happen to be no one's concern but hers.

"Would you scratch my head here, Arial?" Sylvia pointed to the spot with her index finger.

Pop went Arial's comb. Sylvia withdrew her hand quickly and kissed her knuckles.

"There will be no tip for you today. Naughty girls are not rewarded."

"Depends on what the naughty girl is doing. Back to the subject."

"Arial, I don't want to talk—"

"You can hide behind the bush if you want, but your secret is written on the side of every MARTA train, the bathroom stalls at the Hartsfield-Jackson Atlanta Airport, on the walls of the King Center and on the menus at Gladys' Chicken and Waffles. Everybody knows, girl."

"You're exaggerating, Arial."

"I don't know how you failed to give me this little tidbit. Such an important piece of information, and I had to hear it from the lips of gossiping clients. Sister, I was there way back when. Remember? Yeah, you remember because Kenny twisted your brain inside out, and you couldn't eat, sleep or function."

"Hmph. Aren't you the pot calling the kettle black. I heard your ex, Lawrence, was in the shop last week. Come to get a *blow* job?"

Arial yanked the blow-dryer off the counter and turned it on full blast into Sylvia's face, although she made sure it was several inches away. "Oh, you want to be a nasty little heifer, too. This conversation isn't about me and Lawrence. It's about you and Kenny."

"Is there a point to this? I've got a function this afternoon. In fact, you need to buy a barbecue dinner—no, two—from me."

Arial turned off the blow-dryer. "Look, you've proved my point. You've forgotten all those painful times when I had to nurse you and your hair back to health. Hair was so thin, it would break off if you looked at it."

"Hmmm," Sylvia muttered. "Look in your own mirror."

"I'm not through. That man was no good—"

"Hold it, Arial. Let me be the judge. Kenny is a changed man, and I think I'm falling in love with him."

"What, what, what did you say? My Lord, I know you didn't utter something about falling in love with Kenny."

"How's that for news?" Sylvia said snugly.

"They call me the psychiatrist, the psychoanalyst, the motivator, the black Ann Landers. I'm here for whatever ails you, but I don't have any words for you. You're going to have to help yourself."

"Maybe you didn't hear me. The only help I need is from the hairdresser. So unwind that person from your list of personalities and tell her to get to work on my head. And if the psychiatrist wants to say anything, please put some tape across her mouth. Now, I'm a paying customer, and you've wasted twenty minutes of my valuable time."

"Oooooookay," said the muffled voice.

Sylvia laughed until she almost fell out of the chair.

Arial led Sylvia to the sink and washed her hair without one of her super-duper massages. She wrapped a towel around Sylvia's head and marched her over to her chair. She picked up the blow-dryer and began to dry Sylvia's head. She didn't say another word about Kenny.

"I need ten dollars for two dinners," Sylvia said to a now quiet Arial. "Claudette Beasley's shop burned down last weekend. We're having a barbecue fund-raiser to help her with expenses."

"I heard about that. I'll give you the ten dollars only if you can give me a guarantee that you won't make her salon your home."

"Arial, how long have I been coming to you?"

"Sylvia, I've sculptured your mop into what it looks like today. Took a long time to cultivate, and I still have skills."

"Need I say more?"

Brrng, brrng, brrng. "That's my cell," Sylvia said.

Arial turned off the dryer. Fighting with Sylvia had exhausted her.

"Excuse me," Sylvia said. "Hi, Kenny. I'll be ready in…" Sylvia looked into Arial's pouting face…"about twenty minutes. See you then, sweetie."

Arial twirled the irons and curled Sylvia's hair without another word.

xxx

Sylvia slipped on her sunglasses and pulled her BMW away from the curb in front of Mane Waves. Arial had gotten on her nerves today, but her hair looked good. Yeah, Arial was good for another ten years.

It was a beautiful day for a fund-raiser. The sun scorched the sky with its brilliance. The flowers sang the sun's praises, showing off petals in pastel colors that waved to the sky, while tall pine trees lifted their branches in honor.

A smile marked Sylvia's face. *Secrets*, Arial had said. There were no secrets. Simply put, she and Kenny had gone out on a couple of dates. There was no intimacy, no…

Sylvia drove onto I-85. A large black-and-white cow with a milk mustache over its mouth loomed on the billboard in front of her. Images of Kenny draped in her black-and-white polka-dot robe came rushing back to her. She laughed out loud.

Kenny was going to meet her at her house before going to the barbecue. Sylvia's contribution was four German chocolate cakes. It made her feel good that the group would work together to help Claudette get back on her feet.

Thoughts of Kenny invaded Sylvia's mind and wouldn't let go. Going to the fund-raiser with him validated what her heart was feeling, but she wondered whether she was with Kenny because everyone doubted their relationship and she had something to prove. Love seemed to have blanketed everyone—Rachel and Marvin, Mona and Michael—but eluded her. Sylvia dropped the thoughts from her mind and exited the freeway toward Stone Mountain.

When Sylvia pulled into her driveway, the first thing she saw was Kenny Richmond's silver Acura parked off to one side. She adjusted her sunglasses, looked in the rearview mirror and flipped her hair with her hands. Before she could get out of the car, the door handle clicked, and Kenny—dressed in a black crocheted knit top and white shorts—held the door open. Sylvia could hardly contain herself as she cruised this man's body from his sandaled feet, past the muscular, taught legs and the well-chiseled chest she remembered so well to the top of his curly head. And the way he wrapped his hand around her arm caused her butterfly alarm to go off.

Sylvia got out of the car. She tried to rush past the gorgeous man, but he had already read her vibes. Kenny quickly put his arm around Sylvia's waist and drew her to him.

"Not outside in front of the neighbors," Sylvia said with a frown.

"It's not as if you're cheating on your husband," he pointed out. But he dropped his arm and followed her into the house.

"It doesn't matter. I'm not ready to share you with the world, although Arial says that everybody in Atlanta knows that we…"

"We what? I'm anxious to know myself," Kenny pushed.

"That we're an item."

"Are we an item?"

"Let's go in the house, Mr. Richmond. You can put the cakes in the car while I change into something cool. We've got to hurry because Marvin said we were going to start serving right at eleven."

"Do you need help getting into something cool?"

"Kenny Richmond, get those cakes into the car. I'm a big girl, and I don't need any help." *I wish you could help me with the way I feel because I'm falling in love with you.* Sylvia watched as Kenny lifted the boxes with the cakes and headed outside. He was gentle. He was kind. He was a changed man.

xxx

Everyone was there when Sylvia and Kenny arrived. Rachel turned toward Mona and whispered something in her ear, blocking the view of her lips with her hand. Mona mimicked Rachel but added an extra eye roll. Sylvia dismissed them both.

Two large barreled grills stood in the parking lot of where Claudette's shop used to be. The sizzle of the meat made Sylvia smack her lips as she drew near, and Marvin raised his head only for a second to nod hello, before picking up a long-handled two-pronged fork to turn over a slab of ribs. Pork and beef ribs, chicken and links were being prepared. There was a large pot of collard greens, grilled corn on the cob, Mona's fabulous baked beans, bean casserole, and Rachel's potato salad. The aroma was already sending signals throughout the neighborhood.

Claudette prepared dinners to go for those who'd paid ahead. Tyrone was the deliveryman, Kwame his assistant. There was a line of twenty deep—women dressed in cut-offs and short-shorts; neon-colored halter tops; orange, yellow, and blue flip-flops; and leather sandals, while men were dressed in colorful T-shirts, shorts and jogging shorts from Nike to Adidas. Some were Claudette's beauty shop patrons while others were families from the area who wanted to help restore an important landmark in their neighborhood.

As people inched up through the line, fingers pointed to where the shop once stood, recalling the night of the blaze. Others murmured about Kwame and how the police found him at the scene of the crime and arrested him. But the ultimate goal was to get some of that lip-smacking barbecue that you could smell for more than a mile. Some had already been through the line but had come back to get plates for others after sharing firsthand how tasty Marvin's ribs were.

Mona, Rachel, and Sylvia served dressed in picnic aprons over shorts and pastel-colored tees. Every now and then Michael would inch his way up around Mona and peck her on the cheek and rub her backside. He was way overdressed—slacks and a long-sleeved shirt—and stayed as far away from the barbecue sauce as he could.

After the last preorder had been prepared, Claudette joined the others.

"Where is Ashley?" Claudette asked. "Has anyone heard from her today? She was supposed to bring her apple dumpling cake that she's always raving about."

"Maybe she didn't feel well or she was still taking care of her baby's daddy," Mona put in.

"Can you be serious for once, Mona?" Claudette asked.

"Oooh, aren't we a little huffy. I've been slaving all night over the stove just for you and you want to get—eh—on me."

"Come on, Mona," Rachel said. "She's truly concerned about Ashley and so am I."

"I have her phone number," Sylva said. She whipped her cell phone from her pocket and dialed Ashley's number. It rang several times before Sylvia left a voice message. "Ashley didn't answer. She's probably on her way."

"I see you're still hanging in there with your male pal," Mona quipped.

"At least I'm not running off with a man I hardly know."

"Okay, ladies," Rachel said. "We have people in line and they can hear you. And it's not good for business."

"You're right," Sylvia offered. She placed a wrapped piece of German chocolate cake into the next person's hand.

"Don't I know you?" Rachel asked the young lady who held out her plate for a spoon of potato salad.

"You're...you're the lady from the spa. Yes, I remember. I gave you a facial."

"Yes," Rachel said. "Anika...right? I do apologize for not getting back with you about our support group. In fact, most of our members are here today. The fund-raiser is to support the lady whose beauty shop burned down."

"Who, Ms. Claudette?"

"You know Claudette?"

"Yes, she's my hairdresser."

"Well, she's one of our members and the group is out here helping her."

"That's so wonderful. I really do want to join."

"You can, little lady," Marvin said, coming up behind Rachel. "I'm the cook, and I'll be hosting the next meeting of the Ex-Files." He hugged Rachel.

Anika looked puzzled.

"Anika, this is Marvin Thomas. He's also a member of the group. He's a testament that the support group works."

Anika continued to look puzzled. And then she said, "Ooooo-oooooh, I see."

"Look, our next meeting is the second Sunday in August. Rachel, get her number so we can contact her and give her directions. Here's my business card in case you have any questions before then. I've got to get back to the grill; that line hasn't let up. "

"Can I bring someone with me?" Anika asked.

"I'm sure it will be okay. It was good to see you, and you'll be hearing from me."

"Thank you, Rachel. And your complexion still looks good."

"Thank you."

"I think we're doing good," Claudette said to the ladies. "Thanks to Marvin's genius."

"Here, here," Rachel said.

Tyrone whipped into the driveway and got out of the car. He adjusted his baseball cap and moved toward the ladies. Seconds later, Kwame joined him at his side. They moved to where Claudette was standing, excited about the success of the day. Tyrone moved closer and wrapped his arm around Claudette's shoulders.

Three pairs of eyes shifted at the same time. They weren't sure what to make of this display of affection. Claudette hadn't even made an attempt to free herself of Tyrone's embrace. The group smiled. If the Ex-Files were meant to draw families back together, so be it. Claudette, Tyrone and Kwame—a picture worthy of a frame.

Kenny moved behind Sylvia and whispered something in her ear.

"Fix me a plate, somebody," Sylvia ordered. "My man is hungry."

"Did your man pay his five dollars?" Mona twitched her lips in disgust.

"I donated fifty dollars, Mona, but I only want one plate."

You could hear an ant scurrying on the ground and a beetle limping across the cement. Sylvia couldn't believe that Mona was left speechless. Such satisfaction. Then Sylvia gave Mona a look that said, "You're messing with the wrong man. You need to take a look at your own life before you try to judge another's."

Rachel leaned into Mona. "He told you." And still not a word from Mona.

"I need a cigarette," Claudette announced.

"Mommy," Kwame said. "No, you don't. Didn't you learn anything?"

Another moment of silence.

Ashley Jordan-Lewis

Ashley paced the floor with her arms folded over her breasts. She was clad in a pair of white shorts and a pink, green, and white tank top. A pair of jeweled-white sandals adorned her feet. She stopped and stared. William sat toying with the TV remote.

"Ash, I don't know why you want to hang around those people, especially that loud-mouth woman who was at the clinic with you."

"This is a fund-raiser, William, and the group is expecting me to bring this cake."

"The group?" William asked, looking away from the television.

"My support group...for ex-wives."

"Well, you don't need them anymore. I'm back."

"We're divorced, William. It's what you wanted. Remember?"

"I wanted a lot of things, but right now, I want my wife...ex-wife, or whatever you want to call yourself, to stay with me today. We haven't shared a Saturday afternoon together in a long time."

Ashley stared at William. She wasn't sure what planet he had come from, but he wasn't making sense to her. This couldn't be coming from the man who hadn't shared his days, nights or weekends with her in months on end. Not the man who'd paraded his mistress in front of her, waving her around like she was the old red, white, and blue vowing his allegiance to her like he didn't have a wife but shouting there would be liberty soon in a DeKalb County courtroom.

"I need to go, William. You can't hold me hostage in my own home."

"Ashley, let's get remarried."

There was fear in Ashley's eyes. Two weeks ago, she would have screamed her own victory…looking into the face of the dethroned mistress, but now…today…she no longer felt the same way about William. She wasn't sure why she slept with him. There was something bizarre about him, and her gut was telling her to get far away from William. Ashley didn't care that she carried *their* baby inside of her. She was prepared to do it alone. But what was she going to do with William making demands. Well, not quite a demand, but an offer of marriage that didn't have the slightest glow.

"You didn't want the marriage several months ago."

"I've changed my mind."

"You can't turn life on and off like a light switch at your own whim, William."

"Let's stop talking and do it, Ashley. Our baby needs its father…"

"Is this about the baby or…or… "

"Don't try to twist what I said, Ashley. I want my family to be together, and that includes you, me, and our son or daughter."

Ashley looked into William's eyes. He didn't blink or smile, but matched her stare. He blinked and turned his head slightly, Ashley's stare getting the best of him. Ashley walked over to the kitchen table and picked up the cake she had made for the barbecue.

"Don't make a mistake and walk out of that door, Ashley."

"You may have gotten your degree from Georgetown, William, and you may have been in the top percentile of your class. But somewhere on the road from there to here, you lost some brain matter because you are not functioning with a full deck."

"Ashley, I'm going to let you get away with your snide remark for now. Right now, you are a victim of nature—a combination of morning sickness and the heat. I'll forgive you for that, but in the future, you need to refrain from questioning my sanity. I could have had any woman I wanted, but I picked you for my wife. I was clear about that, and now you are carrying my child. Get used to it. I'm going to be around."

William walked out of the room and left Ashley standing in the kitchen with the cake in her hand. Ashley sighed and put the cake back on the counter. She'd make it up to Claudette, but right now she had other urgent concerns.

EX-Files

Smokey Norvel began to sing at eight a.m. Marvin sat up straight in the bed. He stretched, yawned, and looked at the clock on the nightstand. It was past time for him to get up.

Marvin thought about the fund-raiser for Claudette. He smiled, and he felt good about himself. He and Ex-Files raised more than $500 to help get Claudette back on her feet, and she was grateful. When people in the community realized what they were doing, they came from everywhere—the city councilman, several pastors and a recording star stopped by and gave very liberal donations to the cause. It was a very satisfying day.

Skipping church this Sunday made Marvin feel a slight twinge of guilt. Keeping the Lord's day holy was his motto, but today he was host to the Ex-Files, and he wanted everything to be just right. He jumped from the bed and showered, shaved and splashed on his favorite cologne. Next, he walked into his two-tier closet, which was large enough to hold a full bed. There were sections for his slacks, jeans, sweaters, suits, jackets and shirts, and a special section for his shoes.

He thumbed through the row of slacks and pulled out a pair of white jeans and a red Ralph Lauren polo shirt with black and white stripes running along the collar and hurriedly put them on. He slipped on a pair of brown, leather sandals and closed the door to the closet.

The meeting was to be held at the clubhouse on the southeast end of the subdivision. Mona was delighted that Marvin had asked her to cater the event.

Marvin walked to the window. A wide smile crossed his face. He left the window and crossed the threshold into the foyer, opened the door, and stood in the doorway and watched as Rachel made her way up the stairs.

She is ravishing, he thought. Rachel's hair was done up in curls and bounced when she walked. A red sundress with white piping, running along the V-neckline and around the armholes, was draped over her petite body. A large, white carnation appliqué stood hostage at the bottom of the dress.

"Hey baby," Rachel said as she reached him.

"Hey yourself, beautiful," Marvin responded. He leaned down and planted a simple kiss on her lips.

"Oooh, la, la," Rachel cooed.

"We can cancel the meeting, if you like." Marvin kissed Rachel again. He pulled her inside and closed the door.

They held each other and enjoyed the taste of each other's lips. A tiny tear dripped from Rachel's eyes onto Marvin's muscled arms. He opened his eyes and looked into hers and pulled up her chin with his hand.

"What's wrong, buttercup? Why is my Rachel crying?"

"I'm so happy, Marvin. For the first time in my life, I understand what it really means and how it really feels to love someone. The way you give of yourself so freely and so unselfishly just gives me such a warm feeling. It makes me want to do things to help other people. You empower me, man."

Marvin released Rachel and looked at her with a smile on his face. Rachel balled up her fist and lightly tapped him on the chest. Marvin continued to smile.

"I guess we better go on over to the clubhouse. Mona will be here in a few minutes. She was too through when I asked her to cater my meeting."

"That's what I'm talking about, Marvin. You're always thinking of others. My man, my hero." Rachel planted another kiss on Marvin's lips. "What is Mona preparing?"

"I told her to surprise me. I trust her judgment. She really is a good cook."

"That I will agree."

"One more kiss, Ms. Washington, then we'd better go." Marvin pulled Rachel close. "I love you, Rachel Washington."

"I love you too, Marvin Thomas."

xxx

The tires on Mona's red Jaguar scraped the curb when she pulled in front of the clubhouse. Rachel and Marvin watched with amusement. After fixing her face, Mona jumped from her car and pointed to Marvin.

"Help me get this stuff out of my trunk," she said.

Marvin and Rachel assisted Mona, carrying boxes full of delicious smelling food.

"I'm going to hurt myself today," Rachel said, waving her nose in the air and sucking in the aroma that was about to consume her.

Walking into the clubhouse made Rachel feel like she had gone away for the weekend at somebody's nice villa on the coast. The high-ceilinged room sported multiple skylights and tall windows that ran around the circumference of the room. The walls were covered with a brown textured wallpaper. A large marble fireplace sat in the middle of one wall, with a brass poker leaning against it. A mustard-gold leather couch sat opposite the fireplace flanked by matching loveseats. A brass-inlaid mahogany coffee table sat on polished hardwood floors, which glistened in the sunshine.

A large wooden credenza with three sets of doors sat against a far wall beneath a sixty-inch plasma television. Eight high-backed leather chairs sat in a semi-circle facing the credenza. Placed strategically throughout the room were surround-sound speakers that accompanied the home-theater system. The walls were hung with framed pictures of exotic beaches from around the world, casting their spell and enticing you to spend your money on their sandy shores.

A large kitchen sat off to the side of the main room. The trio rushed into the kitchen, set the boxes down on the countertops and left Mona to her devices. After all, she was getting paid for this gig.

"In what part of the room will we have our meeting?" Rachel inquired.

"We'll start out in front of the fireplace. The couch and chairs should fit all of us comfortably. The meeting can't last too long because the football game will be on soon," Marvin said.

"You're gonna watch it all by yourself. These cacklin' hens aren't interested in any football."

"We'll see. At least the plasma is at the far end, and I can move over and sit in one of those chairs where no one would miss me."

"I'd miss you," Rachel cooed.

"Ms. Washington, I'd love to have your company at the fifty-yard line." Marvin and Rachel kissed.

"Okay, there will be none of that," Mona said, shaking her finger as she came out of the kitchen. "You lovebirds will have to contain yourself for awhile. You'll forget all about it after you feast on my mouthwatering crab cakes... "

"What?" Rachel said. "Girl, let me taste one now."

"Not until it's time, girlfriend. Guess what else we're having?"

"Tell me, tell me so I don't have to guess."

"Steamed crab legs, seafood gumbo, jambalaya."

"Marvin, that cost a lot of money," Rachel said with a frown on her face.

"Your man knows how to throw a party, and he pays well," Mona said.

Marvin smiled at Mona's antics, but she was telling the truth. "I wanted it to be special, and this is how Mona interpreted it. You're going to eat, so what do you have to complain about?"

"I hope people don't get the idea this is the way they're going to be eating all the time. Just a few refreshments."

"Sylvia had ribs," Marvin countered. "In fact, she had a pretty good spread."

"Don't you remember what I had at my house?" Rachel asked.

"No, that was the meeting I was not invited to." He raised an eyebrow.

Rachel began to laugh. "I'll make it up to you, baby."

"I had a bottle of wine in my car to get the party started...well, our party..."

"All right, kids," Mona quipped. "I said you two need to stop cooing up in here. It's sickening."

"Don't be jealous," Rachel said to Mona.

"I'm not, but it's sickening just the same."

Muffled voices made the trio turn and look at the door.

"Hey everybody," Claudette said. "I brought a new member."

"What's up, man," Marvin said to Tyrone, giving him the brother's handshake.

"It's a good day, brother. Can't thank you enough for what you did for Claudette."

"I was glad to be of help."

"It sho smells good up in here," Claudette said. "Smells like Mona's hands." The ladies laughed.

"Yeah, girl. My name is written on this meal."

"I think Claudette and I are going to make it," Tyrone whispered to Marvin as they went back into the main room.

"That's great, man. All's well that ends well."

"We sat down and talked about us…our family…intelligently for the first time. It won't be overnight and we know there will be a lot of rough hills to climb. But we have searched our souls and want to make it work."

xxx

"Hey, everybody," Sylvia said, followed by an attractive and well-dressed middle-aged woman. "This is Margo Myles, my pastor's sister. She's going to share with us today. Ms. Myles, this is Marvin Thomas and Tyrone Beasley."

"Pleased to meet you, Ms. Myles," the men said in chorus.

"Please call me Margo." They nodded.

"Somebody has this place smelling good. Where are the ladies?" Sylvia asked, hands on her hips, when she realized that no one was in the room but the men, herself, and Margo.

"In the kitchen where you all like to congregate," Marvin said, laughing.

"Not me," Sylvia shot back walking toward the room Marvin pointed out. "I'll introduce you to the ladies, Margo."

As soon as Sylvia and Margo disappeared through the doorway, the door to the clubhouse opened.

"So how is motherhood, Ashley?" Marvin asked, walking over to greet her.

"As well as could be expected."

"Why don't you sit down and rest yourself," Marvin said.

"I'm all right. Where is everyone?"

"Follow the noise. They're in the kitchen. Tell them to come out; it's about time to get started."

"All right."

"She doesn't seem okay," Tyrone said to Marvin after Ashley was out of sight.

"Yeah, something is troubling that one."

✗✗✗

They filed out one by one wearing shifty grins on their faces—Sylvia, Rachel, Claudette, Mona, Ashley and Margo—as if they shared some secret they vowed to keep away from Marvin and Tyrone. They plopped down on the couch one by one, in the same order they'd filed out of the kitchen. Margo sat on the love seat but quickly exchanged places with Claudette so that she could sit with Tyrone. The ladies chatted loudly until Marvin loudly cleared his throat.

When he had their attention, he announced, "We will start the meeting."

Claudette jumped from her seat. She had on a plain orange top covered by a long burnt-orange duster with Kente cloth swatches forming geometric designs on the front panels and matching wide-leg pants. Claudette's braids were drawn together and neatly tied in an orange, yellow and brown Kente head wrap. Gold earrings dangled from her ears.

A broad smile hung on Claudette's face. "I can't tell you," she began, "how much you mean to me. Each and every one of you gave of yourselves to make sure that I had a head start in re-building my business. I want to especially thank you, Marvin, for leading the pack, helping to get Kwame released from jail with your generous monetary contribution and orchestrating the fund-raiser that was more than a success. I love you"—Claudette began to sob—"for being there for me and my family. I don't know what I would have done if you all hadn't been in my life.

"This group has shown me the way back to my husband, Tyrone. It wasn't all his fault that we were no longer together. I have some growing up to do. Our short time together, believe it or not, has shown me what family really means. Tyrone is here today in support of our family. We have a lot of work to do to get us back on track, and we are ready to make that step…thanks to you." Tyrone smiled.

"I am getting insurance money…" Everyone clapped loudly and whistled. Claudette continued, "I will rebuild in the same spot. In the meantime, I will open up shop at home as soon as Tyrone installs the wash sink for washing hair and my beauty chair. And…I have a surprise. Free hairdos and haircuts for you all."

Clap, clap, clap, clap, clap, clap.

"Thank you for the applause. I want Ashley to know that I do white hair, too. I can give you a nice shampoo, set and curl." Everyone laughed.

"I'll take what I can get," Ashley responded.

Everyone stood up and clapped for Claudette.

"Bravo," Sylvia shouted.

"Bravo," the others joined in.

"Group hug," Rachel chimed.

The group formed a huge ball and laced themselves with one another. Marvin's fingers touched Rachel's and they locked them together. Heavy breathing and a series of gasps came from the tight-knit group that clung on for dear life further sealing their bond. After a few more hugs and squeezes, the group sat down while Ashley remained on her feet.

"First, I would like to apologize to Claudette for being obviously absent from the barbecue fund-raiser. I had every intention of being there—even had the cake I promised I'd bake neatly in its box waiting for me to escort it to the car. I apologize more…" Ashley stopped and tried to suck in the tension that rattled her body, then continued, "I apologize…because I let you down, Claudette. I went against everything my head told me not to do, and that was let William back into my life."

"It's all right, Ashley," Claudette said, waving her hand for emphasis.

Ashley smiled and hung her head. "I thought sleeping with my ex would make me feel better about him leaving me in the first place. Somehow I thought it might hurt the mistress he left to come back home to me. But William has somehow changed. Maybe he had already changed and I had failed to notice. His behavior is erratic and unpredictable."

Marvin got up and moved close to Ashley, while the others sat on the edge of their seats. Marvin touched Ashley's shoulder.

"Has he hurt you, Ashley? I don't mean to pry, but brother Tyrone and I noticed how nervous and jittery you were when you arrived earlier."

"He best not put his hand on her," Claudette sounded out.

Ashley didn't reply. She blew air from her mouth and looked toward the ceiling, then back at the group.

"Well?" Marvin pushed.

"No, he hasn't put his hands on me, if that's what you mean. He's become possessive and makes me feel trapped in my own home. William doesn't…he doesn't want me to be a part of this group. Threatened me if I went to the fund-raiser."

Sylvia stood with Claudette right behind her.

"Ashley, why didn't you call me or tell someone? We are here for you and care what happens to you." Sylvia put her arms around Ashley, and Claudette rubbed her arm.

"I don't believe he is interested in me…just the baby." Ashley paused and began to sob. "Frankly, I'm afraid of him. If he hadn't gone to his sister's birthday party in Charlotte, I would not have been here today. I'm sure he's blowing up the phone, wanting to make sure I didn't leave the house."

"What are you going to do, Ashley?" Sylvia asked.

"I don't have the faintest idea. And…the big and…William wants to get remarried. There is no way that I can remarry him."

A collective gasp came from the women.

"Why did you sleep with him in the first place?" Mona finally spoke up. "Looks like you were asking for trouble."

"Come on, Mona," Sylvia admonished. "Try putting yourself in Ashley's shoes."

"Wouldn't be there if I was in her shoes. I wouldn't have opened my door."

"Easy for you to say," Sylvia said. "This is about Ashley."

"It's all right, Sylvia," Ashley said. "I don't pay Mona any mind."

Mona rolled her eyes while her head danced on her neck. "Mmmm-hmmmm."

Margo Myles stood up for the first time and went to Ashley and embraced her. Sylvia and Claudette moved back to their seats.

"I know what it's like to be in love with someone who breaks your heart. I was married for twenty-five years when I found out that my husband was having an affair with the married neighbor next door, who was my best friend, as well. On top of all that, he was deeply embroiled in a scheme to steal weapons from a military base and sell them to this rebel group in Honduras. He stole money from his clients and stole my heart from me. And, my husband was gunned down by someone in the organization he worked for while he was driving and nearly lost his life.

"It's not an easy thing to let go of someone you spent a lifetime and had four children with. I found myself fighting for what was rightfully mine. I didn't care what people thought. Yes, I wanted to kill Jefferson for making me hurt the way I did, but there were so many good times I could not forget.

"Whatever your relationship is with your ex, you have to assess what it is you really want. There must have been a good reason why you let him in the door. I've already heard some of your explanation, but the bottom line is you haven't really gotten over him yet."

Ashley held Margo tight without uttering a word.

"My husband is paying for his crime. He is spending the next twenty years of his life behind prison bars. I'm paying, too. Aside from all the humiliation that I suffered from the trial and all the news accounts that were in the paper and on TV constantly reminding me that the man I married and held in high esteem had wrecked our happy home, I'm alone without anyone to assuage my wound or my lonely heart. Yes, I could have divorced him. I certainly have more than enough grounds to do so, but I recognized that the man I loved was still beneath all the rubble of his tattered soul.

"I'm not telling you to stay with William nor am I telling you to leave him. The decision is yours. By the sound of this group, they will be here for you no matter what road you chose. Be true to yourself. Don't let anyone force you to do what your head tells you not to do. I'll be a phone call away should you ever need me."

"Thank you, Margo," Ashley said. "I feel much better. I don't know what I'm going to do yet, but I'm glad I have my extended family on my side."

"I also suggest professional counseling," Margo added. "You may need a little more than this group can offer you. They'll be here for the moral support, but you may need the other as well."

"Thanks again. I appreciate your kind words." Ashley touched her stomach. "My baby and I are going to be all right. I know it."

"Group hug," Claudette said, pushing to the front of the line. Everyone jumped up and made a circle around Ashley and squeezed. Ashley felt protected.

Nothing Like an EX

"Time to wet your whistle," Mona crooned. "Let's take a break. I've reinvented the famous Hurricane that they serve down in the French Quarter. Just a little rum in it; won't hurt a fly. Of course, for the devout Christians and mother-to-be, I have a plain, fruity concoction that is equally good."

Margo gave Sylvia a glance.

Mona brought out the drinks on a wrought-iron serving tray. She served the strawberry-colored drinks in tall, hurricane glasses, waltzing around the room like she owned it, extending her arm to each individual as she invited them to take a glass from the tray.

"Let's make a toast," Mona said, looking in Marvin's direction.

"Why don't you make the toast, since you came up with the idea," Marvin said matter-of-factly.

As if Mona was waiting for Marvin to concede, she lifted her glass in the air. "Lift your glass, everyone. To the Ex-Files. To new life, new loves, new beginnings and renewal."

"Hear, hear," everyone shouted in unison.

"While you sip on your drink and I have everyone's attention, let me share this," Mona quipped. "I still don't know why I'm in this group, but I will say that it has awakened a sleeping giant within me. I moved on with my life some fifteen years ago. I've been having a ball since. What I realized from this group was I had dust in my Files. I analyzed it for what it was worth and decided that it was expendable. Once I got rid of the dust, real love was able to sprout.

"You all met Dr. Michael Broussard over at Claudette's. I'm not saying that a man defines me, but for the first time in years, someone has walked into my life that happens to be more than just a pretty face with a fancy car, a fabulous house and lots and lots of money. Dr. Broussard represents a man with principles. He saves lives for a living. This man has his life mapped out—knows what direction he's going. It's not just about today; it is also about tomorrow. His financially savvy stock portfolios are balanced like his checkbook. He can purchase any car outright with the flick of his Monte Blanc. He serves on boards of major corporations, and he gives tremendous amounts for AIDS research and feeding the homeless. Whew."

"Sounds like my Marvin," Rachel said with a straight face. There was sniggering throughout the room.

"Marvin isn't Michael Broussard."

"Well, we've heard about 'Michael Broussard,' but how do you figure into all of this? Did he propose to you? Did he buy you a car? I'm just not getting the correlation," Rachel said.

"I wouldn't expect you to," Mona shot back.

"All right," Sylvia said, forever the mediator. "What are you trying to tell us, Mona?"

"You too? I'm surprised, Sylvia. Well, Mr. Broussard has asked me to go away with him to Louisiana…to meet his family."

"Ohhhhhhh," said Rachel sarcastically.

"Anyway, we will be leaving next weekend, and I'm really looking forward to it. I have feelings for Michael…"

"Finally," Claudette cut in.

Mona rolled her eyes at Claudette. "My feelings for Michael are more than…you know."

"No, we don't know, Mona. Why don't you tell us," Marvin said tactfully.

"You people are just haters. Michael and I are in love. There, I said it."

"You told us that a couple of weeks ago, but we're happy for you, Mona," Marvin said. "While I have the floor, I'd like to say that I couldn't agree with you more that I am not Michael, but you don't know me like that. Don't forget that I'm on my way to being a Fortune 500 company."

"Tell her, baby," Rachel cooed.

"All right, all right," Mona cut in. "Since you people can't think outside the box, let's eat. You'll be singing a different tune once you feast your lips on the New Orleans feast I've prepared at Mr. Marvin Thomas' expense."

"Thanks, Mona. I appreciate you cooking for my party. I do want you to know, Mona, that we love you and are happy that you're happy about the new man in your life." Everyone clapped. "We know that you can't help who you are and that you know how to get on most people's last nerve, but you are consistent."

"Got that right," Claudette put in. Mona stood quietly with her lip poked out.

"Rachel, will you come here?" Rachel looked puzzled but got up and stood by Marvin's side. "I'm in love with this beautiful woman," Marvin continued. Rachel batted her eyes as Marvin wrapped his arm around her. "Sylvia, the Ex-Files was your doing, and it has turned out to be a blessing. It has helped to bring marriages back together, establish new ones…I mean, new relationships, and… "

"Yeah, you said what you meant, Marvin," Sylvia howled. "Give it up for Mr. and Mrs. Thomas."

"Hold on a minute," Marvin interrupted. But he couldn't hold back the chants.

"Mr. and Mrs. Thomas! Marvin and Rachel! Mr. and Mrs. Thomas! Marvin and Rachel!"

Even Tyrone and Margo joined in on the chant. Rachel waved "no" with both hands, but her smile said "yes."

Mona brought in an empty pot and beat it with a wooden spoon. "Rachel and Marvin, Mona and Michael." Waves of laughter washed over the room. Marvin had never seen anything so infectious.

Just before everyone moved to eat, the door to the clubhouse flew open.

"Hello everyone," said the new arrival.

"Anika." Rachel rushed to meet her. Anika wore a pair of white denim stretch jeans that were sculpted onto her full-figured hips and a multi-colored napkin shirt that covered her small top and waist. "So sorry I'm late, but I had to stop and pick up someone I invited to come along. She's a fairly recent divorcee. I met her at the spa while giving her a facial."

"Well, we're glad you were able to come. Where is your friend?"

"She was right behind me."

The door opened again. A woman dressed in a smart military-inspired blazer in camouflage green, a green knit tank, a pair of eggshell-colored slacks and a silk camouflage-patterned scarf tied around her neck stepped into the room. Rachel stiffened at the sight of Marvin's ex-wife, Denise.

Rachel and Denise went into a diva lock.

"We're in the middle of a meeting, and you're interrupting it."

"Rachel—it is Rachel? Why don't you try and be polite. I'm an invited guest," Denise drawled. "I'm here to see my husband… "

"*Ex*-husband," Rachel corrected.

"Whatever. I'm here to see what kind of meeting Marvin is orchestrating. It's amazing what you learn at the spa. I couldn't believe it when Anika produced Marvin's card, talking about he invited her to a support group meeting for ex-wives and husbands. I just had to see for myself."

"Look, Denise, you've seen it; now you can leave. This group is by invitation only."

"Need I remind you again that I was invited?"

"Well, I'm uninviting you," Rachel retorted.

"I am too sophisticated a woman to stoop to your level and give you the behind beating you deserve. I don't know what Marvin sees in you, but you are no match for me, Miss Thing."

"Low is where you go from what I heard." Rachel pointed her finger in Denise's face. "You *had* a good man, and you threw him away. I'm not the clean-up woman, but I'm going to tell you in very clear, audible tones so that your sophisticated ears won't misconstrue what I'm saying... He's my man now. Holler."

"So Marvin likes ghetto girls, now. Holler back," Denise sneered.

"What are you doing here, Denise?" Marvin asked, finally freed from the paralysis of shock her appearance gave him. "This is a private meeting."

Before Marvin could stop Denise, she moved from the back of the room toward the group that sat eating. Denise looked around the room with distaste and sneered as she devoured each person nibbling on their food. She waved Mona over as soon as she was able to get her attention.

"Hey, Denise. What brings you here?" Mona questioned looking around the room.

"Marvin is standing over there with that ghetto woman, if that's who you're looking for," Denise offered.

"I wasn't looking for Marvin. Trying to make sure that everyone has what they need since I'm catering this event."

"What am I interrupting?"

"Denise, this is a group of divorced folk…you know…a support group." Mona sighed.

"So I heard. You mean to tell me you all sit around discussing your problems?"

"Something like that."

"Well, I'd like to join. I've got problems I'd like to discuss with the group. To whom do I speak to about joining?"

"This might not be the place for you, Denise. Marvin is already a member and it might cause a conflict."

"Why, Mona? Because of Ms. Thing back there? I am not afraid of her. I have every right to be here."

"This is an invitation-only group, but I'll introduce you to Sylvia. She's the founder. It's up to her."

"Not a problem. Introduce me."

Don't Look Now

Sylvia was talking to Margo when Mona approached with Denise in tow. The twisted look on Mona's face and her upturned lips indicated trouble was not far behind.

"Sylvia, this is Denise Thomas, Marvin's ex." Mona raised her eyebrows and rolled her eyes so that Denise couldn't see. "She wants to join the group."

Sylvia's look was grave, but she extended her hand to Denise. "Hello, Denise. Welcome."

"I'll talk with you later," Margo said as she walked away and grabbed Mona's arm.

"I was invited to be a part of this group," Denise quickly said before Sylvia had an opportunity to get another word out.

"I'm not sure what your interest is in joining the group, Denise. This is a support group for divorced men and women who are struggling with going on with their lives and feel the need to express their feelings to others. I'm sure you already know that Marvin is a member, and I'm not sure that it would be healthy to have his ex-wife in the same group."

"It wouldn't be healthy *not* to have me in this group. I think having us both might provide the kind of therapy Marvin and I need to get past the reason for our failed marriage and possibly place us on better footing."

"Have you discussed this with him?" Sylvia asked.

"I was hoping I would get an opportunity today. Instead, people in here are trying to undermine what I hoped to achieve."

"And just what do you hope to achieve, Denise? I think Marvin is already on the mend, and I would hate for something to interfere with his progress."

"So are you saying that I can't be part of this group?" Denise questioned. "You know I can call you up on discrimination charges. Do you have a charter, a set of bylaws that govern this group?"

"Let's not get carried away, Denise. If you like, you may stay this evening, but I'd really like for you to think about the reason you're doing this and what you expect to gain. Our purpose is to heal broken and wounded hearts and give one another a sense of purpose so that we can move on and have happy and productive lives. If that's not your purpose, this is not the place for you."

"Well, Sylvia, I'm a perfect candidate for this group. I feel a sense of family already, and I have a broken heart that needs mending."

"As I said, you may visit with us this evening, but let me warn you…I'm sorry, I don't mean to sound so harsh, but no foolishness will be tolerated here. I hope we understand each other."

"Oh, quite well. I'd like to grab a plate, if you don't mind. I'm quite famished and quite fond of Mona's cooking."

"Help yourself," Sylvia said, pointing toward the food. "You aren't fooling me," she added under her breath.

When Denise left, Marvin headed her way.

"You're not going to let her stay, are you?" he asked, stopping in front of Sylvia.

"Your ex is a barracuda, Marvin. It's going to take more than a few words to throw her out. I'm surprised you put up with her as long as you did."

"She's jealous of Rachel…that I got over her so soon. Denise thought I could never love anyone but her. In fact, she had me believing it. I am a simple man, Sylvia. I'm not a player. I don't hang out with the boys. I don't hang out in bars. I love football, basketball and Jesus…and Rachel, too."

Sylvia smiled at Marvin. "You do love her, don't you?"

"I know it hasn't been that long, but I knew it the first time I laid eyes on her at your house. Rachel had a lot of junk in her Ex-Files, but I knew that girl was the one. If Denise thinks that she can come up in her and try and manipulate somebody—"

"Are you talking about me, Marvin?" Denise asked, as she barged in on Sylvia and Marvin in her sophisticated sort of way. She put the plastic fork on the side of her plate and then looked between the two.

"Why would I want to waste my time, Denise?"

"Because you haven't gotten over me. You'd take me back this very moment if I let you. I'll let that rest for tonight. I promised Sylvia that I was going to be on my best behavior."

Sylvia sighed. "Why don't we get started, Marvin."

✗✗✗

Marvin cleared his throat. "We're going to get started everyone." He carefully avoided Denise's eyes while Mona busied herself picking up empty plates and cups. Everyone assembled on the couch and chairs as before, except that Denise sat in one of the private chairs with her legs crossed.

"I've got a wonderful peach cobbler for afterward," Mona said, giving Marvin the thumbs-up.

"Before we get started," Marvin began, "we have two people who have just joined us. Please welcome Anika Matthews and Denise Thomas."

Everyone clapped except Rachel, who sat in the middle of the group with her legs crossed—the crossed leg swinging defiantly. The newcomers raised their hands in acknowledgment, and the room fell silent.

Sylvia moved to the front.

"Today we have a special visitor to our group. We heard a little bit from her earlier, and she will now come in her own way. Margo Myles lives in Fayetteville, North Carolina, and is the sister of my pastor, Pastor Goodwin. She is in town visiting family, and we appreciate her being with us today. Margo Myles."

The group clapped again.

Margo rose from her seat and moved to the center of the group. She surveyed each one in the room.

"I want to thank Sylvia for inviting me to your meeting this afternoon. It's a wonderful thing to have someone you can talk to, lean on and get comfort from when you have been through what might seem to be the worst battle of your life.

"I was told that you all were divorced—some much longer than others—and that this group has been a saving grace for most of you."

"I don't know why I'm here," Mona said for the umpteenth time, waving her hand for attention as she took her seat with the others.

"Okay, Mona, this isn't for you. As I said earlier, I'm married… still married by the grace of God. My husband, Jefferson, and I were married for twenty-five years before he decided he wanted to test the sugar water elsewhere. His infidelity rocked a neighborhood, a town and friendships.

"My husband decided that all that he had was not enough. We enjoyed the good life—a house in the 'burbs, expensive vacations, whatever we wanted after taking care of what we needed. Jefferson also owned a collection of vintage automobiles. Anyway, he began to steal money from his clients to purchase stolen guns from a military base to resell to some rebels in Latin America. The money Jefferson made from the sale of those weapons was so good he couldn't stop. But it nearly cost him his life.

"My husband has served two years of a twenty-year sentence. The judicial system may be kind and reduce his sentence after he's served at least five years. He's due for a parole hearing in three years.

"I was also handed down a sentence—a twenty-year sentence that sent me to solitary confinement. I was without a man for the first time in years. I decided to wait for my husband. I know some of you are thinking 'she's crazy' or 'I would have divorced him.' Jefferson and I were more than an ordinary husband and wife, we were a team who conquered the universe together, had four wonderful children and threw caution to the wind. Now when I try to throw caution somewhere, it seems to come back to me like a message in a bottle to remind me of all the heartaches I went through behind my husband's infidelity.

"When you come to a crossroad in your life, whether you're contemplating divorce, just received your separation papers or had a pronouncement that your marriage is over, it is okay to cry. Go in a corner if you have to and get it out of your system. Take off by yourself to places unknown. Just have the pity party, but when thirty days have passed, get up from wherever you are, take a good look around you and declare your freedom if that's what you need to do. Otherwise, say I'm going to do what it takes to make my marriage work. I'm going to see a counselor, therapist or whatever your wallet can afford. But get up and do something about your situation.

"I invested twenty-five years in my marriage, and I was not going to let my husband or the scum who lived next door or anyone else move me out of my house...my rightful place. Yeah, I was mad as hell at Jefferson, but there was still good in that man. I've been with him long enough to recognize that in him. My husband and I reconciled while he was in the hospital after his horrible accident, and I made a promise...a vow that I would be there for him. And I'm going to honor it.

"I'd just like to leave this thought with you. No matter what your circumstances are, be true to yourself. If you don't have a relationship with God, try Him. God has not failed me through all that I've gone through. Know that you can overcome your hurt, pain and disappointment. We've seen a testament to that today with Claudette and Tyrone. Sylvia, you've done a great service to the members of your group. While I'm not an expert, I hope that my testimony will help you move forward and not backward. Thank you."

Everyone stood on their feet and clapped, clapped, clapped. Anika moved forward and placed her arms around Margo's neck and hugged her tight, while tears fell from her eyes. One by one the others joined Anika, and before long, there wasn't a dry eye in the place as hands swiped at faces trying to hold back the flow of tears, except Denise who sat and watched with interest, her legs still crossed.

Sylvia sniffed and asked everyone to give Margo another hand-clap. A minute passed, and everyone settled down.

"Margo, thank you for those words of encouragement. I believe that sometimes we wallow in our grief because we hope that someone somewhere might save us. Today, your words may have saved someone. Thank you, again."

Ashley stood on her feet. "I've made my decision. I'm moving on without William. Baby or no baby, I no longer want to be afraid of what William might do if things don't turn out the way he wants them to. I'm Ashley Jordan, and I'm taking my life back. Thank you, Margo." Everyone clapped. "I'll need every-one's support because I'm not sure about where I'm going, and there's no turning back."

"You've got our support," Sylvia sang.

"Yes," the rest of the group said in chorus."

And without fanfare, Denise rose from her seat.

"May I say something?"

Rachel looked at Marvin. Sylvia looked at Rachel, then Marvin.

"Ummmmmm," Mona said louder than she had planned.

"Sure," Sylvia said hesitantly, giving Denise the "do not cross the line or I'll toss you out with my bare hands" look.

✗✗✗

Denise moved to the middle of the room with no pep in her step. She looked at the group that was assembled in front of her and rocked her head left to right. Eyes shifted, with everyone wondering what this woman who said she was Marvin's ex-wife wanted to say.

"I'm not sure where to begin, so I'll pick a spot," Denise began.

Rachel sat tall in her seat, balling her hands, then releasing them. She glanced at Marvin, who was scooting around in his seat like his pants were on fire, unable to sit still for more than a minute. Rachel grabbed Marvin's hand and threaded her fingers in his, and they formed a united fist.

"As most of you know, I'm Marvin's ex-wife, Denise. I met

Marvin when he came to New York on a business trip. He seemed so kind and gentle."

Rachel squirmed in her seat.

"It wasn't long before we began dating, although by long distance, but we had enough chemistry to keep our love alive. When Marvin asked me to marry him six months later, you would have thought that we were the only two people left on earth."

Marvin squirmed in his seat and gave Rachel's hand a tight squeeze.

"Marvin and I kissed like we lost our minds right in front of the Times Square marquee. Remember, Marvin?"

Marvin looked in Denise's direction, and Rachel stood and marched to the back of the room with a scowl on her face.

"We could not get enough of each other. That was the moment I understood what people meant when they said they had sex without taking their clothes off. But believe you me, we had lots of sex later that night."

The room was deathly silent. No one dared to look at anyone else until Rachel marched back to the front of the room and stood in front of Denise with her hands on her hips.

"I'm getting to the point," Denise said, dismissing Rachel with a mere twist of words. Rachel scowled at Denise but went to her seat next to Marvin.

"I was an unfaithful wife."

Loud murmuring floated through the room like a tidal wave while Denise's words crashed down on them like heavy steel. Faces turned toward Marvin, no doubt feeling sorry for the place he was now in. No one tried to stop Denise as she moved on with *her* Ex-Files.

"You can't be surprised," Denise said matter-of-factly. "I'm sure Marvin has shared the sordid details of our life."

Eyes stared straight ahead. Denise looked at the stoic faces and shut her eyes, contemplating her next thought. She wrinkled her lips and let out a sigh.

"I did some terrible things to Marvin that he didn't deserve. This man gave me everything, and I'm not just talking about the materialistic. He gave me his heart and his soul, and I took advantage of it. Don't think I'm trying to solicit your sympathy because I'm not. I betrayed the best thing I ever had, and now I'm paying for it."

Sylvia scowled and looked in Rachel's direction. Marvin sighed, but held Rachel's hand even tighter. Claudette moved closer to Tyrone with a placid look on her face. Mona had boredom written all over her body. Ashley watched Denise intently as if she were analyzing her every word and movement, and Margo sat stiffly in her seat.

"Out of all the things my husband did for me," Denise continued, "he only asked one thing of me. Marvin wanted children. And yes, I had promised to give them to him, but it was a lie. No baby was going to disfigure my body; I had an image to uphold.

"I saw so much potential in this brother who was skyrocketing his way up to the Fortune 500 club. Marvin knew what he wanted, and unlike most brothers, he had everything going for him to achieve success. And I needed him to help me be successful.

"When he made me his wife, he lavished me with a fine home—take a peek on your way out. Marvin may even give you a tour." Denise would not look in Marvin's direction.

"He gave me the whole world, but I gave nothing in return but a heartache. I don't know why I'm telling you this, but I feel like I need to unleash this burden. Guilt is partly to blame, and before God and these witnesses, I'd like for your forgiveness, Marvin."

Marvin made a move to get up.

"I'm not finished. When I came back into Atlanta a few weeks ago, it was for my own selfish reasons. I needed Marvin, but what a surprise I found. My husband…who adored the life out of me…had moved on. It was so uncharacteristic of the Marvin I had come to know and love that it threw me for a loop. Seeing him with Rachel in that restaurant disturbed me greatly.

"But this is really not about me and Marvin. I have something else to share. I'm not ashamed to say that in a moment of desperation, I came running back to find the only person I thought could help me." Suddenly, Denise clawed at her head.

Gasps filled the room: Denise stood holding a wig before her, revealing a nearly bald head.

"A few months ago, I was diagnosed with breast cancer. I may only have a year to live. I'm in the first stages of chemotherapy."

There were more gasps, and every woman in the room instinctively touched her breasts, as if guarding against the pronunciation of the Grim Reaper's next victim. They looked at this woman standing before them in disbelief.

"I don't want your pity, just your love." Large tears welled up in Denise's eyes that she tried to control. "I know I should have stayed in New York where I have lots and lots of family, but when it came down to it, my ex-husband was the family I needed."

Marvin rose from his seat, pulling Rachel with him. He stood in front of Denise and looked into her pained eyes.

"We will be here for you," Marvin said to Denise. "Rachel and I will be here for you." Marvin pulled a resistant Rachel closer. Denise sobbed openly.

Sylvia St. James

The front door shook and squealed on its hinges. Sylvia hadn't realized how hard she'd closed it until her body vibrated. She kicked off her five-inch heels as she marched through the living room on her way to her bedroom, dropping her keys and purse on the living room table.

Sylvia sighed. Month after month of helping others find their way to a new and healthy life and believing what she told others was the way to get beyond an unhealthy divorce was something she now questioned. Did she really believe? How could she help others when she wasn't sure what she wanted herself? It seemed to make sense when the idea had come to her in the beginning, but now...Adonis still kept floating back in her subconscious in the middle of the night or at the breakfast table while she nibbled on a bagel saturated with strawberry cream cheese, his favorite. "Damn him to hell."

This afternoon was another matter—one too complicated for Sylvia's fragile heart. Who would have thought that an ex-wife would barge her way into a meeting that was going oh-so-right with testimonies and tell the world that she might have a year to live. It was not what Sylvia envisioned. She wanted healing for the hurt...the pain that Adonis caused her, but it seemed she had to wait in line because everyone else's pain was much greater than hers.

She peeled off her slacks and caught a glimpse of herself in the floor-length mirror. She turned from side to side, admiring what she saw. She was still attractive, even though a slight bit healthier. She blew the mirror a kiss, and her reflection tossed back her round hips as they sashayed around the room.

"I need to get out of this funk." Sylvia sighed and flipped on the radio.

"It's the top of the hour. This is WJZZ-FM, your Hot-Hotlanta jazz radio station. Don't turn the dial. We'll be right back after the news with the soulful sounds of Will Downing and my girl, Jill Scott," the announcer promised.

Sylvia pulled off her cotton blouse and tossed it on the bed. Not sure what to do next, she plopped down on the edge of the bed and extended her arms back to prop up her body, then looked up at the ceiling.

"God, why do I feel so empty? You have to help me. It's been almost a year, and I can't let it go. I say I'm over Adonis, but these meetings are causing me to want him more than I'm afraid to admit. Lord, You've got to help me. I don't want a man who doesn't want me—a man who has gone on with his life with another woman.

"I went out with…I've been with…uhhh…Kenny."

Sylvia sat up straight. How could she talk to God about Kenny? It was an out-of-the-way fling with an old flame. Kenny, Kenny, Kenny. It was nice to have someone's arms wrapped around her.

Rising from the bed, Sylvia walked the few steps to the small table next to the chaise that held the picture she and Kenny took a few weeks ago at a formal gathering Mona gave and catered at an exclusive Atlanta nightclub. She picked up the picture and gazed at the couple with the wide smiles. "Humph, he does look good. And he smelled good, too."

Falling onto the chaise, Sylvia hugged the picture to her breasts and closed her eyes.

"I was just thinking about you," Sylvia sang seductively, then realized that Jill Scott was singing along with her.

She looked at the photo and ran her fingers over Kenny's face. *"You just running across my mind, you just running across my mind, you just running across my mind,"* she and Jill sang.

Visions of dancing with Kenny crept into Sylvia's head. She scooted farther down on the chaise, bending one leg at the knee, and closed her eyes. She felt Kenny's hands circle her waist and Karl Lagerfeld seep through his pores as he inched his face closer to hers. They lost themselves in the melody—the slow, syrupy rhythm that beckoned for them to become one. Oh, but she came alive when his lips touched hers, and she reciprocated like she was Cinderella and the clock was only minutes from striking twelve.

She let Jill continue to sing as she lay there and reminisced.

She recalled the moment Kenny handed her the key to his room, and she stared at the palm of her hand as if an unidentified foreign object had just landed. There was a twinkle in his eyes—she was sure it was lust—but suddenly she was game for whatever. She tried to play hard to get but followed the man into his hotel room. Her heart needed a massage, so she'd let an old friend do the honors. That was the first time, and there was a second, although nothing happened either time. She was having serious feelings for this man.

"How amazing," Jill sang. And Sylvia ran her hand down the

length of her body, over her breasts and down her thighs. *"And kiss this and this and this, and that,"* Jill and Sylvia sang together.

Tears began to well up in Sylvia's eyes. She looked once more at the picture she clutched in her hand, studying it for a long moment. Brushing a tear away from her face, she placed the photo on the table, facedown.

"Lord, forgive me of my sinful thoughts. I know You will give me the strength to get through this mini-depression. Lord, will You be my lover tonight?"

Ding, dong.

xxx

"Hold on, I'm coming," Sylvia shouted. She grabbed her white-and-black polka-dotted robe off the hook on the bathroom door, slipped it on and headed for the front door. She combed her hair with her fingers and tied the belt around her waist. "I'm coming, I'm coming," she shouted again as the pounding on the door became louder.

"Girl, are you going to let me come in or what?" Rachel said when Sylvia got the door open.

"Of course," Sylvia said as Rachel pushed past her.

Rachel's jaw dropped as she tripped over one of Sylvia's shoes. "Uhhh, what happened up in here? Shoes all over the place, papers strewn across the floor and no car outside. Was this a drive-thru? I smell impatience all up in here. And why do you have your robe on, looking like one of the 101 Dalmatians? It's only been an hour since we left the meeting. You got somebody up in here?"

"No, Rachel."

Rachel quickly moved from the foyer into the family room and plopped down on the couch. "That witch is trying to steal Marvin from me," she began. "I don't believe her. Waltzing into our meeting with her sob story to try and get her ex-husband back."

"You saw her hair," Sylvia pointed out.

"So it was short and splotchy. Doesn't prove a thing—she could have done it herself."

"Rachel, I believe Denise is sick even if I didn't particularly care for how she chose to deliver her message. She's a drama queen, and drama queens do what they do best—act it out. Clearly, Denise has issues, but I don't think she's feigning her illness."

"Sylvia, she's not going to take away the best thing that has happened to me with her one-act play. I'll fight her like the disease she has."

"That was not nice, Rachel. You ought to be ashamed for having thought that, let alone utter the words out loud. Listen to yourself. I know you're afraid of losing Marvin. He's a good man, but you have to trust that he loves you. He told me so."

Rachel's shoulders relaxed. "He did?"

"Yes, and it was *before* Denise made her public announcement. But like he helped Claudette, he's not going to abandon Denise during her time of need."

"You're right, but I don't trust her as far as I can see her, Sylvia." Rachel picked up a pillow from the couch and threw it back down. "I hate her," she said, beating the pillow with her fist.

"Hate is a mighty strong word, sister."

"I know I'm being selfish because I want Marvin all to myself. Let's drop it…the subject, that is."

Sylvia looked at Rachel, who sat back on the couch pouting. If it were her man, she would probably be doing the same thing. Her thoughts were on Kenny again; his image was strong in her mind. Misguided messages…no, messages she took to her bosom and pretended to ignore, danced in her head. She wanted him, and as soon as she got rid of Rachel, she would call Kenny and ask him to come and play.

Was she mixed-up? Ten minutes earlier, she was asking God to help her. Now, she was helping herself.

"Earth to Sylvia," Rachel said, popping her fingers. "Where is he? I know you've got a man stashed away in your closet."

"Are you through?"

"Not until I get some answers."

"I don't know what you're talking about, you crazy girl. And stop pulling on my robe." Sylvia slapped Rachel's hand.

"Don't keep any secrets from me, Sylvia. Where's the man? You got him hiding in your closet. I'm going to check. You might as well confess because you know I'll find you out."

"Nothing to tell, darling. And stop snooping around like a beagle. I have nothing to hide."

"Mmm-hmm. See, you can pretend that you don't want Adonis back," Rachel said, as she placed her hand on her hip, "but your best friend knows better. I'm not stupid."

"You're being silly, Rachel."

"Jealous, that's what I say. Jealous."

"Jealous of you and Marvin? I don't think so."

"Sylvia, I love Marvin. I don't know what I would do if he decides he wants to be with Denise, even if it's because he feels sorry for her. Why does she have to have cancer now? Don't say it; I know I'm being mean."

"I understand, sweetie. My advice is to be there for Marvin."

"I will. I just know that at one time Marvin loved Denise very much...maybe he still does. And now Denise's illness may bring them back together."

"You may have to step back and let Marvin help her."

Rachel sat quietly on the couch, deep in thought.

Sylvia sat next to Rachel and rubbed her back. "It's okay. I'll let you in on a secret. I was beginning to have reservations about our support group. I'm not sure that I believe in what I'm doing."

Rachel hugged her. "Girl, you are doing the right thing. If it hasn't helped you, it has helped a whole lot of other folks. Look at me. Look at Ashley, Claudette and Mona. I'm grinning all the time like I haven't got the good sense that God gave me. I've been renewed and I have a little more faith in that creature we call man. There are some good ones out there, Sylvia, if only I had let God pick out my man in the beginning. I'll get through this crisis."

Sylvia smiled. "You are a good friend, Rachel."

"You hang in there and don't even think about going anywhere because we need you. Your knight in shining armor will come."

"He may have already come."

"I knew it, I knew it, I knew it," Rachel crowed.

"You know what, you silly girl?"

"Drive-thru."

"No, not quite a drive-thru."

"Whatever."

They laughed. Rachel picked up a pillow from the couch and tossed it at Sylvia playfully. "Now, tell me."

"Okay," Sylvia began. "I've been reminiscing about Kenny."

"Kenny? He's still hanging around?"

"Kenny is a changed man, Rachel. You may not be able to see the good in him, but I have been with him to know."

"Have you slept with him?" Rachel asked politely with a bit of sarcasm in her voice.

"No, but we have spent the night together."

"I can't believe you kept this from me. Don't blame you for a minute. I would have kept it under wraps, too. And you didn't sleep with him? I don't quite get it."

"You wouldn't."

"Okay. That's the second time someone has said that to me in as many days. I'm not stupid; it's just difficult to understand."

"Nothing difficult about it at all. He is a gentleman—much like Marvin."

"Okay, my sistah. Tell me anything. Was it good to you?"

"Again, we didn't have sex, Rachel." Sylvia's mind was wandering. "I was having those crazy dreams about Adonis leaving me. Kenny's touch was so gentle. He held me like my momma used to do when I hurt myself. He's been good, Rachel."

"I have to respect that. And if my girl feels good about it, who am I to criticize?"

"Exactly what I've been trying to say."

Rachel sucked her teeth. She picked up a magazine that was on the floor next to the couch. "Now, this is what I call *phine*." Rachel pointed to the healthy hunk who was one of the thirty-one most eligible bachelors in *Ebony* magazine.

"Be happy for me. I am for you. It's like this, Rachel. The meeting today was for the most part great, but it made me feel just how lonely I was. All those testimonies about how new life had sprung up in different lives. Look at you and Marvin, Claudette and Tyrone. I'm not settling for Kenny; I am falling in love with him."

"Sylvia, we've been friends a long time. I have made plenty of mistakes in my lifetime, but I know that Marvin not only feels right; he is right. I have no reason to sit in judgment of you. I was thinking about all the strides you've made to get over Adonis only to let a two-time loser like Kenny teeter your totter for a few minutes. But I have to believe you know who Kenny is, and I know you'll do what you think is right for you."

"Great. Now why don't you pick yourself up from my couch and go see about your man so I can see about mine."

"Does this mean you're kicking me out of your house?"

They laughed.

"All right, Sylvia. I'm going to see about my good man."

"Arial said you didn't know how to pick a man."

"She said that?"

"Yeah, but I'll let her know you've got a good one now. So get up and get ready for your drive-thru."

"No...you didn't. I'll have you know that I'm going to the drive-in. There's a world of difference between drive-in, drive-thru and drive-by."

"And...the difference is...?"

"I'll say this." Rachel sighed. "They're all quickies."

Sylvia picked up a pillow from the couch and threw it at Rachel. It was on. Pillows flew through the air.

"You better watch out for my African fertility statue," Sylvia warned.

"Oh, the magic stick. You've been working this statue over-time." They laughed and laid the pillows on the couch.

"I love you, Rachel. You've always been a good friend."

"Honey, you've been there for me more times than I've been there for you. Sylvia, I love you from the bottom of my heart.

I'm serious about our support group. It has helped me to get way beyond where I was at our first meeting, and I have you to thank."

Sylvia smiled and cupped her chin with her fingers, trying to suppress the emotions that wanted to leap out of her soul.

"I just hope Kenny wasn't hiding in one of your closets all this time, rushing me out of here."

"Out!" Sylvia laughingly shouted, pointing the way to the front door. *It won't be a drive-thru tonight*, Sylvia thought.

Rachel Washington

Rachel was in a good mood when she left Sylvia's. She and Marvin were going to be all right. She had to believe. Didn't Sylvia just tell her that Marvin said he loved her? That he'd told her this very afternoon. Yes, she had nothing to worry about.

Rachel turned on the radio; soft jazz floated through the air. She glanced at her watch. It was eight-thirty p.m. Darkness pushed the light from the city, and it was time for her to head home to get ready for another week at BellSouth.

Cars whizzed by. Rachel held the steering wheel steady with her right hand while she rested her head in the other. All of a sudden, she grabbed the wheel with both hands and made a quick U-turn in the middle of the street and headed north.

She made several turns and quickly got on I-85. A patrol car sat on the shoulder of the highway around the next bend. Rachel put her foot on the brake, spotting the car just in time. She hadn't realized that she was going 75 miles-per-hour in a 65 mile-per-hour zone, but she was now alert.

Her freeway exit reached out to her on the highway sign she passed beneath. Rachel immediately moved over into the right lane, ready to get off as soon as her exit beckoned her to do so.

She was only ten or twelve minutes from her destination, and she couldn't keep her foot from hitting the accelerator.

Soon, the entry to the Somerville Estates subdivision was fifty feet away. She sped through the subdivision, oblivious to the speed limit signs posted at the entry and on the street. When she saw Marvin's house, she pulled into the driveway.

The blinds were drawn, and a faint light shone through an upstairs bedroom window. Rachel moved quickly up the few steps to the front door and rapped lightly. After a few seconds she started to ring the doorbell. Then she heard faint conversation. The woman's voice caught her attention. She put her ear to the door, but the voices faded in and out.

Rachel moved backward and stood staring at the door. Her blood began to boil as her imagination got the best of her. Images of Marvin wrapped around Denise flooded her mind. Before her senses caught up with her, Rachel reached out for the doorknob and twisted it hard, leaning hard on the door—which was unlocked. It swung open, startling Marvin—who stood consoling Denise, his arms wrapped around her like Saran Wrap.

Shock registered in Rachel's eyes. Her breathing was labored, and she stood with her feet spread apart, her right hand clutching her chest, waiting for an explanation—any explanation.

Marvin went to Rachel and reached out to hold her. She brushed his hands away and didn't miss the smirk that crossed Denise's face.

"What is she doing here, Marvin?" Rachel asked, tears forming in her eyes.

"Marvin and I were talking about—," Denise began.

Rachel held out her hand. "I wasn't talking to you."

"Hold it, Rachel," Marvin said.

"You're going to take up for her?"

"It's not about taking up for Denise. You were rude. I know what you think you saw, but that's not the way it was at all. Denise is going through a terrible period in her life, and I've promised that I would be there for her. I hope you can help me help her."

Rachel couldn't believe her ears. "Can't you see through her, Marvin? She's just trying to worm her way back into your life. She had her chance when she was Mrs. Thomas. And why were you holding her like that?"

"Let me answer that," Denise cut in. "Contrary to what you might believe, Ms. Thing, my husband is a caring human being. We shared a life together, and yes, we are still friends. Friends help friends, and my friend has graciously agreed to be there for me. I know that Marvin has a thing for you, even though I don't understand it, but let me leave you with this piece of advice. You are going to lose this man if you put a stranglehold on him. I'm not in competition with you because if I were, you wouldn't stand a chance. So get it out of your head. But know I will be in your life as long as Marvin is."

"Are you going to let her just talk to me like that, Marvin?"

"Rachel, Denise is making a lot of sense."

"Oh, is that right? Well, it doesn't make sense to me! You can have your friend, because I'm out of here. You need to make up your mind, Marvin, which one of us you want."

"Rachel, you are being irrational. How many times do I have to tell you I love you? Today alone, I've told you more times than I've got fingers. I love you, Rachel, and I want you in my life, but I'm not going to desert Denise. It could have been you with breast cancer… "

Rachel flung her head around and looked into Marvin's eyes in disbelief as he tried to pronounce a death sentence on her.

"But you don't have it," he continued. "Count yourself blessed that you are among the lucky ones not faced with an uncertain future. Denise has some rough roads ahead of her, and I will be going to chemotherapy with her and—"

"Suit yourself," Rachel barked. She took one last look at the pair and walked briskly out of the front door, slamming it behind her. She waited a minute on the porch, but Marvin didn't follow her. Rachel raced to her car and fled into the night.

Tears ran down Rachel's cheeks. She felt humiliated and isolated. She looked down as her cell phone played Marvin's song. "Let him sweat," Rachel said aloud. "It's going to be on my terms or there won't be a Rachel and Marvin."

EX-tra Curricular Activity

"The door is open," Sylvia sang softly.

"Rather dangerous leaving your door open for any stranger to walk in on—"

Saliva caught in Kenny's throat as the sight of Sylvia caused him to lose his balance and his train of thought. Sylvia stood in the middle of the room clad in a crème-colored satin robe with fur around the collar that came just to her waist, exposing a satin lace bikini and her form-fitting legs.

"Not just any stranger, sweetie." Sylvia smiled at the surprise on Kenny's face.

"Uhh, well, I don't consider myself a stranger, however, if that works, I certainly don't mind being one." He couldn't keep his eyes off of her.

"Well, come in and close the door. You're letting some of the mood I created slip out."

For the first time Kenny relaxed and smiled. It was then that he noticed the dozen or so candles flickering away in the dark, dancing to a midnight sonata.

Sylvia was satisfied that the man she was fast claiming to be hers was pleased and that the night she planned was moving in the direction she intended. She stepped close to Kenny and planted a sensuous kiss on his lips.

"I don't know what I did to deserve this, but I'm happy about it. Oh, boy. Am I happy! Come over here and give me another one of those hypnotic kisses."

"At your service."

"May I ask, if I won't be penalized for disturbing the mood, what has caused this change in you? A month ago, you acted as if you couldn't stand the sight of me, and tonight we've become…"

"Don't flatter yourself. I'm horny and I need a man."

"Okay, Sylvia. Now that you have succeeded in deflating my ego…"

"You pushed. You couldn't just let the night flow."

"Look, why don't we start over?"

"I like the sound of that, Kenny."

Kenny held Sylvia, his gentle hands moving her within inches of him so that he could get a better look. Then he drew her near and held her, caressed her, kissed her lips. Sylvia reciprocated, she'd been longing for this moment.

Peeling his lips from hers, Kenny looked at the beautiful woman in his arms.

"If I was a dog, I'd eat you up right here and right now, but you have been trying to tell me something since that night at the hotel."

"What are you talking about? Kiss me again."

"Wait, Sylvia." Kenny painted her lips with his fingers. "Making love to you is all I think about, and I know it will be wonderful when we do. I don't know what's different tonight from any other night, but I believe your Christian walk with God is being compromised, and I don't want to be the reason."

"I can't believe I prayed. I actually prayed for this moment, and now you want to get religious on me."

"It doesn't make much sense to me, either. Girl, I want you so bad. Whoa, I want you, but you'll thank me later. Besides, I told you that I have changed. If I plan to take these serious steps I've been contemplating about, I want it to be pure…like you are pure."

"Kenny, what steps are you talking about? All this talk of purity… where is the Kenny I used to know?"

"Thought you didn't like him."

"Well, there were some parts of him I liked better than others."

"I'll accept that."

"Look, I would have cooked you a meal, but Mona worked it out today at our Ex-Files meeting. Oh, God, she had some mouth-watering food, and then that peach cobbler that was to die for."

"How about a bowl of ice cream—two scoops?"

"Two scoops of French vanilla coming up."

"May I ask a favor?"

"Ask away."

"Please keep the outfit on. I'm struggling, but it don't hurt to look."

"You know the Lord said, 'Thou shall not tempt.'"

"So what have you been doing for the past half hour? That's why I'm eating ice cream."

"Kiss this and this and this and this and this and this and thattttttt," Sylvia sang.

"What?"

"Jill Scott."

"Oh. Now come here, baby, so I can kiss them sweet, sweet lips of yours."

"Eat your ice cream."

Guilty

Rachel lay awake, the soft down of the comforter not offering much in the way of comfort at one in the morning. Her eyes stared at the ceiling, oblivious to the dancers who gyrated on the flat-screen television that hung on the wall in front of her.

Visions of Marvin and Denise together were frozen in Rachel's mind, and Marvin's harsh words vibrated in her ears. *How could he tell her he loved her in one breath and say that he was going to be there for Denise in the other?*

Rachel fumed and would not allow sleep to take over. Yes, Marvin had called her cell phone more than a dozen times, but he couldn't leave Denise alone for a moment to come out on the porch to see about her well-being. Well, the hell with the both of them.

Rachel turned off the television and darkness engulfed the room. Her eyelids became heavy and sleep found its way.

She was dreaming. There was a shadow…a woman who was of medium height and build. She was walking down a long, dark corridor, groping the walls like a blind person not sure of her way. A mist rose and clouded Rachel's vision, the woman temporarily disappearing from view. Then she reappeared, running, stumbling, crying, calling out for someone to help.

Rachel jerked awake. Her body was covered in sweat. She wiped her face with her arms, shivering, and then saw the face of the woman in the dark hall staring at her. It was Denise, calling out for Rachel to help her.

Kicking off the covers, Rachel ran to the bathroom and drenched her face in water. She dried off with a towel and slowly went back into her bedroom. She walked around the bed wringing her hands. *This must have been how Sylvia felt when she had dreams of Adonis walking out of her life*, she thought.

The telephone lay in sight, and before she could talk herself out of it, she dialed the first three digits of Marvin's phone number and hung up. She dialed again but chickened out once more.

Rachel moved to the side of the bed and sat down. She'd been rude to Denise, but she wasn't putting anything past her no matter how "sick" she was. She picked up the phone again and dialed.

"Hey, Sylvia."

"Rachel, do you know what time it is? You and I both have to go to work in the morning."

"Sylvia, I dreamed about Denise, and she was calling out to me…asking me to help her."

"It must be guilt. Now I've got to get some rest."

"So he's there."

"He, who?"

"Kenny, that's who. You made me say his name. I know that's why you're trying to rush me off of this phone."

"You crazy, girl. It's two in the morning and normal people who have jobs to go to are trying to get their beauty rest so they can deal with the crazy folks at the workplace."

"What a lame excuse, Sylvia."

"Rachel, Kenny is not here. Why don't you disturb Marvin?"

"It's a long story."

"So, what happened?"

Rachael gave Sylvia the lowdown on what transpired at Marvin's house and how she'd left Marvin with an ultimatum.

"I guess your dream means you regret how you treated your man's ex-wife," Sylvia said.

"What should I do?"

"It sounds simple to me. You need to get some rest, then make amends with Marvin. I can't believe you played right into Denise's hands. You need some backbone, girl. Marvin says he loves you. Why don't you believe him? It should be enough for now. I'm only saying this, sweetie, because he is truly a good man."

"You're right. I just don't know how I'm going to do it…since I acted so ugly. Even Denise had the nerve to give me a piece of advice."

"And it was…"

"Something about losing Marvin if I keep a stranglehold on him."

"Heed her warning. Now get some sleep. Make sure making amends with Marvin is one of your top priorities today."

"Thanks, Sylvia. I love you."

"I love you too, Rachel. Good night."

Rachel hung up and closed her eyes—some of her fire now distinguished. She needed Marvin…all of him, without any distractions. Somehow she would find a way to get rid of the thorn in her side.

xxx

Relationships were difficult, in fact they were a whole lot of work. Marriage was a full-time job, 24/7, 365 days a year. Who was she fooling? Sylvia thought as she lay in the darkness of her room.

Kenny was a fresh relief, but Sylvia's thoughts wandered. What if she let this man into her life full time? Would she regret it?

Tonight had erased many of her doubts and fears. She found a man who cared about what she wanted and what she thought. Here was a man who was willing to hold his own lust and desire for her in check...barely. Sylvia laughed out loud as she recalled Kenny trying to hide the great big bulge in his pants.

It scared Sylvia, though, because the Kenny she really knew would have had all the goods, would have asked questions later and would probably be on his way to his next conquest. She shuddered at the thought.

Sylvia had wanted him to stay, but he thought it too tempting. She knew he wanted her. Yes, he wanted her bad. However, her empty bed made her smile. Sylvia was in love, and she was willing to make this relationship work.

Ashley Jordan-Lewis

The air was brisk but gentle. An overcast sky blocked the sun, but it was perfect for a morning run. Ashley slowed down to a trot as she rounded the bend headed toward home. She patted her stomach, assuring the baby growing inside of her that her jog was done for the day.

As Ashley neared her house, William stood in the driveway with his arms folded across his chest. His eyes were glued on Ashley as she walked in his direction with no hint of his real thoughts shining through.

"I just lost a baby a few weeks ago," William reminded Ashley as she passed to the side of him.

Ashley glared at William, disbelief written on her face. How dare he throw up the dead bastard embryo in her face. So that was what this was all about—his coming back home. William wanted the son or daughter his mistress failed to give him.

Ashley continued toward the house.

"You're going to walk past without a word?"

"I didn't think your statement required a response, William. You made yourself clear. But so that you know, it is safe for me to continue jogging for at least another month."

"It doesn't matter who says it's okay—I say it isn't. Today we have a matter we need to handle."

Ashley stopped in her tracks, squinting her eyes against the sun, and swiveled her body around so she could get a good look at William.

"What matter?"

"Get ready. We're going to the courthouse to apply for a marriage license."

Ashley froze.

"William, I'm not going to marry you."

"Our child will have a mother and a father."

"It will, but not at the same residence. It's time for you to leave."

"Ashley, you let me come home, and I have no plans of leaving. Those people in that support group have got your mind twisted. Didn't think I knew you went to your little meeting yesterday, did you? If you didn't want me to know, you shouldn't have written it in your calendar."

Ashley rolled her eyes. "William, I'm not going to remarry you. If I need to move out of the house, I will."

"Don't make a grave mistake by walking out of here."

"And just what does that mean? Certainly you're not going to try and harm me in any way. You'll put your child in danger."

Fire rising in his eyes, he raised his hand and pointed his finger as if he were going to reprimand her, but Ashley had already disappeared into the house.

"You will be Mrs. William Lewis a second time," William said to the wind.

Isn't This What a Support Group is For?

"BellSouth. Rachel Washington speaking."

"Hey, sweetie. This is Sylvia."

"You're feeling bad because you treated me kinda shabby last night."

"Correction—early this morning. I was in a deep sleep with no crazy dreams interrupting me until you called."

"Say what you want, but I'm sure your boy toy was lying next to you."

"Wished he were, but happy he wasn't."

"What kind of sense does that make?"

"It's a long story, Rachel. Besides, I called to see how you're doing. Have you spoken with Marvin?"

"Not yet. Actually, I'm too ashamed. He called me at least a half-dozen times, and I wouldn't answer his call."

"You're going to lose a good man. I know how this Denise thing looks, but you have to trust your instincts. Denise had the man; you've got him now. You've got to keep that barracuda in the water."

"Now look who's being insensitive?"

"I'm sorry that Denise has cancer, and…"

"What, Sylvia? Tell me…"

"A thought just came to me. We should all rally around Denise like we did with Claudette. Rachel, Denise is scared. That's what this is all about. While I may be a tad bit cynical in my thinking, if we rally around her, she'll find the support she's looking for and need. It will take some of the pressure off of Marvin."

"You are so smart, Sylvia. I'll get my Marvin back and Denise will have the support of the group."

"Don't go skinning and grinning, yet. We have to be sincere about this. I'm going to call the rest of the group...ohh..."

"What?"

Sylvia caught a glimpse of Ashley standing in the doorway to her office and waved for her to come in.

"It's Ashley, Rachel."

"Is she all right?"

"Ashley, Rachel wants to know if you're okay?"

Ashley took a seat in the chair next to Sylvia's desk. Her face was pale, and she looked visibly shaken. Sylvia put the phone on speaker.

"She's not all right, Rachel. What's wrong, Ash? Is it William?"

"What did he do to you?" Rachel piped in.

"He made me go down to the courthouse today. We applied for a marriage license."

"What?" Sylvia and Rachel exclaimed in unison.

"Is this what you want?" Sylvia continued. "You said at the meeting you weren't going to marry him. Why don't you just kick him out of the house?"

"William is adamant about us getting remarried. It will have to happen over my dead body. I'm not going to marry him. I feel so stupid because I let him back in my house. I thought William really wanted me. When I saw him at the door that day, I couldn't resist letting him come in. Sure I said all those things at that first meeting about it being just me and my baby, but William came back, and I wanted my husband. But now, I don't know who this person is William has become. He is so possessive, but I'm telling you, it's all about having this baby. He doesn't care about me."

"You know you can come and stay with me, Ash."

"Thanks, Sylvia. I'm not sure what to do. I could go and stay with my parents, but they hate William with every fiber of their being, and I don't want to hear them talk about it day and night."

"Is there anything I can do?" Rachel asked.

"Yes, go get your man," Ashley said with a smile.

There was a brief moment of laughter.

"I better get back to work," Rachel said. "I'll give you the update at six on the continuing saga of the life and times of Marvin and Rachel…a little something from the drawers of the Ex-Files."

The ladies laughed again, and Rachel hung up.

"What am I going to do, Sylvia?" Ashley asked.

"Do you believe in prayer?" Sylvia replied.

"Well, yes. I guess I've never really prayed for anything special. I've always had what I wanted."

Sylvia looked at Ashley with hard eyes.

"What did I say, Sylvia?"

"Nothing," Sylvia replied, realizing she was doing the other woman a disservice by not telling her what she really felt. So what if Ashley had it good all her little life? When things weren't going Ashley's way, who did she come running to?

"You gave me a look."

"Don't worry about it. Just know that you're not going to marry William if you don't want to. You have a place to stay, and we've got to go to the Lord in prayer for the rest. Give me your hand, Ashley. Close your eyes, and let's pray."

XXX

Rachel swiveled around in her seat. She hadn't given BellSouth a good hour of productive work this morning. Chatter coming from other cubicles hadn't calmed her nerves.

She looked at the time posted on the bottom of her computer screen. It was eleven o'clock. Rachel put the end of her pen in her mouth and gnawed on it. She finally got up enough courage to lift the phone from its cradle. She dialed.

"Good morning, Thomas Technical Technology Solutions."

"Yes. May I speak with Mr. Marvin Thomas, please?"

"I'm sorry. Mr. Thomas is in a meeting right now. Would you like to leave a message?"

"No, I'll call again later. Thank you."

Rachel set the phone in the cradle. She continued to turn her chair from side to side. *Was* Marvin in a meeting? She called his direct number, but apparently he had it forwarded to his secretary's line. She had to trust him. For the next three hours, she placed four calls to Marvin, but the meeting he was in was lasting a lot longer than she thought a meeting should.

Life Ain't Fair

S team engulfed the bathroom, clouding the mirrors completely. Denise cleared a space on the mirror—a small circle
large enough to see her face. She stared at the image that
stared back, its face swollen, its hair patchy.

Denise moved in closer for further examination, picking at a
blackhead like it was a new discovery. She wiped the mirror again,
exposing breasts that seemed to have lost some of their perkiness.

Taking her left breast in her hand, Denise examined it gently,
afraid to discover what she already knew she would find. She
pulled her hand back as she hit a tender spot. With the other
hand, Denise glided over her right breast to make sure there was
nothing different since she had examined them last night.

The image in the mirror went from soft to defiant. It also
looked strong and sure. It was ready to do battle against all of her
enemies, even the one called cancer.

The phone interrupted Denise's thoughts. She slipped into a
terry-cloth robe and quickly answered the phone.

"Good morning, Denise. How are you feeling today?"

"Marvin," Denise said in a low, sexy voice. "I feel pretty good,
especially knowing that you'll be by my side when I go for treatment today."

"I said I would. I'll be there in twenty minutes."

xxx

The hospital walls were as drab as Denise felt. Though she dreaded the thought of another chemo treatment that would leave her feeling like dung, today, she rejoiced inside because Marvin was there to give her all the support she needed. She hadn't even told her family that she was diagnosed with Stage II breast cancer.

Even Harold, her lover and Marvin's cousin, passed through her thoughts. Would his family take Danica if…if she didn't make it? Marvin was the one who wanted a baby, but she was the foolish wife who'd had unprotected sex with her lover and produced a baby neither wanted. It never occurred to Denise that she might have to pay the price for her sins. "The Big C" was a death sentence that she never saw coming.

Although Denise was glad Marvin was at her side, he hardly said a word. He was pleasant on the ride over, but it was quite obvious something was on his mind. Denise was sure that her burden had now become his burden and he was overwhelmed with just the thought of it. If Rachel were the reason for Marvin's silence, though, the next few hours would erase her from his thoughts.

The nurses greeted Denise like they were old friends. Marvin stood back until Denise introduced him, though a little awkward. He produced a slight smile, but it quickly faded once one of the nurses ushered Denise toward the room where her chemo would take place.

xxx

Marvin sat down in the waiting room with two other pale-faced men who had probably shouldered their burden much longer than he. He tried to read their faces, but their expressions never changed.

A slight vibration caused Marvin to grab at his side. He pulled his cell phone from its holder and glanced at the number. This was the fourth call from Rachel, with just as many coming to the office. *Now* she wanted to talk, even though he had left more than twenty messages the night before, hoping to explain what had gone down with him. Well, Miss Rachel would have to sit on the back burner today, he thought, and he put the cell back in its holder and rested his head in his hands.

"Mr. Thomas." The voice seemed to boom, jerking Marvin from his wandering thoughts. He looked around to make sure that he was the Mr. Thomas that was being summoned.

"Mr. Thomas," the nurse said again, looking directly at Marvin. Marvin stood up and went to the counter.

"Mrs. Thomas is having second thoughts about her chemo treatment and the doctor is on his way to discuss it."

Marvin cringed slightly at the reference to "Mrs. Thomas."

"What do you mean, 'second thoughts'? We're here to try and save her life."

"Calm down, sir. Follow me and you can discuss this with your wife and the doctor when you get to the room."

Marvin followed close on the nurse's heels. They passed several rooms, making a few lefts and rights before proceeding through a door where Denise lay on a recliner. She looked so fragile to Marvin; the mere sight tugged at his heartstrings.

"What is this I hear about you not taking chemo?" he asked gently.

"I've been thinking, Marvin. My chances may be better if I have a radical mastectomy."

"When did you decide this?"

"I was lying here thinking about Danica and what would happen to her if I died. Marvin, I know I've been a vain woman most of my life, but I've got a little girl I'd like to see grow up and give me some grandbabies. My chance of survival will be greater if I do this, and I don't want to suffer through the side effects of chemo and the bald head."

"Even if it would save your life? You've got that vain thing going again."

"I haven't been a role model, or the best wife, or the best mother I can be. I've lost a lot because of my stubbornness and bourgeois attitude, but if I can increase my chances of being able to raise my child, I want to take it."

The door suddenly flew open and in walked a tall, dark and statuesque physician in civilian clothing—a long white coat draped over it.

"Hello, Mrs. Thomas. I hear you've made a decision regarding your breast cancer treatment."

"Yes, Dr. Sosa. And this is my husband ah…ex-husband, Marvin Thomas."

"Nice to meet you, sir. I'm Dr. Timothy Sosa, Mrs. Thomas' physician."

Marvin extended his hand. "Nice to meet you, Dr. Sosa. I just need to know if Denise's decision is the best one."

"Let's ask the patient."

"Dr. Sosa," Denise began, "I know in the beginning you suggested that a mastectomy might be the best route for me to take considering the stage my cancer is in. I know I wasn't very agreeable to that in the beginning, but after thinking about it and praying about it, this is what I want to do."

"Let me say this, Mrs. Thomas. You have stage II breast cancer, for which we are treating you appropriately. Since we are already on course with your chemo treatments, it's advisable that you complete today's treatment. That way, if you're sure about having a mastectomy, your tumor will have had enough shrinkage for us to consider your request. Right now, we need to get your vitals and blood count so that we can proceed with your treatment."

"Dr. Sosa, am I going to lose all of my hair?"

"More than likely. You don't have much now, which is typical after the second cycle of treatment. Since we are hoping that all goes well, you'll be able to grow your hair out again."

Denise smiled.

"Have you told the rest of your family about your illness?" Dr. Sosa glanced at Marvin. "Other than Mr. Thomas?"

Denise winked at Marvin. He smiled back but was not amused.

"Not yet, but Marvin and I will tell them this week."

Marvin flinched and gave Denise a haunted look. This was harder than he expected. He'd been caught up in the moment of Denise's desperate plea for help. Being the decent man that he was, there was nothing else to do but to be there for her. He was not enjoying the cozy little family environment that she was painting for the good doctor, though. Maybe Denise was scared and was holding on for dear life. Rachel crossed Marvin's mind, and suddenly he wanted to talk to her.

Dr. Sosa briefly placed his hand on Denise's folded ones for reassurance. Then he prepared to administer the IV portacath that would be inserted just under her collarbone. "Let's get started."

Marvin moved toward Denise and stroked her arm. She looked innocent and helpless. "I'll wait for you in the lobby."

"Okay."

"I'll let you know when Mrs. Thomas has finished her procedure," Dr. Sosa said. "Then we can talk about scheduling her surgery."

"All right, Doctor." Marvin shook Dr. Sosa's hand and left the room.

Marvin felt his heart flutter. He would be there all the way for Denise, but he needed to reach Rachel because he was going to need support as well.

Life Support

Denise felt a little weak but much better than she did after her second treatment. First thing in the morning, she would be at the clinic to get her Neulasta shot to boost her white cell count. She adjusted her wig and looked in the mirror, applying a small amount of lipstick. A month from now, she would be minus one breast, but she felt confident that her life would be extended well beyond the one to five years she feared could be her diagnosis.

Her strength and energy came through Marvin. She felt awfully lucky to have this wonderful man back in her life, although it was at her expense. She walked out of the hospital room and smiled as she approached Marvin sitting in the waiting room.

"Mr. Thomas, I'm ready," Denise said.

She wrapped her arms through Marvin's as he led her to his car.

"What're you thinking?" Denise asked. "You've hardly said a word."

"I can't imagine what you're going through. I wish I could wave a magic wand and you would be healed. Too much all at once, I guess. I don't know if I can give you what you need."

"Your being here with me today has meant so much to me. And with advanced technology in chemo treatment, a cancer patient, at least in the early stages, doesn't suffer as much. Marvin, I believe that I'm doing the right thing by having this mastectomy."

"Why haven't you told your family? Does Harold know?"

Denise stopped and pulled her arm from Marvin and held her chest.

"My family has been through a lot with me and my troubles. First a failed marriage—that just doesn't happen in my family. I was the successful one but I had to go and screw it all up by...by making a mockery of my marriage...and then a baby that wasn't ours. My family is a loving group, but heaven help you if you screw up and give the family a bad name. They weren't ready for my sad news. It would have killed them for sure. As for Harold, we only share a daughter between us. You and he are blood, and whether you know it or not, he misses you, Marvin."

"What if things don't go the way you hope? I don't want to sound as if I don't share your optimism; I want to believe that you will be all right. You have a daughter who's depending on you, and you need to be up front with Harold about your health and what it might mean. I will be here to support you all I can, but you'll need the support of your family who loves you dearly and can give you all the extras you'll need."

Denise was silent, letting Marvin's words soak in. She slipped her arm back in his.

"Why don't we go to our favorite restaurant? I'm famished and not quite ready to go home."

"I'd rather not, Denise. I have a lot to do at the office."

"Marvin, I'm scared," Denise admitted. "I'm scared to go home. I'm afraid to go to sleep. I'm afraid I might not wake up."

Marvin pulled Denise close to him, and she laid her head on his shoulder.

"I know you're scared, Denise. So am I." Marvin lifted her chin with his finger and smiled. "Why don't we have lunch, Mrs. Thomas?"

✗✗✗

They settled on Steak and Ale. It was a little early for a steak, but he felt like he needed substance to get him through the rest of the day. He knew that Denise would want him to stay with her, but he had some very important business that needed to be taken care of at the office. And as real as the disease was that racked Denise's body, Marvin wished he could distance himself from the pain of her affair with Harold, which still seeped through his pores.

The waitress took their orders and Denise headed for the ladies' room.

"I'll be right back," she said softly, giving Marvin her winning smile that stole his heart so long ago.

"I'll be right here when you get back."

Marvin watched as Denise disappeared from sight. He surveyed the room and pulled out his cell phone. He looked around again and then dialed the numbers.

"Rachel, please don't hang up. I need you."

EX-travagance at its Best

Excitement made Mona smile as she sifted through her purchases from the last two days of relentless shopping. Bags from Neiman's, Macy's and Saks lay on her king-sized bed. There were dresses in exotic colors, cotton shirts and matching shorts, casual slacks for sightseeing and a sexy after-five dress should an evening that demanded it arise. She pulled more than ten shoe boxes from the box that had been delivered today—everything from the sexiest diva heel to the most elegant sandal.

Prancing before the mirror, Mona tried on outfit after outfit until she was satisfied that her purchases were indeed what she wanted, kissing the point of her dainty index finger and tapping on the mirror that glanced back at her.

"Mr. Broussard, eat your heart out." Mona cackled as she took off her last purchase and neatly folded it and put it into her suitcase. "A new queen of hearts is about to descend upon New Orleans."

Ever since Michael said he wanted to take Mona to meet his family, she fantasized about the moment they would arrive in New Orleans, anticipating the look on their faces when she strolled through the airport on Michael's arm. Their eyes would be fixed on her stunning beauty, sizing her up and taking bets as to her family's standing in society; she was sure that Michael had told them all about her. She would be gracious, not too snooty. You never show all your cards in the beginning. If the Broussards passed her inspection, there was no telling where she would go from there.

Mona's thoughts turned to her family. She had not seen them in ten years. There were several attempts to bridge the rift, especially after Timothy was no longer in her life. It was always Mona going home to see them. Not once had her parents or siblings journeyed to Atlanta to see her. No news was good news, but Mona missed them dearly and she wanted nothing more than to put her arms around her mother and father and tell them she loved them.

A lone paper sack sat on the bed, away from the other pretty packages. She picked it up and looked inside, finally pulling out the contents. She read the package label and started for the bathroom.

Brrng, brrng, brrng. Mona raced for the phone and jerked it from its base, dropping the package back onto the bed.

"Hey, baby. What time are you coming over?"

"Sorry to disappoint you, sweetheart, but this is Sylvia."

"What do you want?"

"I do not like the tone of your voice—but I forgive you. I can tell you are madly in love with Dr. Michael Broussard."

"And what's it to you?"

"Look, Mona. I was thinking about that episode with Denise last night, and I've come up with what I think is a great idea."

"Great idea for whom? Sylvia, I still can't get over her snatching that wig off her head and announcing she has breast cancer. Poor Marvin. He's going to end up taking care of that girl after all."

"My idea, Mona, is we get together and support Denise in

whatever way we can. Ex-Files has to be about something. Look at Claudette and Tyrone. They have found their way back to each other."

"Tyrone probably smelled the check coming after Claudette's shop burned down."

"Girl, you are crazy," Sylvia said, coughing in between laughs.

"All jokes aside, I like your idea, Sylvia. Makes me feel human."

"Michael makes you feel human."

"Got that right. We're going to New Orleans this weekend."

"That's right. Girl, go and have you some fun."

"I plan to do just that. Count me in on whatever you want to do for Denise."

"I'll touch base with Marvin about the particulars of her treatment. Maybe we can take turns going to the clinic with her."

"How's Rachel taking this?"

"Not well. Just as she thought she found the man of her dreams, in walks the jealous ex-wife who has real issues that maybe only Marvin can handle."

"What a drag."

"Oh, oh, oh, today, Ashley's ex-husband dragged her down to city hall to apply for a marriage license."

"Was she kicking and screaming?"

"Not enough, apparently."

"She asked for it, inviting him back into her bed."

"He tricked her, Mona."

"Dumb blonde. Need I say more?"

"Mona, something just came to me. The Gordons…"

"You mean Kohara and…"

"Yes, yes. Her fund-raiser was to raise awareness for breast cancer. Maybe she can help us with Denise."

"Girl, what a brilliant idea. I'll contact her and see what she can do."

"Let me talk with Marvin and I'll get back with you."

"All right. Let's talk as soon as I return from my trip."

"Okay. I've got to call the others. Have a safe trip."

Mona put the phone down. She took time from her purchases to wonder about Denise. She didn't know Denise as well as she did Marvin, but she'd interacted with the woman at several big functions she'd catered for Marvin.

Denise always played the role of the executive of the executive husband. There was no illusion in anyone's mind that Denise was her own woman and that Marvin did not define who she was in society. In fact, Marvin was just an asset that boosted her status among the rich and not so famous. Now she was vulnerable and at the mercy of the little people.

Mona held her breasts tight as Denise's announcement came back to her with a vengeance.

Mona shook her head. So many years had passed, but Timothy crossed her mind. His dream was to be an ob-gyn doctor. Mona wondered what had become of him.

She looked at the clock. She was going to be late for her date at the beauty shop. She moved her empty shopping bags to one side of the room and left her purchases on the bed. She picked up the small package that was in the brown paper bag and disappeared into the bathroom. She emerged ten minutes later without the package. Tying back her braids, Mona grabbed her purse and headed out the door.

Jacqueline Monique Baptiste

"Girl, it's a wonderful day," Mona chirped. "Claudette, I need the full works for my braids. I want them to smell extra spicy. You know I've got to have it going on for my trip to New Orleans."

"So you and Mr. Broussard are going to do this?"

"Oh yes, and you should see what I'm taking on the trip. I am so tired from all the shopping I've been doing the last two or three days."

"So, you've been on Bourgeoisie Boulevard spending all of your money?"

"Claudette, don't hate. It doesn't become you. I am so looking forward to going home to see my family." Mona paused. "It's been a long time, but it will be extra special because I'll have Michael by my side."

"You don't know anything about him."

"I know enough. He's rich, rich and rich."

Claudette and Mona laughed.

"You know being rich isn't everything. It's the rich guys you have to watch."

"Well, how are you and Tyrone getting along? It's never the same when they come back."

"How do you know? Did Timothy ever come back to you?"

"So nasty so early."

"Well, you need to be careful what you say to people. Tyrone and I are doing great. Even the kids have settled down, and I think our marriage has a wonderful chance at restoration. Now sit your ass down in this chair so I can make you pretty for Mr. Broussard."

"That's what I'm talking about," Mona cackled. "Make me pretty for my man; I'll do the rest."

"I know you will." Claudette laughed. "Poor Michael, he is in for it."

"Don't you worry about Michael. I'm the one you need to say a prayer for because that man of mine is a tiger."

"Uhmmm, got your tank full already."

"Let's just say, when you hear the roar, it's my man fully satisfied."

Mona and Claudette laughed and laughed until Mona was about to choke. Mona settled down and caught a glimpse of half of a cigarette crumpled up in an ashtray.

"So you're smoking again, Claudette?"

"Mind your own business, Mona. You know better than to go meddling."

"We stood in the hot sun selling barbecue dinners to save your tail. Don't you get it, Claudette? Your children could have died and you could have lost everything. Besides that, you could get lung cancer. Did last night have any effect on you?"

"Hold it, Mona. I'm trying. That was sad about Denise. Sylvia called awhile ago talking about doing something for her."

"I know. I think it's a great idea. But I don't want to have to have one for you, too. One fund-raiser is enough, although I was happy to be a part of it. Even though I talk crazy, Claudette, I'm happy for you and Tyrone. I'm not jealous; I think I'd just like to have a little happiness in my life, too."

"There's nothing wrong with that, Mona. You deserve it. Speaking of happiness, I've got to check on Ashley. That crazy ex of hers is trying to drag her back to the altar."

"Ashley needs to give him a swift kick in the...well, I won't say it, but she needs to demonstrate to him that it's not happening. She's going to have to get out of the house or have him put out of the house."

"I'm afraid that he might hurt her. She has a doctor's appointment tomorrow, and I'm going to close the shop for a few hours and go with her. I'm really concerned for Ashley."

"Maybe she should take out a restraining order."

"Those are worthless as Monopoly money. One of my best girl-friends took out a restraining order on her ex-husband who stalked her day and night after she left him. They had a son, and the ex vowed that my girlfriend wasn't going to take his son away. He was not to go within two hundred feet of her, but that jackass didn't care what the law said. One night he just went crazy. He went to her house and started banging on the front door. My girlfriend called the police, but they couldn't do anything because all he was doing was banging on the door. Well, that fool went into the yard, picked up a brick, broke the front window and went inside and murdered my girlfriend. I cried for days."

"My God!"

"It was horrible, Mona. I don't know what we can do for Ashley, but we have to do something."

"You're right. We are all in this together."

"I like your spirit, Mona. Maybe Mr. Broussard is the lucky charm after all."

"He is, now get to work on my hair."

"I'm on it because your hair needs all the help I can give it."

"Can I ask you a question?"

"Oh, this has got to be serious."

"Would you be my matron of honor if Michael asks me to marry him?"

"Say what, girl? You're...you're really thinking about marriage? I can't believe you're getting all soft on me."

"Does that surprise you?"

"Well, yes...maybe not. It's hearing you say it out loud is all."

"Would you rather I whispered?"

"Mona married? Girl, yeah, I'd be happy to be your matron of honor."

"Don't tell anyone yet. Nothing is official, but I feel it. I think I'd want to be married in the islands."

"That sounds so romantic. Mona and Michael Broussard. Go, girl."

"That's not all." Silence.

"What do you mean, 'that's not all'?"

A perplexed look crossed Claudette's face and looked into Mona's anxious one. Mona wrung her hands, then settled in a chair at Claudette's kitchen table.

"Speak up, Mona. What are you trying to tell me?"

"Mprgnt."

"I can't quite translate that."

"I'm pregnant."

Claudette's eyes bulged from their sockets.

"Michael and I are going to be parents. Just took the test today. No one but you knows my secret."

"Mona," Claudette sang. "You're going to have a baby?"

"Yes."

"You are a quarter turn of the moon from turning forty years old. What are you going to do with a baby?"

"I'm going to have this baby. This is something I wanted for a long time. Now I have a chance to be a mother."

"But your lifestyle; you're so busy."

"I can take care of a baby and still do the things I enjoy, Claudette."

"So when do you plan on telling Mr. Rich Man?"

"Once we get to New Orleans and we've met each other's families."

"You've got an answer for everything. Give me some love. You never cease to amaze me, Ms. Mona Baptiste."

Mona got up from her seat and turned to hug Claudette.

"Thank you for not judging too harshly. I was glad that I could confide in you."

"Look, Mona, I've always got your back. Now promise that you'll be extra careful on this trip. I heard on the news that a hurricane is threatening to hit New Orleans."

"I thought about it, but that area hasn't been hit hard by a hurricane in years. I hope it will die at sea, but if it does come ashore, my parents have provisions for such a storm. If we ran from every storm that threatened New Orleans, we'd be running all the time."

"You know best. Just go and have yourself a good time."

"We will, Claudette. Just keep my secret tucked away…at least for now."

"No need to worry; it is safe with me. Now, let me fix you up!!"

EX in the Middle

"Well, Mr. Thomas, you've finally found some time to call me back," Rachel said in a sharp tone.

"I've calmed down enough to speak with you." Marvin was snippy right back.

"I was so angry. Seeing Denise all up on you…and then you defending her like I was the Wicked Witch of the West."

"I can explain it to you."

"Actually, Marvin, you don't have to explain a thing. I was wrong. Jealousy got the best of me. I just don't want to lose the best thing that has happened to me in a long time."

"Rachel, I told you a dozen or more times that I love you. I'm not a turn-it-on and turn-it-off kind of guy. You have nothing to worry about."

"That's what Sylvia said. I don't know why I can't be level-headed about that woman."

"Speaking of Denise, I'm with her now." Silence lay on the line. "Are you still there?"

Rachel sighed. "Yeah."

"You have to trust me, Rachel. That's what our relationship is going to have to be about. I went to chemo treatment with Denise today and she wanted to get something to eat afterward."

"Is she sitting in front of you?"

"Of course not, she's in the ladies' room. This is the first chance I got to call you. I need you, Rachel. I don't think I can do this alone."

"Look, Sylvia and I were talking today, and she's going to talk to everyone in the group about doing something to support Denise during her illness—maybe take turns going to treatment with her."

"That would be good. Denise decided to have her breast removed."

"What? Oh, my God."

"The surgery is scheduled two weeks from Friday. Denise thinks this might prolong her life."

"Maybe it will, Marvin. I guess she's scared."

"Real scared. She doesn't want to die, Rachel."

Rachel sighed. "I feel so foolish. She's battling what could be a death sentence, and I was jealous for her wanting to live. I don't deserve you, Marvin."

"Rachel, I love you."

"I love you, too, Marvin. Please forgive me."

"It's been forgotten."

"We're going to help Denise through this, and I promise to be by your side wherever this takes us."

"That means a lot to me. I'll call you later."

Marvin closed his flip phone. His eyes traveled around the room and stopped when he saw Denise staring at him. She had a frown on her face, but Marvin didn't care. For all she knew, he was conducting business.

Denise moved toward the table once she noticed that Marvin was watching her. She flopped in her chair and fiddled with the napkin that contained her silverware.

"So who were you talking to?" she inquired.

"The office," Marvin lied. "I told you I had a lot of business to take care of today."

Denise's face relaxed and she offered a little smile. "I'm glad you're here."

"I told you I would be."

There was truth to the cliché about beauty being skin deep. Denise was a beautiful woman, but the beauty that Marvin once saw in her, mainly because of her infidelity, had long departed. Looking at her didn't make him quiver or his blood boil like lava in an active volcano. There was an arctic chill between them that no amount of heat could warm.

"What's the matter?" Denise asked. "You're looking at me like you saw a ghost. Baby, I'm not going anywhere. I may be getting ready to lose one breast, but I've got so much more of life to live."

"That's a good attitude to have. And just so you know, I'm pulling for you, too. I want you to do something for me."

"Depending upon what it is."

"I want you to call your family today and tell them about your illness. No more delays. And I want you to call Harold, too."

"Look, Marvin. Can we have a pleasant lunch?"

"We can, and we will. I need you to promise me that you will take care of this matter today."

"And if I don't?"

"I will call them myself."

"Even Harold?"

The waitress arrived at the table and placed their plates on the table. "Will there be anything else?" she asked.

"No, thanks," Denise said.

Marvin turned to Denise. "Eat your food, Denise. End of discussion."

Bottoms Up

Claudette pulled up in Ashley's empty driveway. Everything seemed still. The flowers smiled as they drank the liquid sunshine and the towering pine trees in the backyard offered protection.

A bulky white cloth circled Claudette's head, lifting her braids high in a slight twist. A wide smile crossed her face as she recounted Mona's conversation yesterday about getting married. She never thought she'd see the day. Men came and went in Mona's life. The woman was a nomad crossing the desert sand when it came to men, never wanting to settle with one for long.

Claudette pushed the doorbell and waited. She could have easily stayed in the car and honked the horn, but she half expected Ashley to be outside since she was about five minutes late getting to the house. With no answer, Claudette rang the bell again.

Sweat began to form on Claudette's face. It had only been an hour since she spoke with Ashley. Claudette began to bang on the door. Then she remembered the story she told Mona about her girlfriend's ex-husband beating on the door. There still was no answer and she began to pace, contemplating what she should do.

The front door opened suddenly. Out stepped William in a pair of blue jeans and a sleeveless, scoop-neck T-shirt.

"Go home. We don't need you meddlin' in our affairs. I'm taking Ashley to the doctor."

Claudette stared at the towering giant.

"Cat got your tongue? You had plenty of talk the last time I saw you. This is none of your business, so go get in your car and get off of my property."

"I'm not going anywhere until I see Ashley."

"Lady, you are getting on my nerves. Take your…"

"Take my what?" Claudette asked, waiting for an answer with both hands on her hips.

Ashley suddenly appeared at the front door.

"What's going on, Ashley? We're going to be late for your appointment."

"Claudette, William is going to take me. I appreciate you taking time away from work to go with me—"

"Look, Ashley, I don't know what's going on here, but I'm here if you need me. If you didn't want me to take you, you should have told me before I came over."

"You heard my wife," William said, moving closer to Claudette. "I've got this."

"I'm not scared of you."

William moved to within inches of Claudette's face.

"William, stop!" Ashley hollered.

"You better move back or you'll regret the moment you got up in my face. You don't scare me, Mr. Lewis." Claudette raised her finger in William's face. "I will not hesitate to go to the police if something happens to Ashley."

"Get the hell off of my property, you fat ass…"

"Who are you calling fat, you no-good, cheating, wife manipulator!"

"Shut up!" Ashley screamed. "Please stop this!"

"I'll leave if you want me to, Ashley, but I'm not scared of—"

Before Claudette knew what was happening, William picked her up off the ground and single-handedly lifted Claudette to her car. Ashley began to run after them, but William turned around and gave her a "don't take another step" look. He opened the door to Claudette's car and dumped her in it.

"Don't let me ever see you on my property again or I'll call the police," William said to Claudette, slamming the car door.

As soon as Claudette was able to straighten herself up, she started the engine and barreled down the driveway, leaving Ashley to fend for herself.

"Next time, I'll be ready for him," Claudette vowed.

xxx

"I'm going to be late for my appointment." Ashley watched as Claudette drove out of sight.

"That woman is to never blacken my door again. Those crazy braids stuck to her head have suffocated her brain cells—getting all up in my face like she didn't have good sense. She was within two inches of getting her ass kicked."

"That wasn't necessary, William. You were out of order and out of control."

William stopped and looked at Ashley, then headed into the house with Ashley at his heels.

Once they were inside, he grabbed Ashley by the shoulders and stared straight into her eyes.

"Understand this, Ashley: You and I are going to get married tomorrow. You'll probably need an extra hour for lunch. There are no ifs or ands about it. We are going to be a family again and raise our child.

"Your meddling friends are off limits, and there will be no need for you to go to your little meetings any longer."

William released Ashley's shoulders. Words had yet to escape her lips. Ashley just stood there transfixed as if waiting for a spell to be lifted.

"You don't have to say anything, Ashley, so long as you know the rules. Now, go on and get in the car. I've got to get my shirt, and I'll be right out."

Ashley stood in the foyer and looked around. She rubbed her stomach, which showed little evidence that a baby was on board. She picked up her purse and headed to the car through the garage. It would be so easy to just get in and drive off without ever looking back, but somewhere lurking in the shadows would be William, reminding her that she was carrying his baby. She was carrying his baby all right, but she had no plans of meeting him at the altar a second time.

Conference Call

"Hey ladies."

"Hey, Sylvia," Rachel and Claudette said in unison.

"Hold on a moment. Someone else is calling in."

"Good afternoon, divas."

"Hey, Mona."

"Has anyone talked with Ashley lately?" Sylvia asked.

"I was manhandled and thrown off the premises by that big Mandingo she calls an ex-husband," Claudette said.

"Manhandled how?" Sylvia inquired.

"That sorry excuse for a husband put his hands on me when I went to pick Ashley up for her doctor's appointment. He picked me up and threw me in my car and told me not to set foot on his property again."

Laughter erupted across the telephone lines.

"Do you mean…hee, hee, hee, hee." Mona couldn't contain her laughter. "He…heeeeeeee…he picked you up off the ground? Hee, hee, hee."

"It is not a laughing matter!" Claudette shouted. "Something crazy is going on in Ashley's house, and if we don't rescue her soon…"

"He, he, he, heeeeeeeeeeeeeee. Was your tail turned up to the sky?" Mona asked.

"I'm through with you sisters. You don't know how to be serious. But I'm telling you, I'm afraid for Ashley, and we need to be ready to move in and help her as soon as she sounds the alarm."

"I think you're right, Claudette," Sylvia said. "We work in the same building, but I rarely see her. I believe she's even avoiding me."

"How is it that our exes have got us so messed up?" Rachel inquired.

"Because we've settled for less than our true worth," Mona said. "You get what you pay for."

"Look," Sylvia interrupted. "Let's meet for lunch tomorrow around eleven-thirty. Can everyone take a lunch break at that time?"

"You'll have to eat without me. I have a plane to catch," Mona reminded the group. "I'm going to New Orleans with my man."

"What time is your flight?" Rachel asked.

"Four in the afternoon, and I'm not going to miss my flight because I was sitting around snacking and jacking my jaws with you crazy women."

"Mona, we'll meet somewhere close to the airport," Sylvia said.

"No can do on my lunch hour," Rachel piped in. "I can't waste it sitting in ATL traffic."

"Okay, I'll come to you all, but if I miss my plane, all of you will have to answer to me."

"I'm surprised you're still going with that hurricane whirling so close to New Orleans," Sylvia said.

"Nothing's going to stop me from seeing my parents and showing off Mr. Broussard. That hurricane has been unpredictable. It'll probably come close, wave its mighty arms a few good times and New Orleaners will be back gambling, slopping down

Hurricanes—no pun intended—and just living it up in the French Quarter in no time."

"Well, okay, that's settled," Sylvia said. "Rachel, you need to see if Marvin can come and…"

"Uhh, uhh, you and Marvin okay now?" Mona asked Rachel.

"There was nothing wrong with us."

"Not according to what I heard."

"Listen, Mona, don't worry yourself about it. Marvin and I are finer than we've ever been."

"Mmm, hmm."

"So, Sylvia," Claudette asked, "what prompted this lunch?"

"Besides the fact that we just need to come together more often and hang out, I think it is time we put the crap in our lives on the back burner and make way for new and better things. Also, we need to talk about what we're going to do for Denise."

"Sylvia, the Gordon Foundation is geared toward cancer research," Mona interjected. "I think we can take turns going with Denise to her therapy sessions."

"Denise is going to have a mastectomy," Rachel volunteered.

"What?" Mona said excitedly.

"Has her situation turned for the worse?" Sylvia asked.

"According to Marvin," Rachel said, "she decided that she didn't want to continue chemotherapy. I guess she wanted to hold on to her last bit of dignity, being her hair."

"But if it was going to save her life," Mona began.

"She believes she can prolong her life even more if she goes ahead and has her breast removed," Rachel said.

"Who's having their breast removed?" Ashley asked, walking into Sylvia's office.

"Ashley, is that you?" came Claudette's voice.

"I'm really sorry about yesterday, Claudette. I didn't have any energy left to deal with William."

"Did William really turn Claudette upside down and throw her in the car?" Mona asked. "He, he, he, he, he, heeeeeeeeeeee."

"Mona, it's not funny. If I was taller, I would have squashed that Amazon to the ground. What did the doctor say, Ashley?"

"The baby's all right."

"Well, that's good news," Rachel said.

"Ash, we are meeting tomorrow for lunch at eleven-thirty, since Mona has to catch a plane, to talk about how we are going to help Denise."

"Okay."

"Ashley," Claudette called out, "tell us what's going on with you. I hear it in your voice."

"Claudette, I'm all right. I'm tired of fighting with William is all. I will be making some tough decisions about my life soon."

"Does William still expect you to get married?"

"Tomorrow."

"What are you going to do, Ashley?" Rachel hurriedly interjected.

"What I said I was going to do all alone. I'm not getting married."

"How are you going to get out of it, living in the same house and all?" Sylvia probed, getting up from her desk to stand beside Ashley.

"I haven't quite decided, but know that I will not—I reiterate, will not—be getting married tomorrow."

"Ashley, I say punch his lights out and head for the border," Mona said, putting in her two cents.

"If you need me," Claudette said, "call me. I'll throw my curling iron down so fast, and I'll be at your front door before you hang up the phone."

"Thanks, Claudette. I might need you."

"Ohhhhhhhhhh," Sylvia said, "I'll let you all know where we'll meet later on tonight."

"Sounds good," everyone said, in unison.

"Ciao," Mona said

"Talk with you later," Rachel piped in.

"Bye," Sylvia said.

"I'm here if you need me, Ash."

"Thanks, Claudette."

Sylvia hit the off button and turned back to Ashley.

"Do you want to talk about it?"

"No. I feel better just in that brief moment of conversation with you and the other ladies."

"Ashley, I see that you're hurting, but you'll get through this. You have your baby to think about. You are already divorced from William. It's just a question of how you are going to get him out of the house."

"I know. Sylvia, sometimes I do some dumb and stupid things. I never should have invited William back to the house no matter how hard he begged. He's this person I don't recognize, and it frightens me."

"Have you thought about getting a restraining order?"

"What good is that going to do if he lives in the same house with me?"

"I guess that was a bad idea."

"That's all right. I have been giving it some serious thought, but my first thought is about not getting married tomorrow."

Ashley stood by the window that looked out at the Atlanta metropolis that dumped into I-85.

"That bastard grabbed me by the shoulders yesterday and told me I was going to marry him on Friday. A cold chill ran through me, Sylvia. I wanted to slit his throat. He no more cares about me than the man in the moon. He is obsessed with having this baby—you know, the way those crazy folks did in *Rosemary's Baby*. But my baby is not a devil, and he will not be raised by one."

Sylvia went and stood by Ashley and rubbed her shoulders.

"You can come and stay at my house tonight. William will have to come through me."

"I can't involve you in this, Sylvia. I've got to take care of this myself. I'm going to face William head on. There will be no wedding tomorrow. I'll see you at eleven-thirty for lunch."

Ashley hugged Sylvia and walked out of the office. Sylvia stood staring at her until the phone rang, disturbing her disturbing thoughts.

Let's Get Together

"How is the hardest-working woman in Atlanta doing?" Kenny asked.

"Much better now that I've heard your voice."

"I just got back in town, and you were my first stop."

"I'm flattered."

"Don't be flattered, Sylvia. I really mean it. I've been thinking a lot about you, us, lately and to quote my boss, it is affecting my work."

"I certainly don't want to be the reason you don't get that great big bonus at the end of the year."

"Not a chance. Look, why don't I take you out to lunch tomorrow? As much as I'd love to see you tonight, I have to work on a presentation that I have to give tomorrow morning."

"Kenny, I wish you had called earlier. We're having an Ex-Files luncheon tomorrow. Marvin's ex-wife, Denise, has breast cancer, and we're getting together to see how we can help her out."

"I thought Marvin was with Rachel."

"I'll tell you the sordid story later."

"I won't say I'm not disappointed, but that's a good enough reason for not meeting me for lunch. Sylvia, I need to see you."

"What about dinner and a movie tomorrow night?"

"I have a better suggestion. Why don't you take the afternoon off and I pick you up after lunch? There is something I need your opinion on, but I need you to take a ride with me."

"Any hints? You seem so secretive."

"I'll say this: It's one of my new inventions."

"Inventions? You amaze me, Kenny Richmond."

"We've got a date?"

"I'm sure I can work it out."

"See you tomorrow. And food for thought, your opinion matters."

Sylvia hung up the phone for the second time in a matter of minutes. A satisfying smile crossed her face and stayed there like a permanent fixture. Yes, Kenny Richmond was running rampant through her veins. Adonis who?

EX-pired

"From Times Square in New York, it's *Good Morning America* with Diane Sawyer and Robin Roberts."

Ashley looked up as the door that led from the garage into the house opened. Sweat poured from William's face. He blew air through his fingers, and offered a smile.

"I'm making breakfast for you this morning."

"This is the Ashley I fell in love with—so full of love and devotion."

Ashley smiled, but did not say a word.

"I'm going to take a quick shower, and I'll be back. I hope you're wearing my favorite outfit for our special day—you know, the navy blazer with your cream-colored blouse and slacks."

"Just for you, William."

"I'm not sure why your attitude has suddenly changed, but I'm happy. Our baby will be happy."

Ashley managed another smile. She adjusted her robe and went to the stove to turn down the heat under the pot. She picked up the large wooden spoon and stirred the oatmeal carefully, making sure it was free of lumps. She took some sugar and cinnamon and poured the mixture into the cereal. She stirred a minute longer; then, satisfied, she turned the stove down to very low and left the room. Oatmeal was one of William's favorite breakfast foods.

Taking off her robe, Ashley reached for the navy blazer that hung in her spacious closet. She put the blazer on and admired herself in the floor-length mirror. Ashley noted that the water was still running as she passed the master bath on her way back into the kitchen.

Ashley poured herself a cup of coffee, took a seat at the table and waited. The oatmeal was simmering on low and every few minutes she would jump up and stir it with a wooden spoon, making sure that it retained its smooth texture just as William liked it.

A noise made Ashley look up. William was making his way back into the kitchen. She rose from her chair and pulled two slices of wheat bread from the bread box and put them into the toaster. She stirred the oatmeal once more.

"Are you ready for our big day?" William asked, smiling as he entered the kitchen.

"Sure," Ashley said noncommittal. "How about some breakfast? I fixed your favorite—oatmeal—just the way you like it. Your toast should be coming up any minute."

William watched Ashley get up at the sound of the toaster releasing twin pieces of hot bread.

"You shouldn't have gone to all the trouble, but I appreciate you doing so."

"It was nothing. I thought it would be the perfect beginning to our day."

"So you have accepted our getting married again."

"You left me no choice."

"Well, I'm glad you came to your senses. And by the way, I apologize for the way I acted with your friend. You won't be needing her anymore."

"Ready for your oatmeal? Your toast is buttered and the jam is on the table."

"Joining me?"

"Just toast and coffee."

Ashley stood and moved to the stove. She picked up the bowl she had set out on the counter. She stirred the oatmeal one more time before emptying the contents of the pot into the bowl.

"Ashley, we are going to be a happy family."

Ashley looked at William with a forlorn look on her face. "I hope so, William. Now eat your oatmeal before it gets cold. Would you like a cup of coffee?"

"No, maybe some orange juice."

Quietly, Ashley moved to the refrigerator and pulled out a pitcher of juice. She got a glass, poured it full and set it down next to the bowl of oatmeal.

"Umm, this oatmeal is good," William said.

"Just the way you like it," Ashley replied.

"You ought to…"

"I ought to what?" Ashley asked.

"Ash, I don't feel so good. I can't…I can…I can't…catch my…"

"You can't catch…what?"

"Call nine-one-one…"

William fell forward into his bowl of oatmeal. Ashley sat still and watched as he gasped for breath. She picked up a paper napkin out of its holder and wiped her mouth, then stood up and took her near empty cup of coffee and threw the remnants in the sink.

Ashley walked past William. He seemed to be resting comfortably—slumped over in his seat, his face covered in oatmeal. She left the room and returned with her purse, car keys and an overnight bag. Setting the alarm, she took one more look at William and walked into the garage. She whistled as she got into her car. It was going to be a good day.

Overcast skies threatened rain. Ugly and dirty clouds quickly emerged from nowhere and blanketed the morning sunshine. When the light turned green, Sylvia walked briskly across the street and into the restaurant, happy that the slight drizzle had not turned into a downpour.

Sylvia was shown her seat and waited for the others to arrive. Two minutes later, Rachel appeared, offering sister hugs to Sylvia. They ordered water with lemon and sipped until, Mona showed up—alone.

"Where is everyone?" Mona asked, taking off her coat and giving Sylvia and Rachel a hug. "I was hoping everyone would be on time because I have to leave in a couple of hours."

"They'll be here," Sylvia offered. "Girl, we are not going to let you miss your plane."

"Look at Ms. Diva," Rachel piped in. "Going to New Orleans with her man."

"I'm going to share something with just the two of you," Mona said. "I am so nervous. I would never admit that to anyone, but all of a sudden I've got these nervous jitters. Michael is going to pick me up and I want to be calm when he gets here."

"I can't believe that the incomparable Mona Baptiste is nervous about anything," Rachel said. "Miss I've Got It All Together is having taking-my-man-home-to-meet-the-folks jitters."

"I shouldn't have told you," Mona marked.

"Just messin' with you, girl. Right, Sylvia?"

"Rachel, you're doing all the talking."

The trio stopped when an excited Claudette followed by Tyrone headed their way. Claudette waved a piece of paper in the air and danced her way to the table.

"What do you have in your hand, Claudette?" Sylvia asked.

"God is good," Claudette said.

"He sure is," Tyrone echoed.

"Well, tell us before you split in two from grinning so hard," Mona pleaded.

Claudette closed her eyes and kissed the piece of paper. She sat down next to Mona and held Tyrone's hand.

"Is Marvin coming?" Claudette asked looking at Rachel.

"Yes, he should be here any minute."

"Well, I'll wait until Marvin arrives to share our good news."

"Ahhh," Mona quipped. "You got us all excited. You're acting just like someone who's just given a baby a sucker and you take it back as soon as they put it in their mouth because you just realized that it wasn't good for them."

"Here comes Marvin now," Rachel said.

Marvin has eyes only for Rachel, Sylvia thought. He moved so easily and stopped next to Rachel, giving her a quick kiss on the cheek before sitting down. Rachel blushed. They seemed happy.

"Now are you going to tell us what you're bursting at the seams to tell us?" Mona asked.

"Who's missing?" Claudette stalled.

"Ashley. She's probably on her way to the Justice of the Peace," Mona said.

"I let her down," Claudette said.

"So did I," Sylvia interjected. "I was so busy this morning, I forgot to check to see if she made it to work."

"Anika won't be able to make it," Rachel said. "She had several clients this afternoon, and she really needs the money."

"Well, drum roll, please," Claudette shouted while Tyrone banged the table.

Claudette stood up. "Claudette's House of Styles is about to be reborn. I am holding before you an insurance check in the amount of $150,000. And the judge threw out the arson charge on Kwame. They said it was an accident, and the only thing he'll have to do is forty hours of community service."

"What?" Mona screamed.

Tears streamed down Claudette's face and Tyrone stood and squeezed her. Everyone clapped and wiped tears from their eyes.

"God is so good," Claudette managed to say between sobs. Marvin hugged her tight.

"You deserve it, Claudette, and however I can assist you and Tyrone, I'm here."

"Here, here," everyone shouted.

Heads began to turn in the restaurant. Instead of nasty looks, smiles were pasted on the patrons' faces almost as if they were privy to Claudette's wonderful announcement.

"I can't thank my Ex-File family enough for all of your support during one of the worst times in my life," Claudette said. "If you all hadn't been there, I don't know what I would have done. Not only have I been blessed with the means to rebuild my shop, but God has restored my family."

She hugged Tyrone around the waist. "My baby, my rock. I love you, Tyrone. Although it was a tragic moment that brought you back into my life, I thank God that it happened."

Tyrone choked on his words. "I love you, too, Claudette. I don't want to live another day without you."

The entire table was wet with tears. Hugs were the order of the day, while the waitress waited patiently off to the side to take their orders.

"One more thing," Claudette began. "Because of your support, lunch is on me today."

"Now that's what I'm talking about," Mona crowed. "This day is going to be perfect."

"We hope you have a great time in New Orleans with your man, Mona," Sylvia said.

"I plan to." Mona looked up and saw Claudette smiling in her direction. Mona lowered her eyes when Claudette gave her a "your secret is safe with me" wink.

"Well, let's order," Marvin said. "I'm famished."

"Yes, I've…"

"Got to get to the airport on time," Sylvia, Rachel and Claudette said in unison. Laughter followed.

The waitress took everyone's orders and Sylvia began to discuss how the group would assist Denise. In the middle of Sylvia's discussion, heads began to turn as Ashley approached the group.

"What did I miss," Ashley asked, as she sat in the empty seat next to Sylvia.

"Did you do it?" Sylvia asked.

"You mean get married?"

"Yes, that's what we mean," Claudette said a little agitated.

"Don't be 'shamed," Mona interjected, taking a sip of water. "You aren't the first person who remarried their ex. Look on the bright side. You don't have to go through that dating game again. You already know what you got."

"I didn't get married," Ashley said in a rather stoic voice.

"Are you all right?" Claudette asked. "You don't seem yourself. You should be celebrating!"

"I got up this morning, told William I was through and was not going to marry him and walked out of the door. That was a celebration. I hope the offer to stay with someone tonight is still open because I walked out with nothing but the clothes on my back and my overnight bag."

Eyes shifted around the table from one to another. Something very strange was going on with Ashley. She didn't even seem real— talking out of the side of her mouth and pretending that her decision to leave William was like making a decision to buy either regular or decaf.

"Good for you!!!" Sylvia finally said.

"Let's make a toast to Ashley's liberation," Rachel said, lifting her glass of water.

"To Ashley's liberation," everyone said in unison.

xxx

Ashley lifted her glass as if it was weighted with sand. She looked at her friends celebrating her liberation when in truth her freedom was coming to an end. She pushed back the tears that threatened to expose her and tried to make the best of a moment she would forever capture in time.

Ashley jumped when Marvin touched her shoulders. She set her glass down on the table and picked up a napkin to catch the tears she was unable to control.

Marvin said, "I know it was a hard decision to make, Ashley, but leaving William for good is probably for the best. We will be here for you."

"You know you don't have to ask about a place to stay, Ash,"

Sylvia said and then remembered that Kenny was coming by to pick her up. "We'll work out the details later."

"I'm fine…I just get so emotional sometimes and can't think straight. Just a few months ago, I had to sit through a court proceeding and the judge told me my marriage was dissolved. It felt like death." Ashley cried into the napkin. "It is really dissolved this time."

Claudette got up and hugged Ashley. "Ashley, sweetheart, I'll still be available to go with you to your doctor's appointments… and for whatever else you need."

"Thank you all for being there for me. I do appreciate it. Let's order. I'm hungry."

All Alone

"Hush, everyone, it's time for me to depart." Mona pointed toward the entry to the restaurant. "My man has come to whisk me away for our fabulous weekend in New Orleans. Lunch was wonderful, especially since Claudette is paying. Gotta run now. I will be back in time for Denise's surgery."

Michael Broussard advanced toward the satisfied group and stopped in front of Mona, placing a kiss on her lips.

"Good afternoon, everyone. I hate to take this beautiful lady away from you…" Mona blushed. "If we don't hurry, we won't catch our flight, and I don't think Mona would forgive me."

"Take her away," Rachel said. "I've got to get back to work before I don't have a job. It was real, and I love you guys." Rachel blew a kiss.

Everyone put their coats on and prepared to leave the restaurant.

"I'm glad you didn't let that bully take you to the altar again," Mona said to Ashley. "I knew you weren't weak. We're here for you if you need us."

"That means a lot coming from you, Mona," Ashley said. "I appreciate it."

Mona rubbed Ashley's arm. "Gotta go."

Kisses passed around the room. The rain had let up and everyone made a run for it. Sylvia walked to the entrance with Ashley behind her.

"Ash—"

Just then the door opened.

"Tried to get here as soon as I could," Kenny said to Sylvia. "Hi, Ashley."

"Hello, Kenny," they both said.

Sylvia felt awkward. She was ready for her special moment with Kenny, but she felt obligated to help Ashley.

"Look, Sylvia. It seems you already have plans."

Kenny looked from one to the other.

"Well, Kenny and I have plans for this afternoon… but…"

"I'll go to my mother's house."

"You're not going back to work?"

"No, I've taken the rest of the day off. I was not in the mood to sit behind the desk and plan events for people today."

"I can give you the key to my house, and you can make yourself comfortable until I get home."

"Look, Sylvia. We can get together tomorrow." Ashley managed a smile. "I can tell by the sly grin on Kenny's face that he has a special afternoon planned for you. Hook up tomorrow?"

"Thanks, Ashley. I'll make it up to you then."

"Okay."

Ashley watched the couple leave the restaurant hand in hand. She started out of the restaurant, but quickly found a bench and sat down. She clutched her heart and exhaled deeply before placing a hand on her forehead. The rain began to fall again and Ashley's tears right along with it. Ashley's sobs became tremors, but she was going to have to brace herself and handle this alone.

"Are you all right, ma'am?"

xxx

"I really hate leaving Ashley like that," Sylvia said, "but I admit that I am going to be selfish this afternoon. I'm always compromising myself for someone else, but today is my day."

"Admit it, Sylvia. You're curious about what I've got to show you."

"I'll admit that, but we'll talk about it as soon as we get in the comfort of your car." Sylvia placed her arm through Kenny's and they raced for his car as the rain began to pour.

xxx

"Here we are." Kenny opened the door for Sylvia and ran to the other side and got in.

"What's up with Ashley, anyway? She was acting weird—not herself."

"She walked out of William's life for good. They were supposed to get remarried today—or should I say, William was forcing Ashley to get married."

"What kind of craziness is that?"

"Tell me about it. Now I really feel bad because Ashley may need someone to talk to. I'm sure it took a lot of courage for her to do what she did. Truthfully, I believe she was afraid of William."

"We can put this off until tomorrow if you need to be with Ashley. I'll understand."

"Gosh, Kenny. I love you."

Kenny smiled. "You said that like you meant it."

"I do."

"Let's go back to the restaurant to pick up Ashley, and I'll take you to your car. What I want to show you can wait another day."

"Thanks, Kenny." Before Sylvia knew it, she kissed Kenny on the cheek. "That's all for now. I don't want you to wreck your fancy car." They laughed.

Kenny stopped at the curb and Sylvia jumped out and ran into the restaurant. Two minutes later she emerged but without Ashley.

"Ashley's not in there," Sylvia called to Kenny.

"Get in the car. We'll drive around and see if we can find her."

They drove around for ten minutes or more without a trace of Ashley.

"We tried," Sylvia said. "I guess we can continue with our afternoon after all."

"You don't fool me, Sylvia St. James. Secretly, you were hoping not to find Ashley."

"I'm not that shallow, Kenny, but boy, can you see right through me." They laughed.

"Sit back. You are in for a long afternoon."

Up, Up, and Away

"You look delicious, Mona. You even have a glow all over your face."

Mona gave a faint smile. "Fasten your seat belt, Mr. Broussard. You're making me blush."

"Come on, girl. You're talking to me. I know what makes you blush."

"We might have to cut our trip short as I'm sure our families will not give us time to ourselves so that you can make me blush all over."

"You make life so difficult, Mona. I've already got reservations down in the Quarter for Wednesday night. Our families are not going to monopolize *all* of our time. I want this trip to be special and memorable."

"Mr. Broussard, you have everything under control. I do like that in a man."

"Ms. Baptiste, you have not seen nothing yet. And if you're good…"

"What do you mean, if I'm good?"

"If you're a good girl, I have a special surprise for you."

"Hint?"

"It wouldn't be a surprise, now, would it?"

"Welcome aboard Delta flight 1089 to New Orleans," the captain's voice boomed over the loudspeaker. "We may run into some turbulence today, but our hour and a half flight to New Orleans should be uneventful otherwise. In a moment, we will be cruising at an altitude of thirty-seven thousand feet. Enjoy your flight and thank you for choosing Delta."

"Are you ready to meet my family?" Michael asked. "We love to party and have a good time."

"I was sitting here thinking about how my family will react when they see me. Will they run up and hug me—kiss me? I'm excited, but I'm not sure about this. Michael, I haven't seen them in a long time. What if I don't recognize them?"

"Don't be silly. You can age in ten or twelve years, but you'll always recognize family."

"I have a surprise for you, too, but I can't tell you until we get to New Orleans."

"Hint?"

"No, Mr. Broussard. No hint for you."

Michael and Mona watched as the flight attendant attempted to go through her spiel about plane safety. Midway through, she took the cardboard she was asking everyone to refer to for emergency evacuation information and began to fan herself. The flight attendant began her spiel again, and two seconds in she began to fan again. It was so comical.

"That's what Delta gets for keeping the old coffee, tea or me flight attendants around. They probably have ten lines to say during the whole flight, but her menopausal state is going to cause us to not get all of our instructions. Heaven forbid the plane should crash."

"Michael, please. Leave that woman alone. She has a right to a career as a flight attendant if she wants one. She's getting old, but she's not dead."

The plane began to shake. The cardboard safety instructions flew out of the flight attendant's hand. The *Fasten Your Seatbelt* sign flashed.

"What did I tell you?"

"You were right this time, Michael, but you wouldn't have listened to anything she said if she hadn't started fanning herself."

"Well, let's hope we get to New Orleans in one piece."

A Special Lady

The rain was relentless and so was Kenny. He was determined to make this a special day for Sylvia.

"So where are we going, Kenny?"

"You'll see in a moment."

"It looks like we're heading for Buckhead. You're not planning an instant replay of our night at the Intercontinental Hotel."

"Frankly, I don't want to replay that night, Sylvia. It was awkward and we are well past that now."

Sylvia smiled.

"Ten more minutes and you'll get to share in my surprise."

Kenny drove into the heart of Buckhead. He made a couple of left turns and another slight turn to the right and pulled his car to the curb. Sylvia quickly surveyed her surroundings, and Kenny could tell that she was baffled. She didn't say a word.

"Let's take a short walk," Kenny said.

"In the rain? This has better be some surprise."

"I promise you it is."

They turned the corner and walked to the middle of the block and stopped. Sylvia looked at the building, then back at Kenny. He offered her a smile and extended his hand.

"After you."

Sylvia did not move. She stood staring at Kenny unable to comprehend what they were doing there.

"Let's go in," Kenny said, giving Sylvia a slight tug on her arm.

Sylvia and Kenny walked into the store, although Sylvia resisted.

"Hello, Mr. Richmond. I see you brought your little lady with you."

Sylvia stared at Kenny. She puckered her lips and then relaxed them into a great big smile.

"Ma'am, Mr. Richmond picked out the most beautiful and exquisite ring for you. Now I understand why he insisted on it being this one," the jeweler said, opening the safe and pulling a red velvet box from the vault. "She is lovely, Mr. Richmond."

"Thanks, Steven. She is special and I want her to have the best."

"You are doing the right thing! Yes, you're doing the right thing."

"You're thinking about your commission. I'm not fooled."

Steven and Kenny laughed while Sylvia continued to wear her smile.

Kenny took the five-carat, marquise-cut diamond engagement ring in his hand. He got down on one knee and held Sylvia's hand. Steven leaned both elbows on the counter, cupping his face in his hands.

"Will you marry me, Sylvia St. James? I'm so glad you came back into my life. While I may not deserve your love, I know without a doubt that this time is ours. God gave me a second chance at life and a chance to be part of the life of the most beautiful woman in the world."

"Get up, Kenny. I'll marry you."

"Bravo, bravo!" Steven shouted.

Tears of joy raced down Kenny's face. He had no idea he could feel this way for someone else. In his early life, he was a selfish, egotistical, sorry excuse for a man, but now he was a humbled human being and one who knew how to treat a lady.

Kenny stood and wiped the tears from Sylvia's eyes and placed the ring on her finger.

"Aren't you going to buy it first?"

"Mr. Richmond took care of that a week ago." Steven laughed.

"You continue to amaze me, Kenny."

"I pray that I can make all your days like this one." Sylvia smiled. "Why don't we go to Cinnabon and get us one of those sweet rolls to celebrate since you just had lunch. Then a movie and dinner?"

"I'd like that Mr. Richmond, my husband-to-be."

"I like that Ms. Sylvia St. James, soon-to-be Richmond."

"Wow." Sylvia raised her hand and looked at the diamond that sparkled on her finger. "Kenny, let's take our time about getting married…I mean, I don't want us to rush into it. Our wedding will have to be perfect, even if it is the second time. And I'm going to have to tell my daughter. That will be a chore."

"I'm willing to wait. Just don't entice me with those sexy night-gowns you wear. I may not be able to resist temptation."

"Just because I'm wearing your engagement ring doesn't mean you can go tasting the fruit."

"As I recall, you were the temptress and I was the poor victim who was at the wrong place at the wrong time."

"Tell me anything, Mr. Kenny Richmond. You almost broke down. You had to up and leave because you knew your self-control was at its end."

"Excuse us, Steven."

Steven moved to the other side of the store.

"Kiss me, girl," Kenny said to Sylvia.

Their bodies melted together in a long and passionate kiss. Sylvia took a second and extended her hand, staring at the five-carat diamond that sparkled on it.

xxx

Ashley drove around the city not sure what to do or where she was going. It was too late to take back what she had already done. What had given her a moment's satisfaction was now filled with remorse.

She had killed William, and she was going to jail. If Ashley could start the day over, she would have done it differently. She would have gotten up early and walked out, never to return.

The shrill loudness of a siren made Ashley jump even though the police car rushed past her without stopping. Her nerves were on the edge of a cliff, and any moment she was going to fall off. The Ex-Files—or anyone else for that matter—wouldn't be able to save her. She had to find someplace to throw away the vial that contained the remaining arsenic.

How long would it be before anyone discovered that William was missing? He took the day off from work, so no one would be looking for him until Monday. It was a good thing William had not told his family about them getting remarried. His sisters would have come looking. They didn't like her anyway, although they pretended they did.

What a mess she had made. Ashley couldn't go to her parents' house. They would ask too many questions. It was easy to see that Sylvia and Kenny had plans, and she didn't want to spoil their weekend.

Ashley drove around until she noticed a sign on a store awning—
Guns for All Occasions. She quickly pulled to the curb and got
out of the car. Ashley took a long look at the sign, then looked
both ways. Satisfied, she grabbed the door handle and went in.

Mindless of the rain, the afternoon was perfect. Sylvia couldn't stop glancing at her hand and the big rock that sat on her manicured finger. She didn't know if the diamond was glowing more than she, but one thing was for sure: Sylvia was in love with Kenny Richmond.

Dinner was perfect. The revolving restaurant at the top of the Westin Hotel downtown gave a breathtaking view of a breathtaking day. Sylvia and Kenny ate salmon while caught up in the romantic moment they didn't deny. Every moment Kenny could get, he held Sylvia's hands, gawking over the diamond that had set him back but was worth every penny.

"A toast to the most beautiful girl in the world," Kenny said.

"Do you mean it, Kenny? I have gained weight since you met me, and…"

"This is not about Adonis. It's his loss. If he couldn't stay around to love the best part of you, the brother doesn't even deserve a second chance. I love you for who you are, Sylvia. Remember that always. You are smart and have a good head on your shoulders. A little extra weight just adds more to the mix."

Sylvia grinned, then put her hands over her mouth.

"Kenny, that is the kindest thing anyone has said to me in a long time. I trust you with my heart. There was a time when I couldn't say that, but you're living proof that people can change and that God does grant second chances. To Mr. Richmond."

"To Ms. St. James."

They sipped their wine until it was gone, then prepared to leave.

"I still feel bad about Ashley."

"She probably went to her parents. There's nothing like parents when you're in need of a little love."

"Maybe. But something was bothering her. I could feel it, Kenny. I'll make it up to her tomorrow."

"I guess it's back to your house."

"I need to pick up my car."

"As much as I hate for this night to end, it might be better if I let you go home by yourself. I don't trust me. I'm still a carnal-minded brother."

"That's just an excuse. You're hoping I say come on over. Now that we are engaged…"

"Don't start nothing, girl. My temperature is rising and I can't be responsible for my actions."

"How about a kiss?"

"In front of everybody?"

"Are you ashamed of me?"

"No, baby, I will never be ashamed of you."

Kenny and Sylvia offered each other their lips. It was a soft, clean, unassuming kiss. They pulled gently away and looked into each other's eyes.

"You want to come over?"

"Yes, and we'll pick up your car tomorrow."

"Let's go."

xxx

Kenny and Sylvia rode in silence, letting Brian McKnight serenade them. The rain had stopped although the forecast was for more. Every now and then, Kenny stroked Sylvia's thigh, and she stroked his arm in return, taking the opportunity to look at her sparkling diamond every chance she got.

"We're going to be good together, Sylvia."

"I know. I was sitting here thinking about how Claudette and Tyrone found their way back to each other; and while Rachel and Marvin have a few things to iron out, they will be okay. And who would have thought that Mona would fall in love again? She just might beat us to the altar."

"They keep talking about that hurricane that might possibly hit New Orleans. I hope they aren't in harm's way."

"Me, too. Mona was so adamant about this trip. I don't know why it was so important to go now, but it's what she wanted."

"There's going to be some jealous sisters in your group. And Ms. Rachel might as well get over it."

"She'll come around."

"Sylvia, there's a car in your driveway."

"It's Ashley."

Kenny pulled beside Ashley and Sylvia rolled the window down.

"You okay, sweetie?" Sylvia asked.

"No," was Ashley's weak reply. "Do you mind if I stay with you tonight? I left William at the house, and I can't go back."

"Sure, Ash. You're always welcome."

Sylvia rolled up the window and Kenny parked the car.

"I guess that concludes our romantic evening. Good looking out, Lord," Kenny said, laughing.

"The Lord knows you're a no-good heathen—bringing me home so you can play how far can I go." Sylvia giggled.

"Sylvia, don't even go there, woman. You wanted me to push the button so you would fall into my trap and ask for forgiveness later. I know you. Remember that."

"Well, Ashley has seen to it that we aren't going to push any buttons. I was really hoping for a sloppy kiss."

"Woman, you are greedy. Look, I better get out of here because I might have to give Ashley hotel money. You're already pushing my buttons, and you haven't even touched me."

"Kenny Richmond, there are so many things I want to do to you. I might have to push the wedding date up if we're going to stay celibate."

"Oh, Lord, Lord, Lord. I do like the way you talk to me, woman. But right now, Ashley has other ideas because she's standing outside of her car, wondering what in the hell we're still doing in the car."

"Kenny, stop," Sylvia said playfully, letting her hands fall down the length of his chest. "We are not going to act like the horny human beings we are. I think you better take your cue to leave. I'll call you in the morning to remind you to pick me up to get my car.

"Today was perfect, Kenny—even with the rain. You made it so special and I feel on top of the world. I love you, and I thank you for loving me in return. A chance meeting at the supermarket turned out all right after all."

"I love you too, Sylvia. I'm going to make every day special for you. I'll be anticipating your call in the morning. Now go in and see how you can help Ashley."

"Thanks, Kenny."

Sylvia placed a light kiss on Kenny's lips and exited the car. She watched as her man drove out of the driveway, then turned and smiled at a sad, pathetic-looking Ashley.

"What's up, Ashley?"

"I need your help, Sylvia."

Jacqueline Monique Baptiste

The flight had been rather rough, but Mona and Michael arrived safely in New Orleans. Although it was early evening, the city had a balmy feel to it. They picked up the rental car and headed to the heart of the city.

It was a carnival atmosphere when they reached Michael's sister's house. Colorful streamers in salmon, red, blue, and yellow decorated the walls, and a large WELCOME HOME MICHAEL banner hung in the family room. A gathering of some fifty or more well-wishers greeted them, and Caribbean music floated through the air along with the smell of seafood and island spice.

Michael's parents had come to the United States approximately five years ago from Trinidad-Tobago, to live with their daughter. Other relatives had migrated to New Orleans years before.

"That storm is near," Michael's mother warned in her Caribbean accent. "We may have to go to higher ground. But right now, it's so good to see you, my son and Ms. Baptiste also."

"It's so good to see everybody. It's been awhile, Mommy."

"Well, all your sisters, brudders, cuzins, uncles, aunties—everybody—are here to celebrate your coming home," Mrs. Broussard said.

Everyone swirled around Mona, trying to get the four-one-one on the beautiful lady Michael had brought to New Orleans with him. Mona felt their warmth although she wasn't used to people fawning all over her, asking a thousand questions as if she were being interrogated for a crime. She was ready to be alone with Michael at the hotel and perhaps later a stroll in the city ending up in the French Quarter. It had been an awfully long time since she had been home.

Mona watched as everyone made merry. She looked at her watch. They had been in town for more than three hours and she had yet to call home. She didn't know why she was apprehensive about doing so, but the longer she took to make the call, the harder it would be.

Michael was in seventh heaven mingling, eating and dancing with his family. They were a noisy bunch, but there was so much love in the room. Mona reasoned that all families should experience the effects of being in this room. On that note, she knew it was time to call her parents.

Just as Mona turned to go outside and make her phone call, one of the partygoers touched her elbow. "Don't I know you?" the woman demanded, sipping her beer.

"No, I don't think so," Mona replied. "I've never met you."

"Your name sounds so familiar…Mona Baptiste…" The woman rolled Mona's name around on her tongue as if she could taste it.

"Well, if you'll excuse me, I need to make a phone call."

"By all means." The woman took a last look at Mona and left.

Mona trembled. There was something unsettling in the woman's voice. She'd indulge Michael's family a few more hours and then insist on leaving.

The phone rang twice before Mona heard her mother's voice at the other end.

"Hello, Mommy, this is Jacqueline. I'm in New Orleans with a friend, and I'd like to visit with you and Papa."

"Jean Claude, it's Jacqueline on the line," Mona heard her mother say. "Jacqueline, how are you doing, baby? How long has it been? We thought...we thought...it doesn't matter, it's good to hear your voice."

"Yours, too, Mommy."

"Jacqueline, this is Papa."

"Hi, Papa."

"Where are you, my girl?"

"Here in New Orleans, Papa. I want to come by tomorrow and see you and Mommy."

"Come by and have dinner. You know that big hurricane might pass this way. Thought this might be the last time you saw your mama and papa, huh?"

"No, nothing like that, Papa. I just wanted to see you. A friend has traveled to New Orleans with me, and I'd like for you all to meet—"

"Sure, Jacqueline," Mrs. Baptiste said.

"Whatever happened to your husband...what was his name?" Mr. Baptiste asked.

"Timothy," Mona replied. "And I haven't seen him in years."

"Oh. Well, your Mommy and I will expect you at three for dinner tomorrow. Good-bye."

"Yes, and good-bye, Jacqueline. I look forward to seeing you tomorrow," Mrs. Baptiste said.

"Me, too, good-bye."

Mona flipped her cell closed. That was the hardest call she had to make, but she was glad it was over. Her parents hadn't even bothered to say 'I love you.' While she had wanted to, she couldn't bring herself to say it, either.

Laughter filled Mona's ears when she went back inside the house. One of the cousins was telling a joke, and everyone seemed glued to his every word. Even Michael was caught up in the antics as he waited along with the crowd for the big climax. When it came, people stomped their feet and screamed out loud. Mona was not amused, just ready to leave.

Finally getting Michael's attention, Mona strode to him as he stretched out his arm to embrace her and introduce her to another one of his many cousins. Standing off to the side was the woman who had spoken to her earlier. She seemed to watch Mona's every movement; it made Mona uncomfortable.

Mona whispered into Michael's ear. "Who's that lady standing on the far side of the room? She keeps staring at me."

"It's your imagination, Mona."

"Michael, I tell you that lady is watching me. She even asked me if she knew me."

"Her name is Sadie, and she is the ex-wife of one of my cousins. She's been a good friend to the family all these years, and we invite her to all of our family events. She's harmless as a fly."

"If you say so."

"I say so. Now enjoy yourself. Everyone loves you."

No matter what Michael said, Mona knew differently. That woman had not let her out of her sight, but now curiosity had gotten the better of Mona. She needed to know why she fascinated this woman so. Mona picked up a can of soda, braced herself and went over to face Sadie.

"May I speak with you a moment?" Mona said to her.

"What do we have to speak about? You said you didn't know me."

"Then why are you watching me?"

"Curiosity, I guess."

"Curiosity about what? Let's go outside." If this got ugly, Mona didn't want to show her ugly side in front of Michael's family. Once they were out of earshot, Mona said, "So out with it. I don't mean to be rude, but you leave me no choice but to be blunt."

"Your name again?"

"My name? I told you it's Mona. However, my given name is Jacqueline Monique Baptiste. Satisfied?"

"I'm sorry if you feel insulted or whatever, but I just needed to know," Sadie replied.

"To know what?"

"Were you married before?"

"What does that have to do with anything?" Mona was exasperated.

"You'll know in a moment. Indulge me, Ms. Baptiste."

"Yes, I was married, but it didn't last long. I found out that he was already married."

"Was your husband's name Timothy Sosa?"

Mona's drink slipped from her hand. "Who are you?" she asked.

"I'm Timothy's first wife. I thought your voice sounded familiar even after all this time, although it was your name that caught my attention."

"Michael said that you are the ex-wife of…oh, my God…his cousin." Mona covered her face with her hands. "I remember saying to myself that Michael had a strong resemblance to someone I knew. Jesus, never in a million years would I have thought…"

"So you have not seen Timothy."

"No, not since he left me those many years ago and came back to New Orleans."

"So you don't know."

"I don't know what, Sadie?"

"Timothy is a doctor. That was always his plan—his life's goal."

"I remember," Mona said sarcastically.

"Well, he completed medical school and interned in New Orleans. But it was never his dream to stay here. He wanted to go to the big city. In fact, he's on staff at one of the big hospitals in Atlanta."

Mona's jaw dropped. She stared without saying a word. When the cat released her tongue, the question rolled out. "How long has Timothy been in Atlanta?"

"Three years." Sadie hesitated. "That's how long we've been divorced."

In some way, Mona felt the tears that streamed down Sadie's face. This was the woman she silently envied after Timothy left her. This was the woman who had been his wife and had borne his children. This was the woman Mona hated when she thought of her empty womb, her empty bed and her empty soul, when she realized she had forsaken her family to be with a man who was never really hers in the first place.

Mona took Sadie's hands. "I guess we share something in common. While I blamed you for so many things, I know it was not your fault. It was Timothy's. Let's look past that and go on, but I'd like to ask a favor of you, Sadie."

"What is it?"

"Please don't share this with anyone, especially Michael. I really like Michael. In fact, I'm in love with him. I would have never known that he was related to Timothy. I'm not sure why I'm telling you this, but I'm pregnant with Michael's baby." Mona hesitated and went on. "I was pregnant with Timothy's baby."

Sadie let out a small gasp. "He never told me."

"I miscarried. I'm sure it was a relief to him. Now I have a chance again, but if Michael knew that I was married to his cousin, I think things would change between us."

"I will not tell a soul. I'm glad I had the opportunity to meet you, Mona. I always wondered why Timothy liked you so—he talked about you often."

Mona was shocked and unable to hide her surprise.

"You are beautiful just like he said, but you have intellect, too."

Mona smiled. "Thank you, Sadie, for being in the right place at the right time. I hope our paths cross again."

"I'm sure they will," Sadie said and smiled.

"There you are," Michael said. "I've been looking all over for you. I see you and Sadie have gotten to know one another. Mona thought you were watching her, Sadie."

"I was, Michael. I was admiring her beauty. You are a lucky man."

"Indeed I am, Sadie."

Going Home

They awakened to the wind beating against the window. Mona wore a contented smile on her face, and Michael lay on his side watching Sleeping Beauty rise from her sleep. After stomachs were filled with spicy Caribbean food and the dancing subsided last evening, Michael and Mona bid farewell after a long day and went to their hotel. They made passionate love, whispering promises of love and commitment to each other.

"Would you like a cup of coffee, Ms. Baptiste?"

Mona smiled. "Yes, I'd love some."

Mona sat up and moved to the edge of the bed. Her stomach began to churn, and she jumped from the bed and ran into the bathroom, throwing up the contents of last evening's meal. She fell to the floor and placed her arms around the porcelain bowl and vomited again.

"Are you all right, Mona? One moment you were fine and the next minute you—"

Mona waved her hand to stop the battery of questions.

"I'll be fine in a moment. It must have been the spicy food."

"Let me call room service and get you some toast and a hard-boiled egg. That will help to coat your stomach."

"I don't deserve you, Michael Broussard," Mona was finally able to say.

"I don't deserve you, Mona Baptiste."

Mona got up from the floor, washed her face and brushed her teeth. She felt much better now. Today she would see her parents and she wanted to be at her best.

"What time is it, Michael?"

"It's almost noon."

"Oh, my God. We're supposed to be at my parents' house at three. We've got to hurry, Michael. I don't want to be late. This is important to me."

"Calm down, Mona. Everything is going to be all right. We'll get there on time."

xxx

The drive was silent except for the rain that had increased in strength. The rural highway was littered with travelers heading north. The Baptistes lived in a mansion on a four-acre lot surrounded by trees. Michael stole glances at Mona to make sure she was all right, stroking her arm for comfort every few minutes.

"Is this where you grew up?" Michael asked, when the mansion came into view.

"Yes. My home is quite old, but my father has people who keep it in tip-top shape."

"My family was poor," Michael reflected. "We didn't have a fancy house or car growing up. My parents were farmers, but made a decent living. I saw a magazine once that the mailman left by accident. There were pictures in it of beautiful homes like yours. Right then I knew that I wanted a better life for myself, and I set out to get it when I was old enough."

"So you've made your money by working hard."

"It's paid off."

Mona rubbed her stomach. That queasy feeling was trying to return, but somehow she had to get past it. Michael stopped the car in the circular driveway at Mona's instruction. A tall, elderly gentleman came from the side of the house and asked for the keys to the car and drove it away once Michael and Mona were safely out of the way.

They walked up the few stairs to the porch when the door suddenly opened. A large, woman stood grinning as Mona and Michael stared back.

"Come on in out of the rain, Ms. Jacqueline," the woman said.

Michael looked puzzled but didn't say a word.

"Rita, is that you?" Mona asked.

"Yes, child, it's your nanny, Rita. Let me take your wraps. I'm still here with your momma and daddy. You's a sight for sore eyes. It's been so long, Ms. Jacqueline, so long. Your momma and daddy have waited so long for this day."

"Yes, we have, Jacqueline," Ms. Baptiste said softly as she walked up the path that led to the side of the house. Happiness was written all over Mona's face.

"Hello, Mommy. This is my friend, Dr. Michael Broussard."

"Hello, Dr. Broussard."

"Good afternoon, Mrs. Baptiste. It's very nice to meet you."

"Where's Papa?"

"He'll be here in a minute." Mrs. Baptiste seemed short on words and seemed relieved when she saw Jean Claude coming down the path to join her.

Mona jumped, startled by the sudden appearance of her father. He looked old, not as vibrant as she once knew him to be.

"Hello, Papa."

"Jacqueline. It's been a long time, my love. Let me see you." He held his daughter by her shoulders and took a good look at her. "You're so beautiful."

Jean Claude Baptiste turned toward Michael and gave him the once-over.

"Papa, this is my friend, Dr. Michael Broussard. He's an orthopedic surgeon."

"Nice to meet you, Dr. Broussard. Cigar?"

Mona smiled. Her father never offered a cigar to anyone unless he liked them.

"Dinner will be served in five minutes," Rita said.

"Thank you, Rita. Jacqueline, your sisters and brothers would have been here today, but they took their families and headed north. The mayor is talking about evacuating the city because of the strength of Hurricane Katrina. They seem to be sure that it will hit New Orleans," Mrs. Baptiste said.

"I think it's going to bypass New Orleans," Papa said. "Your mother and I will be safe right here. How many of these storms have we survived? Too many to count. Folks are taking all of their belongings just to have to turn around the next day and come back home."

"So this is serious," Michael piped in. "We haven't been looking at television. I know the rain was heavy on our drive out, but it does explain all the cars on the road."

"Listen, young folks. Let's enjoy our dinner. It's so good to see my daughter after all these years of her being away."

"You knew where I was, Papa. You could have come to see me."

"Dinner is served."

Saved by the bell, Mona thought.

xxx

Mona showed Michael the bathroom so that he could wash his hands. Large black-and-white pictures of various people, whom Michael assumed were family members, graced the walls.

An old cherrywood banister led to an upper floor. The rooms were old but airy and were furnished with antique furniture. The house fascinated Michael, and if it weren't for Rita calling again for dinner, he would have enjoyed exploring a little more. Michael was struck by a photo of five young children on the wall—the youngest, a girl, was dressed in purple taffeta and wearing long braids.

"That's a picture of me with my sisters and brothers," Mona said still wiping her wet hands with a paper towel. "That was taken more than thirty years ago."

"You have a beautiful family."

"Thank you. Now we better get to the dining room before we have to stand before the firing squad."

As they walked toward the dining room, Mona and Michael stole glances at each other. Mona was happy to be home, and she gave Michael a quick kiss before entering the dining room.

The dining room table was set with the Baptistes' best silver, and silver serving trays filled with several dishes sat on the buffet. Mr. and Mrs. Baptiste sat at either end of the long dining table and Mona and Michael sat across. Rita served up platefuls of jambalaya and crayfish with pan-fried corn bread on the side. A burgundy wine was served.

"Your mother and I have missed you very much, Jacqueline. I had hoped we would have seen more of you over the years."

Mona sat down her glass of wine—she would need it to get through the night.

"Papa, I've been very busy cultivating my business. I'm a very sought-after caterer of Caribbean cuisine in Atlanta. I don't often have time for personal things."

"Surely, Jacqueline, you could have made some time to come. Your nieces and nephews are growing like weeds, and the oldest will soon graduate from high school."

"I'm sorry, Mommy. I had hoped this trip would make up for the time I've been away."

"Let's not talk about such sad things," Jean Claude interjected. "We are glad you are here now."

"Yes," said Mrs. Baptiste. "Jacqueline is just glowing. Don't you think, Jean Claude? Her face is so full like when I was carrying her in my womb."

Michael glanced at Mona, who sat expressionless and refused to look in his direction.

"Leave her alone, Rosalyn. Jacqueline always did have a contagious smile. Salute," Jean Claude said, lifting up his glass. "Oh, listen to that wind. It is really howling."

"Would you like for me to help you board up the windows?" Michael asked.

Jean Claude looked in Michael's direction as if seeing him for the first time. He took another sip of his wine before replying.

"So tell me, Dr. Broussard. Where did you get your education?"

"Sir, I went to Johns Hopkins School of Medicine."

"Good school," Mr. Baptiste said with a nod. "And I guess you're interested in my Jacqueline."

Michael proceeded slowly. He was not there to ask this man for his daughter's hand in marriage. He wasn't sure where this line of questioning was going.

"Yes, Mona...I mean, Jacqueline is very special to me. We are still getting to know each other."

"I see. So tell me, where are you from—your family, that is?"

"We are from Trinidad-Tobago."

Jean Claude's eyebrows arched.

"I'm sure Jacqueline has told you that she was married before. She ran away and got married to a man 'bout your color who was also from Trinidad-Tobago."

Mona squirmed in her seat.

"Papa, Michael is not interested in hearing about my past. That was so long ago."

Michael put his fork down. "I would be very interested in knowing all about you, Jacqueline." Michael watched as Mona's face changed, like she was trying to hide something.

"He was studying to be a doctor just like you, Dr. Broussard. He and Jacqueline met at college."

Michael watched Jean Claude. He seemed to derive some pleasure out of what seemed to be an uncomfortable moment for Mona. Michael didn't know what was going on, but it had to have something to do with Mona not seeing her parents for a long time.

"Rita, get the dessert, please," Mrs. Baptiste requested, running interference for an awkward situation.

"You might know the young man," Jean Claude continued.

"Papa, enough of this! I don't want to talk about my past," Mona said desperately.

"As you please, Jacqueline. Dr. Broussard, I'll take you up on that help to board the windows. That wind is packing a bigger punch than I expected."

"Sir, I will come over tomorrow after Mona…Jacqueline and I have had breakfast."

"Well, that's settled. There is something about you I like, Dr. Broussard, even though you are a little dark for my liking.

Jacqueline is the black sheep in our family. She's the only one that stayed in the oven too long."

"Mr. Baptiste… "

"Dr. Broussard, I don't mean any harm by it. I like you, and you already know I love my daughter. A father is a protector of his family. He monitors what comes in and what goes out. It was a little tough for Jacqueline growing up, living under my strict rules and regulations, but she turned out all right even though she's a feisty one—headstrong, always wanted to do what she wanted to do. And she did. Why don't we have that dessert now?"

Michael was feeling a little uncomfortable, but Mona's father intrigued him. He would like to get to know this man better— he might just be his father-in-law one day. In the meantime, he would get to know Mona better and maybe unearth the secrets she seemed anxious to keep hidden.

An EX-page out of History

Sunday morning, Mona and Michael woke up to anxious voices. People were milling in the hotel hallway talking about evacuation. Michael turned on the television and watched as the mayor ordered a mandatory evacuation of the city. Hurricane Katrina was on course for New Orleans.

Mona looked out the window. People were scurrying about in the rain and taxis were lined up outside the hotel. Mona's attention was averted when she heard that the airport was shut down.

"I need to check on my family as well as go to your father's house and help him board it up. I'm not sure they are as safe as he thinks," Michael said.

"Yes, you're right."

Mona had been awake most of the night, playing the scene at dinner over and over in her mind—except she watched her father unravel the pages of her life right in front of Michael—the parts she had purposely not shared with him. Mona believed that Michael wanted to know more, but right now she couldn't. She wasn't sure how Michael would react when he found out that she'd been married to his cousin and the circumstances surrounding their divorce. She didn't want to dredge that up ever again.

A Time of Healing

Most of Michael's family had packed their belongings and set off for higher ground. His sister admonished him to leave with them because she feared the worst. He still had to board up windows at Mona's parents' house, and going back to the hotel would not be an option. A long line of cars stretched from Interstate 10 to the Gulf, running away from what had been announced as a Category Five hurricane, destined to leave damage in its wake.

Mona sighed. She should have listened to her friends about postponing her trip. She'd been oblivious to the fact that a hurricane might hit New Orleans because Dr. Michael Broussard was all she thought about night and day, and she wanted to be with him when he went to see his family. Now they couldn't even fly out of the city because their safety net had been grounded, stranding natives and tourists alike.

"Let's hurry. I'm afraid that the roads will be tied up with people trying to get out. I think we should leave, too, Mona. I don't have a good feeling about this storm."

"I don't know if I can leave Mommy and Papa. I've just seen them for the first time in almost twelve years, and I can't…I just can't leave them, Michael."

"Then you must convince them to leave."

"I'll see what I can do. I'm scared, Michael. For the first time in a long time I don't feel safe."

"I'm going to be by your side and we're going to weather this thing together."

Suitcases in the car, Michael and Mona headed toward the mansion. Sunday worshippers piled out of church believing God would see them through. Dark clouds settled in the city while the wind continued to whip its tail.

"You're awfully quiet, Mona. You've barely said a word."

"Just thinking about life, wondering what I'd do if I had a chance to live mine all over again."

"I'd come back filthy rich so that I could help everyone who needed a helping hand."

"You're always thinking of someone else," Mona chided. "You can't save the world, you know."

"That's true, but I would die trying."

"I can visualize it: Black Robin Hood. He takes from the rich and gives to the kids in the hood."

"Not quite as I had envisioned it."

Mona remained quiet. She twiddled her fingers, then caught her throat. She massaged her neck, but she could not control the volcano in her stomach.

"Pull over to the side, quick," she pleaded.

Before the car stopped, Mona threw the door open, leaned over and retched until there was nothing left in her stomach. She wiped her mouth on the back of her hand and closed the door. She looked straight ahead, avoiding Michael's stare.

"Are you going to tell me what's going on?"

"Nothing, Michael, nothing at all."

"It couldn't be nothing since this is the second time in the last twenty-fours you have had an upset stomach. And don't think I didn't hear the remark your mother made about you glowing. I'm a doctor, remember."

"I'm pregnant. I'm carrying your child."

"Somehow, I already knew. I was just waiting for you to confirm it."

Mona said nothing—afraid to look at the expression on Michael's face, afraid joy would turn to disdain, afraid the man she loved would run away.

✗✗✗

The wind continued to whip and small raindrops hit the windshield. Mr. and Mrs. Baptiste were in the yard when Mona and Michael drove up.

"I was afraid you all weren't coming," Mr. Baptiste said as Mona and Michael got out of the car.

Mona almost fainted as her father came around and gave her a hug and shook Michael's hand followed by her mother.

"Lots of traffic on the road, sir," Michael responded, taking back his hand from Mr. Baptiste's firm grip.

"Papa, Mommy, why don't you come with us? Michael and I think it might be too dangerous for you to stay here. It's starting to rain again and the wind hasn't let up at all. We would feel better if you would come with us."

"You going to help me board up these windows, young man?" Mr. Baptiste asked, ignoring Mona's plea.

"Yes, sir, but I do believe Mona has a good point."

"Jacqueline has always been a scared and overprotected little girl. Jacqueline, take your mother into the house and wait for us there. It shouldn't take us too long."

Mona looked at her father in despair. But she put her arms around her mother and Mrs. Baptiste put her arm around Mona's waist. They turned and went into the house and then the kitchen.

Mrs. Baptiste put tea bags in two porcelain cups and poured hot water from the kettle that sat on the stove. Mrs. Baptiste nursed her cup and turned to Mona.

"I've looked forward to this day for a long time, Jacqueline. So much time has passed and I thought I might not see you again. I'm sorry for the way things were back then—not understanding your desire to be a cook… "

"Chef, Mommy."

"All right, chef. I wanted you to have the best like your brothers and sisters. I had such high hopes for you because you were such a good student, so full of promise. I know now that my children are individuals, and your papa and I couldn't dictate how you all live your lives. We wanted each of you to marry well so that your lives would be prosperous, but it doesn't always turn out that way.

"At first I wanted to point the finger when your marriage didn't last. Maybe it was our fault that you ran off. If we hadn't been so critical, maybe you wouldn't have made such a rash decision. If we'd kept our noses out of your business, maybe you would have taken the time to get to know Timothy better."

"Mommy, Timothy and I were not meant for each other. I should have listened to you and Papa. He was married to someone else when he married me. He was just using me to get a visa. I'm the one who should apologize.

"I've wasted a lot of years. I'm not proud of myself. I was so bent on hurting you and Papa the way you had hurt me…but all I did was hurt myself. You and Papa mean the world to me, and if I could do it all over…"

Mona began to sob. Mrs. Baptiste put her cup of tea on the table and held her daughter as Mona fell into her arms. They hugged each other for what seemed hours, although it was barely five minutes.

"I love you, Mommy."

"I love you, too, Jacqueline. So tell me about this Michael. Is he real nice? He seems very intelligent."

"I love him, Mommy. He's a doctor just like Timothy."

"You've seen Timothy?"

"No. I met someone a couple of days ago who knows him well."

"You have a new man now. Timothy is the least of your worries."

"Mommy, I have something to tell you."

"What, Jacqueline? You sound serious."

Mona took her mother's hand and laid it on her stomach. Mrs. Baptiste's eyes twinkled.

"I knew it. I knew it. Jacqueline, you are pregnant."

"Yes, Mommy. It's Michael's baby. I have another chance to be a mother—something I always wanted to be."

Her mother gasped. "You were pregnant before?"

"Yes. Timothy and I were going to have a baby. I was so happy and I thought Timothy was, too, but that's when he began to act strange, staying out late and finally not coming home at all. That's when I found out he had another wife. I don't know if it was the stress that made me miscarry our baby, but it happened so soon after. It's the only thing I can equate it to."

"You should not have had to bear that all by yourself, Jacqueline. If you had not been so stubborn…I'm sorry."

"It's okay, Mommy. You're right. If I hadn't been such a mean-spirited person, I would have had the support of my family. I suffered for it, though. But now, Mommy, I'm a totally different person. I'm so glad I'm able to talk openly about my feelings with you. You don't know how often I needed my mother's love to carry me through."

"You have me now, Jacqueline. Let's not waste time dwelling in the past."

"You're right, Mommy, but I must tell you about the person I met a few days ago. It was Timothy's ex-wife, and she said that Timothy is a doctor practicing in Atlanta. But he's also Michael's cousin."

"You know Timothy?" Michael said, startling Mona and Mrs. Baptiste as he and Mr. Baptiste walked into the room.

"Yes. Timothy Sosa. He's the guy Jacqueline ran off with and married. It didn't last long. Jacqueline's mother and I tried to tell her she was making a mistake, but she wouldn't listen—and she blames us. That's why we haven't seen Jacqueline all this time. Her mother and I were distraught, but we are happy to have her come home at last."

Mona stood there feeling the heat from Michael's wrath.

"Why don't we all have some tea," Mrs. Baptiste said.

"Doesn't Michael favor Timothy, Jacqueline? They could be brothers."

"I don't see the resemblance," Mrs. Baptiste replied.

"Same height, same color and they are both from the same place."

"Timothy Sosa is my cousin," Michael said without looking at Mona. "Mona, we're going to spend the night with your parents and head out tomorrow. If we can't get a flight back to Atlanta, we'll drive back."

Something's Wrong at this House

The newspaper carrier cursed. Three days' worth of papers were crammed in the tube.

"They should have had someone pick up their papers if they weren't going to be home," the route carrier said to no one. "If I leave this on the grass, the first thing they'll do is call the newspaper. Oh, hell with them."

The carrier put the paper on the ground just below the metal receptacle that held the others. It wasn't his fault they hadn't picked them up. He pulled his digital camera out of his pocket and took a picture. This was cause for an occasion like this. You had to protect your tail from vindictive customers because it was your word against theirs. The carrier made sure he captured the address on camera so there was no mistake if and when he had to present proof.

Hurricane Katrina

The house shook and faded to black. Mona wrapped herself around Michael as the wind's fury lashed out at the house. The howl of the wind was like an angry voice, deep and commanding, sounding the alarm that trouble was near. The rain came down in torrents, pelting the ground like an atomic bomb.

Boom, boom. Mona ran to the window.

"Get away from the window," Michael shouted. "I'm sure that was a tree. One might fall through the window."

"Let's go see about Mommy and Papa."

Mona and Michael stepped into the pitch-black hallway. Mona tried flipping the light switch, but nothing. They carefully went downstairs to check on Mona's parents; as they reached the bottom, a loud thud hit the door.

"What was that?" Mona asked.

"I'm not sure."

The loud banging at the door persisted. Michael walked to the door and peeked out.

"JESUS!!! It's water! Let's get your parents!"

Mona froze. The door blew open and water began to rush in, driven by the force of the wind.

"Michael, Michael! Mommy! Papa!"

Mona began to retreat upstairs as the water ran the length of the house. It began its ascent, rising as fast as it poured into the house, cutting off all connection to Michael and her parents. Mona was not a swimmer.

"Michael, Papa, Mommy!" Mona shouted. But no one replied.

She ran farther up the stairs as the water continued to rise, tripping once on the stairs. She rubbed her knee and continued her climb to the second floor, hoping to hear a word from someone.

The wind had not let up. Glass began to shatter and Mona could hear objects clang against each other. The family Bible floated by, along with other whatnots that used to sit proudly on the coffee table. She called once more into the darkness, but the house was silent save for the howling of the wind and the gurgling of the water that continued to rise.

Mona sat on the landing with her knees up to her chest, praying that God would see them through. *Where are Michael, Mommy, and Papa*, she wondered. Out of nowhere a dark figure emerged from the shadows, stayed afloat on the water. It was Michael.

"Michael!" Mona stood up. "Where are Mommy and Papa?"

"I tried, Mona. I tried."

"You tried what, Michael? Tell me, what did you try?"

Using the banister, Michael pulled himself to the top landing. The water seemed to settle. He looked away, unable to look into her face. Mona began to beat on Michael with her fist, demanding to know where her parents were.

"They're dead, Mona. I tried to save them. A tree fell on that side of the house, causing the roof to cave in on them." Tears formed in Michael's eyes.

"No! No, they can't be. I've just found them again!" Mona began to wail, pulling at her hair.

Michael reached out to her, but she slapped his hands away.

"Don't touch me. Why didn't you save Mommy and Papa? Why, Michael, why?"

Tears streamed down Michael's face. He stood helpless, unable to console Mona.

She stood at the edge of the second-floor landing. "I want my mommy and papa," she wailed like a child. Then her foot slipped. Mona let out a blood-curdling scream as she hurtled into the debris-filled water—debris that dated back several hundred years.

An EX Crisis

Sylvia woke to the sound of running water. Three days had passed with no sign that Ashley would be leaving any time soon. Sylvia looked at the clock on the nightstand. If she intended to get to work on time, she needed to hustle her behind out of bed.

Before her feet touched the floor, there was a faint knock at the door.

"Come in."

Ashley appeared at the door, her wet hair glued to her head.

"Sit down," Sylvia said, patting the side of her bed. "What's up?"

"I don't think I'm going to work today. I'm just not feeling up to it."

"You did the right thing, Ash. You made a brave decision and you should not feel bad about it. Now things can go back to normal. Do you want me to go to the house with you?"

"No, no, that's all right."

"What is it, Ashley? You're acting weird and jumpy."

"Nothing. I mean, William might still be at the house. I left everything, and I'm not comfortable going back yet."

Sylvia patted Ashley's shoulder. "I'm going to get up and get ready for work. Take all the time you think you need to get yourself together. I'm going to turn on the television. You don't have to move."

Ashley sat back on the bed as if she was in her own house and in her own room. Sylvia picked up the remote from the night-stand and turned the television on.

"Hundreds are missing in the worst storm to ever hit New Orleans. At dawn this morning, Hurricane Katrina ripped through the city of New Orleans, breaking levees that separated the Gulf from lower portions of New Orleans. Lake Pontchartrain spilled its bowels into the city, devouring whole neighborhoods and leaving many stranded on rooftops. The City of New Orleans sits like a punch bowl—its elevation many feet below sea level."

"My God!" Sylvia cried out. "I wonder if Mona and Michael were caught in the storm?" She held her face with her hands not believing the images that flashed on the television screen. "I'll call Rachel to see if she's heard from them."

"And she called *me* a dumb blonde," Ashley said.

Sylvia jerked her head in Ashley's direction.

"What was that for?"

"Everybody told Mona that hurricane was coming, but she went anyway."

Sylvia said nothing. If she had, she might have slapped the taste out of Ashley's mouth. It was definitely time for Ashley to pick up the pieces of her jacked-up life and go home. She dialed Rachel's number.

"Sylvia, what is it?" Rachel asked. "I'm running late again. Can I call you when I get to my car?"

"Don't hang up. Did you see the news this morning? Hurricane Katrina devastated New Orleans. The levees broke and the city is under water. People were on rooftops trying to get help—that's how high the water is."

"Jesus!" shouted Rachel.

"Katrina flooded houses," Sylvia said.

"Oh, my God. Mona and Michael are out there somewhere in that mess. Have you heard from them?"

"I called you to see if you heard anything. They said the power is down."

"I'll get back with you, Sylvia. I've got to find out."

✗✗✗

Rachel dialed and redialed. No answer. It was not like Mona to not pick up on a call. Rachel hit the steering wheel with her fist. Although she and Mona had their differences, Mona was a dear friend. There was no way Rachel would entertain the thought that something terrible had happened to her.

Just as Rachel began to dial again, a call beeped in. Claudette's frantic voice was at the end of the line.

"Girl, did you hear about Hurricane Katrina? I've been calling Mona all morning but haven't been able to get an answer. I'm afraid, Rachel."

"Don't think the worst, Claudette. Our Mona is a survivor. She's probably feeding catfish and crab cakes to the hungry."

"That would be a relief if I didn't know better. It's so sad. Those poor people stranded on their rooftops pleading for someone to come and save them. Do you truly believe Mona and Michael are all right?"

"My heart wants me to believe they are fine, but my gut says something different. I do know one thing: We've got to be strong for them and believe that they will be okay."

"Let me know if you hear anything."

"Likewise."

Rachel closed the cell phone and drove blindly through the streets. She couldn't go to work. She wouldn't be able to concentrate until she heard from Mona. Rachel picked up the phone again and called Marvin.

Hoping for the Best

Marvin sat in his underwear, contemplating whether to go into the office or work at home. He had a major presentation to give to a potential customer on Thursday, and working from home might allow him to get more done with minimal interruptions.

His mind wandered to Denise. Friday was D-day, and Denise was getting anxious as the day approached. She called every hour wanting to talk about her treatment and how she wished that she and Marvin were still together. Marvin looked at the clock and made the decision to stay home.

Marvin called his assistant and prepared to turn off his cell phone. Just before he hung up, Marvin heard the beep—an incoming call—and opened the line before he thought about what he had just done. To his surprise, Rachel was on the other line.

"Rachel, sweetheart, what a pleasant surprise so early in the morning."

"There are many more surprises where that came from."

"Well, keep them coming. Are you at work?"

"No, but I'm supposed to be. Have you seen the news this morning?"

"No, why?"

"Hurricane Katrina blew New Orleans away. Marvin, it's so devastating. Whole neighborhoods are underwater."

"What?"

"Yes, you heard me. Bodies floating, people wading through water trying to get to safety."

"Hold on a moment. I'm turning the TV on."

"Marvin, remember Mona and Michael flew to New Orleans on Friday."

"You're right. Has anyone heard from them?"

"No one. I've been frantically dialing Mona's number, but no answer."

"Hold on, sweetie, the broadcaster is saying something."

Rachel held on, driving aimlessly through downtown Atlanta.

"No power at all in the city," Marvin said, his eyes still glued to the TV. "People are making their way to the Superdome for shelter."

"I have a bad feeling about Mona. I can't shake it."

"Rachel, we've got to remain positive. Mona is somewhere trying to figure out which outfit she's going to wear to the Superdome."

"Marvin, you are crazy as a bedbug, but your thought is probably not far from the truth. I can see Mona now, strutting her dreads in some cutesy style tied with a scarf that matches her outfit. I want to believe that so bad. If she would just call us!"

"I'm sure she is looking after her family. She'll contact us after she's taken care of business."

"So what time are you going to work, Mr. Thomas?"

"I've decided to work from home today."

"Would you like a little company? I don't think I can concentrate on work today."

"You would be a distraction but a nice distraction. Come on, girl, and keep me company."

"Marvin, you know we have not…"

"We have not what, Rachel?"

"You're going to make me say it?"

"I guess so since I'm not sure what you're trying to say."

"You are a big liar. I'm sure you have often wondered what it would be like to make love to me."

"Oh, so you've been in the brother's head and knows what he's thinking. To be honest, I think about it daily—what you feel like, taste like… "

"Hold it until I get there. Don't say another word. I feel a hurricane coming on."

"There's something you should know."

Rachel's mood changed. Every time Marvin started talking in that way somehow Denise was involved. "What is it?"

"Ohh, we've got a little attitude."

"Umm," Rachel muttered.

"All I was going to say was that I'm sitting in my bed with nothing on but my briefs. In fact, I'm flexing my six-pack. Firming them up so your mouth will hit the floor when you take this all in."

Rachel dropped her cell phone. She laughed and laughed. She had to pull over to the curb to pick it up. When she put it back to her ear, all she heard was "Rachel, you all right…Rachel, you all right…Rachel, Rachel." Rachel patted her chest to keep from laughing again.

"Baby, I'll be right over. Don't move. I'm coming."

"You will be," Marvin said as he hung up the phone.

xxx

Michael jumped into the water. He only had a few precious seconds to try and save Mona. She couldn't swim.

Michael pulled himself down the stairs by holding onto the banister. The constant movement of the water made it difficult to move, but Michael was counting on finding Mona on a step fighting her way to the top. Then he was at the bottom—no Mona—and he had to come up for air.

Portraits of Mona's family floated around him, paying tribute to the life and times of those who once lived there. Treading water, Michael screamed out Mona's name.

Tears formed in his eyes. He didn't want to believe that he had come all the way to New Orleans to lose the woman he loved— a woman who also was carrying his baby.

Suddenly, he heard a faint noise from somewhere close. Michael lifted his head and strained to hear above the screams of the storm. There! He thought he heard his name. Michael swam toward the sound, toward what he thought was the front door. Finally, in the gloom, he saw Mona, clinging to a ten-foot curio cabinet, afraid to move.

The cabinet was anchored to the wall. Mona held on tight, not releasing her grip even upon seeing Michael. Michael swam to her and tried to get her to put her arms around his waist, but Mona stayed fastened to the cabinet and didn't utter another word. Michael was full of relief but knew he had to somehow get the both of them out of the house before it was too late.

Make My Day

Rachel tried calling Mona several more times and gave up. Mona would call soon; she was sure of it. Rachel threw Hurricane Katrina temporarily to the back of her mind and focused on the man she would find waiting for her. She raced through the streets not wanting to waste any more valuable time.

They had known each other for almost four months. For the first time in her life, Rachel was going to get it right. Yes, her relationship with Marvin had started out a little rocky and all of the kinks had not been ironed out, but her heart told her Marvin Thomas was hers for keeps. And if that meant seeing Denise through her illness, Rachel would be right there.

Marvin was the perfect gentleman. He treated her like a lady with class and style, was attentive to her needs and always doing thoughtful things. However, the one thing Rachel wanted eluded her. She should have been happy because it proved that she could love someone without the sex. But Rachel had fantasized about making love to Marvin every night of her waking day and how he would act when she threw it on him.

Rachel was a freak, but she was an educated, employed and intelligent freak. Behind closed doors, Rachel liked to satisfy and be satisfied. The sky was the limit. This was probably Rachel's toughest assignment, but Mr. Marvin Thomas would have the experience of a lifetime when she was through.

Rachel rang the doorbell, and the door flew open.

"Whoa," Rachel said after adjusting her eyes.

Marvin's body was polished. He looked like a WWF wrestler with that fabulous body.

"Are you going to come in?" Marvin asked.

"Uhh, uhh, yes," Rachel finally said, not taking her eyes away from Marvin but managing to give him her coat and purse. She straightened the thin belt that circled her crème crepe de chine shirtdress. "I feel overdressed."

"You won't for long. I promise you," he said, closing the door.

Rachel fell into Marvin's arms and found his lips. They kissed passionately where they stood oblivious of all else around them as if the mood would suddenly evaporate if they ceased. Five, ten minutes passed and they were still discovering each other with their lips, pausing for only seconds at a time to look into each other's face and enjoy the taste of each other's lips again.

Heat seared through their bodies. Rachel was pleased at the way Marvin touched her, felt her although not a stitch of clothing had left her body. She pawed his chest and drew lines across it in quadrants like she was sectioning off a side of beef—separating the tenderloin from the ribs in anticipation of the final meal.

Without fanfare, Marvin lifted Rachel from the floor—to her delight—and carried her up the stairs to his bedroom. He kissed and gently laid her across the bed, her dress falling and draping her like a fan.

Marvin lay next to Rachel, pressing his body close to hers. He squeezed her shoulders and pressed his lips against hers once more. Rachel wrapped her arms around Marvin's neck and held on for dear life. She felt every groove, nook and cranny, pushing her body further into his. It felt wonderful just to lie with this man, exploring the possibilities of further exploration.

The sun peeked through the blinds, shedding light on the morning interlude. Marvin brushed Rachel's hair with his hand, pulling it back to get a better look at her. Then he unbuckled the belt that circled her waist and unbuttoned the buttons on her dress.

Rachel lay back as Marvin kissed her neck down to the top of her breasts. He took his time and savored every moment, watching Rachel respond to his touch. Rachel squeezed the comforter with her fingers and let her head roll slowly from side to side. She was in the moment, and it wouldn't be much longer before she unleashed her pent-up passion.

Brrng, brrng, brrng, brrng.

"Let it ring," Marvin said between his teeth, teasing Rachel with his kisses.

Brrng, brrng, brrng, brrng. Brrng, brrng, brrng, brrng.

"Damn," Marvin said, moving away from Rachel to retrieve his cell from the nightstand. He glanced at the number. "It's Denise. She calls like this several times a day to talk about her illness. They must have told her I didn't come in today."

"She still loves you."

"Rachel, please don't start. Denise does not love me. I'll agree that she does not want to see us together, but it isn't about love. I don't think she's even been to see her daughter.

"Denise is feeling alone, needy—it's her own fault. I tried to be the best husband I could be, but it wasn't enough for her. Rachel, I wanted my marriage to work, but in a strange way, I believe God gave me an out when I wasn't looking because he knew I deserved better. And then I found you. And I don't want all this talk about Denise to ruin our future, because it looks pretty bright to me."

"Marvin Thomas, I love you. God gave me a second chance, maybe a third, but I don't want to blow it. I had already made up my mind that I would be by your side where it concerns Denise. She deserves the love the members of this group give one another. Now about my man, I'll have to fight her on that one."

Brrng, brrng, brrng, brrng. Brrng, brrng, brrng, brrng.

"Let me get this. I promise you a day you won't forget. It won't be about the sex because I will make pure love to you, Rachel."

Rachel threw Marvin a kiss, pressing her fingers to her lips and flinging them his way. She watched as Marvin took the phone call and finally the smile evaporating from his face. He looked up, then away and ended the phone call. "Denise is on her way over."

Rachel sighed.

xxx

"Denise is at the door. I'm going to have to be firm with her. She can't just show up here anytime she gets ready."

Rachel remained silent.

"Sweetheart, hand me that shirt on the chair next to you. I'm trying to be patient and do right by her, but I've just about had it. She is not going to dictate my life."

"Calm down, sweetie. You'll get through this. I'll hang out here until she's gone."

"No, you're going downstairs with me. We have nothing to hide. I'm in charge here."

"That's my baby. Got any aspirin? I'm getting one of my head-aches."

"We've got to see someone who can help you."

"Taking charge of my life? I ain't mad. In fact, I kinda like it, boo."

"I kinda like it, too. Now let's go downstairs before Denise rings the doorbell again. How about a little kiss to get me through this moment?"

"There will be a whole lot of those kisses. But here's to the moment."

They pecked and went downstairs.

"What took you so long?" Denise shouted when Marvin answered the door. "I've been standing out here waiting for almost twenty minutes." She pushed her way in, then froze when she saw Rachel.

"Hi, Denise," Rachel said.

"So this is what this is about. A booty call, Marvin?"

"Denise, you came to my house. What goes on here is my business."

"I stopped by to tell Marvin that we have not heard from Mona or Michael," Rachel explained.

"What about Mona?"

"She's in New Orleans, and if you've listened to the news you know that—"

"Hurricane Katrina. Oh, my God."

"Has Sylvia heard anything?" Marvin asked.

"No, and everyone is worried. We don't have her parents' number so we can't call them, either."

"Remember, the power is down and I believe one of the newscasters said something about no phone service, either."

Denise sat down. "I don't believe this."

"Neither do we," Rachel said. "I wish there was something I could do. I feel so helpless."

"Why don't you call Sylvia again?" Marvin said. "Maybe she's heard something."

"I'm sure she would have called with the news, but I'll call her anyway."

Rachel dialed Sylvia's number while Denise and Marvin looked on. For the first time, Rachel saw compassion written in Denise's face. *So she is capable of caring.*

"Sylvia, this is Rachel. Any word?"

"No, girl. I'm a nervous wreck. I ended up not going to work."

"You and me both. I drove around downtown for God knows how long this morning. Then I finally called Marvin to see if he had heard anything. I knew I was grasping for straws, but I had hoped someone had heard from her."

"Look, why don't you and Marvin come on over? We can continue this vigil together."

"Come over to your house? Well, Denise is here at Marvin's and she may not feel like coming to your house."

"I'm part of the group. I'm in," Denise said, then began saying a prayer for Mona.

"It looks like we'll be over. We'll see you in a few. Don't forget to call Claudette and Tyrone. Do you want us to bring anything?"

"Just your faith. I'll order pizza."

Rachel ended her call. She had faith, but it seemed as if Denise had more faith than she did. Denise was pouring her heart out to God, and all Rachel could do was listen. Rachel stood behind Denise and placed her hand on her shoulder. Marvin followed suit.

"Lord, please protect Mona and everyone else who's been affected by Katrina," Denise prayed. "Keep her safe from hurt, harm and danger, we pray. Amen."

Rachel began to weep.

Marvin sped through the streets of Atlanta anxious to join the other members of Ex-Files to await word from Mona. Light music floated through the Escalade while Mona and Denise stared at the scenery that flew by, no one willing to make small talk to pass the time. The days were getting shorter, but there was still plenty of good light left on this September day. There was no hint that the remnants of a devastating hurricane had come and gone in Atlanta save for the broken limbs and leaves that were scattered across rain-soaked lawns.

Several cars were parked in Sylvia's driveway when Marvin turned the corner and pulled up in front of Sylvia's house.

"Ashley and Claudette are here," Rachel announced. "I don't recognize the other car."

"That's Anika's car," Denise said in a low voice. "She's a sweet girl, and she deserves better than the jerk she had for a husband."

"She told me her story when were at the spa," Rachel said not wanting to be outdone by Denise. "Her parents spent a lot of money on her wedding and it didn't even last two years."

Denise was silent again. She didn't stir until Marvin came around and opened the door to the truck. She hesitated and frowned when Marvin held out his hand for her, but turned her frown into a smile when Marvin smiled back. Rachel watched from the sidewalk, but ignored Denise's attempts to seduce Marvin. For the very first time, Rachel was confident in the fact that no matter how many times Denise threw herself at Marvin, he was in love with her and only her.

The threesome walked together. Sylvia hugged each one as they entered the door, taking coats and scarves. They found the rest of the group lounging in the family room in front of the television, holding their post while waiting for word about Mona and Michael.

"Hey, everybody," Marvin said, followed by Rachel and Denise.

Hugs went around the room, some holding on longer for their sister Mona.

"I've got pizza," Sylvia said. "And if you all plan to camp out here all night, dinner will be on you."

"Dinner will be on me," Marvin said, not giving it another thought.

Marvin and Rachel sat in the love seat, while Denise reluctantly sat in the recliner that Tyrone gave up for her. Denise glanced at Marvin and Rachel and turned away. She kept her eyes glued to the television.

"How are you feeling, Denise?" Claudette asked.

With surprise in her eyes, Denise said, "I feel pretty good. I can't wait for the surgery to be over."

Everyone's attention was on Denise.

"You are brave," Claudette said.

"It's not about being brave, Claudette; it's about survival. I don't want to die; I want to see my daughter grow up." Denise swallowed while fighting back tears. "I don't want to die."

Everyone gathered around.

"We are going to be with you during your surgery," Sylvia said.

"And we are going to be there to help you when you come home," Rachel interjected.

"Whatever you need, we will be there for you," Marvin said. "We mean it, Denise."

"I'll be there to give you massages and make you beautiful," Anika added. "Not that you aren't already beautiful."

Ashley remained silent and looked on.

"We're family," Tyrone said, wanting to put his five cents in.

"Thank you all. I really do appreciate your support. I've never had friends like you all." Denise looked at Marvin. "Thank you, Marvin, for what you have already done. I owe a lot to you. I would not have made it this far without you."

She looked at Rachel and back to Marvin.

"Marvin, you are extremely lucky to have Rachel. She's given me a run for my money."

Rachel frowned.

"Don't worry, Rachel. It's clear to me now that the two of you belong together."

"Okay." Rachel still didn't trust Denise and wasn't planning on letting her guard down anytime soon.

Dinnng, donnng, dinnng, donnng. The group jumped at the sound of the doorbell. Sylvia went to the door with a smile on her face.

"Hello, everyone," Kenny said upon entering the room.

"Hey, Kenny," everyone said in return.

"I'm Denise Thomas," Denise said, as she stood and extended her hand for the handsome gentleman to shake.

"It's nice to meet you."

"Kenny, this is Anika," Sylvia pointed out. "She keeps our faces in tip-top shape."

It was then that Rachel noticed it. Long, extended fingers found their way around Kenny's neck as Sylvia stopped to give her man a hello kiss. Sylvia seemed to be flaunting her ring as the noon-day sun captured its essence. It was probably Rachel's imagination, but the rock that sat on Sylvia's finger was not.

Rachel grabbed Sylvia's hand as she passed by the couch.

"So when did this happen?"

"When did what happen?" Sylvia smirked.

"I mean, this rock on your hand must weigh a ton," Rachel said, her eyes passing back and forth between Sylvia and Kenny.

"We were engaged on Friday," Kenny stated.

Denise was immediately disappointed.

Rachel was shocked, and it registered on her face. She looked at Marvin, who stared straight ahead.

"Well, damn," Claudette said. "Somebody say congratulations! You know Mona, uhh…"

"Mona what, Claudette?" Rachel inquired. "Is Mona engaged, too, and you just 'forgot' to tell us about it?"

"Rachel, what is wrong with you?" Marvin asked. "We should be happy for Sylvia and Kenny."

"Kenny, I don't know what it is about you," Tyrone said, "but the drama always begins when you show up."

"What can I say?" Kenny said, giving Tyrone a brotherly hand-shake.

And Denise began to laugh. She laughed and laughed and laughed. She couldn't stop. "Oh…Rachel, you should see your face." And she laughed some more.

Ashley remained silent. No one seemed to pay her any attention.

"Folks, we are gathered here this afternoon to await word about our friend Mona and her boyfriend, fiancé, whatever he is," Sylvia said. "Kenny and I are going to be married. We love each other very much and we hope that you will join us in celebrating that love. If you don't like it, oh well. This is my life, and I'm going to live it with Kenny Richmond—maybe have his baby, if I'm not too old. Bottom line is we are more than just an item. We love each other and we'll let you know when the wedding date has been set."

Rachel bit her bottom lip. "I'm sorry, Sylvia."

"No need to be. Kenny and I know what we've got. Come here, baby."

Kenny came and stood next to Sylvia, an arm around her waist. She kissed Kenny long and hard in front of everyone. This was out of character for Sylvia.

"Forget it," Rachel said. "You're right, Mona is our number-one concern."

Denise began to cackle uncontrollably, and the others just stared at Rachel.

"Congratulations," Anika said. "I wish you a long and happy life together."

"Thanks, Anika." Sylvia hugged her. "Thanks, again."

"Congratulations to the happy couple!" Claudette hollered. "Now give me my hug."

Everyone clapped and passed out hugs. Ashley left the room and Rachel stood in the corner sulking. Rachel watched as Kenny stopped in front of her.

"I know that you and Sylvia are close, Rachel, but I'm a different man now. The person I was when Sylvia and I were together back then is long gone. You don't have to like me, but I'm going to be with Sylvia for the rest of my life—when we're sitting on the front porch watching the young folks, when we're old and wrinkled, when Medicaid has said they will no longer service us because we've lived too long. I love her, Rachel, and I hope in time you'll be able to accept that. Besides, you've got a good man yourself, so don't hate on Sylvia."

Rachel's face softened and turned into a smile. "Thanks, Kenny. I needed that slap in the face. I love Sylvia, too, and I want her to be happy. If she says she's happy with you, I'm happy for her."

"That's all I need to hear, Rachel. Time will bear me out."

"It better." Rachel and Kenny hugged, and Sylvia's smile radiated across the room.

Concerned

"Has anyone tried calling Mona again?" Marvin asked.

"Just three times in the last half hour," Rachel replied.

Dusk had settled over Atlanta, and there was still no word about Mona. Denise was asleep on the recliner. Claudette, Tyrone and Anika were glued to the television. Sylvia and Kenny sat in the kitchen away from the others, sharing moments of love and tenderness. Ashley lay across the bed in Sylvia's guest room with her eyes wide open.

"Look!" Claudette shouted. "Look, look, look! There's Mona and Michael!"

Sylvia and Kenny flew from the kitchen into the family room. Denise wiped her eyes as she sat up to see what Claudette was making all that noise about. Ashley got up and came to the doorway.

"That is Mona!" Rachel exclaimed. "They're stranded on top of the house."

"Somebody help them," Rachel cried out. "Somebody help them. Can't you people see them on the rooftop?"

"Calm down, Rachel," Claudette said, rubbing Rachel's back. "I'm sure if the cameraman is shooting this picture, the rescuers are not far behind. Thank you, God, for this blessing."

"Yes, thank you, God, for this blessing," Denise repeated, now standing in front of the television. "If you can do this for Mona, surely you can make a miracle happen for me."

Marvin went to Denise. "God will be right with you, along with the rest of us. You're going to be all right." He hugged her.

"Can you believe all that water?" Kenny said. "As much as I like the ocean, this is unbelievable. How can a whole city be swallowed up like that?"

"You see who has been affected the most," Sylvia said. "The poor black folks that didn't have a way to get out of the city. They're saying the whole Ninth Ward is underwater. It's so devastating that so many didn't get out of the city."

"What a shame," Tyrone said.

"Look!" Claudette exclaimed. "Rescuers in a lifeboat are helping Mona and Michael off the roof. Jesus, You are so good. Mona looks fatigued."

"And looks like she had on one of her nice sundresses," Rachel chimed in. "Should have known that Mona wasn't going to look shabby when it was time for the spotlight."

"I hope she didn't lose the baby," Claudette said without thinking.

"*Baby*?" Sylvia shouted. "What baby?"

"What's the use of hiding it now?" Claudette said. "Just before Mona left, she told me she was pregnant with Michael's baby."

"Damn," Rachel said. "Everybody has good news to share except for me."

"Rachel," Denise began, "you get on my nerves. You have a good man standing by your side—a good man who loves you. If I could have a second chance with Marvin, I would stop at nothing to give him what he deserves. But I won't get that chance because he's in love with you. Don't take that love for granted. It must be nurtured. There must be trust and understanding, and first of all you must be friends.

"Sister, you need to hang up that constant whining before you wind up with nothing at all. I told you that once before, but I guess you thought I didn't know what I was talking about. Believe me, I know what I'm talking about. It's time for you to be happy for someone else, and when your turn comes they will celebrate with you. When that happens, don't mind me if I sit that one out. Now can we get some love for Mona and Michael?"

"That was beautiful, Denise. Your level head was what we were missing with this group. Sylvia's got a level head, but two level heads ain't bad. We're going to be celebrating your miracle soon."

"Thanks, Claudette. I feel…" Denise began to cry. "I feel like God has already worked a miracle. Being in y'alls company today has been an eye-opening experience. It's okay to be angry as long as you replace it with love. I'm happy for Mona."

"We all are," Sylvia said.

Everyone watched as Mona and Michael were rescued. They were placed in a boat and paddled away.

"I wonder if Mona's and Michael's families are okay. They didn't show anyone else," Marvin said.

"Shhh," said Claudette. "Let's hear what the broadcaster is saying."

"Another courageous rescue marred with tragedy. Mona Baptiste and Michael Broussard were just rescued from the top of Ms. Baptiste's parents' home. Ms. Baptiste has sustained some injuries and will eventually be taken to a hospital in Houston.

"Ms. Baptiste's parents, who were also in the house, did not survive the ordeal. Rescuers found the bodies of Jean Claude and

Rosalyn Baptiste in a first-floor bedroom. It appears a tree fell on the house, causing the roof to cave in on them."

"Oh my, God," Rachel said. "Mona's got to be devastated. She's been through so much."

"She can stay with me when she returns," Claudette said. "No ifs, ands or buts about it. Since I work at home, I am better suited to do this."

"That's if she wants to stay with you, Claudette. She may want to stay with her fiancé," Rachel said.

"Whatever, but if she doesn't go with Michael, she's staying at my house."

"You got it, Claudette," Sylvia said. "Nobody's going to mess with your thunder."

"Where's Ashley?" Claudette asked, suddenly remembering that Ashley was in the house.

"Over here," Ashley said from the doorway.

"Come in here with us. You should be celebrating your freedom—unless you really want to be with William. And the way he treated me the other day at your house, I sure hope you don't want to be with him. I certainly have something to say about that."

"It's not that I miss William, Claudette; I just feel so lonely."

"You have us, Ashley," Marvin interjected. "We have been with you from day one. Divorce can be a traumatic experience for some, but you're over that, and you have made your decision final as to your being with William."

"Come on in and sit with us. Group hugs are in order."

Ashley left her perch at the door and walked into the room. She allowed the love of her fellow members to envelop her. Marvin was right about one thing. The decision about William was final, but that decision was weighing heavily on her heart. So much so, she couldn't join in on the celebration for Mona, Sylvia or even herself. Her celebration was about to come to an end.

"Dinner is on me," Marvin shouted, happy about Mona and Michael's rescue. "It's going to be Chinese takeout or Kentucky Fried Chicken."

"Chinese," was the unanimous vote.

"Write down what you want, somebody call it in, and I'll be more than happy to pick it up and pay for it."

"All right, now," Kenny said to Marvin. "Brother, I would be more than happy to help you with the cost."

"Think nothing of it, Kenny, my man. Don't worry, there will be plenty more times for you to foot the bill." Marvin and Kenny laughed.

Dinnng, donnng, dinnng, donnng.

"Who is it now?" Sylvia asked. "Don't forget to put down spring rolls," she hollered.

Sylvia opened the door. Two white men in suits, one tall and the other short, stood at the door.

"You must want my neighbors next door," Sylvia said, pointing to her right.

"Does a Sylvia St. James live at this residence?"

Sylvia pulled back with a distressed look on her face. "I'm Sylvia St. James."

"Are you familiar with Ashley Jordan-Lewis?"

"Who are you, and may I see some credentials?"

The men took out their badges and flipped them so Sylvia could see.

"We're homicide detectives with the Atlanta PD."

Sylvia frowned again. "Atlanta PD? What does the police department want with Ashley?"

"Have you seen Mrs. Jordan-Lewis?" the short detective asked.

"Yes, she's here."

"We need to speak to her," the other detective said.

"What's wrong, Sylvia?" Kenny asked as he approached the door. "Everyone's wondering what's taking you so long."

"These gentlemen want to see Ashley. They're detectives," she whispered to Kenny.

"Ashley," Sylvia said upon returning to the family room, "there are some gentleman in the foyer who would like to see you."

"Gentlemen? Like who?"

Sylvia whispered in Ashley's ear, "Detectives."

Ashley froze, and all attention centered on her.

"What is it, Ashley?" Sylvia inquired.

"I tried to talk to you all weekend, Sylvia. Your mind was elsewhere."

"Look, don't try and put the blame on me for whatever is going on with you. I can't read minds, Ashley, and I certainly wasn't going to beat it out of you. I care for you, but you have to help me to help you."

"It's too late now."

"What's too late?" Marvin cut in.

"Never mind. I better go talk to the men at the front door."

Sylvia watched Ashley. "Where is William? Where is William, Ashley?"

The others watched as Ashley walked away and went to the door where Kenny still stood talking with the men.

The detectives looked puzzled as Ashley approached them.

"Ashley Jordan-Lewis?" the tall detective asked.

"Yes."

"I'm Detective Wallace, and this here is Detective Kelley. We need to ask you some questions about your husband, William

Lewis. Is there some place private that I can talk with Ms. Lewis?"

"You can go in my library," Sylvia said as she walked up on the group. She extended her hand and pointed in the direction.

"What is this all about?" Kenny asked Sylvia, more confused than ever as Ashley was led away.

"I don't know, but it has to do with William. She is not going to ruin our perfect weekend because she did something she wasn't supposed to."

"You're making assumptions, Sylvia."

"Kenny, the homicide detectives are giving me the assumptions, and I don't have a good feeling about it."

"We'll stand here just in case Ashley needs us."

"Kenny, I hope that what I'm thinking is not true. I think William is dead."

✗✗✗

The group gathered in the foyer and stood with Sylvia and Kenny. Speculations about Ashley's visitors and their interest in her conjured up questions the group wanted answers to.

An hour had passed since the news of Mona's rescue, but now the group was faced with a new dilemma. Before one fire could be put out, another one cropped up. It seemed their being together was for some other purpose than being a support group for those whose lives needed mending after divorce. The Ex-Files had become a catch-all for whatever their sordid lives faced.

Silence enveloped the room. The door to the library opened, and the detectives appeared with Ashley in the middle and her arms pulled back. Hands went over mouths as they watched the detectives escort Ashley outside.

No one moved but they glanced at one another without saying

a word. The tall detective came back inside and faced the group.

"Mrs. Jordan-Lewis has been arrested for the murder of her husband, William Lewis. That's all I can say to you now. I will need to interview each of you so I ask that you don't go anywhere. We can make this as painless as possible if you cooperate."

"May I speak with Ashley?" Sylvia asked.

"Sure, why not?"

Sylvia followed the detective to the unmarked car. Ashley would not look up, even when Sylvia called her name.

"Ashley, whatever you need, we'll be there for you. Whatever you need."

Ashley kept her head down and didn't utter a word. Tears rolled down Sylvia's face. Maybe if she hadn't been so absorbed with Kenny asking her to marry him, she could have been there for Ashley. Sylvia looked at Ashley again and went inside the house.

The detective was writing down the names of everyone in the room. Suddenly the idea of Chinese food wasn't so appealing, Sylvia thought. Everyone sat around like they were the accused. In fact, she felt like she was on pins and needles. *Did Ashley kill William? How?*

Sylvia St. James

Sylvia was drained. She couldn't think straight. She couldn't sleep. She had harbored a murderer. The papers sensationalized the story because of how William died. Arsenic?

The detectives questioned the group for five hours. The answers were the same. Everyone was together for lunch on Friday, and Ashley showed up. Ashley was supposed to get married, but decided she wasn't going to do it.

Claudette told the detectives about William throwing her in the car and kicking her off the premises. He was nuts but didn't deserve to be killed. Everyone agreed that Ashley was advised to leave William, but not once did anyone say she should kill him. Ashley had the best lawyers money could buy, and if anyone could get her off, Ashley's dad had the power and influence in Atlanta to make it happen.

Sylvia let her thoughts move to Denise. Her surgery was in the morning. Sylvia couldn't imagine having a breast removed or having cancer for that matter. She would pray extra long this evening for Denise's miracle.

Brrng, brrng, brrng.

"Sylvia speaking."

"Hey, this is Rachel. Do you want me to pick you up after work to go to the hospital?"

"Sure, why not."

"Bad day?"

"Bad week."

"You've got that right. I still can't get over Ashley killing William. Can you believe she poisoned him with arsenic in his oatmeal? I never would have believed she had it in her."

"You're innocent until proven guilty."

"She's guilty, and she didn't even try to hide it."

"If we had only known what she was going to do so we could have talked her out of it."

"She would have been married to the bully."

"Yeah, but she wouldn't be sitting in jail because she killed the bully, Rachel."

"I know. Maybe her father's money will get her off."

"It'll help, but I don't know how much. Pick me up. I'll be outside in ten minutes."

"How does that hefty rock feel on your finger?"

"Rachel, I don't want to get into any discussion with you about me and Kenny."

"I mean well, Sylvia. I've come to peace with my issues with Kenny. He seems changed. It's about time to let that twenty-year-old grudge go."

"It's time. As for my finger, it feels so good because everything is so right. I look at this ring every day. It makes me smile because of the love Kenny and I have for each other. I think back to that chance meeting in the grocery store that changed my whole life. Adonis who?"

Rachel laughed. "You're crazy, girl, but I love you. Maybe one day Marvin will ask me to marry him."

"Rachel, it's not a race to the finish, but how you run the race.

Marvin is still learning and discovering you. When the time comes, and it will come, you better be ready."

"But look at you and Kenny. You've only been in each other's lives for three short months as well."

"Kenny and I have a long history, although we've created some new history. Let's stop talking about this, please."

"Okay. I just want to be happy."

"Hey…will you be one of my bridesmaids? I'm going to ask Maya to be my matron of honor—after I tell her I'm getting married."

"You haven't told your daughter yet? What are you waiting on? She's going to give you plenty of lip."

"I'm going to plan a nice little dinner party and invite Maya and Carlos. Kenny will be there, of course, and I'll tell them then. I believe Maya expects it anyway."

"Well, I'll be there in ten minutes."

Return from the Brink

The hospital was fairly quiet. Sylvia and Rachel anxiously went to see Mona. She had been flown to Houston, but Mona had insisted that she be moved to Atlanta. Her records were there, and she knew she would get the best care.

A host of people was in the room when the pair arrived. Michael was in deep conversation with Tyrone. The room was filled with flowers and cards. Claudette stood off to the side so that the other well-wishers could kiss and love up on Mona. She was fortunate to be alive.

"Sylvia, Rachel," Mona called, her voice scratchy. "I want you to meet my sisters and brothers and their families."

Sylvia and Rachel shook each person's hand as Mona rattled off their names.

"Sylvia and Rachel have helped me so much," Mona told her family. "We're part of a support group for divorced people. They helped me to get back my self-esteem."

Sylvia patted Mona's arm. "Girl, we were praying for you and Michael. We didn't take our eyes from the television until we saw you rescued from atop of that house."

Mona squeezed Sylvia's hand. "My mommy and papa died. Michael and I tried to get them to leave but they wouldn't. Mommy and I had the best talk. We got everything off our chests and were starting over. Papa really liked Michael. Michael helped him to board the house up. I can't believe they are gone. I just can't believe it."

"We are so sorry for your loss," Rachel said to everyone. "Your family is in our prayers."

"When they are able to get back into the city, my sisters and brothers will be going back to New Orleans to bury my parents. I can't go back there, not now. I'm glad I went because it might have been too late if I had waited. I know everyone thought I was crazy, especially Ashley, since I knew Hurricane Katrina might come that way. By the way, how is Ashley?"

Sylvia and Rachel looked at each other.

"They arrested her a few days ago."

Mona tried to sit up. "Arrested Ashley? For what?"

"She poisoned her husband. Killed him," Rachel said.

"Shut up! She must have just done it before meeting us for lunch. She was acting strange. Oh, my God."

"Surprised us all," Sylvia said. "Everyone was at my house watching the news to see if there was word about any more survivors when the detectives arrived. She was a scared chickadee."

"I can't go away for a minute without some drama."

"Well, Denise is going into surgery tomorrow. We'll all be here with her."

"I might as well tell you both now. I'm going to have a baby."

"Congratulations," Rachel said, trying to hide the fact she already knew.

"Congratulations," Sylvia sang. "I'm excited for you."

"This is my chance to be a mother again. Thank God for my miracle. Michael wasn't excited at first, but I think he's adjusted to the idea."

Michael walked over to Mona's bedside and gave her a kiss. He thanked Sylvia and Rachel for coming. "I'm going to take your family back to your house now," he said to Mona.

"See you, Jacqueline," everyone said.

"Bye, everybody. I'll see you tomorrow."

They waved and were gone.

"I'll be back in a minute," Tyrone said to Claudette. "I'm going to get some air." He followed the others out of the room.

"What's up, Claudette?" Mona asked. "You look like you've been carrying some baggage. Smell her fingers to see if she's been smoking again."

"Yuck," Rachel and Sylvia said in unison.

"I was just thinking about all this little group has been through in the past three months. But if I didn't have you all, my world would be different. I got my husband back, and Tyrone has been so helpful and loving. He's helping with the kids, and he's making sure that my new shop is put together right. I'm blessed."

"Speaking of blessings, I'm engaged, Mona. Kenny asked me to marry him last Friday. It was so beautiful how he asked me. The main thing is, I'm truly happy."

"That's wonderful, Sylvia, and I'm happy for you. I'd jump up and down if the doctor hadn't ordered me to rest. And what about you, Rachel? Marvin pop the question yet?"

"No, but he will. I know he will. I'm sure he will."

Everyone laughed.

"Marvin loves me, and I love him. We have a lot of getting to know each other yet, but we'll get there. We've got to see Denise through her recovery until she's back on her feet. This one thing I can say, Mona, is that I trust Marvin. He loved Denise, but he loves me now. I'll be with him in whatever way he needs me for Denise because while she may try to hit on Marvin, he's all mine."

"Dang, girl, you've grown since I saw you last. I thought you were going to beat Denise's tail at that meeting. I know I would have and—wouldn't have thought nothing of it. But you handled yourself with dignity because you would have been looking bad when Denise pulled that wig off her head."

"Yes, Mona, I have grown. We all have grown. A new man and a baby on the way. Blessings."

"Excuse me, ladies," the nurse said as she breezed into the room. "The doctor will be here in a few minutes to examine Ms. Baptiste. You can stand outside."

"I'll be back tomorrow," Claudette said.

"We all will," Sylvia chimed in. "We are so glad to have you back with us. We love you. Get some rest."

"I love you all, too."

✗✗✗

Mona dozed off as soon as Sylvia let go of the doorknob. The attending nurse walked in followed by the doctor, surprised that her patient was already fast asleep. She lightly shook Mona not wanting to startle her, but it was time to make sure she and baby were all right after such a traumatic ordeal.

The doctor moved close to the bed and held Mona's wrist, checking for a pulse. He put down Mona's hand and stared at her for several minutes before shaking her again.

She began to stir and moaned lightly. Seconds later she brushed her forehead with her hand. Sensing someone at her bedside, she willed her eyes open.

Shock then recognition registered on Mona's face. She might have been dreaming, but the dark handsome face spoke to her before she had time to blink.

"Hello, Mona."

Mona didn't speak—couldn't speak. She kept staring at the face of her ex-husband, Timothy.

"I'm here to check and make sure you and your baby are all right. I'm going to listen to the baby's heartbeat."

"Where's my doctor?" Mona demanded.

"Your internist will be along shortly. Since I'm ob-gyn, I will be monitoring the baby while you're here."

Timothy took his stethoscope and leaned over to listen to the baby's heartbeat.

"Don't," Mona said, raising her hand for effect.

"I must check the baby's heartbeat. You've been through a traumatic experience."

"I didn't get a chance to carry our baby to term—"

"Nurse Brewer, would you give us some privacy, please? The patient is my ex-wife."

Nurse Brewer looked at Mona and then at the doctor, and walked out of the room.

"Timothy, I saw Sadie right before Katrina hit New Orleans. She seemed to be very sad. She told me you were in Atlanta, but I never expected that I would see you so soon after that discovery. You've been here for three years."

"Mona, you and I were a long time ago."

"But I loved you, Timothy. I left my family for you. They didn't want me to be with you, but I went anyway, against my parents' wishes. I didn't have a relationship for almost all those years I've been gone, and the moment that I go home to make amends, a lousy hurricane takes them away from me."

"Surely you can't blame your relationship with your parents on me. You were the one who made the decision."

"Still a pompous ass. If I had listened to my parents, I would not be hurting so much inside. I'm glad our baby died because I would not have wanted it to know what kind of lousy person you are."

"I can recommend another doctor for you," Timothy said, sighing in exasperation.

"Did you ever love me, Timothy? Look at me. Did you love me? Or were you merely entrapping an innocent young lady who could help you become an American citizen? You don't have to answer the question. I already know the answer."

Timothy sighed, again. Suddenly, Timothy reached for his pager that vibrated in his coat pocket. "I'll be right down," he said in the pager. "I must go to the nurses' station," he said to Mona.

"Saved by the bell. I don't need you or your services ever again."

Timothy turned to leave the room. Before he opened the door, someone else walked in. Timothy couldn't believe his eyes.

"Hello, cousin."

"Michael? What brings you here? We can talk outside. I'm finished with this patient."

"Do you know who this patient is?"

"Yes, her name is Mona Baptiste."

"It's Jacqueline Monique Baptiste."

"So you know Mona. I'm sure she's tried to trip you into her net."

"Trip me? No, cousin Timothy. I pursued her like a hunter. She was hard to catch and just as hard to tame." Michael winked at Mona, who was not amused.

"Well, I wish you well. You have a handful."

"I sacrificed my family for you and I lost my baby because of you. Don't go and get high and mighty. Everyone knows all about you. Michael knows how you cheated on Sadie with me. Michael knows you used me to try and get your green card. Michael knows that you threw Sadie away after she sacrificed for you to go to medical school. And when you had turned all of that into success, you dropped her like a bad dream. I don't care if an 'MD' is after your name, I don't want you to ever touch me again," Mona shouted.

"You heard the lady…cousin," Michael said.

"I'll get Ms. Baptiste another doctor." And Timothy left the room.

"Mona, don't cry. Everything is going to be all right. We survived Katrina," Michael soothed.

"But Mommy and Papa didn't. I can't forgive myself for not making them leave the house."

"They made their choice, Mona. They would have stayed no matter what. Good news. Everyone in my family is accounted for although they lost everything. I'll have to help them for awhile, which may mean bringing some of them to Atlanta."

Mona said nothing. She was going to miss her parents more than she knew.

"I need to go to their funeral, Michael. I need to say my proper good-bye."

"You did, Mona, the last night we were with them. You are not able to travel right now, and your siblings aren't sure when they'll be able to get back to New Orleans since the city officials aren't letting anyone come into the city. I'm sure your mother and father are satisfied that they got to see their little girl before they left this earth."

"Think so?"

"I know so. Now get some rest. Everything is going to be fine, and I'm not going to ever leave you."

"Those were the words I needed to hear."

It's All in the Family

"What time is it?" Rachel asked Marvin. "They've been in there for three hours."

"They should be about through. They'll take her down to recovery first."

"I'm going to see Mona since it will be a while before we get to see Denise," Claudette said. "You coming, Sylvia?"

"Yeah, I think I will. How about you, Rachel?"

"I'll stay with Marvin."

"Baby, you can go with the ladies, if you want. It looks like it might be a few hours."

"No, I'm going to stay with you, Marvin. I promised you and Denise that I would. I want her to know that I was here when she wakes up."

"Rachel, Rachel, Rachel. What am I going to do with you?"

"You don't want me to answer that."

"Too much information," Tyrone said. "You and Marvin work that out somewhere else."

Rachel laughed. She didn't know Tyrone well, but she could tell that Claudette was the one who'd messed up that marriage. Yes, there are two sides to every story, but it was as plain as looking through a glass window that Claudette was lucky to reclaim her Prince Charming. He was a good man.

The waiting room was small. The chairs were not cushioned to accommodate a long stay, but after five hours, Marvin and Rachel dozed off. Tyrone worked on a crossword puzzle.

Forty-five minutes passed. Marvin sat up and yawned, stretching his arms outward. He got up to stretch his legs when a middle-aged man walked into the room, carrying a baby no more than eight or nine months old. A pretty woman with a slight limp followed him.

The man gave the baby to the woman, and he stepped forward.

"Hey, Marvin. How are things going?"

"We haven't heard anything yet, but we're praying for the best. Harold, this is Rachel Washington, my fiancée, and Tyrone Beasley."

Everybody shook hands, but Rachel looked hard at Marvin who didn't give her the satisfaction of looking at her. Rachel smiled. In fact, she grinned.

"Harold is my cousin."

No one said anything.

"Uhh, this is Ms. Re Re Bridges. We're very good friends, and she's holding Danica, Denise's…and my little girl."

Marvin reached out for the baby. The woman pushed her into Marvin's arms. Danica looked just like Harold, but pretty, like Denise. Marvin kissed her cheeks and made baby sounds with her. Danica blew bubbles and patted Marvin on the face.

"She's beautiful," Marvin said.

"Yes, she's a handful. I never realized what a responsibility it was having kids. Diapers, milk, daycare."

"The price we pay for having little ones." Marvin passed Danica back to the woman.

"So you're engaged?" Harold asked.

"Yes, Rachel and I will be getting married next year. She's the love of my life."

Rachel smiled. In fact, she wanted to run down the hall and scream in delight. She didn't have a ring, but Marvin was making public announcements about their engagement. Rachel saw that Tyrone looked just as surprised as she was.

They all stood as the doctor made his way into the waiting room.

"Mrs. Thomas did fine. She's in recovery now, but you may go back and see her for a moment, Mr. Thomas."

"Thank you, Dr. Sosa."

"She is very drowsy and probably won't know you're in the room. It'll take some time for the anesthesia to wear off."

The others sat as Marvin went in to see Denise. Sylvia and Claudette returned just as Dr. Sosa was leaving.

"Who was that hunk, Rachel?" Sylvia asked.

"That's Dr. Sosa, Denise's doctor. She's in recovery now, and Marvin went to check on her. This is Marvin's cousin, Harold, his friend Re Re and little Danica—Denise's little girl."

"Ohh," Sylvia said, remembering Marvin's story. "Nice to meet you."

The room was quiet until Marvin returned an hour later.

"They've moved Denise to her room. We can go up to the room now. The doctor advised us not to stay long. It's been a long day for her. Ready?"

XXX

The small party of seven and a half walked like they were going to the guillotine with shackles on their ankles, two by two, shuffling along silently. No one knew what to expect.

They reached Denise's room and Marvin turned to the group as if he were in charge.

"Rachel and I are going in to see if she's up to visitors. We'll be right out."

Rachel held Marvin's hand tight as they went into the room. Denise was resting, but her eyes opened just as they walked in. She managed a smile and then looked toward the area where the surgery was performed and tried to lift her hand to point.

"Hey," Marvin said. "How are you feeling?"

"Like cancer has been lifted from me." An answer only Denise would come up with.

"Hey, Rachel," Denise said, looking around the room to see if there were any other visitors. "You said you would be here, and you are. Thank you. It means so much to me. I thought the others were going to be here."

"Marvin and I just wanted to make sure you were up to having company. The others are outside waiting to come in."

"Let them come in. I'm ready. I'm going to be honest with you two. I wasn't sure that I was going to survive this. Reading is powerful but sometimes scary because you come in to so much information. The doctor told me that everything went well, and I should have a full recovery. For that I'm eternally grateful. Marvin, Rachel, thank you. Now let my well-wishers come in."

Rachel kissed Denise and stroked her arm. "I'm so glad you're going to be all right."

Both Marvin and Denise watched Rachel in amazement as she went to let the others in.

"There's a surprise outside. If it's too much let me know."

"What is it, Marvin?"

The door opened and in walked Sylvia, Claudette, Tyrone, Harold, his friend and Danica. Denise locked in on her precious Danica. She reached out her arms.

"Danica, my sweet Danica."

Harold brought Danica to Denise but sat her on the edge of the bed. Danica drooled on her bib and made cooing sounds.

"She's teething," Denise said to Harold not looking in his face.

"Yes, and she's crawling, too…"

Denise was not able to move her body, but she kept staring at her baby, her precious baby. She took her hand and traced the contours of Danica's face.

"I love you, Danica. Mommy is going to get well, and she'll be able to see you take your first steps. You are so pretty."

Marvin moved away. Denise watched Marvin as she talked baby talk with Danica. How could she have messed up the best thing she ever had? And now it was too late. He loved Rachel, and Rachel loved him. There was no use fighting it. She smiled at Danica and thanked God for this gift.

"Sylvia, Claudette, Tyrone—it's so good to see you."

"We said we would be here for you, Denise," Sylvia said, "and we meant every word."

"If you want, I'll be more than happy to do your hair," Claudette offered.

"Claudette, I would love that. Would you? I feel so special. By the way, what's going on with Ashley?"

"She has been arraigned for William's murder," Claudette said. "You know her father has put together some of the most high-powered lawyers in the country to argue her case. Her family never did like William."

"I felt so bad for Ashley that night at your house, Sylvia. We were worrying about Mona, and me having my operation, but no one really asked about Ashley."

"I feel like I let her down," Sylvia admitted. "She came to the house because she needed a friend, but she found a selfish woman instead because it was all about me and Kenny."

"That's that fine brother," Denise said.

Everyone laughed.

"You can't feel that way, Sylvia," Rachel said. "You were in your moment. Kenny had just proposed to you, and you were celebrating love at its finest. Now what do you have to say for Ex-Files? It has brought love as well as drama into all of our lives, and I don't know what I'd do without my newfound sisters and brothers."

"I second that," Denise said. "Although I had an ulterior motive coming to the group, I found some genuine and loving people, and I apologize for the ass I was. I was not in my right mind."

Rachel looked at Marvin and they laughed together.

"Oh, Mona is doing fine, Denise," Sylvia said. "She's on the floor above you. She'll be in the hospital for another couple of days. She had a few broken bones, and she's pregnant."

"Mona, pregnant? This I've got to see."

Harold and his girlfriend had stood in the background, but now took command of the conversation.

"Denise, this is Re Re Bridges."

"Hi," Denise said coolly.

"She's been helping me take care of Danica."

Denise's eyes shifted between the two of them. "Don't get any ideas, Harold. I will be taking Danica back as soon as I get on my feet."

"Since I haven't heard from you in awhile, I thought you had given Danica to me," Harold retorted. "She's a sweetheart, and I've fallen so in love with her."

"Harold, don't even go there…don't even think about getting custody of Danica."

"You dumped her on my doorstep with six Pampers and two bottles of milk! What kind of mother just drops off their child without another word? Until something happens to them and suddenly they want another chance."

"Harold," Marvin stepped in, "this is not the time. Denise has just gotten out of surgery and she needs time to recover."

"But I want to talk about it," Denise said. "If he thinks he's going to take my child away from me, he better get prepared because I'll declare war on him. He's giving me back my baby."

"Danica is my baby also."

"We're going outside and give you all some privacy," Sylvia said.

"No, don't go," Denise begged. "I need your support. This can't be happening to me." The tears welled up in her eyes.

"Everyone out," Marvin said. "Denise needs her rest. You can come and see her later."

"We'll be in Mona's room," Rachel whispered, and left with the others.

"Don't take my baby, Harold. You'll be sorry. I may be down now, but I'm on my way back. Don't mess with me."

"Calm down, Denise," Marvin said.

Harold took Danica and left the room.

"Don't take my baby. Please don't take my baby from me!" Denise cried.

Before Marvin could leave the room, Dr. Sosa entered.

"What's wrong, Mrs. Thomas? You seem stressed."

"They are trying to—"

"Doc," Marvin began, "we've had a small family crisis is all. We're leaving for now."

"Marvin, don't let Harold take Danica from me," Denise cried.

"I won't, Denise."

xxx

Marvin looked at Harold holding Danica in his arms. He seemed so natural, like he had done this many times before. The last person Marvin wanted to see was his cousin, but he had to face him, if not for himself but for Denise.

"Man, I know this is not a good time," Harold began. "I didn't come here to start no mess. I heard that Denise was having the surgery today, and I wanted her to see her daughter. That's all."

"Harold, as much as I don't like you, I understand your dilemma. I just ask that you not keep Danica away from her mother."

"Marvin, you don't know what the last five months have been like for me. I didn't know anything about caring for a baby."

"You did everything to get one."

"I've apologized over and over for what went down with me and Denise. It's over. I've learned."

"Would it have been over…would it have been over if I hadn't caught you?"

"Eventually. Let's get back to Danica. I've fed, cleaned and clothed this little girl. I've watched her grow. She knows that I'm her daddy because she sees me every day when I come home from work. I play with her. I give her baths. Not once since I've had her did Denise call to check on her."

"You knew she would be back for her," Marvin protested.

Harold laughed bitterly. "Did I? She forced that baby on me, and now I'm glad she did. Danica is my sweetheart. I love her, Marvin. Denise wants a fight? Well, she can just bring it on. What's going to happen the next time she gets a whim? Who will she drop Danica off with next? There's a pattern with that woman. You should know."

"Don't go there, Harold. I'm just tolerating this conversation. Oh, my sisters tell me that you've got your own business in

Birmingham, and you're doing well. Every now and then I wonder where would we have been if you had just kept your pants zipped."

"Marvin, I made a stupid mistake, for which I've apologized over and over. I wanted to do some good by bringing Danica here. I wonder how long it would've taken Denise to contact me after everything was all right with her?"

Harold reached in his pocket and took out a card.

"Here's my business card if you need to reach me. Tell Denise she can call me at any time to discuss Danica's future. I'm leaving Atlanta and don't plan to come this way again soon. It was nice seeing you again, cousin. I just hope that one day we can become friends again."

Marvin watched until Harold, Re Re and Danica were out of sight. Something inside of him hurt so bad. He and Harold were like brothers once. They were so close. No one thought they could ever be separated.

The door to Denise's room opened, startling him.

"Mrs. Thomas is resting now. It would be best if you all left now," Dr. Sosa said.

"Thanks, Doc. I'm going to just peek in on her and be on my way. Everyone else has gone up to Mona's room—she's another friend of ours that's in the hospital."

"Oh," Dr. Sosa said. "Don't be long."

Marvin went to Denise, who was asleep. "I won't let Harold take Danica away from you. I promise," he whispered.

Girls' Conversation

"Mona, Marvin's cousin that slept with Denise showed up at the hospital," Claudette said, wanting to tell the tale before the others got a chance. "Had a little girlfriend with him and guess who else?"

"Tell me," Mona cried. "I'm stuck in this bed and missing all the action."

"That ain't the half," Rachel threw in.

"Marvin's cousin brought the little girl he and Denise had together. She's a doll-baby."

"Since Claudette is taking so long to tell the story," Sylvia interjected, "let me finish up. There was a scene. After Harold let Denise see the baby, he told her in a nice way that he was going to get custody of the little girl. It was a pitiful sight—Denise begging for him not to take her baby."

"It wasn't that bad," Rachel said.

"You don't even like Denise. I can't believe you're taking up for her," Sylvia said.

"Sylvia, please. I agree Denise has issues, but I feel her pain as a mother."

"But sweetie, she left the baby with Harold and didn't bother to check on her in all these months."

"Okay, Sylvia. I'll give you that, but it was the cancer."

"I'm with Sylvia, Rachel. Whose side are you on? Denise barely likes you. She likes Marvin better. Remember that? Have you forgotten?"

"Claudette, who are you talking to? You just barely got your own husband back. It wasn't as if you were the model mother."

"Okay, I've heard enough," Claudette said, steam coming from her nostrils. "If that's the way you feel, screw you."

"I'm sorry, Claudette. Why are we at each other's throats? We were kicked out of one hospital room. We've got to at least stay here until Marvin gets here."

"You hens are crazy. You should see yourselves—acting just like sisters." Mona began to laugh and couldn't stop. "They need to hurry up and release me from this hospital. I don't want to catch whatever you wenches have."

Mona, Sylvia, Claudette and Rachel stopped and looked at one another and started laughing. They laughed until Marvin and Tyrone showed up in the room.

"What are you all laughing at?" Marvin asked.

"You don't want to know," Mona said. "I will say this: All of you will need a room if you don't relieve some of the stress you guys have choking you. I don't need any more.

"Thank you Lord for giving me a chance to see my parents before they left this earth." And Mona kissed the sky.

"Let's plan that ski trip we've been talking about," Rachel said. "That's something I've always wanted to do."

"You better get your invitations picked out. I don't know what possessed me to agree to a double wedding."

"Who would have thought that Kenny would have joined forces with Marvin? We are going to become the Fortune 500 wives."

"Four short months ago, you didn't even like Kenny."

"I was wrong, Sylvia. Your man is da bomb. He and Marvin have so much in common. It's almost frightening."

"I know. We're just lucky like that. I remember when you and I were talking sometime ago, and I wondered if I was doing the right thing by organizing this group because it seemed to be helping everyone but me. You can't rush time."

"Amen. Speaking of time, Ashley's trial is coming up."

"I know. Kenny and I plan to go and see her this weekend. Claudette and Tyrone went up last weekend. Ashley wasn't doing too well—the confinement and all. She told Claudette that she killed William because she knew that would be the only way she could be free of him. If only I could have been there for her. It's probably taking me so long to visit because I feel so guilty."

"Don't beat yourself up about it, Sylvia. You gave Ashley a safe haven for a few days, and if she wanted you to know, she would have told you then. We'll all be there for her at the trial, although it doesn't look good for Ashley. Did you know that Claudette agreed to raise her baby? I think there's some controversy with Ashley's parents because William was black."

"They better give up some money so that Claudette can take care of it."

"I think that's being arranged."

"I've got a gown fitting next week on the twenty-eighth—my birthday. It's also my and Adonis' wedding anniversary. Ms. Maya reminded me of it."

"She's always going to love her daddy, Sylvia."

"You're right, but I'm glad that she's cool with Kenny as her stepdad. After all, if things had of gone right, he might have been her daddy."

Rachel laughed.

"I saw Denise the other day. She's coming to the meeting tonight. She's getting a lot stronger. Marvin still takes her to her doctor's appointments."

"You better watch that wench. She's not sick now, and she may use that as an opportunity to move in on him."

"*I'm* walking down the aisle," Rachel reminded her.

"I say watch your behind. It happens all the time," Sylvia shot back.

"Marvin says she's consumed with getting full custody of Danica."

"She's hooking Marvin in her mess."

"Sylvia, I trust Marvin. Isn't that what you told me to do?"

"Yes, but I didn't tell you to be a fool. No woman should let another woman be with her man all the time like that; I don't care how much you trust them. You need to go to some of those appointments with him—let Ms. Denise know that you care and are standing by your man in his decision to help her."

"Okay. I read you loud and clear. I must make sure the man I'm planning to marry has eyes only for me. You make a lot of sense, Sylvia."

"Of course I do. Now let's clean up our mess. I'm looking forward to going to Michael's house. This meeting is also going to be their official engagement party. They are going to wait until after the baby is born to get married."

"May is only four months away."

"And then there's June."

"You and me—June brides."

"I'm happy, Rachel."

"So am I."

✗✗✗

Michael's two-story brick house sat on a hill and boasted a swimming pool, a movie theater and a tennis court. Sylvia and Kenny *oohhed* and *ahhed* as Michael led them through the 5,500-square-foot home; it was elegantly decorated but yet simple.

Rachel, Marvin, Claudette, Tyrone, Anika and Denise were in the great room sipping Chardonnay when Sylvia and Kenny arrived. Mona was running around making sure that the meal was perfect.

"Hey everyone," Sylvia and Kenny said in unison.

"Sylvia," Mona said as she walked into the room from the huge kitchen on the other side of the house, "the meeting is all yours. Of course, Michael and I have a special announcement at the end."

Everyone smiled.

"Wow," Sylvia began. "Look at us. We have been together for

almost eight months, and look at how far we have come. Some of us have cleaned out our Ex-Files and moving on. Others are on their way to bigger and better things. I know that I would not be where I am or feel the way I do if it wasn't for your love. Rachel and I are getting excited about our pending weddings."

Sylvia saw Denise fidget in her seat.

"We've been blessed with the most wonderful men in our lives. I recall when we first met as a group; I said something like 'I vow to never look back.' From this day forward, I am moving straight ahead. I don't care if my Ex marched in here right now, declaring his love for me, and told me he wanted me back. I don't care if he was crawling on all fours, I would never go back. I don't know if I really believed that then, but today, at this very moment, I can truthfully say that my ex is just that—my ex. I will be the lovely Mrs. Kenny Richmond soon, and I can't wait.

"Before everyone gets a turn to say what's on their mind, Rachel and I—actually, it's Rachel's idea—think that we should plan a ski trip. We've talked about it before, I think it's a great idea. We need a fun outing. How about it?"

"I can do the ski thing," Marvin said. "Put me down."

"Claudette and I may watch y'all at the bottom of the slopes, but we're down, too," Tyrone said.

"I'll try and get the time off," Anika said. "Put me down."

"Mona and I might be sitting with Tyrone and Claudette. Mona won't be able to ski because she'll be so close to her due date," Michael interjected.

Mona rushed in from the kitchen. "Baby, you can ski. Claudette will keep me company. Don't even think about counting us out."

"You may not be able to fly, Mona," Michael cautioned. "After all, you'll be too close to your due date."

"We'll just wait and see how I feel," Mona said, pouting.

"Okay. Denise, what about you?" Sylvia asked.

"You guys go ahead. I need my strength for fighting. When you all get back from that ski trip, I'll have babysitting schedules made out for you."

The room was quiet.

"The only thing on my mind," Denise continued, "is getting Danica. I can't get her skiing down a slope. I've talked with my family in New York, and they're working on getting the best attorneys to represent me. Whether you all believe me or not, I want Danica's father to have a place in her life; if he plays fair, that will happen. If not, I'm bringing all my guns, and he will not win. I love my baby no matter what you heard in that room, and no one, *nobody* is taking her away from me."

The mood in the room changed. The gaiety fizzled, and the excitement of going skiing was put on the back burner.

"Hey, guys. Lighten up. I'm not mad. I'm just not going on the ski trip—at least this one. I hope that won't be the only one you plan."

"Okay," Mona said. "Michael, I think this is the moment."

"You're right, Mona. Friends, we have gathered here today…"

"Come on, Michael," Mona prodded.

Michael put his arms around Mona. "This is a special day. I have asked Ms. Jacqueline Monique Baptiste to be my wife."

"Yeah!!!" Claudette shouted.

"Shhhh," Mona chided.

"This woman is very special to me. I remember the day I first set eyes on her. She was catering an event for some good friends of mine. She had the grace and style of a goddess.

"The woman I've come to know is more than that. She is passionate, she has dreams, she's intelligent and she knows how to throw a great meal together. Mona has been through a lot, but it has only made her stronger. Her will to live when Katrina had announced death makes this day that much more special."

Tears were falling from every eye. Sylvia passed a tissue box around the room, taking a good supply for herself.

"Although Mona has already said she would marry me, we wanted to recapture the moment before our special friends." Michael dropped to his knees and kissed Mona's hand.

"Will you marry me, Jacqueline Monique Baptiste?"

Mona began to cry and couldn't turn it off. Sylvia, Rachel and Claudette went to her and held her.

"It didn't go like this, guys," Michael said, "when I originally asked her."

Giggles went around the room.

"Michael," Mona began. "You've made me the happiest woman. There's no one I'd rather be with than you. I'd be honored to be your wife—to love and to cherish, till death do us part."

"Sounds like a yes to me," Marvin said. "To Mona and Michael."

"To Mona and Michael!" everyone shouted.

"A toast is in order," Kenny said. "Everyone get your glass."

The Chardonnay flowed until every glass was full again.

Kenny began, "I remember meeting Michael at the same function he met Mona. Although the meeting was casual, I knew that this man stood for something. I also saw the way he looked at Mona. It might have been lust, because she was looking good, but I could tell he was observing the whole person.

"While Mona and I were not the best of friends, I knew that she's a hard worker and a go-getter. Mona stops at nothing to get what she wants and doesn't take no for an answer. Now I see her as a sister and a dear friend, and I'm happy that my sister has found true happiness in her life.

"I pray that the two of you will have a long and prosperous life together and that you grow in knowledge and love each other to death. May your child be blessed with the best parents I know you will be. To Mona and Michael."

"To Mona and Michael!" everyone shouted again.

"Kenny, thank you for that wonderful toast," Mona said. "You brought tears to my eyes. If anything, you've taught me something. God can change anyone, and it is not for us to judge. I love you. I love you, too, Sylvia."

"Thanks, man," Michael said to Kenny. "You're a good man."

Tissues were passed around one more time.

"This is the most boo-hooingest group I've ever met. Can we ever go a minute without crying?" Marvin asked.

Everyone laughed.

"I have another announcement," Mona said. "Our baby is going to be a girl, and Michael and I are going to name her Katrina. I know you're wondering why in the world would I name my baby Katrina, but Katrina brings thoughts of my parents. Just before the storm hit, my parents and I had come to peace with many things, so that time will always resonate with me. Katrina not only took life, it brought life. So don't look so gloomy."

"I think that's beautiful, Mona," Denise said. "Maybe Danica and Katrina will be able to play together someday."

"That sounds great, Denise. We'll have to arrange it once Katrina is born and on her feet. Now let's get this party started, unless somebody else has some sharing to do!!"

"I'm with, Mona," Michael said. "DJ Marty Marvin"—everyone laughed—"spin those records."

"And the buffet is ready," Mona shouted.

Old-school music floated through the house. Rachel and Marvin were the first on the floor, while Sylvia, Kenny, Claudette, Tyrone and Anika headed for the food. Denise got up and danced by herself. She was feeling the groove.

"Was that the doorbell?" Mona asked. "Baby, see if someone is at the door. I don't know who it could be."

"Okay, baby," Michael called out. "I'm on my way."

Michael opened the door. A tall, thin caramel-colored gentleman stood on the porch.

"May I help you?"

"Is this the meeting of the Ex-Files? I was given this address and was told you accept men in your group."

"Well, come on in, brother. You've missed the main part of the meeting, but some good eating is going on now. Come on in. Let me take your coat. We'll just follow the noise. I'm Michael Broussard."

"Nice to meet you, Michael. My name is Adonis St. James."

No He Didn't

The music was jamming. The food was slamming. Everyone was having a good time. No one looked up when the tall gentleman first walked into the room.

"Excuse me, everyone," Michael interrupted. "We have a potential new member."

The music was still going and a few hellos went around the room, but the looks on Sylvia's and Rachel's faces said something was wrong. Sylvia dropped her plate on the floor and fell right behind it.

"What's going on?" Kenny asked, trying to help Sylvia from the floor.

"Kenny, this is Sylvia's ex-husband," Rachel explained. "How did you get here, Adonis?"

"My daughter Maya was gracious enough to give me the address. Her mother left the directions at her house."

"This is getting interesting." Denise chuckled. "This group never ceases to amaze me."

"Hey, Mona."

"Hey, Adonis. We're having an engagement party. You met my fiancé, Michael."

"Well, I heard that this was a support group for ex-husbands and ex-wives. Sounds like something I want to join. My daughter tells me it has done wonders for her mother. Maybe she can tell me herself when she gets up from the floor."

Sylvia began to stir and sat up. She blinked to make sure she was seeing correctly. Kenny lifted her up from the floor and held her close.

"I'm Kenny—Sylvia's fiancé."

"Aren't you the old no-good boyfriend—treated my girl terribly, if my memory serves me right."

"That's in the past."

"They tell me a tiger doesn't change its stripes."

Kenny said nothing. It wasn't worth it.

"So…Sylvia, what's going on girl?"

"Adonis, this is a private party. We were having a celebration before you walked through the door."

"I heard this was a support group meeting. Maya told me all about it, told me how it has helped you. Hmmph. If hanging with old dude has helped you out, you're in bigger trouble than I thought."

"Mr. St. James, I don't want to have to ask you to leave, but I will if you insult any more of my guests," Michael said.

"I didn't mean no disrespect, man."

"He's drunk," Rachel said. "I think he needs to be escorted out."

"Rachel, Ms. Rachel. I'm trying to be nice here. There's no need to bash the brother. Which husband are you on now? Five, six, seven?

"Look, I won't stay long. I'll say what I have to say and move on. I came to get my wife back. I'm home, Sylvia. Home to stay. I love you, girl; I always have. I didn't mean all those things I said to you."

Sylvia let go of Kenny's arm and moved in front of Adonis. "Turn the music off, Marvin. I want Adonis to hear this."

"Let me get a good seat first," Denise said.

"Adonis, I'm engaged and will marry Kenny Richmond in a few months. Your time has come and gone. There is nothing left of our marriage. I don't love you anymore. Words are powerful, my friend, and I will never forget what you said to me before you walked out the door. Whether you meant it or not, you said them and now our life is done.

"So good-bye, Adonis. Go back to your stank ho, your prehistoric fossil. The two of you deserve each other, and I wish you all the best. As I said earlier, this is a private party, and you are not welcome. Michael, show him to the door and let's resume this party."

Adonis looked around. "No need. I'm gone." He stopped, saluted Sylvia, and left quietly without another word.

"Party over here," Claudette sang. "Party over there. Do that thang. Do that thang."

Kenny embraced Sylvia. "That was so brave of you. I was praying to God that you wouldn't leave me again."

"You had nothing to worry about, Kenny Richmond. I love you from the bottom of my heart. I can't wait for us to be man and wife. It just wasn't our time years ago, but now that it is, let's not waste it talking about the past. Kiss me."

Sylvia and Kenny stood in the middle of Mona's engagement party and kissed the night away. Rachel and Marvin, Claudette and Tyrone, Mona and Michael had found their own special spot, singing love songs to each other.

No They Didn't

It was quiet in the room. Sylvia pulled her lips from Kenny. Anika was gone and Denise was getting her coat. The other lovebirds were still nesting.

"You got your ex's number?" Denise asked Sylvia. "God, girl, he's fine. I don't know how you messed that up."

"I don't have his number, but you're welcome to him—that is, if you like sloppy thirds. Ain't even worth it," Sylvia said.

"Well, hold it down. I'm calling it a night. Too much love in the room for me. Good night."

"Good night," Sylvia said. Kenny nodded. They watched as Denise walked down the hallway and out of sight.

"Why don't we leave these good folks and head over to your place?" Kenny asked, placing a kiss on Sylvia's lips.

"Wise decision," Sylvia said. "I'm feeling awfully…wanting you…"

"Girl, why don't you just say horny?" Kenny held Sylvia's shoulders and let his hands glide down her arms. "I feel the same way."

"We could get lost in Michael's big ole house." Sylvia chuckled at her thought. "And at the next meeting we could say…we conceived Kenny III in the West Wing of the Broussard Estate."

"That's not a bad idea." Kenny laughed.

"You can't be serious, Kenny."

Kenny stood up and took Sylvia's hand and pulled her up from the loveseat. "Let's explore. There are so many rooms in this house, no one would ever find us."

"I don't know, Kenny. This isn't my style, but I do feel a little sneaky."

"Relax, we're not going to do anything. Steal a few kisses here and there. I feel romance in the air."

"Like you know what romance is when you see it."

"Follow me, girl."

Sylvia and Kenny tiptoed through the family room. Michael and Mona were sitting out on the enclosed deck snuggled under each other. Rachel and Marvin had found their way to the Jacuzzi. A long spiral staircase led upstairs, and they took them and disappeared from view.

There were three large bedrooms, a weight room and a movie theater complete with a popcorn machine. Sylvia and Kenny gawked at it all.

They avoided the three bedrooms that seemed to beckon them and found themselves in the weight room. Sylvia straddled the Bowflex machine and pretended to pull down the weighted rings. Kenny sat in front of her, taking the rings from her hands, straightening the five-carat diamond ring on her finger and threading his fingers with hers. Their upper bodies touched, and Kenny found Sylvia's waiting mouth and kissed her hungrily. They untangled their fingers and made a full circle with their arms, wrapped around each other like the rings around Saturn.

Sylvia's body fell back on the upright board—Kenny's body following as their kisses became intense. Kenny reached up and unbuttoned her white cotton blouse, her breasts now exposed and pushing beyond the border of her white lacy bra. Beads of sweat began to form on Sylvia's chest, but he found it intoxicating and began mapping his way with his tongue. Tasting the mounds of her swollen breasts, Kenny successfully navigated his way beyond the covering that held her ripe nipples. He sampled and played until Sylvia let out an uncontested moan of pleasure.

Kenny moved on top of her, still pelting her with kisses. She felt his hardness through the thin material of her skirt and moved her lower body just enough to let him know that she was pleased.

Sylvia tore away the shirt from Kenny's body, his sweat dripping in torrents. She kissed his mouth, his neck, letting her tongue trail the length of his upper body until she circled the dark portion of his nipples, while she held his hands captive. Kenny groaned with pleasure as Sylvia continued her assault, and with one swift motion he loosened his hands from her grip and eased her breasts from the bra and sucked them.

Sylvia's free hands ran up and down his back, squeezing his shoulder muscles time and again. And then he took his hands and drew the sides of her free-fall skirt up to her waist, examining her bent legs with his hands. He charged up her leg again and moved past her thighs until he touched the rim of her bikini panties. Kenny hesitated, then looked around the room as if it suddenly dawned on him that they may not be alone or that he was not in the comfort of his own home.

"I want you, Sylvia. I want you bad, but not here."

"I'm disappointed, Kenny, because you've messed with my groove once again. I was so ready to have all of you and repent for it later. You do these crazy things to my body that got me not thinking straight. Whoa, boy, I don't know if I can wait."

"Sylvia, why are you pretending?"

"Pretending?"

"Girl, don't play those theatrics with me. I'm glad you didn't share with the Ex-Files, especially Rachel, about what happened the night Ashley was arrested. Scared they wouldn't look at you quite the same?"

"What they don't know won't hurt them. Why are you doing all this talking anyway, Kenny? We could have successfully executed our covert operation without any suspicion."

"Sylvia, you are a freak. As bad as I wanted it, not in Michael's house."

"Just testing you. I wouldn't dare make love to you in someone else's home."

"Sylvia, you almost did."

"We might have to move the wedding up," she whispered, ignoring Kenny's last statement.

"What are you talking about, Sylvia?"

"Rachel will be disappointed."

"Talk to me, Sylvia."

"I believe I'm pregnant."

Kenny lifted his body and sat upright on the weight bench. "Do you know for sure? Did you take a pregnancy test?"

"Will it change things between us?"

"Of…course not, baby," Kenny said hesitantly.

"No, I haven't taken a pregnancy test, but my body has given me all the signs—a missed period that was as regular as the mailman and my very tender breasts. Are you disappointed?" Sylvia asked again.

Kenny held her face in his hands. "Baby, I love you. And if you're carrying our baby, I'm happy about that, too. I just want you to be happy, for us to be happy with no misgivings about what we've done and where we're going."

"No misgivings, baby. I'm more in love with you, Kenny Richmond, than I've ever been. I can't begin to tell you how happy I am. I haven't had a nightmare since the night you came to my rescue. I feel like I've betrayed God, though. All that talk about waiting until I was married, and in a moment of weakness I jumped at the carrot dangling in front of me."

"It wasn't a carrot."

"No, it wasn't." They laughed.

"My life is with you and my Lord, Kenny, and I will love and cherish you both until the day I die."

"And, Sylvia, I will cherish you and our Lord until the day I die."

"I love you, Kenny. Now that our hearts and minds are clear, who's going to tell Rachel?"

ABOUT THE AUTHOR

Suzetta Perkins is the author of *Ex-Terminator: Life After Marriage*, *A Love So Deep*, and her riveting debut novel, *Behind the Veil*. She is also a contributing author of *My Soul to His Spirit*, an anthology that was featured in the June 2005 issue of *Ebony* magazine. Suzetta is the co-founder and president of the Sistahs Book Club in Fayetteville, North Carolina and is Secretary of the University at Fayetteville State University, her alma mater. Visit www.suzettaperkins.com and www.myspace.com/authorsue or email to nubianqe2@aol.com

EX-Terminator:

Life After Marriage

■ When a marriage breaks up, it can be a very emotional time. This may be the time to get advice from a professional counselor or join a support group. A support group may get together and share information and experiences, solve problems, and share resources. Sylvia needed a support group and started one she dubbed the Ex-Files, gathering a few of her friends who were in the same predicament. Did Ex-Files accomplish its mission?

■ Who do you think in the Ex-Files gained the most by joining the group?

■ Who do you think it helped the least?

■ What reason did Sylvia give for her husband leaving her?

■ Why do you believe Mona never went home to see her family? Why do you think she picked the time she did to finally visit them?

■ Rachel Washington seemed to look for love in all the wrong places. How many times was she divorced? Do you think she deserved a second chance with Marvin?

- Marvin was a good man—some would say "too good." On several occasions, Marvin's ex-wife, Denise, shows up and finds her way into Marvin's heart. Were Rachel's actions justified?

- What was the real reason Denise came back to Atlanta?

- What event brought Claudette and her husband, Tyrone, back together?

- Do you feel the group let Ashley down? What could they have done differently? Was Ashley the cause of her own fate?

- A chance meeting found Sylvia face-to-face with an old flame—one whom she fell in love with all over again. Would you have given Kenny a second chance? Did Sylvia give him a second chance because she was on the rebound or for a totally different reason?

- The old cliché about the "grass is not always greener on the other side" rang true again as Adonis St. James comes to reclaim Sylvia at the eleventh hour after leaving and divorcing her to be with a previous ex-wife. Should she have left Kenny to reclaim her life with her baby's daddy or do exactly what she did?

Excerpt from

A Love So Deep

by Suzetta Perkins

Available from Strebor Books

PROLOGUE

It was early fall, and weeping willows bowed to sun-baked lawns while giant redwoods spanked the skies, casting a lazy-like setting about the Bay Area. Maple trees were adorned with leaves of gold and reddish brown while squirrels scampered up twisted branches in preparation of the winter months that lay ahead. It was an enchanting feeling—a movie set backdrop. The summer was coming to an end, but its remnants were still very evident.

It was five in the morning when Charlie Ford, Dexter Brown, Bobby Fuller, with Graham Peters bringing up the rear, strode onto the Berkeley Pier, carrying tackle boxes, bait, chairs, and insulated coffee mugs filled with steaming coffee. The sun was not due to come up for another hour. The calm and peacefulness the water yielded was just right for the few fish that might nibble on their hooks.

Not much talk passed between the four men. This was to be a short trip—a two-hour excursion to help lift the spirits of a friend. Then it would be back to Bobby's house for his wife's hot, homemade biscuits with honey oozing from their sides along with a plate of soft-scrambled eggs, a couple pounds of bacon, and fresh brewed coffee to wash it all down. If they were fortunate to catch a few fish in the process, that would be all right, too.

Their poles were extended, lines laying in wait, birds chirping signaling the day to begin. An hour passed, and the sun rose like a yellow monster ready to devour the city. Its reflection illuminated the water a little at a time as it rose over the Oakland and Berkeley Hills to sneak a peek at the four men.

"Something's biting," Charlie yelled, reeling in a three-pound halibut. "Hey now, I got me a fish for dinner."

"Who you gonna get to clean and cook it for you?" Dexter chimed in. "See, I've got me a woman that'll clean my fish, fry it up in a great big pan, and serve it on a platter with homemade potato salad, collard greens, and hush puppies."

"But you don't have no fish for your woman to fry," Charlie countered, letting out a great big howl and slapping Bobby with a high five.

"I wouldn't eat the fish from the bay anyway. Heard there might be mercury in the water," Dexter said. "These puny little bass and halibut out in this water is just for sport—test your skills."

"Amanda!" Graham shouted, jumping into the water, causing the other men to gasp out loud in alarm. Graham gasped for air, his arms flailing around like he was cheering on his favorite offensive end, Jerry Rice of the Oakland Raiders.

"My God, Graham. What's gotten into you? What are you doing?" Charlie shouted at the top of his lungs, ditching his pole and jumping in. Graham could not swim.

Dexter and Bobby threw down their poles and ran to the water's edge. Sixty-two-year-old Charlie was the only one in the bunch who could swim, and he was giving it his all in the cold, murky water to save the life of his best friend.

Three feet out into the water, Charlie's muscular arms grabbed onto Graham, pulling him up. Bubbles came out of Graham's mouth. Charlie gave him a quick glance while paddling back to shore.

Anxious faces looked down at Charlie as he neared the shore. Dexter and Bobby extended their arms and pulled him onto the bank.

Graham's body trembled as he stood facing the group. His wet clothing stuck to him like Saran Wrap. His teeth clinked together in rapid succession, making a chattering sound. Bobby took off his jacket and placed it around Graham's shoulders.

Graham appeared tired and worn as he stared back at the alarmed men who were unable to utter a word. He looked at each one individually—Charlie, Dexter, and Bobby—then shut his eyes, clasping his hands over his face. He let out a sigh and his shoulders slumped with the weight of his grief. Amanda's death sapped the life straight out of him.

"What's wrong with you Graham?" Charlie shouted out of fear. "You could have drowned out there? Talk to me."

"Stop it, Charlie," Dexter cut in. "I know you're still hurting," he said, turning to Graham. "It's gonna take some time, but you hang in there buddy. It'll be all right after awhile."

"Manda, Manda, Manda," Graham moaned over and over again, his tears flowing like a busted fire hydrant. He fell to his knees, shaking his head, unashamed of his outburst. Life didn't seem worth living now that Amanda was gone. Charlie held onto him. His crying was so uncontrollable that his body shook violently as if he had been injected with a thousand volts of electricity.

"It's gonna be all right, man." Charlie hugged and squeezed his best friend. "If I could, I'd bring Amanda back, but that is not humanly possible. I loved Amanda, too. I wish I could somehow drain the pain from you, but for now, you'll have to trust that I'll be there for you."

"I can't go on without my beloved Amanda," Graham wailed.

Charlie, Dexter, and Bobby sat down on the bank next to Graham and wiped tears away from their own eyes.

CHAPTER 1

She was everywhere. Everywhere Graham turned and in everything he touched, she was there. Her reflection peered back at him when he looked in the mirror. She was a glimmer of light on a distant ocean. He felt her hand graze his while placing the oversized pillow on her favorite spot on the sofa. On the day he'd gone fishing, there she was in all her radiant beauty, staring back at him through the ripples in the water, and he had jumped in to try and save her.

❖❖❖

It was almost two months to the day since Amanda died. Graham had not ventured out of the house except for the day he'd gone fishing with his buddies. He sat home day in and day out waiting for Amanda to return so they could resume their life together. But with the passing of time, his obsession left him scraping the bottom of loneliness.

Today was going to be a new day, Graham promised himself. Self-pity had its place, but now he was ready to rise from its shadow. As he lay on the couch trying to make good on that promise, he was suddenly twenty again— a young man recently come to the Bay Area from St. Louis to follow a dream.

❖❖❖

Graham's best friend, Charlie Ford, had arrived in the Bay Area a year earlier. Charlie's Uncle Roscoe, or Roc as he preferred to be called, migrated to California after the war, finding work at the Naval Air Station in Alameda. Uncle Roc had invited Charlie to come out west after high school.

Graham and Charlie went way back. They met at junior high school. Charlie was one year older and seven inches taller than Graham, although Graham swore he was six feet tall when he had his Sunday-go-to-meeting shoes on. Charlie had coal-black, wavy hair that appeared an iridescent blue depending on the light. Graham had a thick crown of self-made waves with the help of a little Murray's hair pomade and a stocking cap. They were a pair. You'd rarely see one without the other. And yes, they could turn the charm on and were not accustomed to being without a girl wrapped in each arm.

Graham and Charlie played football in high school and were the main ingredient in a singing group they formed. Now Graham found himself in the Bay Area by way of Southern Pacific Railways with a shoebox filled with all his worldly possessions under his arm. Graham's mother, Eula Mae Perry Peters, had died suddenly of a brain aneurism, one short year after his father died. So Graham set off to see the world, leaving his two younger sisters behind with his Aunt Rubye to care for them.

It was Graham's first week in Oakland. The city was all a-buzz—a little like St. Louis, except that there were more jobs for Negroes and maybe a chance to strike it rich. Striking it rich didn't seem to be a likely event in Graham's immediate future unless he accidentally fell into it, but he did like the feel of the place he now called home.

Charlie subletted a small room from his Uncle Roc and asked Graham to stay with him until he got on his feet. There would be no problem with Graham getting a job. Hire notices were posted all over the black community. Everyone was looking for young, strong Negro men to work in the Naval shipyard, lifting heavy cargo.

But this was the weekend, and Graham was ready to see the sights. It had been a long, tedious ride on the train. The bright lights of the San Francisco Bay were a wonderful welcome mat for a young kid a long way from home.

"Come on, Graham," Charlie shouted. "The show's gonna start in about an hour. Man, you and me will be back in business in no time—all the babes we want."

"Church, Charlie? You've gotta be kidding. All of those clubs we passed on the way in. I'm sure we can find some good-looking girls there. I'm ready to unwind a little, kick up my heels."

"Relax, Graham. They say if you want a real woman, go to the church house. There's a convention going on at this big church up on Market Street that's about three blocks away and in walking distance. My man, Curtis MacArthur, swore up and down that there's gonna be a lot of babes at the convention. They come from far and wide. Graham, man, you can take your pick—short ones, tall ones, skinny ones, fat if you like, but there's enough to go around for seconds, thirds if you want. There's gonna to be good music, eating and even a little preaching, but this is the place to be if you want the cream of the crop."

"Charlie, you are crazy. You should have been a car salesman. Anyway, I don't have anything to wear."

"That's no problem. Uncle Roc got plenty of suits. They might be a tad bit too big, but they'll do for tonight." Charlie laughed and hit Graham on the back. "You're my buddy, and we're a team. Now what kinda friend would I be strolling with a fine babe on my arm and my best friend sitting back in the room all by himself?"

"You don't want me to answer that…?"

"Go on, tell me."

"What makes you so sure any of these girls are gonna even look at you? They're lookin' for preachers so they can become first ladies. No slick, jive-talking, unrepentant, tall, dreamy-eyed, dark-haired boy without an ounce of salvation got half a chance."

"I was counting on that tall, dreamy-eyed, dark-haired boy to do the trick." They both laughed until it hurt.

"You're right," Graham continued, "we are a pair, but you run on tonight. I'll catch you in church another time."

"Suit yourself, buddy. You're gonna wish you were there. And don't let me have to tell you I told you so."

"Get on and get out of here. I might take a walk later."

"Gonna try and sneak a peek, eh?"

"Catch you later."

Graham sat in the room contemplating life—what he was going to do tonight and then tomorrow. An hour had passed since Charlie left. It seemed the whole neighborhood had evaporated into the night—a hushed quiet that made Graham a bit wary. He jumped up and went to the window, but only the stars and the moon dared to stare back at him, the moon illuminating his face in the windowpane.

Graham grabbed his jacket off the chair and headed out the

door. He wasn't sure where he was going, but he knew he needed to get out of that noiseless house—maybe hear a little music, ahh maybe some preaching, but he wanted to be where there was life and a little reminder of home.

He headed West passing a few couples out strolling. Then he noticed the cars—so many lined the street. He continued another block, and the cars—Buicks, Packards, and Fords, inhabited every available space on either side of the street. Yeah, he would own one of them one day. Then he heard it, felt it reverberate throughout his body. It reminded him of thunder, cymbals crashing. Yes, someone was having a good time, and it didn't sound like the blues they were playing back at Slim's in St. Louis.

As Graham neared the big church on Market Street, a flurry of activity surrounded it. The building seemed to sway on its cinder blocks, careful not to empty its precious cargo from inside. It was ten p.m., and although there seemed to be a lot going on inside the church, there was a lot happening outside as well. Small circles of young people milled about holding conversations. Suddenly, Graham was converged upon by a sea of purple and white choir robes which dutifully stretched into a single line waiting to march into the sanctuary. Graham looked around, but Charlie was nowhere to be found.

As Graham inched closer, a beautiful girl in her late teens emerged from the fellowship hall. She was about Graham's height, give or take an inch. She wore the prettiest white silk suit and a white pill hat with a bow made of lace attached to the front. The ends of her hair were turned up in a shoulder-length flip that accentuated her nutmeg-colored skin. But it was the nut-brown legs that made Graham come from his hiding place.

Graham stumbled over a workhorse that had been placed over an open manhole. He regained his composure and followed her right into church.

He'd forgotten for a moment that he was not dressed appropriately, but that didn't matter. Charlie was right; "the crème de la crème" resided here. Someone called "Amanda," and the girl with the nut-brown legs waved her hand. What a pretty name. Graham would have to move closer if he was going to say anything to her at all. She looked his way and then quickly away, bobbing her head to the music as the choir marched in. She looked his way again, and Graham locked upon her gaze and didn't let go.

She seemed shy in a girlish sort of way, but Graham forged ahead. He pushed closer to her, the crowd unyielding until he was within an inch from touching her nose.

"Hi, Amanda," he said above the noise.

She sneered at him, wrinkling up her nose.

"Who are you, and how do you know my name?" Amanda Carter demanded.

"That's a secret," he said, even more mesmerized by her beauty. "My name is Graham." He extended his hand. "I'm going to be a preacher one day."

Graham saw the puzzled look on her face. "What does that have to do with me?" she retorted, leaving his hand in mid-air.

"Well...I...Would you like to go outside and talk for a few minutes?"

Amanda cocked her head back hesitating before she spoke. Her eyes cut a path down the length of his body and rested on his wrinkled khaki pants and blue pea coat that had doubled as a pillow on his trek to the west.

"Sure, why not," she said nonchalantly. "You seem harmless enough, but after this choir sings. They are so good."

Oh, if Charlie could see him now. Graham could tell Ms. Amanda liked the attention he was giving her, although she pretended she didn't. When the choir finished singing, they quietly went outside. They made small talk, but Graham was transfixed by her beauty (eyes the color of ripe olives embedded in an oval, nutmeg-colored face) and those beautiful nut-brown legs that he wished he could wrap his own around. Actually, he wanted to reach out and touch her, maybe place a kiss on those fine chiseled lips of hers that smelled of sweet berries when he got close enough to catch a whiff.

There was something about Amanda that was different—unlike those other girls who stumbled over themselves vying for the chance to be his lady. Graham Peters became a different person that night—his heart ached for Amanda Carter, a girl he had just met. If given half a chance, he would cherish her until the end of time.

CHAPTER 2

Two hours had elapsed when the telephone's ring brought Graham out of his reverie.

"Who's wanting me now?" he said aloud. "Don't they know I just wanna be left alone? Shut up!" he hollered at the telephone as the caller made no attempt to give up its quest to be heard. Graham made no attempt to answer. "All people want to do is give advice and get in your business," Graham grumbled. And he was having no parts of it.

Graham walked listlessly around the house, finally retreating to his bedroom. "Why Amanda, why?" Graham cried out loud, throwing his hands in the air. He sat on the edge of the bed, closed his eyes, and shook his head. He would not fulfill his promise to himself today. *Maybe tomorrow*, Graham thought.

Graham stood up and ran his hand along the dresser where Amanda kept her things. There were photos of their two girls, Deborah and Elizabeth, now fully grown with families of their own. The pictures were taken when they were five and six years old, respectively. Sitting next to the pictures was Amanda's jewelry box. It held everything from precious gems to costume pieces. Many were gifts the girls or Graham had given her. Amanda cherished each and every piece and would often tell people she couldn't part with them.

Graham rifled through the box until his heart stopped where his finger had also stopped. In the midst of all those trinkets was the rose pendant Graham had given Amanda on their first date as a token of his love and affection. Graham picked up the pendant and twirled it in his hand. He clutched it tightly, finally bringing it to his chest. The memory was so vivid—that first date. Graham fell on the bed and let time take him to the moment when he knew for sure that Amanda was his true love.

❖❖❖

It had been three weeks since Graham set eyes on Amanda at the big church on Market Street. Amanda lived not far from Charlie's Uncle Roc, but it was difficult to see her. Since Graham worked during the day at the Naval shipyard, it was next to impossible for Amanda to meet Graham. Mr. and Mrs. Carter kept a tight rein on their daughter. The best that Graham and Amanda could hope for was a phone call here and there.

As fate would have it, Graham got a weekend off and vowed to see Amanda. After giving Charlie what he owed for rent, Graham took five dollars from his remaining salary and set off to find something nice for her. A man bearing gifts had to amount to something. He'd show the Carters what he was made of.

There was an H. G. Grant store downtown that sold nice little trinkets; hopefully, he would find something befitting Amanda. He had called her the night before and asked her to meet him there for a fountain soda. Then he would give her the gift.